Windamere's Rose

Barbara Wilson

ACKNOWLEDGEMENT

A special thank you to my husband, Eddy, for his unwavering support, encouragement, and patience throughout this journey—I couldn't have done it without you.

CONTENTS

CHAPTER 1 - NURSE ASHFORD

Princess Alexandra Military Hospital

Major World War II, hospital providing care for injured soldiers. Its red brick structure, arched windows, and well-kept gardens reflected the era's architecture, while the sight of military vehicles and personnel emphasized its critical role during wartime.

"Rose, come over here," Sue called, her voice tinged with urgency yet gentle as a breeze, beckoning her towards one of the new casualties.

With deliberate care, Rose completed the dressing on her current patient. She tenderly patted his shoulder and adjusted the blanket around him, ensuring he was warm and comfortable. The soldier's weary eyes softened, taking solace in her radiant smile, a beacon of light in the harrowing darkness of the hospital. She had a unique way of making each one feel irreplaceable, a jewel amidst the rubble of War. For Rose, every patient was a friend—each recovery a silent triumph, and each loss a deep, wrenching sorrow that lingered like an unhealed wound in her heart.

Peering down at Sue's patient sprawled on his stomach, Rose's senses were assaulted by the sharp tang of antiseptic mingling with the spicy scent of the cream, yet neither could fully mask the disgusting odour of burnt flesh. The acrid smell alone painted a vivid picture of the severity of his burns. Infection, the relentless tormentor of soldiers, hovered like a dark cloud over his precarious fate.

"Get closer and listen," Sue said, moving aside to let Rose lean in and catch the faint murmurings. Her voice was filled with urgency, the worry etched in the lines of her face. "Doesn't it sound like Windermere? Isn't that where you're from?"

Rose bent lower, her ears straining to catch each barely audible word. There it was.

"Windamere, Windamere, Windmere," he repeatedly whispered as a chant anchored in desperation, as if clinging to the name could somehow pull him through.

"Yes, it's Windermere," Rose confirmed, eyes scanning his sun-darkened face. Deep etchings of pain marked his expression. His brows furrowed intensively over tightly shut eyes, every muscle tensed in a battle for life. Each whispered word was a lifeline. "But I don't recognise him."

"His name is Rory Anderson. Does that ring a bell?" Sue inquired, her brow furrowing as she leaned over the bed.

Rose paused, a puzzled expression crossing her face as she tried to dig through her memory. "No, afraid not," She finally replied, shaking her head. The name could have been anyone, a ghost from the past or a stranger she had never met. Sue's persistence only added to the mystery surrounding this elusive Rory.

"Pity, he's dark and handsome, just my type." Sue quipped with a light-hearted laugh, though her eyes betrayed a flicker of concern. "I was hoping for an introduction when he comes to."

"His burns are severe," Rose replied somberly, her gaze sombre. "He will need to fight to survive," she murmured, almost to herself.

That indomitable will sometimes carve a path between life and death. She resolved to visit him tomorrow, reflecting on the familiar towns scattered throughout the Windermere district. Did he come from one of them?

Calm washed over her as she replaced the blood-soaked dressing, lost in the thought of 'Windamere.' Each whisper of the name reminded her of peace, but the chaos of the ward was an ever-present truth.

The ward was a cacophony of suffering, filled with soldiers in various stages of agony. The air was thick with the nauseating stench of burnt flesh mingling with the clammy scent of impending death, evolving the space into a harrowing purgatory for nurses. Still, Rose pressed on, her steps heavy but filled with an unyielding resolve.

Every inhale brought a stinging awareness of the possibility of another life slipping away under her care. "Someone has to fight for those who have fought their last on the battlefield," she reminded herself, her voice barely a whisper over the relentless sounds of anguish.

Each soldier she rescued delivered a brief yet potent rush of euphoria, a fleeting glimmer that life might conquer after all. However, every passing soul gnawed a piece of their spirit away, leaving behind the sad recognition that soon enough, another would occupy the vacant bed. The vicious cycle of hope and despair perpetually renewed itself, tinged with the scents, sounds, and weight of suffering that enveloped every corner of the ward.

Rose thought of her cherished Windermere with a glimmer in her eyes. It was not just Windermere's haunting beauty that called to her, but her family.

There in the graveyard lay her parents at rest, where the crisp air carried the fragrance of damp earth and blossoming wildflowers. The serenity, the rich green of the surrounding hills, and the occasional bird song created a symphony of nature that enchants all who visit. It comforted her that they had such a final resting place.

She pondered what made his Windermere so special, wondering what could drive him to such lengths, its importance profound enough to spur his relentless fight. Who was he? It puzzled her why he lingered in her thoughts after, little more than a whisper in the cacophony of her troubled mind. Yet, he stood out against the backdrop of chaos, an enigma wrapped in the folds of her uncertain emotions.

Drained from another punishing shift, she collapsed onto her bed. The sagging mattress and rough sheets faded into insignificance as her body screamed for respite, a need so urgent it drowned out any discomfort.

Yet, as she teetered on the edge of sleep's tenuous embrace, the relentless shadows of her past tightened their grip. Like relentless phantoms, the memories she had fiercely fought to bury clawed their way to the surface, turning her refuge into a battleground.

In the profound silence of the night, the horrors she had endured reawakened as vivid nightmares, pulling her back through the visceral anguish and dread she believed she had escaped.

Her mother and father—gone, claimed by the explosion that obliterated their London home. She heard her mother cry, "Get Rose," a desperate command piercing through the chaos. The acrid smell of gas hung in the air. They dragged her through what was once the front wall. Then came the explosion. Every pounding heartbeat, every ragged breath in that darkened room mirrored the monumental psychological odyssey that had led her to this precarious moment of solitude. Her mother and father perished in the wreckage of their home, victims of that fateful bomb.

The morning light crept through the window too soon, casting a pale glow that did nothing to soothe her weary soul. Her mind, a tempest-ridden battlefield, was worn to the edges by the relentless assault of a war that should have never been.

For three long years, she had devoted herself to stitching together shattered bodies and offering a fragment of hope to wounded souls clinging desperately to the promise of a reunion with their loved ones.

Today, she would once again step into the storm. Why? Because she couldn't stand the thought of them suffering alone, adrift in their sea of pain. She refused to become a reflection of the cruelty that humanity had unleashed upon itself. Where had the kindness of humankind vanished?

Before facing the growing list of work tasks, she reached out to her lifeline, Aunt Rosemary, whose wisdom and love had always been a steady anchor in her life.

The old, rotary phone on the wall was a relic of times past, yet it was her lifeline to cherished voices. She gingerly lifted the receiver and began to dial, each click of the numbers blending with the gentle hum of dawn outside.

The familiar ringtone echoed in her ear, a

symphony of anticipation and nervousness, until a warm but slightly crackled voice finally emerged, filling the space with comforting familiarity.

"Hello, Rosemary Ashford."

"Aunt Rosemary, it's me, Rose."

"Rose, how nice to hear from you," her cheerful voice brightened the day. "How are you faring? I hear they have been bombing London again."

"Yes, it does not seem to stop. We scuttle like crabs into the bunkers every time the siren sounds."

"You keep yourself safe," her Aunt's voice was filled with concern.

"I will. I was calling to find out if you knew of any Andersons in Windermere." Her Aunt was silent, so she continued, "An Australian soldier was admitted with burns. He's in a bad way and keeps murmuring 'Windermere.'"

Her Aunt's voice came back on the line, breaking up. "Yes... Yes, I knew the Andersons. Hugh went to Australia."

"Are you okay?" Rose asked, concerned. "Your voice sounds different."

"Just the line," her Aunt's voice came clear. "He went to Western Australia."

"Thanks, that's great. If the patient survives, I will find out. He said something about my Windermere not being the same as his." Another nurse was waiting for her to finish. "I must go. Jenny wants to use the phone. Bye, I will keep in touch."

"Please do. I would like to know how Hugh's son gets on."

Aunt Rosemary sat at the worn oak table, the faint aroma of freshly brewed coffee lingering in the air. The room was bathed in soft, golden light, filtering through the lace curtains and casting delicate shadows on the patterned wallpaper.

Hughes' son was injured and in London—a sombre expression crept across her face as she delved into her memories. Hugh couldn't lose his only remaining son, especially after the heartbreak he'd already endured.

A lone, glistening tear traced its way down Aunt Rosemary's cheek, mingling warmth with the coolness of her skin. She shivered slightly at the thought that it could have been her child if things had been different, but that was the past.

She stood, determined to shake off the memories. They were only ghosts of the past. A smile gradually lit her face as she moved to the sink, ready to tackle the dishes. She knew the past had to be kept in its place, or it would overshadow the present. Today— she reminded herself—was a day to be savoured, not clouded by yesterday's pain.

As she surveyed the ward, she looked at the soldier from the night before, a figure suspended on the delicate thread between life and death. Memories washed over her of their intertwined past and the grit he embodied. Was this the same man who had braved tempests of hardship, driven by a steadfast love for Windamere, a cradled in a tranquil that beckoned him home?

Did the prospect of reuniting with beloved faces stir his spirit, or was Windemere's silent call summoning him towards a long-sought peace? She had to know. It was the same man who had braved tempests of hardship, driven by a steadfast love for Windamere and cradled in a tranquillity that beckoned him home.

As she approached the bed, his dark eyes tracked her every movement, remarkably keen and vibrant with life. It was a testament to the tenacity that had carried him through a lifetime of hardship in the Outback, where survival was not a given but a hard-won battle.

"So, you survived the night?" she asked, her voice tinged with relief and the weary resignation from years of witnessing the fragility of life.

He grimaced, a shadow of dread flitting across his rugged face, etched with lines that spoke of countless brushes with death. "Ah, the English Rose from last night. Didn't think I'd make it, did you?" His Australian drawl was low and musical, like the distant hum of the bush at twilight.

He remembered her, yet he had been semi-conscious. Rose covered her surprise, recalling the way his fevered skin had felt beneath her fingers, and leaned down, her hands now tenderly examining his bandages. "I've lost so many patients that I've learned not to get my hopes up," she confessed, thinking of the small graves scattered across the windswept cemetery.

"I will survive." His voice held a fierce resolve forged in the unforgiving heat and isolation of a lifetime in a far-off land. "I want to see this 'Windamere' you come from. If fate is kind, perhaps I will show you mine." He gazed at her with a look that spoke of distant dreams and untamed lands, a promise of adventures neither had imagined.

In his eyes, she saw a fiery determination that defied the grim statistics she had often faced in her career. Memories of past failures flickered through her mind, each a blow to her hope. Yet, there was something uniquely determined about him, and for a fleeting moment, the fragile light within her flickered but did not extinguish. "I will hold you to that," she said, clinging to the slim hope that this time might be different.

He watched her retreat, the rhythm of her footsteps a welcome distraction from the relentless pounding in his back. She moved with unwavering grace, her serene face radiating a fresh innocence that seemed incongruous in this grim setting. Yet, beneath that veil of steadfastness, he sensed her weariness, her quiet capitulation to the burdens of this harsh reality. She was his solitary beacon in this chasm of despair—an angel guiding him through this inferno.

She returned with fresh dressings cradled carefully in her hands, her expression a battle between steely determination and understated worry.

"This will hurt," she whispered, her voice tinged with an earnest gentleness. Her eyes, shadowed with fatigue, flickered momentarily with regret as she continued, "I will try to be gentle."

Internally, she chastised herself, her thoughts a tumult of frustration and guilt, knowing that nothing could truly alleviate the pain except for the morphine that lay in such short supply—a cruel irony, for its long-term consequences, were as fearsome as its immediate relief.

"Ready." His face, tense with resolve, portrayed an unwavering determination to seize victory.

Rose was grateful when the pain claimed him, and unconsciousness had once again claimed him; she gently peeled back the bandage, revealing the raw, angry red burns beneath.

Her heart pounded as she meticulously examined the wounds, her breath hitching each time she detected an unfamiliar spot. Relief flooded through her when a thorough search found no signs of infection.

She exhaled a shaky sigh, her shoulders loosening slightly from the weight of her fear.

Determined, she carefully changed the dressings, each action a silent plea for healing.

The antibiotics offered a glimmer of hope, standing as guardians against the looming threat of infection. Despite all her efforts, an uneasy dread lingered; only time would unveil the actual outcome.

Another shift was over, and again, she found herself lost in thoughts of Windamere—a name wrapped in mystery and allure. Windermere is where she grew up, and she has memories of her father and mother. It was the sanctuary where her dear Aunt had nurtured her through the formative years of her life, a nurturing presence now aged and frail whom she missed deeply.

The beauty of Windermere held a special place in her heart, serving as a sanctuary away from the chaos of the War. The serenity of its shores and the tranquillity of its waters gave her a sense of peace and solace amidst the turmoil of the time. It was where she could escape the harsh realities of the conflict and find a temporary respite from the upheaval that had disrupted her life. Windermere's pristine beauty and timeless charm symbolised hope and a connection to happier memories, making it a place of immense importance to her during such trying times.

She cursed the War for cruelly separating them, for this conflict had uprooted so many lives, thrown the world into chaos, and kept her from the comforts of her past. The War had been a series of battles and a relentless force that altered destinies and scattered families. Its repercussions echoed through every facet of her existence, imbuing even her cherished memories with a shade of sorrow. Still, Windemere was deeply rooted in her childhood dreams and recollections, a constant amidst the turmoil.

Yet, she couldn't help but ponder about his Windermere. What kind of landscape shaped his memories? What stories from his past are interwoven with his family's history to bestow that name upon their estate? The thought intrigued her, binding her nostalgia with a broader sense of shared human experience amidst the relentless backdrop of War.

The ring stops with a resonant click. "Aunt Rosemary, it's Rose." She tries to infuse her voice with a touch of cheerfulness.

"Good morning, dear. You don't sound as bright today," Aunt Rosemary's voice ripples with concern.

"Just a little down," Rose murmurs, knowing that disguising her true feelings from her perceptive Aunt is futile.

"How is Rory doing?" Aunt Rosemary inquires, her voice tinged with worry. "He's doing better than expected; he's a fighter," Rose replies, suppressing a sigh.

"I thought he would be," Aunt Rosemary responded, the relief palpable in her words.

Silently, she knew he had the Hughes' resolve. "Better go. Catch you tomorrow."

"Goodbye, love," Aunt Rosemary's voice wavered as it faded down the line.

CHAPTER 2 - RECOVERY WARD

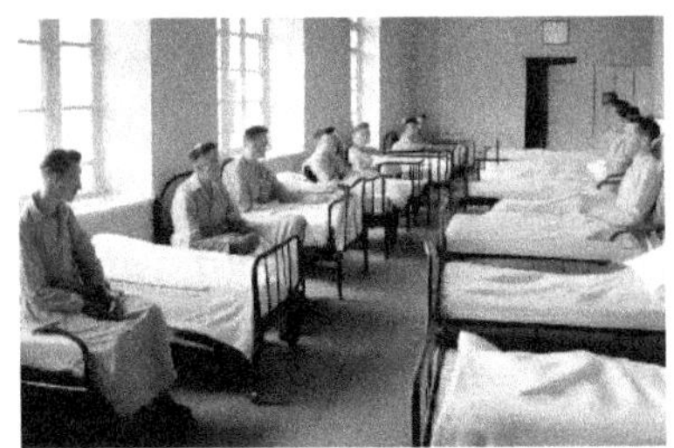

Princess Alexandra Military Hospital

The ward typically featured rows of simple metal-framed beds, each with minimal personal storage, separated by curtains for privacy. The atmosphere was functional but compassionate, with medical staff providing care for war-related injuries such as fractures, burns, and shrapnel wounds.

Rose had been observing Rory's recovery closely and noted daily improvement. His lopsided grin, a heartwarming sight, greeted her warmly each morning, sealing a silent bond between them.

"Good morning, Rose. Still hanging in there with me," Rory greeted. His voice was a deep, soothing melody that resonated with a comforting warmth she had grown to cherish. His eyes crinkled at the corners as he spoke, reflecting his genuine affection for her.

"Good morning," she responded softly, her voice barely above a whisper. Her eyes twinkled with a familiar warmth, a connection that spoke of shared moments and unspoken understanding.

She moved with practised grace, placing fresh dressings on his bed as her fingers worked gently, ready to change them as part of her comforting routine. Her every movement spoke of her dedication and the quiet strength beneath.

"Is that all I get? Just good morning?" he teased gently, his voice a soothing murmur, eyes dancing with a mischievous sparkle that caught the morning light. "Perhaps some conversation. I want to know more about your Windamere."

She smiled, her lips curving into a playful mimicry of his Australian accent, "My Wind-er-mere."

Rory's rich, endearing laughter echoed through the sterile hospital ward, infusing it with warmth. "You mean 'Wind-a-mere'!"

Their banter, a cherished ritual, transcended mere accents. It was a tapestry of shared moments, interwoven with an unspoken affection—a testament to the deep connection that had blossomed between them.

"No, it is 'Windermere,'" she insisted, her eyes twinkling with determination. "Not my 'Windamere,'" he countered with a playful edge in his voice.

"What is your 'Windamere' like?" she asked, emphasizing his pronunciation.

Rory's eyes glazed over, lost in the memory of home. "It's hot, with plains that stretch endlessly, eucalyptus trees rising from the dust, and a farmhouse standing tall like a sentinel in that vast, native land." His voice softened, carrying the warmth of his homeland.

"Not mine," Rose countered, her words painting a vivid picture. "Huge lakes, rolling hills, green valleys, ancient forests, and the quaint village where I grew up." She ticked them off on her fingers like a meticulous teacher.

"Different," Rory quipped, a grin spreading across his face.

"Nurse Ashford, have you finished yet?" Matron's authoritative voice interrupted the moment.

"Oops," Rose murmured before responding, "Just about."

His grin widened, eyes gleaming with understanding. "These Windameres are worlds apart."

"Windermere," she corrected him gently, a smile playing on her lips.

He shifted his gaze to the side, his expression a mix of exasperation and amusement. "The English," he muttered with a wry smile, "They always believe they're infallible."

In just a week, he had improved enough to be transferred to the rehab ward. On the ground floor, a sense of hope pervaded the atmosphere. The ward was bathed in natural light from large, arching windows offering a serene view of the sprawling gardens. These meticulously manicured gardens, with their winding paths and blooming flowers, served as a therapeutic escape for the patients, and exercise, deemed crucial for recovery, was routinely encouraged.

Within the confines of the ward, it was as if a tapestry of human endurance unfurled before one's eyes. Each bed held a story of suffering and survival, where the weary and wounded began their arduous journey toward recovery.

The walls, painted in soothing shades of blue and green, bore witness to this epic struggle. They were adorned with vibrant artwork depicting scenes of nature and hope. The air was filled with a hum of patients engaged in animated conversation, each voice a beacon of resilience. Their laughter and shared anecdotes spoke of bonds forged in the fires of hardship, a testament to their resilience.

The side door led to the garden, where every flower seemed to mirror the patients' determination to rise from the depths of their suffering. Each step taken along these paths, each story shared beneath the blooming canopies, wove a narrative of physical and emotional healing, transforming the ward into a sanctuary of recovery and renewal.

After one of Rose's first visits, Noel, lying in the bed next to his, watched her walk away with a longing in his eyes. Her presence lingered like a gentle fragrance, almost palpable in its absence.

Observing his friend's sad gaze, Rory couldn't help but issue a playful warning, "She's already taken."

Noel's eyebrows shot up in surprise. "Like that?" he asked, a hint of disbelief. "Are you sure?"

Rory nodded with unwavering confidence. "I am one hundred per cent sure," he declared, his voice firm and resolute. I am taking her home with me."

Noel cocked his head, puzzled. "Head over heels?"

"Yes," Rory replied, his eyes softening as he spoke. "Head over heels in love." His words carried the weight of undeniable truth.

Noel held out his hand, and Rory shook it. "Don't let her escape, or I will catch her." Rory laughed. Looking at his friend's plastered leg, he commented, "I can run faster than you."

With a smirk, Noel agreed. "Undeniable."

"Where are you from?" Rory asked, curiosity sparking in his eyes.

"Melbourne, Victoria," Noel responded, a hint of pride in his voice. "And you?"

Rory smirked, the typical interstate rivalry flashing through his mind. "Well, I won't hold it against you," he quipped. "Midjal, Western Australia."

"Where is that?" Noel asked, raising an eyebrow and leaning forward slightly. "Not the bush?"

"Yes, the bush, wheatbelt country," came the

reply, the speaker gesturing with a slight nod as if pointing to a distant horizon.

"Ah, a farmer. I was a photographer," Noel's tone shifted, a hint of nostalgia colouring his words.

"Where's your camera?" Noel inquired, furrowing his brow in curiosity.

Noel paused, his eyes narrowing thoughtfully. "Must be in my luggage. I'll have them find it," he said, his fingers tapping lightly on his chin as if punctuating his resolve.

This simple exchange was where it all began. Despite the well-known rivalry, something about Noel's straightforwardness and Rory's easy-going nature just clicked. They soon discovered shared interests beyond sports and politics. As common grounds unfolded, their budding friendship deepened, defying the often superficial state-based tensions. It was a moment that marked the beginning of a bond neither would have anticipated.

Once Noel's camera was unearthed, he dedicated countless hours to capturing the world around him. With each click of the shutter, he documented not only the tangible elements of their existence but also the intangible essence of their ongoing battle. Every fleeting moment that stirred in the vicinity was meticulously recorded, weaving together a rich tapestry of visual memories that chronicled the trials and tribulations they faced. In this way, Noel became both an observer and a participant, his photographs assembling an intricate narrative of their shared struggles.

Every day, Rose's arrival felt like a sacred ritual, intertwining solace and torment that seeped into the very essence of Rory's existence. Initially, the salve she applied was merely a balm, a fleeting escape from his persistent discomfort. Yet, with the passage of time, it morphed into something deeper—an intricate tapestry of pain woven with hints of ephemeral joy. Her touch, once clinical, evolved into a gentle caress that ignited a roiling tempest within him.

"Off with your shirt," Rose chirped her voice light as a breeze, blissfully unaware of the havoc she was unleashing on Rory's fragile soul.

With a heavy sigh, Rory peeled the shirt from his body, meeting her gaze with eyes laden with unspoken words—a silent cry she seemed unable to comprehend. His shoulders slumped, a gesture thick with yearning and frustration, as he sank onto the bed, turning to face the mattress, his heart burdened with turmoil that went unexpressed.

"It's looking good," she commented, a note of satisfaction lacing her voice, oblivious to the storm raging inside him.

He struggled to hold back a wave of confessions, fighting against the constraints of self-restraint. What seemed like progress to Rose felt like a torturous exercise in self-control to Rory, one that he was afraid he would ultimately fail.

His only comment was a "Hmm." Looking sideways, Noel caught his eye. The raised eyebrows and cheeky grin confirmed Rory's growing suspicion: Noel had uncovered his secret.

"That's it," Rose declared, satisfied, and wiped her hands on a towel. Rory turned his gaze toward her, noting the satisfaction lighting up her face.

She had no idea that her touch conveyed more than simple care; it was a soothing balm to his restless spirit.

"What are you grinning about?" Rose asked, her curiosity piqued. "I would say you did a real good job," Noel butted in.

Rory bristled silently, wishing he could erase that cocky grin from Noel's face. Being the subject of amusement was not his forte; he preferred to keep his vulnerabilities well-guarded.

"Thank you, Noel," Rose replied, accepting the remark as a genuine compliment. Rory silently appreciated her, grateful for her unaware comfort amidst the subtle tension within him.

The following day, she arrived with a sense of purpose, ready to shoulder her responsibilities. However, she was met with the unwelcome news that the task had already been done. A wave of confusion washed over her as she stood still, the nurses around her exchanging knowing glances that spoke of her unfulfilled duty.

"Rory, what's happening?" she asked, her voice tinged with bewilderment.

Stepping forward, Noel took charge, his tone steady, "Old Fran made her rounds early today."

He chose to leave out the background of his own decision, a detail that hung in the thick air between them.

Old Fran was a formidable presence, her physique resembling a solid brick fortress, strong enough to withstand any storm. While Noel spared no words on the lines etched across her face, a testament to her years, everyone recognized the warmth of her heart, shining like pure gold beneath the surface.

It hadn't escaped Rory's notice that he'd picked her, joking about his back pain while desperate for someone who could balance toughness with care—much to the amusement of the entire ward.

"How about a stroll in the garden?" Rory proposed, eager to shed the skin of his unofficial role as the ward's jester, even if just for a moment.

As he guided Rose through the ward, the weight of unspoken camaraderie hung in the air, punctuated by the unvoiced chorus of laughter from the men.

On their daily walk in the garden, Rory drew her closer with his arm around her back. "They are discharging me back to the barracks next week," Rory announced.

Rose felt a sharp pang of sadness coursing

through her. Rory had become the unexpected light in her otherwise predictable and grey existence, his humour and warmth etching unforgettable moments into her heart. Now, as his days in the hospital waned to a close, the looming reality of his departure filled her with a profound reluctance to let him go.

"You're not going back to the war, are you?" she asked, her voice trembling. Visions of Rory's lifeless body sprawled on a distant, violent battlefield seized her mind, and a cold wave of horror gripped her heart.

"Not quite," Rory responded, his grin faltering as a chilling wind tousled his hair. *Home,* he thought, but what did that even mean? The words echoed in his mind, each a reminder of the emptiness that had settled in his heart.

He felt the burden of his years pressing down on him, a relentless tide of bitter wisdom and the crushing weight of war's weariness. He glanced at the world around him, its colours muted, stripped of vibrancy by the memories of fallen comrades and the haunting spectre of unending conflict.

"Is there a place for me in this chaos?" he wondered, the question an ache deep within his soul. Rory's thoughts spiralled into the labyrinth of his past, vivid flashes of those he had lost flickering before his eyes. Faces of forever young comrades haunted his dreams and waking moments alike. Each smile lost, each voice silenced, tugged at the frayed edges of his sanity. He could almost feel the weight of their sacrifice on his shoulders, a mantle he found too heavy to bear.

His heart clenched with fear at the thought of returning to the battlefield. The very idea of donning his uniform once more, of stepping into the war, filled him with dread. What if he wasn't strong enough? What if he couldn't protect those around him? The self-doubt gnawed at him, festering into a wound that refused to heal.

Did he even deserve Rose's affection, to be loved by someone untouched by the horrors he had seen? The hospital's sterile walls offered a temporary sanctuary, a refuge where he could hide from the chaos of war. But leaving meant facing his demons, confronting the phantoms that trailed his every step.

The thought of leaving Rose behind shackled him to his fears. Rory hesitated, the spectre of his past gripping his soul with icy fingers as shadows of the battlefield loomed ever more prominent in his mind.

He wrestled with the tempest brewing inside him. How could he ever repay a beautiful woman to whom he owed his very life? Though a grin flickered across his face, it couldn't mask the sorrow that shadowed his eyes as memories cast a darkness over his heart.

"I am going home to Windamere?" she asked, a smile playing on her lips despite the flutter of excitement and anxiety. "I'm taking a week off to visit my Windermere."

"I suspect they are quite different," he replied, as her voice pulled him back to the present. His uneven grin failed to hide the fear in his gaze.

"Why don't you come with me?" she blurted out, startling herself. Where had that come from?

They had struggled for his survival, each minute a gruelling test of fortitude and faith. Perhaps the triumph they shared encouraged her, the feeling that they had already conquered so much together. Did he sense the same pull, the complex and suffocating tangle of emotions that now enveloped her in a storm of inner conflict?

Rory pondered this momentarily, a familiar pause descending upon her like the weight of a thousand unspoken words. Each decision and every adjustment demanded thorough scrutiny. He was a man of caution, a quality perhaps honed during the turbulent war years that had scarred their lives and reshaped their very beings. The brutal lessons of the battlefield had deepened his vigilance, moulding him into someone who measured every step with almost eerie precision.

"Yes, I would like that," he replied softly. His grin returned, though it was now merely a ghost of the broad, joyful smile that used to light up his face, hinting at the shadows of happier times long past.

Later, back in the ward, Noel's eyes sparkled with mischief as he challenged him. "Well, did you ask her?" he demanded, anticipation curling in the air.

The entire ward seemed to lean in, waiting on tenterhooks for his reply.

A lump formed in his throat as he uttered a reluctant "No."

Disappointment rippled through the room, and a chorus of boos swallowed his voice, sealing his shame. "Coward," someone hissed from the corners, "what's wrong with you?"

Before the gloom fully descended upon him, he quickly added, "But she invited me to go to Windermere, her home." He felt a flicker of hope ignite, offering him some solace against the tide of disapproval.

"That's better," Noel said, his voice taking on a teasing edge. "Even a slow country boy like you should be able to achieve that." Despite Noel's ribbing, he felt a sense of warmth and camaraderie. The words stung, but beneath the teasing, he sensed a small amount of encouragement, and that was enough.

It was time for Rory to leave, time for goodbyes. "I am going to miss you guys," he announced, a profound sadness settling in the room like a heavy fog.

He shook Noel's hand, their grip lingering for a moment. "Victoria may be the end of the earth," he teased with a bittersweet smile, "But keep in touch."

Noel's eyes widened with a mix of sorrow and surprise. "Yes, I will do that. I will write," he said, his voice trembling slightly. Then, attempting to lighten the mood, he added, "You can write, can't you?"

Rory chuckled softly, tousling his hair in a self-conscious gesture. "Sure can. Even country boys get an education in Aussie."

He turned away, addressing the entire ward to sound cheerful.

"Good luck, guys." The room echoed with heartfelt wishes and tearful goodbyes.

As Rory approached the door, the group broke into an off-key chorus of "We'll Meet Again," resonating with hope and desperation, "I don't know where, I don't know when. We'll meet again some sunny day."

As he was about to step out, the cheers intensified into a unified shout, "For God's sake, ask her."

CHAPTER 3 - AUNT ROSEMARY'S COTTAGE

Aunt Rosemary's Cottage

A classic Windermere cottage set in a picturesque countryside, 1945. The cottage showcases traditional architectural features typical of the Lake District, including a steeply pitched roof with thatch or slate tiles, small dormer windows, and whitewashed stone walls. The neatly framed windows with flower boxes add charm and warmth to its appearance.

At last, they stepped onto the train platform, where a vibrant whistle sliced through the air, announcing the arrival of the steam train. A dramatic plume of mist rose, curling around them like a ghostly embrace, as the weariness of their five-hour journey faded into the backdrop.

Rose's eyes twinkled with excitement as she turned to Rory, her voice bright against the backdrop of flitting birds and rustling leaves. "Isn't it wonderful, Rory? This place feels like a dream."

Rory's gaze drifted over quaint houses with

chimneys releasing warm wisps of smoke, signalling comfort and home. "It does. They're like scenes from a storybook," he replied, their charm igniting his senses.

Rose pointed towards the hills, her arm sweeping over the horizon. "Look at those hills! They stretch out like a green quilt. It's so peaceful compared to London." She inhaled deeply, savouring the crisp air, a content smile breaking across her face as she relished the calm far removed from the city's relentless pace.

Rory admired Rose's enthusiasm for the simple beauty of Windermere and pulled closer into her orbit of excitement. Rose's gaze shifted to the shimmering lake, her wonder immense. "Did you know it's England's largest natural lake? Isn't it incredible?" Light danced on her face, illuminating the captivating scene

"Rose, you're back!" a voice burst forth, electrifying the air.

A smile bloomed on her face, yet worry flickered in her eyes as she replied, "Windsor!" They embraced the warmth of familiarity like a soft blanket, yet a storm brewing beneath the surface.

Rory observed an itch of resentment gnawing at his insides as Windsor swaggered in, the embodiment of effortless aristocracy, clad in his rustic finery.

As they parted, Rose made the obligatory

introductions. "This is Rory Anderson, Windsor Hubert." The air grew thick with unspoken tension as Windsor extended his hand, a gesture of camaraderie that made Rory instinctively recoil.

Hesitation hung between them like a taut wire before Rory clenched Windsor's hand, scepticism rippling through the touch.

"Windsor," he replied sharply, the name slicing through the air, heavy with implications. "An Australian," Windsor remarked, his voice dripping with polished English precision.

"Yes, from Australia," Rory shot back, the sharpness of his tone revealing an unseen edge. There was no need for niceties; each word felt like a duel, a clash of worlds colliding.

"And a soldier," Windsor continued, his gaze lingering on the uniform that spoke volumes in silence.

Rory held his tongue, allowing the weight of his unspoken truth to hang in the air. He wanted to bark back, 'We fought for England.'

"He was wounded in Normandy," Rose offered quietly as if the admission could dissolve the tension thickening between the two men.

"You did not fight?" Rory's piercing gaze locked onto Windsor, a tempest of intensity in his eyes.

Windsor felt a wave of discomfort wash over him. The question landed heavily, resonating with an unsettling truth. No, he had not gone to war; his mother had forbade it, declaring him the heir. How often had he endured the weight of judgment for his mother's unwavering refusal? Each word felt like a dagger, igniting the turmoil within him as he grappled with the haunting shadows.

"No, I had to manage the estate; my parents are aging," Windsor replied, but the explanation felt flimsy in Rory's judgment. Memories of his mother's solitary toil on their farm gnawed at his conscience.

"Really," Rory said, his gaze drifting into recollections of shared hardships and unrelenting responsibilities.

"Let's go. Aunt Rosemary is waiting," Rose interjected, sensing their shifting animosity. "Are you here only for the weekend?" Windsor's inquiry dripped with ulterior motives, curiosity intertwined with something more profound.

"A week, then back to work," Rose replied, her hesitance echoing the uncertainty that cloaked the moment.

Windsor's eyes bore into hers with an earnestness that felt urgent. "Join us for dinner on Sunday," he insisted, warmth mingling with an underlying tone of pressure. His invitation extended to Rory as if he were an afterthought, "All of you, even Aunt Rosemary."

"Will your mother approve?" Rose asked, a flicker of doubt tainting her voice.

"No worries," Windsor waved off her concern,

yet the dismissive gesture did little to ease the tension that rippled through Rory. Although he doubted his mother would be impressed by the company.

"Thank you," she responded, a smile attempting to mask her lingering hesitation. Windsor's sudden interest unsettled her—was it sincere affection or veiled competition? She felt a dissonance between his surface charm and the storm brewing in Rory's heart, a deep understanding of love that Windsor seemed to lack.

Beside her, Rory's displeasure simmered like lava beneath a fragile crust. The invitation festered within him, an unwelcome intrusion.

"I'll send a car for you at six," Windsor announced, turning to descend the hill, leaving a wake of unresolved feelings behind.

Rory watched him leave—resentment across his features. The bitterness of Windsor's cavalier mention of servants sting like a fresh wound. The insidious threads of superiority wove themselves through their exchanges, each word a reminder of the societal gulf yawned before him.

While Rory had always found pride in his humble beginnings, the yawning chasm between their lives stung sharply. His childhood home was one of toil— a realm where every small triumph demanded grit and blood, while Windsor glided through life on paths of gold, his every whim effortlessly satisfied.

Beneath the surface, Rory wrestled with feelings

of inadequacy, haunted by the notion that no matter his efforts, the shadows cast by men like Windsor would forever loom ominously over his ambitions. The stark divide they represented tormented him, barriers he feared he would never, indeed, evade— not in England, at least. Thank the stars for Australia.

But what of Rose? He hoped bringing her to a land of meritocracy would fulfill their dreams, yet dread lingered.

These thoughts enveloped him as they walked along the road toward Rose's Aunt's home, the unsteady pulse of their burgeoning connection weaving between them like a delicate thread, poised to either strengthen or fray at any moment.

"What do you think?" Rose inquired, her voice tinged with eager curiosity. As they turned the corner and Aunt Rosemary's home came into view, the autumn wind whispered through the trees, carrying the scent of fallen leaves and the distant chatter of woodland creatures.

"It's like my Windamere!" Rory laughed when he saw the house at the end of the lane. He grinned widely. Rory studied the roofline; it was his Windamere. There were differences; he had a big porch, and the roof was less steep. He concluded, "Our Windameres are alike in spirit. Mine is an Australian version. They are similar."

His excitement surprised Rose. "What do you mean by similar?" she asked, furrowing her brow in confusion.

"My father built our Windamere and modelled it on your Aunt's house," Rory explained, his eyes sparkling with nostalgia and pride. His hand reached up to scratch the back of his neck absently, a wistful smile touching his lips. "Or as close to it as possible, considering the different country and climate."

As the memory flickered to life, he felt himself swept away, back to Windamare—the sprawling homestead in the heart of Australia's vast plains. There, the golden grass swayed like a sea, and the sky was an endless expanse of deep, inviting blue. How long had it been since he'd stood there, feeling the sun's warmth on his face and the whisper of the breeze enveloping him?

Now, the only anchor he had left was his father— the sole remnant of the family they had once been. His heart ached as he considered the fragile connection, a thin lifeline tethering him to a past brimming with love and warmth. The war had ravaged their world, snatching away his mother, Albert, and Guy, leaving behind an emptiness he struggled to comprehend.

The sounds of their laughter, which used to fill the air with palpable joy, had faded into a haunting silence that would cling to the walls of Windamare like an unwanted guest.

Could this place ever reclaim the essence of home? Would it ever again resonate with the spirit of the love they had shared?

The price of the war, so steep and unforgiving, demanded more than he could bear, and in its wake, it offered nothing—only echoes and shadows of what once was.

Rose took a deep breath to calm herself. The air was thick with the scent of freshly cut grass and eucalyptus, the symphony of a distance with the wind-whispered secrets of the ancient oaks.

Silence enveloped them as Rory's gaze lingered on the house, a familiar yet subtle version of his home.

"Father was trying to capture your Aunt's home, but the setting is so different," he mused inwardly, his eyes reflecting the myriad emotions cascading through him like autumn leaves caught in a gentle breeze.

Rory could see the sun's golden rays shining on the veranda boards, casting shadows that seemed to whisper tales of the past.

Windamere was his father's pride, as it stood out amongst smaller homes in Midjal. His father had built it to honour love with perseverance. This home must have meant much to him for him to use it as the model.

"So you have my Windermere." Rose's eyes sparkled with a mischievous glint as she tried to coax more out of him.

There was a playful energy about her, a cheeky

side that Rory found both surprising and endearing, especially considering the hardships she had faced during her nursing experience. The contrast between her light-hearted demeanour and the gravity of her work made her all the more intriguing to him.

"No, mine is Wind-a-mere." He raised an eyebrow, pronouncing the 'a'.

As they approached the end of the lane, the anticipation of home wrapped around them like the sweet scent of autumn leaves.

"So this is where Father's idea came from?" Rory murmured, viewing Aunt Rosemary's house for the first time. It was different but enough alike to be recognisable.

"Aunt Rosemary's house?" Rose asked, puzzled.

"Windamere is bigger and adapted to the hotter climate, but you can see the likeness in the roofline." His grin widened.

The door opened, and Aunt Rosemary stepped out, opening her arms to Rose. Their affection was obvious, but not so their appearance. Aunt Rosemary was robust and shorter, her face open and happy. Rose was younger, taller, and more beautiful, her dark hair gleaming in the sunlight.

Remembering Rory's presence, Rose stepped back. "This is Rory," She introduced him.

Aunt Rosemary caught sight of Rory. He resembled Hugh, but his mischievous grin hinting at his father's spirited nature was absent. The war still weighed on him.

Memories of her youth surged as she recalled the laughter that once filled her childhood home. She turned to face Rory, her heartwarming emotions long forgotten.

"You must be Hugh's son!" she said, her voice rich with excitement and nostalgia. Her eyes sparkled, full of untold stories. Her smile felt like a hug, bridging the past and welcoming the future. Her greeting was heartfelt: "Welcome to our family, welcome home."

"Thank you," he replied, stepping to shack her hand only to find himself in her embrace.

Once free, he grinned widely. "You must be Aunt Rosemary!" he laughed. "From the Ashford side, I assume?" His eyes gleamed with curiosity.

"Indeed, an Ashford," she replied, her voice brightened by merriment. "The last of the Windermere Ashfords," she added softly, nostalgia washing over her. "And you are Hugh's son, just like him."

Gathering herself, she ushered them through the door into the cozy cottage.

"You show him to the guest room while I set up tea." Aunt Rosemary commanded.

Rory trailed behind Rose down the corridor, her cheerful footsteps echoing softly against the walls. As they reached the final room, a warm and inviting glow enveloped him, starkly contrasting the shadowy corners of his home, where the tight grip of financial worry stifled laughter and warmth. A longing surged within him, a bittersweet reminder of the comforts that felt perpetually out of reach, making the cozy space seem almost foreign in abundance.

"I'll unpack for a bit," she offered, her fingers brushing against the worn fabric of the suitcase as if it held more than just clothes; it was a vessel of memories waiting to be released. "Go on," she encouraged, her tone laced with warmth and a touch of mischief. "Aunt Rosemary's going to want to hear about your dad." Her eyes sparkled with intrigue, a hint of unspoken secrets lingering in the air, weaving an invisible thread connecting the past.

Rory corrected her with a cheeky grin. "Windamere," he emphasised before departing.

"Not 'a' but 'er,'" Rose called after him.

Aunt Rosemary guided him to a chair at the table and then went to the old stove, where warm scones were ready.

Rory couldn't help but compare it to his home, "Windamere." Her place felt cozy and warm, while his 'Windamere' felt empty and unfinished. Although the houses looked similar outside, her Windemere felt alive and welcoming, a natural family haven.

"Rose mentioned the 'Windamere,' an intriguing Australian variation of the word," Aunt Rose mentioned, her voice lingering softly in the air.

"No," Rory asked with interest.

Aunt Rosemary gracefully placed a large, ornate teapot on the table, its surface reflecting the soft afternoon light. Alongside it, a platter of freshly baked scones was set with care, emitting a warm, buttery aroma. Cups and saucers rattled as she arranged them delicately, and the fine china plates gleamed subtly.

"The story starts in 'Calcutta'. Kings, Queens, Aristocrats, high-ranking Raj diplomats, and Tea Planters stayed at a top-notch establishment. Local business people bought the Villa and made it a Private Limited Company hotel. One of the shareholders was Mrs. Gertrude Bearpark from Windermere. Her partners liked the name, but she thought it would confuse people, so she objected. They changed "Windermere" to "Windamere." And so, the Windamere Hotel was created." She paused to take a sip of tea. "So your Windamere came from here, but your father wanted no confusion, so he named it Windamere."

They laughed together.

Her warm and nostalgic eyes met Rory's. "I knew your father. We were best friends many moons ago," she added, a tender smile touching her lips as memories seemed to flicker like golden leaves in the autumn of her mind.

"You knew Dad?" Rory's curiosity was piqued, and now he felt the pieces clicking together. "Yes, I knew him well. He dreamed big, always talking about turning your barren land into a thriving farm. And he did it," she reflected with admiration.

"He certainly poured everything he had into building our home. Every brick and beam carry a piece of his dedication," Rory added.

He left out that despite his tireless efforts, his father never succeeded as a farmer. The harsh reality was that the crops often failed, the livestock dwindled, and financial struggles were a constant shadow. Yet, none of that dimmed the significance of the house he had built for them.

Aunt Rosemary remembered when Hugh Anderson asked her father for permission to marry her. Her father said no: "A miner's life is only poverty and despair. I want more for Rosemary." These words hurt them both in different ways. Hugh was brave and determined, asking her to move to Australia. But she couldn't be as bold as he was, and she cried as she said goodbye. Was there regret it? Torn between sorrow and comfort, she chose the latter. The memory hurt her with what-ifs and missed chances. But the life she chose brought her peace with its familiarity and stability. She often wondered how things might have been if she had gone with Hugh.

"He has a life that would have always escaped him here," Rosemary whispered, feeling the heavy weight of her father's shadow. Her fingers traced the worn edges of an old photograph, imagining dreams that had turned cold.

Tears welled as she remembered her father, blind to Hugh's true self beneath the miner's grime. That fleeting clarity vanished like mist. Her heart ached, each beat a testament to the courage required now. Love felt like a fleeting memory, a fragile dream dissolved.

"Yes, he has achieved much, especially as a miner," Rory added.

"Enough memories," she commented, her voice tinged with a hint of finality. "Tomorrow, Rose will show you our Windermere." A flush of colour bloomed in her cheeks, like the first blush of dawn over the tranquil lake beyond the rolling hills, and a broad smile spread across her face. She buried the past, now just memories.

But Rory was not finished. "Do I have any relatives?" he asked, his eyes searching for a way out of the oppressive tension that hung like a dense fog.

"No, they are all gone," Rosemary replied, her voice tinged with a bittersweet sadness. As she spoke, memories of her father's sombre words replayed, each syllable painting a stark picture of their lives. Poverty, he had often remarked, was an unyielding affliction that gnawed at both the body and soul, with death as the sole deliverance.

This bleak destiny felt inevitable for a miner trapped in his worn-out boots, the relentless wind whistling mournfully through the cracks of his decrepit shack in Windermere. Dust clung to his skin, mingling with sweat, as he toiled in the suffocating darkness of the mines, his breath echoing against the cold, unforgiving walls.

Despite the heavy pall of their shared history, Rosemary was resolute in her desire to give Rory some measure of belonging. "But we will show you where your father lived and introduce you to the people who knew him."

She felt the inadequacy of her offering, like trying to fill a hollow void with small tokens of the past, but it was the best she could offer.

Thankfully, Hugh had escaped the fate of his kin.

CHAPTER 4 - WINDERMERE'S SECRET

Rorys Grandparents Cottage

Constructed from local stone, the walls bear the marks of time and harsh weather, with the uneven texture telling stories of its past inhabitants. The roof, partially worn, is made of slate tiles, some of which appear to have shifted or deteriorated, adding to the building's abandoned charm.

Aunt Rosemary, known for her warm demeanour and sharp wit, had gracefully declined the walk around Windermere, attributing it to the frailty of her aging legs. However, the real reason was far more poignant. She saw this as a precious moment for Rory and Rose that she should not intrude upon.

Standing just outside the door, she watched them stroll down the road, a bittersweet smile touching her lips. The panorama of her past unfurled before her— memories of lost opportunities and Rose's dreams never entirely realised.

Her love for Hugh had always been a unique

tapestry of shared history and unspoken words. Their connection was strong, yet neither had ever put it into words. As years passed and life left its marks on Rosemary's face, she reflected more on the potential for love to bloom fully in Rory and Rose's newfound companionship.

She could picture them growing closer through evening strolls in the park, hearty laughs shared over dinner, and whispered conversations by the fire. She hoped that, unlike the wistful dream that had lingered unfulfilled between her and Hugh, this relationship could find its happy ending.

They stood before his grandparents' home, where his father had grown up, with a feeling of overwhelming despair. The despair clung to the crumbling walls while the wind mourned through the broken windows. They were gone, lost, and only surviving in memories. His father had survived, and his decision to make Australia home was wise.

His existence here had been riddled with relentless trials, honing his skillset and determination. Day after arduous day, he used those skills to delve into the unforgiving earth of Kalgoorlie, his hands bruised and weary from the countless hours spent chipping away at stubborn rock faces that guided him to hidden veins of gold.

Every nugget discovered was a hard-won victory, a testament to his painstakingly acquired expertise and steadfast resilience. In this crucible of sweat and grit, he forged a modest fortune, an indomitable spirit, and deep, hard-earned respect from fellow miners.

Driven to surpass his parents, he succeeded beyond measure, building Windamere as a testament to emulate Aunt Rosemary's home, which must have held special memories. Aunt Rosemary's home was warm and welcoming, safe and gentle, far removed from the house he had. It was everything he desired. She represented a world of refinement, stability, and gentle aristocracy to him. Her manor was filled with light and laughter, embodying a sense of belonging and warmth his home lacked.

It was not merely wealth that drove his father, but the pursuit of an ideal, the longing to recreate the tender memories of summers spent in Aunt Rosemary's gardens, where roses and camaraderie thrived equally.

A profound sorrow settled within Rory as he reflected on his father's accomplishments. Vivid memories of his father's ever-present smile, masking the depths of his struggles, played through his mind. He couldn't help but wonder if his father had ever truly grasped the magnitude of what he had achieved.

How much deeper would his father's sorrow be now, knowing he returned as the lone surviving son? Albert, who always shared stories of their childhood escapades at Windamere, and Guy, whose laughter could brighten even the darkest days, were now buried in a foreign field. The relentless war had claimed so many lives, and those who perished did so far from the sanctuary of home.

He felt the chilling slick of sweat bead on his forehead; each drop was a harbinger of the war memories surging forth—the gut-wrenching terror, the visceral sight of endless carnage with blood-soaked fields and haunting cries. He stood there, pallor seizing his face as his eyes glazed over, lost in the riptide of recollection.

"Hugh," Rose called, her voice tinged with worry, as she gently shook his arm. "Hugh," she repeated, her grip tightening and her shaking more insistent. She had witnessed this agonising scene countless times, the grip of war dragging him back into its darkness time and again. Her earnest voice pierced through the grim haze, yanking him back from the abyss. Today, they'd escape to Windermere, where the rolling verdant hills kissed the tranquil lake, starkly contrasting from the horror to sheer beauty.

"Sorry," he murmured, placing his trembling hand over hers. He gazed into Rose's eyes and saw the depth of concern in her furrowed brow and trembling lip.

"Don't be sorry; it is the men who conjured this abominable war who should apologise," she said with a gentle yet fierce conviction.

"Sorry," he murmured, placing his trembling

hand over hers.

"That will never happen," he uttered with a note of grim finality.

The aftermath of his experiences left him fragile and profoundly nostalgic, a deep ache for home gnawing at his core. An insistent and overpowering desire surged within him — to craft a family, to breathe laughter and joy into the halls of Windamere. This yearning pulsed through him, a sincere wish to drown out the lingering whispers of sorrow with a radiant harmony of laughter and vitality to usher in a new dawn of life.

"I think it is time for a break," she added with a spring in her step." A drink at Riggs."

They walked in silence, the crisp, fresh air filling their lungs while their eyes lingered on the quaint charm of the village. The muted sounds of birdsong and distant chatter provided a soothing backdrop as they took a moment to gather their thoughts.

The cobblestone streets, lined with ancient oak trees, seemed to hum with stories from a bygone era. The day before, they had passed the old hotel that stood a short distance from the railway station, but Rose had been eager to see her Aunt.

Opened initially as a coach house, it once catered to weary travellers using the newly completed railway from Oxenholme to Windermere. Now, the hotel has become a beloved landmark among the locals. Its peaks, sharply outlined against the sky, accentuated the attic windows and roofline. At the same time, the sturdy stone facade stood proudly against the edge of the roadway, adding a sense of stability to the village. Flowering vines clung lovingly to its walls, and the garden, bursting with colour, seemed like a scene from a painter's canvas. Inside, the warm glow of lanterns allows guests to pause and enjoy the timeless elegance preserved over the years.

The bar's warm glow beckoned them inside. "Rose, back from London," the barman greeted with a broad smile.

"Just for a few days. Then back to the hospital," Rose replied, her eyes reflecting a tired resolve.

"So many lost," the barman sighed, focusing on Rory. Have you seen action?"

"Yes," Rory confirmed, extending his hand."

"Jack," the barman responded, shaking Rory's hand heartily.

"Australian, eh? I don't see many of you around here. Take a seat," he gestured towards a table by the window overlooking the bustling street. "Hugh went to Australia. Haven't heard from him in years," he added, nostalgia colouring his voice.

"My father," Rory stated.

"Your father," Jack's face lit up with recognition. "Did he do well?"

"Found success in the gold mines," Rory shared. "He was a good miner," Jack reminisced, hinting at wistfulness in his tone. "Pity Rosemary's father didn't let them marry. He had ambitions for her that she did not share." Snapping back to the present, he indicated the same table by the window. "Only a half pint, I'm afraid. Ration's."

They sat at the table, their minds turning over his words. "Your father and Aunt Rosemary," he had said. Rose seemed mesmerised by this revelation.

Rory murmured a thoughtful "hmm" as he wrestled with the revelation's implications. His mind wandered to his mother.

Had she been aware of this all along? How did she fit into this complex tapestry of connections? Windamere was the culmination of his father's dreams, a lifelong project into which he had poured his soul. But what of Rosemary? Was she part of this vision, a partner in the dream, or was Windamere a testament to a different kind of love—an attempt to vindicate himself in the eyes of her father's disapproval?

"She never married," Rose murmured, her voice tinged with curiosity and sadness. "Do you think that's why?"

Rory's thoughts churned with the day's revelations. Each discovery pressed upon his mind like a weight, making it difficult to think straight. Today was overwhelming—a treasure trove of histories and secrets unearthed, each raising more questions than answers. He felt a pressing need to make sense of it all, to understand how each piece fit into the larger picture.

"Drink up. Time to walk home," he said, trying to force a reassuring smile. He took a long gulp of his ale, the bitter taste sharp against his tongue. He hoped it would help clear the fog in his head. "I could use a moment to think," he added, looking towards Rose, hoping she would understand his need for respite.

"Just one thing on the way," Rose interjected, putting down her glass as she stood up. "I want to visit my parents' graves. You can head straight home if you'd prefer."

"No, I'll come," Rory replied quickly. He didn't want to miss any opportunity to understand Rose better.

Rose paused at a roadside stall to buy wildflowers as they wandered past the railway station. Rory watched as she carefully selected each flower, her face a mixture of sadness and resolve.

"These should be nice," she whispered, almost as if she were talking to her parents directly.

St. Mary's church was just a short walk downhill from the railway station, with a panoramic view of the shimmering lake and majestic falls rising. The Gothic Revival architecture of the church boasted pointed arches that seemed to reach towards the sky, intricate stonework that felt cool and rough under the fingertips, and stained glass windows that reflected the sunlight.

As Rory strolled through the serene, contemplative atmosphere of the well-kept graveyard, the earthy scent of damp grass and the distant melody of chirping birds filled the air. He noted the variety of tombstones, tracing his fingers over the names on weathered, ancient stones and admiring the polished, gleaming new ones that stood resolutely amid beds of fresh flowers.

As they walked, Rory couldn't help but compare this graveyard to the one back in Midjal. "The graveyard at home... it's so different," he said, almost to himself. "Windswept hillside, dry ground, barely any vegetation. The headstones are newer and far from ornate."

"Over here," Rose guided him, stopping before a well-kept grave plot. She laid the flowers in a corner, her movements slow and deliberate.

"Your family has been here a long time," Rory murmured, reading the headstone inscriptions, some dated back two centuries.

"Yes," Rose replied softly, her voice tinged with pride and sorrow. "This is our family plot; it's almost full." She kneeled to touch a newer headstone, marking the resting place of her mother and father.

Rory watched her silently, the stark difference to Midjal weighing heavily on his mind. "So different from Midjal," he mused again, this time aloud as if trying to find some understanding in the disparity.

As they departed, Rory's gaze fell upon a row of newly turned graves, their gravestones starkly contrasting with the older ones nearby. The stone was light, almost glowing under the mid- morning sun.

He stepped closer and squinted to read the inscriptions, quickly realising these were the graves of soldiers. The air seemed to grow heavier as a profound sadness wrapped around him, squeezing his heart.

His mind drifted to the image of his brother's final rest, buried deep in the soil of Normandy. The thought of his brother without a headstone, so far from the embrace of home, sent a shiver down his spine and caused his throat to tighten. The muffled hum of the world felt distant.

Upon their return, they discovered that Aunt Rosemary was not at home, much to their collective relief. Rory had been hoping to avoid confrontation, but that wasn't in the cards. Rose approached him, carrying some salve. Though Rory resented the necessity and his reliance on it, he understood that ignoring the well-healed burns would be foolish.

He must have dozed off, for he was stirred awake by the clatter of dishes and the mouthwatering aroma of a hearty meal wafting through the air. The familiar scent signaled Rosemary's return. As he roused himself, the lingering warmth of sleep clung to his skin, and he hurriedly dressed. His mind raced with anticipation and a hint of unease about the conversation ahead. He then made his way to join her, heart thumping gently.

She turned from the stove, a waft of rich, savoury spices swirling in the air. Her cheeks flushed a rosy hue, and a warm smile spread. The soft sizzle of something delicious frying filled the cozy kitchen. "Hello, how did the day go?" she asked, her voice blending with the comforting clatter of pots and pans.

Rory sat at the table opposite Aunt Rosemary, who held the teapot. "It was good; we visited my father's home and had a half pint at Riggs."

Rosemary laughed. "Rations are part of what we must endure because of the war," she replied. "You must have met with Jack then."

"Yes, he mentioned you wanted to marry my father," Rory said.

Rosemary's face froze momentarily before a sunny smile broke out. "That's bound to come out—village gossip," she concluded. "Yes, I was in love with your father, and we wanted to marry, but my father had other plans. It's funny. I thought last night when you mentioned that he is now a farmer. My father only saw him as a miner."

Rory, sensing her relaxed demeanour, felt his tension dissipate. "I was worried about asking you; I thought it might bring back bad memories."

Aunt Rosemary laughed, a sound that carried a mixture of wistfulness and joy. "No, on the contrary, it brings back good times—the best times," she said, her eyes lingering in a distant, dreamy gaze. "Your father was the love of my life, but it was not to be." She paused, sipping her tea slowly, savouring each memory and her drink's warmth. Her hand reached for a biscuit, its crunch a momentary distraction in her trance. "We kept in touch, you know. Even when years had passed, he didn't forget. He asked me to be with him again, but by then, my father had fallen ill," she explained, her voice softening. "I chose to stay and nurse him. It was a difficult time, watching someone you love fade away." Despite the sorrow laced in her words, there was a poignant acceptance in her demeanour. Rather than harbour resentment for what life had denied her, she cherished the fleeting moments of happiness she had shared with him. She saw him in a new light, a beacon of cherished memories rather than a source of regret, and carefully tucked away the extraordinary times they had without a trace of bitterness.

"He built Windamere for you," Rory said softly, his voice tinged with admiration and melancholy.

"Yes, he was proving to my father that he could provide everything," she replied, her eyes reflecting a blend of gratitude and wistful sorrow. "Even the chance to become a farmer's wife, which I still find unimaginable." She giggled, but there was a hint of disbelief in her laughter. "I never thought he would follow through. He was always a miner at heart, dedicated and relentless."

Rory tilted his head, his thoughts drifting back to memories of his father. "It was Windamere that he truly loved, not the farming," he said, his words heavy with understanding. He knew his father's flaws well; the man's stubborn nature clashed with the gentleness required for tending the land. "Farming was never his passion, but building Windamere, giving you a dream realised, was the love that drove him."

"How is he now?" Rosemary asked. "I have not seen four him in years, and in that time, we have endured much heartbreak," he began, his voice tinged with sorrow. Though hesitant to delve into the painful memories, a part of him wanted Rosemary to understand the depth of their suffering, to feel as though she was a cherished part of their family. "My two brothers," he paused as if the weight of his words were too heavy to bear, "they died in the war." The silence that followed spoke volumes, encapsulating the immense grief he could not bring himself to explain.

"He must be missing you." Aunt Rosemary mentioned softly.

"Yes, I want to get home." Rory's voice carried a calm assurance, but beneath the surface, a storm roiled within him.

The farm was waiting for him, its fertile fields now a symbol of solace and burden. It wasn't just about reclaiming his father's legacy but facing the daunting reality that life had irrevocably changed.

The wounds of war had scarred more than just the land—they had left deep furrows in his heart, seeding doubts and fears. Would he be able to rebuild what was lost? Would he recognise the person he had become? A heavy sense of unease emerged as he envisioned the battered economy and the challenges looming ahead. The battles had ended, but the struggle was far from over.

CHAPTER 5 - SIR REGINALD

The ancestral home

Reflects the timeless elegance of a grand estate. The symmetrical architecture features a stately façade with tall chimneys, large multi-paned windows, and a central entrance framed by columns. The grounds are meticulously landscaped, with a serene pond in the foreground showcasing an ornate fountain surrounded by trimmed hedges and flowerbeds. Towering trees frame the scene, emphasizing the secluded and prestigious nature of the estate.

The car arrived promptly at 6 p.m.—a sleek Bentley with a poised chauffeur, immediately stirring a wave of disdain within Rory. Every polished surface and impeccable detail of the vehicle seemed to mock him, amplifying his discomfort.

As he sank into the leather seat, a heavy silence enveloped him. Each breath was fraught with a storm of conflicting feelings as the car journeyed toward the Manor.

When they arrived, a gasp lodged in his throat.

The Manor loomed before him, its magnificent and suffocating grandeur nestled amidst a garden so meticulously trimmed that it felt like a testament to meticulous control over nature's wild beauty. The sight was breathtaking and stifling, a heavy weight settling in his stomach, an ominous premonition of the evening awaiting him.

The butler stepped back as the door opened, revealing Windsor's standing in regal splendour. The hallway stretched before them, its immaculate tiles shimmering like polished gemstones beneath the sparkling chandelier's glow.

Rory yearned to brush aside the extravagant display, yet he found himself ensnared by its allure. It clashed violently with his ideals of equality; here, there was no trace of fairness or justice.

In stark contrast, Aunt Rosemary's cottage floated into his thoughts—an embrace of genuine warmth and intimacy. This opulence felt hollow beside that memory, a vehicle for societal validation rather than a true home. The difference was palpable, igniting the tension within him, a reminder of the chasm.

"Good evening," Windsor beamed at the Ladies, gazing at Rose and Aunt Rosemary, bestowing them praises that hung like sweet perfume.

Not a flicker of acknowledgment graced Rory's direction as Windsor added, "Thank you, John. I'll guide them through." He offered his arm to Rose, leaving Rory to accompany Aunt Rosemary in a role that again felt secondary.

A tempest brewed inside Rory; the familiar volatility of comparison ignited his spirit, a sensation of being eclipsed again by Windsor. It wasn't merely the sting of being overlooked—it was Windsor's uncanny ability to render him invisible, a dismissal so artful and casual it burrowed under Rory's skin, igniting flames of frustration that simmered just beneath the surface.

Aunt Rosemary tapped his arm. "Don't let him get to you," she murmured. "That is what he wants."

"By playing Lord of the Manor?" Rory responded quietly, trying to suppress the biting resentment in his voice, but he could not help but feel the sting of condescension.

"Yes, remember his family has been here for centuries," she smiled, her eyes compassionate yet knowing the brittle pride Rory carried. "You will, Sir Reginald, be more palatable," she predicted. Rory knew she was trying to reassure him. But the weight of Windsor's shadow Windsor's present a legacy of dominance he was struggling to accept.

Raised in a Midjal where everyone shared the same modest means, he was taught from a young age that every person deserved equal respect and opportunities. His father ingrained This ethos in him; he recounted stories of communal efforts and collective triumphs.

59

However, it wasn't until he found himself amidst the chaos of the battlefields that he encountered the stark contrasts of the English ruling class. There, the elite's deeply entrenched hierarchies and privileges sharply opposed the egalitarian beliefs that had shaped his upbringing.

Aunt Rosemary possessed a keen intuition for discerning character, and her evaluation rang true.

At first glance, Sir Reginald was not the arrogant aristocrat one might anticipate. Instead, he presented himself as a dignified elder with meticulously styled grey hair and a pleasant demeanour that put others at ease.

Windsor gave them a perfunctory introduction, handing Rose like she was one of them.

In stark contrast stood his wife, Clarissa, her coiffed blonde hair perfectly poised and her smile dripping with condescension—an apparent snobbery on display. It became all too evident when Aunt Rosemary, with her characteristic warmth, introduced Rory to the couple, and Clarissa's dismissive remark hung in the air like a cloud.

Aunt Rosemary, never fussed or outdone, addressed Sir Reginald. "You may remember his father, Hugh. He was a miner who bravely ventured to Australia." Her pride was evident, her stance firm amidst the nobility.

"A miner," Lady Clarissa sniffed, her disdain unmistakable. "I doubt we would have had the pleasure of meeting him."

"I remember him well," Sir Reginald interjected, his tone warming with genuine admiration. "He was a remarkable miner known for his skill in uncovering gold veins. I assume his efforts brought him success?" His gaze turned expectantly to Rory.

"Indeed, he struck gold in Kalgoorlie," Rory replied, a mischievous glint in his eyes. "With his newfound wealth, he transformed our three-thousand-acre farm." There was a satisfaction in his voice, a sharp contrast to the modesty of English estates, even as he delivered his subtle jibe.

Lady Clarissa's dismissive "Oh" was promptly disregarded by her husband. "Good for him. I always enjoy seeing my men prosper," Sir Reginald commented.

Aunt Rosemary remained silent, memories of the miners' harsh working conditions weighing heavily on her.

"Time for dinner," Lady Clarissa suggested, her eyes lingering on the butler, signalling him with a pregnant and weary glance.

"Certainly, let's go through. Miss Ashford," Sir Reginald said, a touch of tenderness in his voice as he held his arm out to Aunt Rosemary. His gesture was more than mere politeness; it spoke of a longing to protect and cherish.

With a burst of adrenalin, Rory turned to Rose, holding out his arms, which she readily accepted.

There was no way Rory was escorting Lady Clarissa. He could not suppress the look of triumph as Windsor was left to escort his mother.

The dining table sprawled elegantly, capable of hosting a much larger gathering than the mere six who would occupy it. The tabletop was adorned with an exquisite display, with candles flickering softly and vases overflowing with fresh flowers, creating an enchanting atmosphere.

Rory approached, intending to claim his spot at the far end, but just as he was about to lower himself onto the chair, Sir Reginal's voice pierced through the ambient chatter. "Rory, come join me at this end," he beckoned, gesture emphatically gesturing seat at his right. His tone was inviting yet charged with a palpable curiosity. "I would like to learn about Kalgoorlie and Australia."

Rory's heart quickened at the unexpected attention, his apprehension melting away under the warmth of Sir Reginal's enthusiasm. A smile broke across his face as he felt welcomed into the inner circle of conversation, the camaraderie between them sparking an instant connection.

"Certainly, Sir, I would like that." Rory's voice quivered slightly, betraying a mixture of eagerness and trepidation as he took his seat. He cautiously glanced at Rose and Aunt Rosemary on the opposite side of the grand table. He was acutely aware of the moment's weight; Sir Reginald deserved utmost respect with his distinguished presence, and Rory felt a quiet pressure to uphold that decorum.

The elegant surroundings only heightened the tension. Rory's heart swelled with admiration as the attendants glided in their crisp white uniforms—each movement perfectly choreographed. Their matching hats were like crowns atop their heads, emphasizing the grandeur of the affair.

He couldn't suppress a smile, feeling a surge of joy amidst the opulence. Yet, beneath the surface, he grappled with a whirlwind of emotions—wonder, respect, and a touch of envy—each competing for his attention as he absorbed the lavish scene.

So, this was how the other half lived. It was all very grand but not to Rory's taste. He could not fathom how one could ever relax in this environment.

To Rory's astonishment, the evening was a success. He was drawn to Sir Reginald, whose passion for farming illuminated their discussion. As they exchanged ideas, their conversation meandered through the lush fields of England and the sun-drenched expanses of Australia, uncovering the challenges each faced. With each shared experience, the warmth between them deepened, making the night feel alive with possibility.

They departed with the promise of exploring the sprawling fields of Sir Reginald's farms and the mine that had once echoed with his father's labour. The air was thick with anticipation as memories of toil and resilience flickered like distant lanterns in the recesses of their minds.

Rory's gaze shifted inward, drawn toward the passions that once ignited his spirit. He struggled to push the haunting echoes of war into the shadows of his memory.

The following morning, he awoke with the sun barely stretching its golden rays across the room, only to be greeted by the delightful clatter of utensils and the rich aroma of breakfast wafting through the air. Aunt Rosemary was already at the table, her warm smile illuminating the cozy kitchen.

"Good morning, Rory," she beamed, the cheerful tone of her voice mingling with the soft bubbling of water on the stove. "An early riser today. But then again, perhaps that can be attributed to your new friend, Sir Reginald."

Rory settled into his chair, the wood excellent against his fingertips, and glanced at Aunt what I expected after meeting Windsor."

"Indeed, Windsor presents a fascinating contrast," Aunt Rosemary reflected, her spoon idly stirring the porridge that warmed her hands.

Memories surged within her, vivid images of Windsor basking in the relentless adoration of his mother—a situation that struck her as both endearing and troubling. Lady Clarissa, his mother, saw her son as an epitome of perfection; he could do no wrong in her eyes. "His mother has sheltered him, often at the cost of his father's role in his life. Although somewhat unremarkable, Sir Reginald embodies what we expect from the upper echelons—fair, affable, and a loyal supporter of the societal hierarchy."

Rory, taking a moment to ponder over his spoonful of porridge, finally interjected, "I think your perception of class distinction is misguided. Surely, all men should be regarded as equals."

With a dismissive wave, Aunt Rosemary countered, "That ideal is nothing but a dream. Men will always be ranked by the rigid social structure we abide by or by their talents and merits."

"While I can accept merit as a measure, I will not subscribe to the notion of enforced class," Rory pressed, his brow furrowed in thought. "Besides Windsor, he seems intent on courting Rose."

"On the contrary," Aunt Rosemary snapped, irritation colouring her words. "His true aim lies in securing your downfall, dear boy. Rose is nothing more than a pawn in his mother's game. His mother, Clarissa, deems us beneath him, and he dances to her tune."

As Rory absorbed her pointed observations, an unsettling truth began to crystallize. Aunt Rosemary had indeed touched on something profound—Lady Clarissa's influence loomed large, casting long shadows over their lives and dictating their standing within her world.

With a contemplative sigh, Rory finally pushed back from the table, the lingering warmth of the porridge punctuating his senses. The flavours and the conversation swirled within him, igniting a myriad of conflicted thoughts about ambition, love, and the inexorable chains of expectation that bound them all.

'Well, I am off to take up Lord Reginald's farm tour,' he announced, his voice carrying a hint of excitement that danced in the steam rising from the kitchen.

He gathered his empty bowl and walked to the sink, the early morning light streaming through the window and casting a golden hue over the room. As he rinsed his dish, the fresh scent of the farm wafted through the open door, stirring a longing for the sprawling fields that awaited him.

"Thank you for breakfast. I wish you a good day," he said, his voice warm yet tinged with a subtle longing. "And please extend my regards to Rose; I should return by lunchtime."

"I will," Aunt Rosemary replied, her voice carrying a depth of affection that seemed to wrap around the words—the moment hung delicately between them, like the final notes of a melody echoing through the stillness of the morning.

"Ah, you're early," Sir Reginald remarked, a joyous smile illuminating his face. The absence of his usual butler added a moment of intimacy to the encounter.

"I trust it's not too early," Rory replied, a flicker of concern crossing his features as he registered the aging lines on Sir Reginald's face, reminding him of the passage of time.

"Not at all, my boy. Though I may be on the other side of my youth, mornings are charming for me. They have a certain crispness as if the world is breathing anew." Rory revelled in the English mornings, where the invigorating chill enveloped him like a brisk hug, each breath sharp and alive with potential. The air was laced with the earthy scent of dew- kissed grass, awakening his senses and stirring new dreams.

In stark contrast, the mornings of Australia, though charming in their own right, felt parched and predictable. Each dawn was a whisper of familiarity, a mere turning of the pages in a well-loved book, lacking the thrill of rebirth that the English sun ignited.

"Well, time to go," Sir Reginald remarked, gesturing towards the jeep that awaited their departure.

It lacked the usual pomp of a dedicated chauffeur; instead, two men stood by—one older, weathered by years, and the other younger, whose attentive demeanour bore witness to the respect he held for Reginald, transcending mere social status.

Their presence offered a glimpse into the subtle dynamics of admiration and duty simmering beneath the surface, hinting at untold stories and connections forged through shared experiences in a world often dictated by rank.

The contrast between Sir Reginald's English farming and Rory's Australian expanse was strikingly vivid.

Rory envisioned his surroundings—endless fields stretching beneath an expansive sky, the golden hues of wheat swaying in the breeze. Such was the reality of Australian wheat and sheep farming.

The farms sprawled across the land, necessitated by an unforgiving climate characterized by relentless heat, arid conditions, and scant rainfall. Farmers were forced to acquire vast tracts of land to ensure the survival of their crops and livestock.

Wheat farming was a colossal endeavour, marked by the whir of machinery efficiently sowing and reaping the golden grains. Meanwhile, the sheep roamed freely over the sprawling terrain, their woolly forms dotting the landscape as they grazed on the sparse vegetation. Australia's agricultural endeavours were firmly rooted in export, with trucks laden with wheat heading towards distant Asian markets. At the same time, bales of wool found their way to buyers across the globe.

"Rory, have you taken a moment to reflect on how profoundly our farming practices have been altered since the war?" Sir Reginald inquired, a hint of concern threading through his voice as he adjusted his monocle while they ambled through the sun-drenched fields.

"You mean the shrinking plots, Sir?" Rory replied, casting a sorrowful glance at the diminished lands. "It's clear that farmers are scrambling to make the most of the scarce land we still possess."

"Indeed, my dear Rory," Sir Reginald continued, his brow furrowing with worry. "The government's intervention has been less of a lifeline and more of a burden. Those subsidies and the so-called advanced machinery—it feels like they expect us to pull sustenance from the air around us!"

Rory chuckled, though the sound held a bittersweet edge. "It's certainly become a pressing matter. We've all felt the harsh reality of food insecurity after the war. It's almost miraculous how quickly we've had to change course."

"Ah, the transition to mixed operations," Sir Reginald mused, a reflective sigh escaping him. "Embracing a blend of crops, livestock, and even the rare dairy cow—it feels like a necessary strategy given the shortages that still haunt us."

"Quite a stark difference, isn't it?" Rory added, his voice tinged with nostalgia. "Back in Australia, we've stubbornly clung to single-crop cultivation, primarily for export. It makes one truly appreciate the gravity of our current situation."

"Exactly! We must prioritize feeding our

people," Sir Reginald said, his voice rising with conviction. "As stewards of the land, we have a deeper responsibility—to nourish our nation before all else."

"I'd like to introduce you to one of our tenant farmers," Sir Reginald offered, skillfully maneuvering the jeep towards a nearby field. The air buzzed with the scent of rich soil and sunshine.

"In Australia, farms are colossal enterprises, vast expanses that thrust their bounty onto the world stage," he continued, emphasizing the vibrant pulse of agrarian life that filled the atmosphere.

"Absolutely! It's remarkable. You gaze upon England, and it transforms into an entirely different narrative," Sir Reginald elaborated, his voice rich with the weight of tradition.

"Indeed, you still cling to that historical landowner-tenant system," Rory noted, the contrast sparking curiosity.

"Precisely! Our farmers toil upon rented patches, each plot a testament to resilience and stewardship," Sir Reginald affirmed, the landscape around them whispering stories of labour and harvest.

Meeting the farmer was interesting. To Rory, he seemed content with his status as a tenant, as his family had for generations—something foreign to an Australian.

For Rory, the disparity was nothing short of astonishing. The spirit of autonomy flourished in

Australia, reminiscent of golden wheat dancing in the wind, standing tall against the azure sky. He could vividly envision the warm sun embracing herds of sheep, grazing blissfully, their produce destined for bustling international markets—a brilliant canvas showcasing the tenacity and ingenuity of the farmers.

Driving back from the farm, Sir Reginal felt compelled to explain.

"Ah, my dear Rory, allow me to clarify this for you simply. Picture this: our English farmers navigate a terrain deeply intertwined with governmental oversight. Historically, this involvement has proven essential, propelling farmers toward higher yields. They are armed with abundant support – from cutting-edge machinery to efficient fertilizers, not to mention assured pricing for their wares. The noble intent behind this framework is clear-cut: to stave off the looming spectre of hunger that could cast a shadow over our society."

"Where I hail from, you'll be struck by the sheer expansiveness of our sprawling paddocks, which seem to reach towards the horizon," Rory replied, his eyes wide with the imagery conjured by his memories. "We own our land and farm with little government assistance.

"But in England, farms are more minor, yet brimming with diversity—crops, livestock, and dedicated hands working earnestly to extract every possible yield from every inch of earth. It's not so much a panorama of open fields as it is productivity and dedication needed.

Sir Reginal insisted on escorting Rory back to Aunt Rosemary's quaint cottage. A silent understanding passed between them, laden with the weight of new beginnings and unresolved paths.

"I can't thank you enough, Sir, for your time and company," Rory said, his voice tinged with gratitude and lingering uncertainty.

Sir Reginal's grip was firm, a tangible reminder of the bond they had forged in such a brief encounter. "Son, you journeyed from the other side of the world for our cause—a choice I admire deeply," he replied, his tone imbued with sincerity as if he was acknowledging a shared mission that transcended mere duty.

"Thank you," Rory managed to say, the warmth of the commendation washing over him, stirring something deep within—the realization that his efforts and sacrifices were recognized by someone so esteemed.

"I can't accompany you to the mine where your father worked, but I can arrange for Jake to show you around tomorrow if that suits you," Sir Reginal continued, a hint of kindness lighting his features.

"I would appreciate that, Sir," Rory responded, a flicker of hope igniting within him at the thought of connecting with his father's legacy.

"Tomorrow at seven, Jake will be waiting for you," Sir Reginal assured him, his eyes holding a weight of promise as he observed Rory preparing to part ways. "And, Rory, should you ever find yourself in need, don't hesitate to call. I will do everything in my power to assist you."

Rory stood watching as Sir Reginal's vehicle disappeared down the lane, his heart tumultuous. Despite his scepticism towards the aristocracy, there was something undeniably reassuring about this man. In that fleeting moment, Rory felt his faith rekindled, the flicker of hope transforming into a robust flame that illuminated the shadows of doubt lingering in his mind.

CHAPTER 6 - HIS FATHER'S PAST

The Slate Mine- set amidst rugged, dramatic landscapes of rolling hills and quiet valleys. Small clusters of stone-built miners' homes dotted the remote terrain near the mines. A tranquil lake, reflecting the surrounding slopes, added stark contrast to the industrial activity. Stone walls and simple structures highlighted the region's harsh yet resourceful environment, symbolizing the legacy of slate mining.

As Rory entered the room, his heart raced at the sight of Aunt Rosemary and Rose sharing an intimate moment over lunch.

"I'm sorry it took longer than I anticipated." The words slipped from his lips, laced with a hint of anxiety. He cast an anxious glance at Rose, searching her expression for any sign of concern, but her calm demeanour left him uncertain. Was her indifference a relief or a source of deeper worry?

Aunt Rosemary's voice broke through his thoughts as she gracefully placed a plate before him. "I kept a plate for you." Her warmth enveloped him like a soft embrace, but he couldn't help but feel the weight of anticipation in the air. "How was Sir Reginald?"

"He is outstanding. He is very knowledgeable about farming," Rory replied, the chatter around him fading as he began to eat. Surprised by the ferocity of his hunger, he realized it was not just the food he craved but a sense of connection, a simple affirmation that life continued to gift him. "What did you do?"

"Winston finally regained his senses." Rose confronted him, her tone sharp and laced with challenge. "So, we found ourselves at the café, sharing a cup of tea."

A storm of anger surged within Rory. He was acutely aware that Windsor was fully conscious of his plans to be with his father. "Good. I feared you might feel forsaken," he replied, masking his rising frustration with a veneer of calm.

"Not at all," Rose shot back, her irritation bubbling beneath the surface, challenging her attempts to maintain composure.

"Ah, so you found Sir Reginald's farm tour captivating," Aunt Rosemary interjected, smoothly steering the conversation away from their earlier disagreement.

"Indeed, English agriculture is very different from what we have back in Australia," Rory replied, a hint of relief washing over him as the topic shifted. "He also rekindled a bit of my hope in the English aristocracy—if only more of them were like him."

"Sadly, they are few and far between," Aunt Rosemary sighed, her eyes narrowing as she shared her insight. "His influence stretches quite a bit, both in the local community and within the House of Lords."

Rory's curiosity was piqued at this revelation, "Does he, now?" He pondered her words quietly for a moment. "He offered his assistance should I ever require it. Not that I foresee needing it, but it was a kind gesture nonetheless."

"He will keep his word," Aunt Rosemary replied, her voice steady yet imbued with a quiet confidence that wrapped around the words like a warm embrace.

"Speaking of which," he continued, excitement flickering in his eyes, "he has arranged for my visit to the mines tomorrow." He paused, letting the moment's weight settle between them, then turned to Rose, anticipation dancing on his lips. "Would you like to come?"

Rose's heart fluttered at the thought. She had never set foot in the mines; they were a world filled with dark secrets and untold wonders. Would the sights and sounds enchant her or chill her to the bone? "Can I think on that?" she ventured, her voice barely above a whisper, as if afraid to disturb the lingering mystery.

"Of course," he assured her, his smile broadening. "You have until 7 a.m. tomorrow to decide; that's when Jake picks me up. I'm certain they wouldn't mind an extra set of eyes in the depths."

The following day, as dawn broke with a cool, crisp air at precisely 7 a.m., Rose and Rory stood side by side with anticipation as the jeep rolled up. Jake, with a confident stride and an easy smile, introduced himself.

They were ready to embark on a journey that promised to reveal the hidden layers of their world. "You intend to go underground, Rose?" Jake inquired, his tone laced with curiosity as if probing the depths of her resolve.

Rose hesitated momentarily, the weight of expectation pressing down on her. "No," she replied, her voice steady yet contemplative. "But I want to see what the women do above ground." There was a flicker of determination in her eyes, a desire to connect with the strength of those who carved their paths in a male-dominated realm.

Jake's relief washed over him like a warm tide. "Good," he said, a hint of appreciation in his expression. The war had cast its dark shadow, leading to labour shortages, and he knew the significance of women's contributions above ground in this arduous time.

Standing slightly apart, Rory interjected enthusiastically, revealing his internal struggles. "I want to see underground," he declared, his words tinged with longing and rebellion.

"Yes, Sir Reginald mentioned your father worked here," Jake acknowledged, recognizing the weight of legacy tied to Rory's ambitions. "Some of his mates still do. Though we work slate now, the gold ran out." There was a camaraderie in the air, a connection built on shared histories and the echoes of dreams unfulfilled.

Rory felt a rush of memories engulf him, particularly his father's insatiable hunger for gold— an obsession that had driven him into the deepest mines. The thought of the slate they now dug felt like a betrayal; his father would have loathed it. Yet, amid those reflections, a glimmer of hope remained. His father had found fortune in Kalgoorlie, and perhaps Rory would, too, carve his path in the shadow of his father's legacy. He was forging his own identity in farming in a new world shaped by history and ambition.

"The mine you will see today is an underground mine, but some mine from quarries," Jake explained.

"Is it a good life as a miner?" Rory queried, remembering his grandfather's humble abode.

"It's a relentless existence beneath the surface," Jake began, his tone heavy with the weight of unspoken stories. "The danger is ever-present, and it demands not only physical strength but a mental fortitude to endure those gruelling hours in the dark underbelly of the earth."

Rory's brow furrowed as he asked, "Are they paid

well?"

Jake leaned in, his voice becoming more serious, "In many mines, wages are set to a piecework system. Miners earn based on the slate or minerals they extract rather than receiving a steady hourly wage. This method adds immense pressure, pushing them to work harder and longer to make ends meet, often compromising their safety."

Rory nodded, reflecting on his father's choice to seek fortune in Australia, realizing it was the right path.

"Given the nature of mining and the economic landscape, families often navigate a precarious financial existence. Mines can shut down overnight due to market shifts, and the demand for slate can vary wildly. When times are tough, a miner might find himself without work, leaving the family in a difficult position," Jake continued, his voice trailing off as they veered off the main road toward the mine. He paused, remembering the countless families he had seen hold each other up amid hardship. "In many mining households, women must step in, taking on jobs on the surface—sorting slate or working in local services. Added income is vital, particularly when a miner is injured or during downturns when mine production slows." He concluded that the jeep had come to a stop. "In this life, mining families learn to rely on one another."

As Rory descended into the underground depths,

the dim, oppressive air enveloped him like a suffocating shroud. The hard hat perched atop his head felt heavy, a hollow reminder of the dangers that lurked in the shadows.

Around him, miners toiled with unyielding determination, their faces glistening with sweat under the faint glow of carbide lamps strapped to their helmets. This flickering light offered only the faintest comfort, revealing the grim contours of their faces drawn tight with fatigue and the grime that caked their skin.

The cavernous space echoed with the rhythmic sounds of picks striking rock, each strike sending a shiver through the earth that resonated in Rory's bones. The air was thick with the earthy scent of damp soil, mingling with a metallic tang hinting at the relentless struggle against the ground they tried to conquer. It was a world steeped in darkness, where isolation gnawed at their thoughts, distorting perceptions, while the oppressive weight of the rock above pressed down on their weary shoulders.

Rory's heart ached as he imagined his father enduring the same gruelling toil daily, trapped amid the silence. He could almost hear the echoes of despair that must have echoed through the relentless hours.

In this cavernous underworld, the soul could wither, leaving only shadows of once-bright spirits. It was no wonder his father had found solace across the ocean in Australia; in this bleak abyss, escape was not just a desire—it was a desperate yearning for light, life, and liberation from the relentless grip of the earth.

A wave of relief washed over him as he broke through the surface.

"Not quite your scene?" Jake inquired, his expression brightening with a playful smile.

"No, I'm a farmer at heart. I thrive in the open air, where I can truly connect with the world around me," Rory replied, the weight of the earth still fresh in his mind.

"I get that," Jake acknowledged, a hint of understanding in his tone. "But in places like this, our choices are limited."

"My father found a way to escape this life," Rory said, his brow furrowing as he struggled to envision his father in the depths of a mine. It seemed impossible, given his father's evident passion for mining. But why?

"Was it wealth he sought?" Jake asked, intrigued.

"Indeed. My father amassed quite a fortune, purchasing land and constructing a grand home —a stark contrast to the place he once called home," Rory answered, pride lacing his voice.

Jake mulled it over, a contemplative look crossing his features. "He must be a man of great vision. Not many of us miners think beyond the daily grind; we go underground to scrape a living, not to chase dreams of fortune. Such aspirations feel distant, even unimaginable."

"Ready to go?" Rose inquired, her voice breaking through the tension that enveloped them as she approached.

"Yes," Rory replied, his eagerness to leave palpable. The weight of his father's hidden past pressed heavily on his chest, a chilling reminder of the shadows that lurked beneath their shared history. Memories of countless hours spent alongside his mother on the farm twisted in his mind, and he couldn't shake the feeling of having dismissed their struggles, unaware of the burdens that had shaped his father's existence.

"I will take you home then," Jake said, his tone resolute. Yet, when Rory opened his mouth to voice his concerns, Jake answered, "Sir Reginald's orders."

As they bid Jake farewell, relief and unease settled over them. With silent glances exchanged, they made their way to Aunt Rosemary's cottage, each step heavy with unspoken thoughts. Arriving to find her absence, Rose recalled the key tucked beneath the red pot—a small source of comfort amidst their uncertainty. "That was certainly… an experience," Rose remarked, her voice laced with contemplation as she set the kettle to boil.

"Experience?" Rory echoed, a frown crossing his features. "Life in the mines is grim. I can't understand how my father endured it and still found joy."

"Yes, the women bear countless responsibilities," Rose replied gently, her hands skillfully preparing the tea. "They sort slate, operate machinery, and manage the mine's surface. Their role is crucial." As the tea brewed, Rory retrieved two cups, the routine now tinged with Aunt Rosemary's absence.

"It seems like a step above the underground," Rory observed, scepticism mingling with a faint glimmer of hope.

"Indeed," Rose agreed, steam rising gracefully from the kettle. "While their work is undeniably taxing and rife with challenges, I share your sentiment. It feels preferable to the darkness below." The air between them hung heavy with awareness of the sacrifices inherent in their lives—both tethered to the earth yet longing for the light.

Rory held his cup of tea close, allowing the warmth to envelop his face as he wrestled with unsettling thoughts. "I still can't believe my father was one of them," he murmured, disbelief and sorrow roiling in his gut. The disparity between his father's cheerful nature and the harsh reality of his past gnawed at him. "Always so joyful, but for me, down there…" He shivered, unable to fathom the hell it represented.

Rose studied him, her brow knitting as she considered her reply. "Perhaps he finds solace in Australia, a land that offers him a life so different from his past." Her tone was gentle, almost hesitant, as if wary of the burden her words might add to his turmoil.

Rory pondered her insight, a flickering light of understanding igniting within him. "That could be true," he replied slowly, yet uncertainty lingered in his heart. His father still loved mining. The more he tried to fathom his father's choices, the more fragmented his thoughts became. Would he ever fully grasp him?

After a poignant silence enveloped them, Rory's voice broke through, tinged with longing. "I want to find my family's graves. Maybe in that sacred space, I could piece together the fragments of my past."

"Of course, we could go now," Rose suggested, her gaze softening with empathy. "But I think tomorrow would be more fitting. That way, I can also pay my respects to my parents."

"Yes, that sounds ideal," he replied, warmth blooming at the thought of her company. Together, they would embark on a journey towards remembrance, seeking understanding in the echoes of their shared past.

The past loomed before them, a poignant tapestry woven into the very soil of Windamere Cemetery. Weatherworn stones stood like sentinels, their surfaces etched with the stories of lives once vibrant now etched in silence. Newer graves, marked by solemn military headstones, paid tribute to local soldiers lost in the throes of war, their sacrifices etched in the hearts of those who remembered. The older gravestones, relics from the 19th and early 20th centuries, bore the weight of time, adorned with moss and ivy that curled around their bases like a lover's embrace, imbuing the place with eternal remembrance.

"They are at peace now," Aunt Rosemary murmured, her voice barely above a whisper, heavy with sadness as her gaze drifted over the sea of stones to the shimmering lakes beyond. The gentle rustle of leaves in the cool breeze seemed to echo her sentiment, wrapping around them in a comforting embrace.

It was a spontaneous decision to join them on this pilgrimage, a fragile thread connecting the living to the lost. It was a moment to reflect and acknowledge that while they were here, the essence of those who had departed lingered still, woven into the very fabric of this sacred ground.

"How do I locate my family's graves?" Rory inquired, his gaze drifting over the myriad of gravestones that stood silent and solemn, each a testament to loss and remembrance.

"The vicar?" Rose proposed, her voice barely above a whisper, perhaps sensing the weight of grief in the air.

Aunt Rosemary brought her thoughts back to the moment, her heart heavy with echoes of the past. "Yes, he will have all the records," she replied, tinged with bittersweet nostalgia.

As they approached the quaint church, Rory nodded to the soldier's grave that stood sentinel by the path. With each step, the sharp edges of sorrow that he experienced when Rose visited his parents' graves on their arrival at Windermere softened. His longing to find his family is now the priority.

The elderly Vicar, clad in trousers and a cozy cardigan, welcomed them with a warm yet weary smile as they approached the door.

"Good morning, Miss Ashford," he said, his voice rich with familiarity and a hint of concern as he turned his attention to Aunt Rosemary. "And Rose, I assume you've taken leave? It's good to see you."

"Yes, indeed. I want to introduce you to Rory Anderson."

They lapsed for a moment as they exchanged polite greetings, the air thick with the weight of shared histories and unspoken emotions.

"Rory is Hugh's son, and together, we're hoping to find his family graves," Aunt Rosemary added, her tone carrying an underlying sense of purpose mixed with nostalgia.

"Hugh... how has he been?" The Vicar's inquiry hung in the air, a subtle acknowledgment of the bonds that tethered them all, a connection forged through loss and remembrance. "I hope his dreams come true."

"Well," Rory responded, remembering the mines of yesterday. He added, "Really well, he made a fortune mining, and now we have a farm."

"I am glad to hear a happy outcome in these times of sadness." He stood aside, ushering them into the church. "Let us have a look at the records."

He delved into the records, his fingers tracing the inscriptions with an intensity that mirrored his inner turmoil. "You're fortunate they have a family plot down here," he remarked, a hint of reverence in his voice as he pointed them toward their heritage.

Thank you," Rory replied, his eagerness palpable, a spark of excitement flickering in his chest.

They approached the plot, and the sight struck Rory before him: ivy entwined delicately over the weathered stones, instilling a sense of tranquillity that wrapped around him like a gentle embrace. The melodic notes of birdsong and the whisper of leaves danced harmoniously, amplifying the serene ambience of the surroundings and urging him to reflect on his connection to this sacred place.

The neatly arranged headstones, with the older graves standing silent in the back and the more recent ones in the foreground, created an intimate tableau of lives intertwining through time. A prominent central stone bore the words "In Loving Memory of the Anderson Family of Windermere," while the others whispered tales dating back to the 16th century.

Rory gazed upon the graves in awe, his heart swelling with the weight of generations of miners whose struggles were etched into the very fabric of his existence—something he found difficult to comprehend fully. They were his ancestors, an intricate web of sacrifices and resilience. He pondered how vastly different the next generation's life in Australia would be.

Open landscapes stretched before them, a promise of freedom and a life unbound by the chains of class—an opportunity to forge their destinies without the burdens that had anchored their forebears to years of servitude and hardship.

CHAPTER 7 - V-DAY

V-Day celebrations in 1945

Jubilant crowds filling city streets to commemorate the end of World War II. The atmosphere was electric, with people dancing, embracing, and waving in joy. Streets were adorned with flags, banners, and impromptu parades, while the air resonated with laughter and music. It was a poignant mix of celebration and reflection, as communities came together to honour sacrifice, resilience, and the dawn of peace.

"It's almost time for the hospital again," Rose murmured, a tinge of melancholy colouring her voice.

"Why not take a couple of extra days?" Aunt Rosemary suggested with a hint of concern.

"They are understaffed and overloaded with patients," Rose explained, her tone resolute. She was deeply committed to her duties, with a sense of responsibility etched into every word.

"And what about you, Rory?" Aunt Rosemary's gaze shifted to the young man. "My ship sails in ten days, so I have a brief reprieve." He paused, contemplating his following words. "The war is almost over."

Both women looked up at him with a mix of hope and disbelief.

"Are you sure?" Rose sought clarification, her mind racing. She tried to envision life after the war. Would she continue nursing? The answer came swiftly—yes, without a doubt. But what would London be like? The thought filled her with despair; so much needed to be rebuilt, and so many lives had been lost. Nearly every family had endured the pain of loss. The road to recovery was daunting. England was facing bleak and challenging times ahead.

"Yes, they are assembling troop carriers, a sign of a new offensive or the war's end. The Germans are retreating; soon, it will be Berlin."

"Life after the war will be hard," Rose voiced her concerns, her voice tinged with the weariness of countless restless nights.

"Yes," Rory agreed, his gaze distant. "England has taken a hammering. It's a wonder we're still standing."

"I am lucky," Aunt Rosemary mentions with a hint of pride in her voice. "I help the war effort, of course." She pauses, nostalgia softening her expression. We are the base for the Flying boats built on the Calgarth Estate."

"I didn't know that," Rory says, genuinely

impressed. "Those boats play a critical role in the North Atlantic Campaign. They protect convoys carrying vital supplies to Britain and hunt German U-boats." "Yes, the Calgarth Estate boasts one of the largest hangars,"

Aunt Rosemary continues, her voice is more animated. "It's not just an estate; it's a lively village with factory shops and bustling activity. The air is filled with the hum of industry and the chatter of busy workers. The scent of machine oil mixes with fresh timber. On match days, the local football team's cheers echo through the streets, mingling with the smell of fried snacks from stalls. At its peak, the factory buzzed with over 1,500 employees, many from nearby villages. Workers' laughter filled the air, creating a vibrant atmosphere. You can feel the energy, see their sweat, and hear the hum of work everywhere."

She brimmed with pride, knowing the profound impact their considerable contribution made. It was not merely the scale of their endeavours that was impressive; it was the profound transformation in the lives they impacted.

Take, for instance, Anna, whose newfound access to education lifts her family out of poverty, or James, who finds a renewed sense of purpose and belonging through their community initiative. These stories, among many others, are lasting testaments to the indelible mark left on individuals."

She paused, taking a sip of her tea before continuing. "What will the people do once the war is over?"

They stood in heavy silence, letting the enormity of the war's impact seep into their very bones, contemplating the profound changes it had wreaked on their lives and the daunting uncertainty of its aftermath.

"London won't conjure many happy memories," Rose murmured, eyes glistening with the lingering pain of loss. "Only the oppressive shadow of death and the relentless scars of destruction haunt its streets." "But amidst the swirling heartache, there glimmers a faint beacon of achievement," Rose interjected softly, her voice echoing with sorrow and indomitable resolve. "They endured, pushing through the searing pain, and in the end, England emerges free, its spirit unbeaten, ready to rise and rebuild. That is our collective triumph."

"Not mine," Rory countered, his tone void of the joy that once coloured his words. "Australia has remained untouched by the ravages of invasion, though the looming threats were ever-present. When I return, I know we will have so much to catch up on, as the burden of work fell upon too few shoulders. Our task will be to catch up." He feared the fate of the farm left to his father. He was no farmer, something only confirmed by his visit to Windermere. What condition would the farm be now? He knew the house "Windamere" would be fine; his father would have ensured that.

Their reflections on the future echoed a more profound resonance—a yearning to restore the shattered buildings and mend their fractured lives.

Rory's prophecy, uttered with eerie clarity, blossomed into reality on May 8, 1945—a day that forever changed the fabric of time and is now inscribed in the collective memory of humankind. This moment marked the end of nearly six gruelling years of conflict, a period rife with anguish.

The war had devoured millions of lives, turned vibrant neighbourhoods into ghost towns, and shattered families, leaving behind a trail of heartache and desolation. Entire cities lay in ruins, their once-thriving streets now silent testimonies to the horrors witnessed.

As the world held its breath on that fateful day, each bore its emotional burden, a tapestry woven with threads of sorrow and hardship.

Years spent in the grips of wartime adversity had stolen their comforts—food and clothing confined to meagre rations, evenings suffocated by dreary blackouts, and the omnipresent dread of aerial assaults looming overhead.

Yet, amid this backdrop of despair, a glimmer of hope ignited in their hearts. The yearning to celebrate—the desire to erupt in joy without restraint—was palpable in the air, electrifying and deeply resonant. A shared longing surged through the masses as a testament to their indomitable spirit.

Rory stepped through the doorway, and without hesitation, Rose flung herself into his embrace. "It's finally over," she exclaimed, laughter bubbling up as she pressed her lips to his. "Yes," Rory replied, his voice tinted with a sad undertone. "But what an immense tragedy—so many lives lost."

"I know," Rose answered, her eyes shimmering with defiance against the weight of his words. "Yet, let's not allow that to shadow this moment. Today, we celebrate as though none of it ever happened."

"Yes, we will," Rory agreed, fully aware that such denial was fleeting. Yet, cradled in her warmth and radiant spirit casting away the darkness, he found solace in postponing those haunting memories.

Rose finally took a step back but paused. "First, I need to call Aunt Rosemary," Rory observed her, trailing her gaze as she made her way toward the public phone, a mix of joy and concern swirling within him.

As Rose dialled her Aunt, a thrill of anticipation danced within her.

Aunt Rosemary's laughter spilled joyously through the phone, wrapping around Rose like a warm blanket.

"It feels as if the entire nation is sharing in a magnificent celebration! Bonfires flicker against the night sky, strangers embrace in jubilant dances, and the pubs overflow with laughter and song." Her voice crackled with affection, bringing a smile to Rose's face. "Thank God it's finally over," she added, her glee unmistakable.

"I know! The scene in London is surreal. For the first time, we can sway through the streets without worry, unburdened by fear," Rose replied, the weight of the past lifting just slightly as she shared this moment.

"Go on then, enjoy every bit of it!" Aunt Rosemary's giggle harmonized with the vibrancy of the evening. "Is Rory still by your side?"

"Yes, we're off together! His return was delayed as everyone awaited the final news," Rose's heart skipped at the thought of Rory, a captivating mix of excitement and warmth flooding through her.

"Send him my love. Now go! Celebrate this newfound freedom—may it remind us never to tread down that darkness again," Aunt Rosemary urged before the call ended. Rose hung up, her heart swirling with hope.

With Rory still beside her, perhaps this time, their story would carve a path toward a brighter future together.

"Come on." Rose seized Rory's hand, hauling him onto the bustling street. The air was thick with the cacophony of voices and the melody of exuberant celebrations. People were all around them, a whirlwind of vibrant chaos—singing, dancing, weeping, and embracing. The weight of the moment—the sheer relief of it all—unleashed a torrent of repressed emotions, bursting like fireworks into the night.

As he enveloped her in his arms, the vibrant world around them dulled into a soft blur, replaced by the delicate sigh of the wind and the gentle whispering of leaves swaying in harmony. His embrace enveloped her like a warm, protective cocoon, isolating them from the world's chaos and infusing her with a serene refuge. Their lips finally met in a kiss that transcended the ordinary— a profound, lingering connection filled with the weight of unspoken promises. The kiss ignited an intoxicating spark, sending electric tremors through their beings, awakening something raw and beautiful. She felt his heartbeat syncing with hers, an intimate melody that anchored them firmly in this fleeting moment, rich with the delicious thrill of untapped possibilities just waiting to unfold.

Reluctant to fully accept the turbulent emotions within her, Rose gripped his hand once more and gently pulled. "Let's go to the Jazz Club," she suggested, her voice mixing hopeful anticipation and underlying tension.

Rory responded with a firm shake of his head, his gaze steady and determined. "No, the hospital, I am sure they are celebrating," he countered. His arm, warm and reassuring on her back, guided her forward with a sense of purpose.

The city around them buzzed with life, yet it felt like a distant hum compared to their electric connection. Neon signs flickered in the dusky twilight, and the aroma of street food drifted through the air, mingling with distant laughter and clinking glasses.

"Perfect," Rose smiled as he pulled her back into his embrace for another kiss. The street lamp above cast a soft glow, wrapping them in a tender cocoon of light amidst the urban chaos.

"But first, there is something I want to ask you." His soft, embracing eyes met hers, filled with a sincerity that seemed to make the world around them fade away.

Rose's lips curled into a loving smile, her eyes soft and dewy, waiting. Behind her, a blaring car horn and the chatter of passersby seemed to lose all significance.

"Will you marry me, Rose Ashford?" It had been a long time coming, but now the time was right. The war was over, and a sense of peace settled in the air, even in the heart of the bustling city.

She reached up and kissed him on the lips. "Yes, Rory Anderson." Her voice was a whisper, yet it resonated louder than any of the city's myriad sounds.

He laughed, lifted her into the air, and smiled at her. The world spun around them, a blur of city lights and distant voices, but in that moment, all that mattered was each other.

After one last lingering kiss, he gently lowered her to the ground, an almost imperceptible sigh escaping his lips as their bodies parted. The moment's intensity still tingled on her skin, a soft blush warming her cheeks.

"Then let's go and celebrate," he said, his eyes sparkling with excitement and affection. Around them, the evening air was cool and fragrant, filled with the subtle scents of blooming flowers, while the sky above blushed with hues of pink and orange as if reflecting their own shared tenderness.

As they stepped into the hospital, an unexpected symphony of laughter and joy washed over them, breaking the cold sterility of the hallways with vibrant life. It was a sound that seemed almost out of place amidst the looming shadows of illness, yet it beckoned them forward, stirring within them a curiosity they couldn't ignore. They followed the jubilant sounds to a long dormitory, where the atmosphere had experienced a delightful upheaval. The usual arrangement of beds, symbols of vulnerability and rest, had been pushed aside, making way for an impromptu dance floor brimming with spirit and camaraderie. In the heart of this vibrant gathering, Nurse Fran and Noel became the focal point of an electric moment; Fran's movements were an enchanting blend of graceful twirls and vibrant energy, while Noel's awkward hopping and shuffling added a note of endearing lightness.

Fran, known to everyone as a beacon of unwavering hope, was a woman whose history was marked by the trials of her own family; she had once sat in a waiting room not so different from this one, hoping for miracles that came wrapped in silence. Her passion for life became her refuge, and today, it enveloped Noel, drawing him out of shadows that often clouded his spirit.

Noel, a young man whose laughter had been drowned by the weight of illness and isolation, felt the buoyancy of Fran's joy lifting his heart. As he stood there, a wisp of a smile flickering at the corners of his lips, the warmth of the celebration seeped into his bones, reminding him of the vibrant life waiting just beyond the confines of his struggles.

"Hey, look who's joined us!" boomed one of the patients, his voice a mix of surprise and warmth, echoing off the walls as the camaraderie rippled through the room, a testament to the unbreakable bonds formed even in the most challenging of times.

Turning to look, Noel nearly stumbled, but Old Fran's sturdy frame kept him steady. "If it ain't the boy from the bush and his..." Noel trailed off as the ward fell silent.

"My fiancée," Rory supplied with a grin.

A cacophony broke out. Cheers, comments of "About time," "never thought he would," and "You owe me a quid, told you he would" filled the room.

Amongst it all, Noel and Fran made their way over. Noel shook Rory's hand and hugged Rose warmly.

"For a real slow county boy, you did it," he exclaimed, raising Rory's and Rose's hands like prizefighters, prompting more cheers from the ward.

Old Fran, eyes brimming with tears, enveloped them in a bear hug, from which they were lucky to survive.

Then Noel scuttled across the floor, "Where is my camera? This news calls a celebration, Fran, and I will record the memories."

John limped to the keys of the old piano and started to play 'Waltzing Matilda.'

Returning with his camera, Noel snapped a quick photo before gently guiding Rory and Rose onto the dance floor. "It's not a waltz, but you know this tune well," he whispered with a knowing smile.

They stepped onto the floor amidst the vibrant clamour of cheers that rose like a swelling tide. The exuberant noise nearly drowned out the music, but Rose's laughter rang clear. "Our first dance," she giggled, her voice filled with joy and excitement.

Rory glanced down, his cheeks flushed a rosy hue. His eyes shone with a luminous love, each second a tender eternity. He silently wished that Noel had captured that moment.

As the evening deepened, a palpable energy

overtook the hospital floor. Partners, nurses, and patients mingled in a vigorous dance of camaraderie. Whether robust or frail and better suited to bedrest, no one could resist the allure of this extraordinary night. The air was thick with a sense of occasion, and for once, the hospital walls seemed to pulse with life rather than illness. Who could remain dormant with such a vibrant atmosphere swirling around them?

The war had finally concluded, a battle of unparalleled ferocity that exhausted both body and spirit. Once thick with the acrid scent of gunpowder and the cries of the fallen, the air now held a melancholy stillness, a prelude to the dawn of a new beginning. Soldiers who had once stood shoulder to shoulder, united by the promise of victory and the fear of oblivion, now felt the weight of their triumph and loss. Tomorrow would bring fresh challenges, but they would confront them with an unyielding resilience and a pride forged in the heat of combat, for they had emerged victorious from the abyss of conflict.

CHAPTER 8 - REFLECTION

London Station 1945 reflected the post-war atmosphere.

The grand arched windows for natural light, the polished floors, creating a mix of shadow and brightness. The station's high, steel-framed roof, a hallmark of Victorian engineering, loomed over travelers, adding a sense of scale and grandeur. Passengers carried suitcases, Some were reuniting with loved ones after years of separation, while others began new journeys. Signs with bold lettering hung from beams, directing travelers to platforms and destinations.

The shrill sound of the alarm jolted Rose from her restless sleep, her hand instinctively reaching out to silence its relentless cry. A dull throb pulsed in her head, and keeping her eyes closed felt like a fleeting reprieve. Yet, as the haze of the night began to unravel in her mind, a kaleidoscope of memories emerged.

Accepting Rory's proposal—what had spurred her to such an impulsive decision? It felt so abrupt, so foreign to her nature. Was it that Rory had stepped into her life during one of her darkest hours, filling a void she had long endured? The allure of Australia, with its sprawling, uncharted landscapes seemed to beckon to her spirit, promising the fresh start she desperately craved.

But did she truly know Rory well enough to stake her future on him? Their fateful meeting in the casualty ward played in her mind; his fervent appeals for Windamere ignited something in her, but the nurse in her was all too aware of the scars that war leaves behind, both seen and unseen.

Their romance had unfolded with dizzying speed, and now she dared to ponder if they had cast their lot too hastily. Could she risk her heart with someone wrapped in a cloak of enigma, aware that Rory's essence held the potential for exquisite joy and shattering sorrow? The weight of his past loomed large, and the uncertainty that circled her thoughts gnawed at her resolve—a persistent murmur of anxiety intertwined with flickers of hope, fighting for dominance.

Looking up, Rose caught sight of the clock, its hands mocking her. There was no time to linger on her thoughts now; she was already late for work and had to call Aunt Rosemary.

The familiar beeps of the phone seemed to amplify her anxiety, but when Aunt Rosemary's voice filled the line, warmth washed over her. "Good morning, Rose. You must have had a late night," she chirped, her tone like a cozy blanket on a chilly morning.

"Yes," Rose replied, the weight of her situation pressing down on her chest. How did she start the conversation that carried the burden of her unspoken fears? The thought fluttered uncertainly in her mind.

"Did you go out?" Rose continued, hiding her inner turmoil.

"Yes, I went to Rydes. What about you?" Aunt Rosemary laughed "What about you?"

"We went to the hospital," Rose mentioned, her own memories flooding back as she spoke. "Rory has many friends there."

"It sounds like you enjoyed it," Aunt Rosemary offered, "Yes, I did—a night to remember," she said, her pulse quickening. There was no point in delaying the inevitable. She needed Aunt Rosemary's counsel now more than ever. "Rory proposed."

"That is wonderful!" Aunt Rosemary exclaimed, her delight starkly contrasting the uncertainty churning inside Rose.

"I'm not so sure," Rose admitted, her voice faltering. Each syllable felt like a weight dragging her deeper into her doubts. "I hardly know him... and Australia?" The very thought seemed to pull at her heartstrings, unravelling her courage a little more with each breath.

"Rose, do you love him?" Aunt Rosemary's question was gentle yet penetrating, stirring emotions Rose had tried to contain.

"I think so…? Not that I have much experience in this," she confessed, the confusion mingling with a fragile glimmer of hope. Was that love she felt, or just a fleeting moment of affection?

"Love can twist the mind and entwine the heart. For some, recognition is instant; for others, it grows and deepens over time." Aunt Rosemary's voice was soothing. It wrapped around Rose like a delicate thread of understanding, coaxing her to explore the true essence of her feelings.

"Thank you. I'll catch up tomorrow," Rose said, her heart racing as she realized she was late for work. The phone clicked off, and she was thrust back into reality, the shadows of her decision lingering on the edge of her consciousness.

Rose sat quietly, surrounded by the hospital's mechanical murmurs. The antiseptic air felt stifling, a constant reminder of her sterile confinement. The distant chatter of nurses and beeping monitors deepened her isolation as time stretched into eternity. Thoughts of Rory tangled in her mind, the weight of uncertainty pressing heavily on her heart. Diving into work became her refuge, a fleeting escape from her worries. Each fluid movement soothed her anxious thoughts. The familiar sounds of the hospital formed a symphony that momentarily silenced her doubts.

With each patient, she found purpose, losing herself in their worlds. Nursing was her passion, a legacy honouring her father's vision, yet her compassion defined her. Every gentle touch felt like his presence beside her.

Patients became fragile in her care, demanding her full attention and empathy. She revelled in the sharp scent of alcohol, the soft hum of machines, and the weight of her responsibility. Their lives balanced delicately on her skill, a fragile trust she vowed never to disturb.

Each night stretched endlessly, a canvas smeared with doubt as she wrestled through the week. The spectre of procrastination loomed large, a relentless adversary whispering its insidious temptations. She broke her thoughts into fragments, each vying for her attention. Did she love Rory? The question hung heavily in the air—yes, no, perhaps, yet finally solidified into a definitive yes, like a heartbeat that would not be silenced.

Could she bear the ache of distance from Aunt Rosemary? She hesitated, feeling the familiar warmth of family slip through her fingers like grains of sand. Yes, it would be a bitter departure, but deep within her, hope whispered she could endure it.

And what of life in Australia? A flicker of excitement ignited within her at the thought of escaping London, that city shrouded in the shadows of war, where anxiety swirled like a tempest.

With each sunrise, she immersed herself in caring for her patients, their struggles momentarily diverting her from her tumultuous journey.

Finally, the weekend—the moment she desperately needed—a break. She was escaping to Windermere.

Her heart skipped a beat when she spotted Rory waiting at the train station. Was this Aunt Rosemary's doing, urging her to confront the matter and potentially find a resolution?

"How was your week?" Rory inquired, a warm grin illuminating his face. He drew her close, enveloping her in a soft kiss.

"Good," she replied, though she withheld the truth of her torturous nights. Yet, as she settled into Rory's embrace, a soothing warmth washed over her, dissipating the anxiety that had clung to her. Her fears seemed to dissolve in his arms, replaced by a serene sense of safety and correctness.

Rory had the tickets and called out over the cacophony of the bustling station, his voice rising above the clamour. "That's our train!" he declared, moving with gentle urgency. His fingers brushed against her arm as he took her bag; the air around them thrummed with bustling engines and murmured conversations while the crisp scent of coal smoke mingled with the cool breeze of the early evening.

They arrived at Aunt Rosemary's home just after dusk, the sky painted deep blue and purple. The warm golden light from the windows spilled out into the twilight, creating a beacon of warmth in the gathering darkness.

"Aunt Rosemary is waiting for us!" Rose laughed, her voice ringing with eager excitement. The familiar scent of blooming gardenias and freshly baked bread greeted them, blending with the crisp evening air. Aunt Rosemary was not just her only relative; she was the comforting embrace of family and the heart that made this house a home.

They knocked on the heavy oak door, its weight echoing through the silent hallway. Rory hesitated, her heart pounding with a mix of nervousness and anticipation. As the door creaked open, Aunt Rosemary appeared, her face beaming with a joyful glow. Standing behind her were her special friend and a few of Rosemary's childhood companions, their faces reflecting the warmth of shared memories.

"My apologies, I simply couldn't contain myself," Aunt Rosemary declared, her laughter echoing like a delightful tune. Aunt Rosemary, a woman known for her vivacious spirit and a heart as vast as the ocean, had witnessed many milestones in the family. Growing up in a close-knit community, she was always the nucleus of warmth and joy during family gatherings.

"My niece getting engaged is such a momentous occasion, so I arranged a small celebration." With her nurturing arms stretched wide, Rosemary enveloped them in her hearty, comforting embrace, sharing physical warmth, deep-seated love, and vibrancy.

Rose introduced Rory to her friends and neighbours, feeling hopeful and apprehensive. To her delight, he blended seamlessly into their gatherings, his easy-going nature drawing smiles and laughter from those around him. With each story he shared, his confidence shone through, captivating her audience and forging connections that made Rose's heart swell with pride. The warmth of their interactions painted a vivid picture of a budding camaraderie that promised to deepen over time.

But crossing paths with Windsor felt like a foregone conclusion. He had been waiting to curtail her, An intertwining of fates that seemed unavoidable and fraught with tension.

Windsor's gaze pierced her with a sardonic edge as he asked, "So, you've decided to marry him." The words dripped with disbelief, a challenge more than a statement.

"Yes," Rose replied, her voice steady though her heart raced. She felt no urge to justify her decision to someone who had always doubted her choices.

Windsor leaned closer, a hint of disdain in his eyes. "You could curate a far better life in England. What compels you to follow him to the other side of the world?"

At that moment, a fire ignited within Rose, her frustration bubbling to the surface. "Because I love him," she declared, her voice laced with defiance and yearning.

"A romantic dream," he retorted, the bite in his words punctuating the air like a knife.

Taken aback, Rose felt the weight of their shared past press upon her. "Isn't it beautiful, after everything we've endured?" Her voice softened, but there was an underlying strength as she delivered that final quip.

For Rosemary, the air was thick with the mingling scents of blooming flowers and rich food, each note of celebration weaving through the laughter that filled the room. Her extraordinary niece's laughter rang like chimes in a gentle breeze.

Yet, each shared glance brought a sharp sting, a reminder that their cherished moments were slipping away, soon to be separated by the ocean's vastness.

Rose's heart, deepening the ache of impending loss. The joyous sounds felt almost mocking against the heavy silence that awaited her, amplifying the emptiness that would soon settle in, leaving behind only echoes of love and laughter—memories that would linger like a fading melody in an empty hall.

After the whirlwind of Aunt Rosemary's celebration, Rose and Rory found some quiet time together on the balcony of Aunt Rosemary's home. The stars twinkled overhead, and the calm night contrasted with the chaos of their recent engagement.

Rose leaned against the balcony railing, taking in the night air filled with the scent of gardenias and the soft rustle of leaves. She toyed nervously with the ring on her finger, her heart racing with joy and anxiety.

Rory stepped up beside her, sensing her tension. "Are you okay?" His gentle voice broke the silence. "You've been quiet since we got here."

"I'm just... thinking," Rose replied, her gaze fixed on the stars. "About everything that's happening so fast. I never pictured my life this way, Rory." She paused, searching for the right words, feeling the weight of her emotions.

"I know things have moved quickly," he responded, his gaze shifting to the horizon. "But I believe there's a reason for it. Sometimes, you must jump in, even when the water seems cold." His arms crossed over his chest, a subtle indication of his unease.

Rose: "But what if I'm not ready?" An edge of frustration coursed through her voice. "Do you think we know enough about each other to make this leap?"

Rory turned to her, his eyes reflecting the depth of his emotions. Rory: "Honestly? There's so much I want to help you understand about me—about my past." He took a deep breath, the tension visible in his jaw. "But every time I try to share, it feels like I'm just pouring more darkness into your light."

"You're not darkness to me, Rory. You're complicated," Rose admitted, stepping closer to him. "And I've been struggling with that. I feel drawn to you but fear what's hidden beneath the surface."

Rory ran a hand through his hair, the weight of unspoken words hanging between them.

Rory: "I thought being with you would chase away the ghosts, but they linger, reminding me of who I used to be and all I lost. I... I don't want you to carry that burden with me."

"You don't have to fight it alone," Rose said softly, reaching out to place a hand on his arm, her touch grounding him. "We can face it together. It may not be perfect, but I want to know every part of you—the light and the dark."

Rory's expression shifted, hesitating momentarily before looking deeply into her eyes. "You make me want to be better." The sincerity of his words rang through the stillness of the night.

"I want you to be proud of me, but I worry I won't live up to what you deserve."

"What do I deserve?" Rose mused, tilting her head with a gentle smile. "I think I deserve honesty—about the battles we're both fighting. If we can share that, we can build something real, even amidst the chaos."

Her words stirred something inside Rory, filling him with hope yet tinged with doubt. "I want that too. But can you truly handle the scars I carry?"

"I'd rather be with you, scars and all, than hide from the truth. Your past doesn't define you, Rory; it shapes you. And if you let me in, we can create new memories together."

The air between them quivered with unspoken promise, their hands inching closer until they finally intertwined.

Rory murmured, "Then let's face whatever comes next together—starting with Australia."

"Together," Rose agreed, a smile breaking through the uncertainty that had gripped her heart.

As they stood united under the vast sky, it felt as if they had forged a new path—a bridge between their complexities and the understanding they would cultivate in one another, ready to face the uncertain future together.

Aunt Rosemary moved through life like an unstoppable force, shifting from an engagement party to wedding plans before Rose could catch her breath. Within, Rose simmered a storm of indecision, yearning for a pause to gather her thoughts, but the whirlwind of events allowed no such luxury. The pressure weighed upon her chest, a constant ache that she could not escape. The more she tried to grasp clarity, but the more it eluded her, the more it left her adrift in a sea of anxiety and doubt.

Enveloped in Rory's embrace, she felt the warmth of his arms tighten around her. The subtle scent of pine and leather intertwined and filled her senses, creating a sanctuary that softened the worries of her restless mind.

"Aunt Rosemary is relentless," she murmured, her voice tinged with frustration and fatigue.

Rory chuckled softly, the sound warm and

reassuring. "Yes. Feeling the need for space?" he asked, his eyes searching hers for a deeper understanding.

She sighed, her brow creasing as she struggled to find the words for her tumultuous emotions. "Yes, it's all so rushed," she finally admitted, her voice trembling slightly.

Sensing her distress, Rory gently kissed her hair soothingly. "Relax," he murmured tenderly. "I know this is a big change for you," he continued, attempting to ease her mind. "You will love Midjal and the people will adore you."

"Do you think so?" Rose asked, worry evident in her voice. Rory gave her another soft kiss. "I'm certain they will."

Rose's doubts surged back to the surface, as relentless as the salt-scented tide crashing against a rugged shoreline. Moving to Australia loomed as a formidable, storm-clouded horizon.

The scent of Aunt Rosemary's lavender garden, the soft, weathered wood of the porch swing, and the warmth of her guardian's loving gaze flooded her memory, only deepening her unease.

Now, she ventured to a distant, sunburnt land she had never seen, accompanied solely by a man who remained shrouded in the mists despite their blooming rapport. Her heart wrestled with the palpable uncertainty, yearning for the comforting embrace of the familiar and the safe.

Later, as he sat with Aunt Rosemary over

morning tea, a sense of unease gnawed at him. "Aunt Rosemary, I think Rose is getting stressed," he confessed, his voice tinged with concern.

Aunt Rosemary's eyes softened with understanding. "Yes, I thought she might be. Rose has always been steadfast, but the end of the war and your engagement must feel overwhelming for her." She took a delicate sip of her tea, her warm, reassuring smile never leaving her face. "She'll get through it, though. Which reminds me, you need a ring."

Abruptly, she stood up with a newfound urgency. "I have just the thing," she said, disappearing through the doorway.

After a few suspenseful minutes, she returned holding a small, ornate box, her eyes sparkling with pride. "This belonged to her mother—both the engagement and wedding rings," she revealed, her voice filled with emotion. "I've been keeping them safe for her. Rose will be overjoyed."

At Rydes Hotel, Rory felt the pulsing rhythm of the band's lively tune resonating through the air as he sat, sipping a frothy ale that offered a comforting warmth. The soft hum of chatter and clinking glasses painted a lively picture all around them. He nestled his hand warmly over Rose's across the polished wooden table, the flickering candlelight casting playful shadows upon them.

"I forgot something," he remarked, his voice mingling with the ambient sounds while his gaze remained tender and focused on her. "Most girls would mention it, but you have not."

Her eyes, gleaming with curiosity and a touch of confusion, met his. "What?"

"A ring." Gently releasing her hand, he reached into his pocket. The music almost drowned out the faint sound of fabric rustling. With a sense of anticipation, he extracted a small jewelled case. "Aunt Rosemary came to the rescue." He opened it with practised care, revealing the glinting treasure inside. In one fluid motion, he slipped the ring onto her finger.

Rose held her breath. There it sat, sparkling in the candlelight. "It's Mother's ring." Her face lit up in the soft glow of the candlelight, and for the first time in days, laughter spilled from her lips, filled with genuine affection. "Thank you both. Nothing could be better." Tears sparkled as she gazed down upon the small but perfect diamond, a beacon of love.

It was official: She had her mother's blessing, and all lingering doubts dissolved. The ring she wore, a cherished heirloom passed down through generations, held more than sentimental value —it carried the weight of her mother's dreams and sacrifices. Removing it would be akin to severing the invisible thread that connected their hearts, a bond far too precious to break.

As her fingers delicately traced the intricate engravings of the ring, vivid and poignant memories of her mother's ring surfaced.

She had been enveloped in their warmth, nurtured as their one and only daughter, and encouraged relentlessly to chase her dreams. This legacy was not only a privilege but also a heavy mantle she felt obliged to honour.

Yet, the burden of upholding such an exquisite legacy weighed heavily on her shoulders. It loomed like an immovable shadow, reminding her that anything less than perfection would tarnish the beautiful love story her parents had crafted. Her upcoming union with Rory must emulate that elevated bond, a standard she found increasingly daunting to meet.

But deep within, an unsettling truth began to unfurl. Their relationship was distinctly marked by imperfections and vulnerabilities, far from the idyllic connection she longed for.

The scars of war had intricately woven themselves into their lives, the evidence of suffering etched into their very essence. The metamorphosis they had undergone was inescapable, and the remnants of their experiences would echo through their hearts indefinitely. A tumultuous clash of yearning for flawless love and grappling with painful acceptance raged within her, an internal struggle.

CHAPTER 9 - THE WEDDING

The post-WWII wedding in Windermere, England.

The groom in a formal military uniform adorned with medals and insignia, reflecting his service and dedication. The bride wears a modest white dress with a matching hat and veil, holding a bouquet of roses and baby's breath, symbolizing hope and new beginnings. Their radiant smiles exude joy, standing as a testament to love and resilience in the aftermath of war.

Rose giggled, trying to handle the flood of emotions inside her. Her Aunt Rosemary was unconcerned about the war-induced shortages. Despite these constraints, the day was full of promise and new beginnings.

Aunt Rosemary had thoughtfully planned every detail, from the church so close that her parents' graves, their souls, would be there. Rose held on to a flicker of hope, praying for clear skies and feeling that her Aunt had somehow included that wish in her plans.

Tears of love and gratitude filled Rose's eyes as

she thought about the day's importance. How would she survive without her Aunt? Rory's home was so far away.

"Tomorrow. It's hard to believe." Rory's voice drifted from behind Rose, causing disbelief and excitement.

Rose turned and smiled warmly at him as he placed a hand on either of her hips. "Yes. Aunt Rosemary is in her element," she remarked.

Rory's lips curled into a grin, reflecting his deep admiration for Rosemary. "Yes," he agreed, his eyes sparkling with affection. "Wonder if we could take her with us? She would marshal Midjal like never before. Her presence would ensure everything ran smoothly."

Rose sighed, a soft murmur escaping her lips. "If only," she whispered. Despite the anticipation of tomorrow, the thought of leaving Aunt Rosemary behind dampened her excitement. Rosemary had been more than an Aunt to Rose; she had been her guardian and mentor, and their bond was deep.

Aunt Rosemary had expelled Rory the night before, forcing him to take refuge in a hotel. He accepted the dismissal with a grin that belied the swirl of emotions within him and a quick yet tender kiss for Rose that lingered longer than intended.

"Until tomorrow," he murmured, his voice a soft promise swallowed by the shadows of the lane as he trailed off toward the village, each step echoing with the unspoken tension of the evening.

Rose watched him leave, feeling both regretful and determined. The tradition she thought brought bad luck now felt like a heavyweight, made worse by Rory's absence. The once lively house seemed sad and quiet, waiting for the next day's activities.

Noel met him in the dimly lit hotel lobby, the low hum of muffled conversations and the clinking of glasses filling the air. Camera in hand, Noel methodically captured candid moments of everyone he could see.

"Drink?" he offered abruptly, then limped to the bar without waiting for a response. The sharp smell of whiskey preceded his return, a glass brimming with amber liquid in hand. "You look like you could use it."

Rory accepted the glass, its calm surface a temporary distraction from his turmoil. Anxiety coursed through his veins, thoughts of doubt and guilt swirling like an unstoppable tide. What was he doing? How could he justify tearing her away from everything she cherished? He forced himself to focus, reminding himself that his love for her was paramount.

"Last minute nerves?" Noel's laughter mingled with the distant jazz arrangement playing in the background.

"You could say that," Rory admitted, feeling the weight of his decision. "I'm uprooting her from everything she loves. Australia is a long way from here."

"Hey, none of that talk." Noel's tone was a blend of reprimand and reassurance. "Rose wouldn't have agreed if she had any doubts. She'll love Australia."

Rory took a sip of the whiskey, warmth spreading through his chest. He desperately hoped Noel was.

Her wedding day was perfect, with a clear sky and shining sun—just right for an English Rose to get married. Aunt Rosemary moved around nervously, her busyness hiding her worry.

Rose stood before the mirror, her heart beating with both anxiety and longing. She had chosen her mother's wedding dress, feeling deeply connected to the woman she admired. Though cream due to age, the dress wrapped her in its history and warmth, making her forget any worries. Her pride in honouring her mother outshone any minor flaws the dress might have.

When the door creaked open, Aunt Rosemary entered, her eyes misty with unshed tears. "You look lovely, just like your mother," she whispered, her voice trembling with emotion and quickly wiping away a stray tear, steeling herself against nostalgia. "She would be so proud," she said with a sad, soft smile, her own heart heavy with the absence of her beloved sister. The two women shared a moment of silent understanding, their mutual loss and love binding them even closer.

"No time to dither," Aunt Rosemary muttered, the fleeting moment of respite dissipating like mist in the morning sun as he departed for her room.

With unwavering resolve, she dashed into her room to dress. She hastily donned her maroon velvet dress. Each movement was brisk and purposeful, smoothing the fabric and buttons with her fingertips. Her fingers, though deft, trembled slightly, the urgency of the moment sending a ripple of electricity through her veins.

They walked down the aisle, Rose and Aunt Rosemary, the final Ashfords making their way forward; after today, one Ashford would remain. They were followed by Fran, who had accepted the maid of honour position with tears. It was not what she had expected.

As Rory looked down the aisle, his heart swelled with emotion. The church was decorated with white lilies and small white flowers. The fresh smell of the flowers mixed with quiet conversations from the guests. Colourful light from the stained glass windows shone on the shiny marble floor, making a glowing effect around the bride.

Next to him, Noel, leaning on his stick, murmured, "About time."

Rory grinned. "I would say it's overdue."

Rory sent Rose a smile of encouragement, deep affection, and admiration. Memories of their journey flooded his mind—the challenges they had faced, the doubts they had overcome, and the love that had relentlessly grown stronger through every trial. Rose stood at the altar, resplendent in her cream wedding dress, embodying every hope and vision Rory had ever held for this moment.

More than just a beautiful bride, she was solid, having weathered the storms of their past with unwavering resolve. This day was a testament to their love and a celebration of their unyielding commitment.

He had observed her tending to the wounded with an unwavering dedication that spoke volumes about her character. Each gesture, from her gentle touch to the earnest concern in her eyes, revealed a compassionate nature that shone brightly even in the darkest times. She approached every person as if they were the most essential individual in the world, offering medical aid, comfort, and solace.

Then there was the Windamere Rose, who found joy in the simplest pleasures. She embraced the freedom of the open air, walked with a light spirit through the village, and expressed a profound love for her Aunt. In every interaction, she demonstrated a deep, abiding respect for her community and the sanctity of their bond.

Here, in this sacred space filled with the grandeur of nature's beauty and the warmth of familial love, she embodied all he had ever dreamed of and more, making a memorable connection.

Rory knew Rose needed all her strength to settle in Midjal on the Australian plains. She didn't just want to survive; she wanted to create a place of beauty and kindness. Her journey was driven by deep determination from her upbringing. This mix of inner strength and learned perseverance made her unique. Rose aspired to live, thrive, and stand apart.

Her lips curled into a sensual smile that threatened to shatter his restraint.

His heart raced, and the room seemed to close in. He felt trapped in all the questions he had not answered. He silently prayed for the torment to end quickly.

As the priest led the ceremony, Rose felt excitement and nerves, finally realizing she was getting married."

"Will you, Rory Hugh Anderson, take Rose Amber Ashford as your wife?" The priest's words blurred. Rose's mind was in chaos, realizing they were getting married. No longer Nurse Ashford. No longer alone.

Walking down the aisle, Rose scanned the familiar faces that carried the echo of her childhood—all those friends she had grown up with in Windermere.

Their presence mingled seamlessly with Aunt Rosemary's cherished companions, creating a tapestry of past and present. This harmonious blend felt right, like two halves of her life had merged into one unified memory. She took a deep breath, her heart swelling with nostalgia and gratitude.

She recognized that this day held significance not only for her but also for her Aunt—an Aunt who had been her steadfast rock, her confidante, and her world. Every smile she saw, every nod of acknowledgment seemed to honour the woman who had given her so much silently. At that moment, she felt a profound sense of unity, as though every step she took was a testament to her Aunt's enduring love and unwavering support.

Outside, the soldiers stood vigil in immaculate formation, their rifles raised high, forming a magnificent archway that spoke volumes of Rory's unwavering respect for his military legacy. As she gazed upward, her eyes locked onto Rory's grave expression.

Yet, amid such solemnity, a mischievous grin flickered across his lips, a fleeting whisper of hidden amusement that ignited a spark of joy within her.

At that moment, an overwhelming realization washed over her—she was about to commit her life to an extraordinary man.

Rory's gaze drifted toward the hallowed ground where his ancestors rested. Though his family was absent today, their spirits lingered nearby. He quickly amended his thoughts; only his father remained, and the rest were lost to time.

Beneath the sun's brilliance, the vibrant buzz of

conversations filled the air as introductions flowed seamlessly and old friends embraced with heartfelt warmth. Rose lost herself in the joy of these reunions, relishing the connection with cherished companions from her past.

Meanwhile, Rory revelled in hearty discussions with his comrades—Major White and the valiant soldiers from his dragoon unit. The memories of their shared trials in Normandy erased the years of separation, rekindling a camaraderie that time could never extinguish.

When Aunt Rosemary made her address to the crowd, they migrated to the reception hall next door.

As they stepped inside, they were greeted by a breathtaking scene that felt almost surreal. The hall, draped in exquisite local flowers, transformed into a vivid canvas. There, amongst the vibrant arrangements, the emblem of Rory's brigade stood tall, a silent guardian over the cherished memories shared within these walls.

The air buzzed as laughter danced through the room, a melodic undertone to deeper conversations. Tears glistened at the edges of joyful smiles, each emotion ebbing and flowing like the tide. The intoxicating aroma of Aunt Rosemary's culinary masterpieces drifted lazily through the air, invoking nostalgia and warmth, reminding them of shared meals and laughter-filled evenings.

The connection between friends and family, each

clink of glasses echoing the unspoken bonds that tied them all together, was profoundly felt in this unforgettable gathering. Not just connections but the very essence of who they were as they shared this space, this experience, and their lives were deepened.

Standing at the threshold, Rose and Rory welcomed their guests, a gentle mix of excitement and anxiety swirling around them. Rory's heart swelled with pride at the sight of Sir Reginald among them, but he could sense the tension radiating from Windsor as he approached.

"Sir Reginald," Rory said, his voice laced with warmth, "it means a great deal that you're here today."

"Ah, my boy, how could I miss this momentous occasion? I've come to witness you unite with our lovely Rose," Sir Reginald replied, a twinkle in his eye that hinted at a deeper connection to their union.

Rose looked up at him, her smile tinged with wistfulness. "Soon to be Windemere's Rose," she said softly, the weight of her new title hanging between them.

"Windamere?" Sir Reginald inquired, arching an eyebrow, curiosity mingling with concern. "My father chose that name for our home," Rory explained, his tone shifting to one of reverence. "It's a homage to our heritage."

"That's a good choice," Sir Reginald remarked, nodding appreciatively. "Your father hasn't forgotten where he comes from or the generations of his family who lived here, indeed." His words felt heavy with unspoken memories.

With a knowing smile, he moved on.

As Rory watched him walk away, a heaviness settled in his chest, echoing the weight of Sir Reginald's words. He turned to greet the next person, but his mind was ensnared in thoughts.

Could it be that Windamere was not just another name but a tribute to his family's legacy? A testament to the years of shared struggles—an emblem announcing that the cycle of despair had finally been shattered. The concept lingered within him, stirring both hope and apprehension in equal measure as he pondered the significance.

When the toasts began, Major White rose to speak on behalf of the groom.

"I'm thrilled to speak at the wedding of a great Australian soldier. In both war and life, he always put others before himself." He paused and looked proudly at Rory. "Rory, I am honoured to present you with a medal for outstanding service."

The room went silent for a heartbeat, a sense of awe washing over the guests. Then, a wave of applause and cheers erupted, filled with heartfelt admiration.

Rory stood, his face a mixture of humility and pride as the Major approached him. The Major's hands trembled as he pinned the medal onto Rory's uniform.

"Congratulations, son," he said, his voice thick with emotion. "May your life be full, and may the memories of war one day fade into the distance." Rory's eyes glistened with unshed tears, a rare softness replacing his usual stoic demeanour. The room buzzed with warmth and solidarity, honouring a hero among them.

Rory faced the crowd, his voice heavy with emotion. "This medal isn't just mine; it belongs to every man who fought in this war. Many of us have lost dear friends, and for those of us who survived, the memories are etched deep, leaving scars that will never fade." As he finished, he slowly returned to his seat, a solemn silence hanging in the air.

His speech took Rose aback. All the time they had known each other, he had never shared this side of himself. It seemed strange that he had kept this hidden, for she had always seen him as someone of few words.

Yet here he was, eloquent and expressive, shattering her preconceived notions and leaving her to reconsider the depth of their relationship. The moment felt surreal, as though the room around them faded away, and only his articulate presence remained, bridging the gap between who she thought he was and the man standing before her now.

When Rory sat at the table, Noel greeted him with a handshake, showing rare solemn respect.

"Congratulations," Noel said, his tone filled with admiration. This departure from his usual cheerful demeanour indicated the weight of the moment. The warm glow of the chandelier cast a golden hue over the polished mahogany table, intensifying the gravity of the exchange. In that instant, the camaraderie between them deepened as Noel's eyes conveyed a mix of pride and sincerity, uncharacteristically serious.

Rose watched the exchange with keen interest, her mind racing with questions. He had not confided in Noel either, leaving her to wonder how many secrets were buried within him. These hidden truths seemed to form an intricate web, each strand adding to the mysterious depths of his character. She had already unearthed numerous facets of his concealed world, but each discovery only hinted at the vast unknown beneath. The significance of these secrets weighed heavily, suggesting that their revelation could alter everything she thought she understood about him.

The band played The Blue Danube waltz as Rory and Rose danced gracefully in the grand hall, with Aunt Rosemary watching with tears. The ornate chandeliers glow warmly as the couple move elegantly across the polished wooden floor. Unlike his father, Rory was a confident and poised dancer.

Fran and Noel joined them, blending seamlessly into the rhythm of the dance. A gentle tap on her shoulder caught Fran's attention, and as she turned, she found herself face to face with the Major, his eyes gleaming with charm and mischief.

"Miss Ashford, may I have this dance?" he asked, extending his hand with a respectful yet inviting gesture.

Her face brightened into a broad, genuine smile. "With pleasure," she replied.

Soon, they, too, were whirling around the floor, their movements harmonious and fluid. Much to her delight, the Major proved to be an exceptional dancer, every step an embodiment of grace and finesse.

"Look at this," Rose giggled as they entered the bedroom, her eyes widening at Aunt Rosemary's careful touch. The room was bathed in a warm, flickering glow from numerous candles, and the bedspread was delicately adorned with crimson rose petals. "She truly is a romantic."

Rory's laughter blended with hers as he gently caught her by the arm and embraced her tenderly. He looked deep into her eyes, his voice soft with sincerity, "Then we had better make sure we don't disappoint her." His gaze lingered, full of unspoken.

Rory watched the light filter through the curtains. How would Rose like Windamere? Sure, it stood like a mansion on the plains, enough to ensnare anyone, but would they be able to make it into a home again? His childhood memories show what could be. He had a family, and he wanted to capture that again with his father and their children. It was a dream, but would it come true?

The next day, Rose gazed around the room with dreamy eyes, reflecting the remains of countless unspoken dreams. The soft, golden light of dawn filtered through the gauzy curtains, casting dappled patterns on the aged furniture. Each sunbeam seemed to hold the tender memories of a wedding night that had fulfilled every yearning Aunt Rose had ever expressed to the stars.

Their honeymoon would take place on a grand, majestic vessel, a troop carrier carrying tired soldiers back to the sun-drenched soils of Australia. Amidst the rhythmic lull of the ocean waves and the hum of the ship's engines, Rose would wear her crisp nurse's uniform, tending to the wounded and the weary with tender hands. Meanwhile, Rory would bring vitality to the journey, organizing lively activities and infusing every moment with his irreplaceable charm, ensuring their voyage was filled with laughter and life.

Leaving for Windamere weighed heavily on her heart. Aunt Rose had been a pillar of strength and wisdom throughout her life, and her home was a sanctuary filled with the warmth of countless cherished memories.

After their untimely passing, she stepped into the role of a parent, instilling important values and moulding her character profoundly. The thought of leaving her, especially in her later years, brought forth a deep yearning and a sting of sadness.

Who would care for Aunt Rose, that steadfast guide, as she slipped further into the twilight of her days? This pivotal choice was laden with complexity.

The allure of a new beginning at Windamere, teeming with possibilities, beckoned her like a siren's call. Yet, the shadow of doubt loomed large, consuming her thoughts. What awaited her in Windamere?

Would the vibrant promises she had heard be fulfilled, or would they dissolve into mere phantoms of hope, leaving her clutching at dreams abandoned? The tightrope she walked between familial duty and her quest for identity had never felt so precarious, with her heart and aspirations hanging in the balance, each pulsing beat a reminder of what she was leaving behind and what might come to be.

CHAPTER 10 - BONN VOYAGE

The HMS Orontes - Built in 1929 for the Orient Line, was used as a troopship during WWII. It transported thousands of soldiers, including Australian servicemen, back to Western Australia. The ship featured spacious barracks-style accommodations and dining areas, adapted from its original luxury design. After the war, it played a vital role in repatriating troops, marking their return to peace and loved ones in ports like Fremantle.

Emotions swirled within her as she faced the daunting task before her. She had one week— just one week—to pack her cherished belongings and muster the courage to bid farewell to Aunt Rosemary—an endeavour that seemed impossible. Her heart ached with every passing minute at the thought of leaving behind the comforting presence of her dear Aunt. Yet Aunt Rosemary, ever the pragmatic soul, viewed the situation through a different lens, her mind already brimming with new plans and unexpected twists.

Aunt Rosemary stood at the threshold, taking in the details of her niece's room. The faded lavender wallpaper, adorned with tiny, whimsical stars, seemed to sigh with memories. The scent of vanilla and lilies lingered in the air, a subtle reminder of the girl's presence. Her gaze fell on the antique ballerina figurine poised delicately atop the oak dresser, its porcelain features frozen in timeless grace. The cozy quilt, stitched with patches of cherished fabric, draped softly over the bed. Each item held a story, a fragment of a life now distant. How much would she take?

A part of her longed for the room to remain untouched, as if Rose had just stepped out for a moment. The faint scent of Rose's lavender perfume still clung to the air, mingling with the musty aroma of old books stacked on the shelves. The gentle play of sunlight filtering through the curtains cast a warm glow on the bedspread, giving it a sense of false comfort. She could almost hear Rose's laughter echoing in the silence, a delicate reminder that, for now, she could pretend Rose was merely in London and not separated by the vast expanse, a world away.

She drew in a trembling breath and stepped forward, the cool touch of the floor sending a shiver through her body. The weight of the past pressed on her shoulders, but she could feel the fire of courage igniting in her chest, warming the cold spaces that fear once occupied. The echoes of her hesitant past were drowned out by the resounding beat of her determined heart.

"Where do we start?" Rose's voice from behind.

Aunt Rosemary's eyes widened, her breath hitching for a moment as the weight of the situation crashed upon her like a rogue wave. She stood frozen, the air thick with tension, before she managed to compose herself. She turned to Rose with a determined nod, her voice steady yet carrying an undercurrent of urgency. "The books. You will need to take your father's medical manuals," she instructed, her gaze intense.

Aunt Rose felt a sharp sting in her heart, even at the thought of losing her brother's book. Although dimming with time, the memories still carried a bittersweet weight, unlike the fresh pangs from losing her cherished niece. She longed to cradle and safeguard these remnants, to linger in this room bathed in the soft, golden light of dusky afternoons, where the past and present could meld, and for a fleeting moment, they would be reunited once more.

Rose stood gazing wistfully at the boxes filled with her beloved books. A heavy sigh escaped her lips as she murmured, "I can't take too much luggage on board."

The weight of her words hung in the air, laden with the unspoken hardships of her journey. Each book represented a cherished memory, a piece of her past she could not afford to carry into the uncertain future. Her heart ached at the constraints of her voyage, which left her with no choice. She felt the tug of sacrifice, knowing the limited space couldn't hold the fragments of her life she wished to bring along.

With her characteristic pragmatism, Aunt Rosemary swiftly dispelled the group's concerns. "Then we'll have them transported," she declared with the air of someone who'd unravelled trickier quandaries. Her eyes glimmered with the resolve of a seasoned problem-solver. "I am sure there are shipping agents in London."

At that moment, it was clear why Aunt Rosemary was the steadfast anchor of their family. Beneath her composed exterior lay a reservoir of resourcefulness, brimming with solutions to every conceivable crisis. Her past was peppered with tales of perseverance—a younger Rosemary who had weathered the storms of uncertainty and emerged wiser and more resilient. Now, as she stood in the room orchestrating yet another plan, her practical wisdom imparted a sense of security and hope, making her indispensable,

Rose felt a surge of anxiety, her heart pounding in her chest as she stood in the bustling streets of London.

It all felt too rushed, too sudden. Aunt Rosemary had stumbled upon a shipping agent, a chance encounter that set the wheels of fate in motion. The arrangements were made and finalised before Rose fully processed them.

Rose had always imagined her future differently,

tethered to her homeland's familiar landscapes and comforting routines. Now, she found herself on the precipice of an unknown journey. Australia loomed ahead, a vast, alien land she neither knew nor understood—the excitement of a new adventure warred with the deep-seated fear.

Her husband, Rory, was an enigma wrapped in familiarity yet perpetually shifting like sand in the winds of time. When she thought she had unravelled the layers of his quiet, patient demeanour, he would transform again, revealing a new facet of his intricate nature.

For instance, there was a time he surprised her with his knowledge of the Windermere trees and plants. Then, when she least expected it, he spoke of Australia, capturing depths of emotion she had never glimpsed in him. Each change left her with bewilderment and more profound admiration, as if she were perpetually meeting a new person who lived inside the same familiar body. So much about him remained mysterious, making her realise how little she knew.

Embarkation came too soon.

The moment of goodbye to Aunt Rosemary cast a gloomy veil over the bustling dock. With trembling hands, Rose wrapped her arms around her Aunt, holding on as if to imprint this fleeting moment forever in her heart.

Standing beside them, Rory felt the weight of the

impending separation just as profoundly. He had asked Rose to marry him, a question laced with hope and uncertainty. What could he truly offer her? A land that he adored, yes, but would she fall in love with it too? It was not England, a place steeped in the deep-rooted comfort of history. This was an unfamiliar frontier where they would carve out their own story, a new tapestry waiting to be woven with the threads of their love and dreams.

Rose turned a tear-stained face that glistened in the soft, waning light. "Time to go," she murmured, her voice trembling like an autumn leaf barely clinging to its branch.

He wrapped a comforting arm around her waist, feeling the slight shiver that coursed through her body. With the other arm, he gripped their worn, heavy luggage and gently urged her forward, the subtle scent of Aunt Rosemary's lavender perfume mingling with the sea's salt.

He turned, a determined look in his eyes as he faced Aunt Rosemary. "I promise to look after her," he said, his voice steady but filled with unspoken emotions.

Aunt Rosemary's smile was gentle, yet her eyes betrayed a depth of relief and affection. "I know you will," she replied, her words carrying the weight of her trust and hope, mingled with the bittersweet acknowledgment of change.

Rose stood by the rail of the HMT *Orontes,*

gazing forlornly into the distance. Beside her, Rory gently wrapped his arm around her in a comforting gesture. The colourful streamers that once fluttered joyously had long since vanished, and the ship's horn was now nothing more than a distant echo haunting her memories. "In time, you'll see her again," Rory murmured, his voice barely audible over the sound of the waves. "She's strong, just like you."

Aunt Rosemary had become a mere speck on the horizon, yet one that lingered painfully in Rose's mind. Her Aunt's once warm and enveloping embrace, a touch that had always been so full of comfort, felt now like a cold and fleeting memory, leaving only a faint, familiar scent in its wake.

"She would want you to be happy," Rory continued, his gaze fixed on the disappearing shore as if willing to bring comfort. "Remember how she always said that life is about the moments we spend with those we love."

Rose nodded, though the ache in her heart only grew stronger. Would she ever see her beloved Aunt again? The heartache welled within her, and tears streamed freely down her cheeks, mingling with the salty sea breeze. Rory gently wiped one away with his thumb, his eyes glistening with unshed tears.

"We'll make new memories, Rose. Together," he promised, squeezing her shoulder reassuringly.

But Rose could only stare out at the endless expanse of ocean, where the horizon seemed to hold all the answers yet remained frustratingly silent. All she could do was stand there, lost in the bittersweet recollection of a love that had shaped her, and pray silently that the future would bring them back together.

Without Rory's support, she could not have done it. His arm was supportive, and their love would see them through.

Rory's mind was a turbulent sea of doubt and fear for the future. How on earth would she manage to survive? His love for her was unquestionable, steadfast, and accurate, but his actions burdened him with uncertainty. Had he truly made the right decisions for her sake? The life he'd crafted for them was meagre—a home made possible by his father's generosity. But beneath that fragile roof, the fate of the farm loomed like a dark cloud.

Every day, Rory wrestled with the absence of his mother and brothers, who had been the backbone of the farm's operations.

How had the land, the crops, the livestock—how had any of it held together in their absence?

He revered his father, a man of immense skill and unwavering dedication in the mines, where he had accumulated a fortune. Yet he was also a dreamer+- who let visions of a better future drain away his hard-earned fortune. Everything his father had managed to gain was spent as swiftly, leaving Rory anxious about their home and future stability.

The burden of these thoughts bore heavily on Rory's heart, colouring his every waking moment with a pall of unease as he grappled with the consequences of their shared sacrifices and the uncertainty.

An able seaman, his weathered face etched with lines from years of sun and salt, walked steadily along the creaking deck of the ship. The wooden planks groaned under the weight of his worn boots, echoing the rhythm of the restless waves below.

As he approached, his steady gaze fixed on the tall figure standing near the helm, he hesitated momentarily, taking a deep breath to steady his nerves. "Sir, Major Anderson?" he queried softly, his voice carrying respect and trepidation. The seaman's tone betrayed his uncertainty, yet his posture remained steadfast, a testament to years. "The captain would like to welcome you aboard."

"Certainly."

Rose pushed herself off the rail and turned her back to the sea. There was a finality in her step as they followed the sailor.

The sailor opened the wooden door with a creak, allowing them to enter the Captain's office. The room was large and filled with the scent of polished wood and aged maps, lending an air of authority and history to the space. The Captain stood as they entered.

He introduced himself smoothly to Rory before

turning to Rose. "You must be the new bride," he said.

"Yes," she replied with a cautious smile, taking the seat as directed. Her senses were heightened, and she could feel the subtle rocking of the ship beneath her feet, a constant reminder of the sea that encircled them.

"I hope the boarding and your cabin are satisfactory." His voice was gentle and reassuring. He was a product of countless conversations with troops and civilians, sculpting his tone to comfort and command simultaneously.

"Yes, thank you," Rory responded.

Rory noted the Captain as he leaned back behind the large mahogany desk. His gaze fixed on Rose with an intensity that spoke of serious business. "I believe you were a nurse at St. Catherine's, and your father was a Doctor."

"Yes," she confirmed, noting that he had done his research. The mention of her father brought a slight ache of nostalgia, but she pushed it aside, focusing on the present. "We are desperately short of nurses on board." He introduced the topic gently but with a hint of urgency in his eyes. "Would you be interested in taking a position with us for the voyage to Fremantle?" Realising she had not addressed Rory, her husband. "perhaps you would like to discuss it."

Surprise quickly dissolved into excitement for Rose, lighting up her face. "I would love to," she responded, feeling joyful. The long voyage had seemed like a looming stretch of monotony, but now it shimmered with purpose. This was her calling, an opportunity to slip back into the comforting routine of care and compassion, like stepping into a familiar, worn pair of shoes.

Rory's agitation simmered just beneath the surface. He couldn't shake the feeling that he should have been consulted before making decisions. After all, it was their honeymoon—an experience meant to be shared and cherished. Yet, Rose had given her acceptance without seeking his opinion, a gesture that left him feeling sidelined and undervalued in their burgeoning marriage. "Good," the Captain said, and for the first time, a genuine smile softened his stern features. "You will be paid, of course. I will get the paymaster to fill you in on the details." He rose, signalling the end of their meeting, and she followed suit. "Thank you for helping us out."

Rose smiled warmly. "Thank you. I've always worked, and the thought of six weeks of idleness was not appealing." Again, she felt the rhythm of the ship beneath her, but now it seemed to echo with the promise of purpose and the steady beat of duty fulfilled.

She left the office with unwavering determination. Emotions swirled within her, but she squashed any temptation to overthink.

Rory was less impressed as he followed behind.

Back in the cozy cabin, she wrapped her arms tightly around Rory's neck, his skin sending a shiver down her spine as she kissed his lips tenderly. "This is wonderful," she murmured, her voice barely above a whisper, as the scent of pine filled the room.

"It is our honeymoon," he pointed out, his breath brushing against her ear.

She laughed, a melodic contrast to the stillness around them. "There will be time for that; we have the rest of our lives, too," she dismissed his objection, her eyes sparkling with joy.

Rory caught between the simmering annoyance in his chest and the effervescent joy radiating from her, decided to keep quiet. She allowed her heart's gentle, rhythmic beat against his to soothe his unease before easing away.

"I must go and report below deck," he mentioned, his voice steady but urgent, as the dim light flickered against the ship's wooden interior.

She felt a wave of resolve wash over her and nodded decisively. "Yes, and I will unpack my uniforms," she replied, already envisioning the crisp, neatly folded garments that awaited her, ready to be donned for whatever lay ahead. The subtle rocking of the ship echoed their shared urgency, the scent of salt and sea air thickening in the passageway.

She was already retrieving the case as he left the cabin.

Her hands trembled slightly as she reached for

the case, holding the uniforms, symbolising her true self. With each piece of clothing she retrieved, a sense of reassurance washed over her. She was reclaiming her identity, step by step, transforming back into Nurse Rose.

Tea time had come and gone, yet she hadn't stepped outside the confines of her cabin. She sat there, her uniform sprawled across the bed, and gradually drifted into a restless slumber. In the haunting depths of her dreams, memories of her parents came rushing back.

She relived the devastating moment when a German bomb obliterated their home in London, tearing them from her life in an explosion of fire and sorrow. The room seemed to shudder with the weight of her grief, the walls closing in as if to echo the claustrophobia of her despair.

A memory lay hidden within her, one she meticulously tucked away in the recesses of her mind, yet the Captain's words had unearthed it. This recollection, steeped in anguish, had shaped the very contours of her existence. Though she had navigated the currents of life with resilience, beneath the veneer of normalcy, the wound remained tender and unhealed, a silent echo of a past she could never truly escape.

She woke in Rory's arms. Her eyes opened to the cabin lit by the moon shining a single beam through the porthole.

"Bad dream." He murmured sleepily. She must have woken him.

"Yes, the blitz," she murmured, burrowing into his arm. She needed to tell him, but not tonight, while the memories were real.

With a world of possibilities stretching out before them, their future was woven with threads of countless conversations waiting to unfold, each holding the promise of deepened connections and shared dreams.

CHAPTER 11 - FREMANTLE

Fremantle Port HMS Orontes diembarking

Australian servicemen returning home after World War II. The ship is docked against the bustling harbour backdrop. A long gangway stretches from the vessel to the pier, crowded with soldiers in military uniforms descending to meet their eagerly awaiting families and loved ones. Cheering crowds, waving hats, and joyful embraces paint a poignant picture of relief and celebration. Reflecting the historical moment when peace and reunion became a reality for so many.

Nov 1945

Dear Aunt Rosemary

I hope you are well. I miss you and our daily phone calls. I had hoped to call you when we docked, but calls are complex and expensive. Long-distance international calls require booking in advance, often days or weeks ahead, so that I will reserve them for special occasions.

I am jotting a letter as we dock tomorrow, and I hope

to post it.

While Rory was clearly in command of activities to keep everyone entertained, Rose was surprised he did it so well.

The voyage seemed to slip away. There was scarcely a moment to breathe, let alone to indulge in the luxuries of a honeymoon.

Luckily, Rory's presence lit up the otherwise dreary journey, and his laughter and energy proved infectious. But now it is over.

Tomorrow is Australia, or as Rory points out, Western Australia. I have found this to be very distinct from the East, as they call it. I am nervous about meeting Rory's father, even though you told me not to worry.

It's all new to the country, especially the way they talk. I will never pick up the Australian drawl.

That is it for now. Keep well, and I will write again from Windamere. I am sure you will be interested in discovering if everything Rory said about Windamere is true.

Love Rosemary

ps. Have the camera will have the shots onboard developed and send them next time.

Rory and Rose leaned against the deck rail, their eyes watching the shore. Their journey would soon come to a close.

A swirl of anticipation and trepidation gripped Rose as she inhaled deeply, uncertain about what awaited them.

Fremantle Harbour unfolded before them like a living canvas, vibrant yet chaotic. Military ships and submarines docked alongside cargo vessels, creating a jigsaw of steel and purpose. Cranes danced overhead, tirelessly lifting supplies with a mechanical efficiency that seemed almost alien to the shoreline's natural beauty. The throng of service members, dockworkers, and civilians moved like a tide, each person a vital part of this busy ecosystem. Amidst this temporary invasion of humanity, the presence of military trucks and guards added an undercurrent of tension to the scene.

The cacophony enveloped them—sharp horns blaring, engines roaring to life, the rhythmic clatter of cranes mixing with the salty smell of the ocean, and the pungent scent of diesel. Rose's heart raced as she took in the enveloping atmosphere; it felt as though the air itself buzzed with the weight of stories and secrets waiting to be uncovered. Beyond the fray, the modest skyline of Fremantle loomed, its colonial-era buildings standing resilient against the tide of modernity, a reminder of history's enduring presence.

"Look, there's Dad," Rory exclaimed, gesturing towards the sea of faces. The chaos of movement blended with the figures of the armed personnel near the gangplank.

"Where?" Rose questioned, her brow furrowing as she tried to make sense of the shifting silhouettes, shadows weaving illusions that made identification nearly impossible.

"Right at the back, beside the pillion," Rory said, his tone tinged with a mingling of excitement and deep-seated relief that threaded through his words.

As they descended the gangplank to the bustling wharf, Rory led Rose forward, anticipation thrumming in his chest.

"Dad." Rory's voice broke as he enveloped his father in a warm embrace, his towering frame overshadowing the man who had raised him. A rush of emotions flooded through him—relief intertwined with a bittersweet joy that reverberated in the tender communion.

It dawned on Rory just how much he had longed for this moment. As they stood entwined, Rory felt an awakening within himself, as if he were rediscovering his father, seeing him through a new knowledge of their family history. So much lay between them, waiting to be shared and understood, echoing in the silence surrounding their reunion.

After a moment, Rory stepped back and turned towards her.

"You must be Rose." The gentle and welcoming voice immediately eased the anxiety that had been gnawing at Rose since her arrival. "Rosemary's niece." His eyes softened with recognition, and she felt an unexpected wave of comfort.

"Yes." She had expected a handshake, a formal gesture, but he pulled her into a quick hug instead. The brief gesture disarmed her and created an instant connection.

"Welcome. I know it can feel intimidating," Hugh said, his smile a bridge to distant and cherished memories. I recall the first time I made this journey." His grin, reminiscent of Rory's, sent a flutter through her heart, awakening a resonance of understanding that felt familiar yet new. It isn't quite what you envisioned," he noted as if he had plucked the very thoughts from her mind, revealing a more profound connection that transcended words.

"Yes," she replied softly, a warmth spreading as she reflected his sentiment. In that moment, she and Hugh experienced the comforting embrace of old friends despite their companionship's fresh and unexplored nature.

He laughed a rich sound that rolled through her, enveloping her in the sense of ease. "Were you expecting South Hampton?" he suggested teasingly, his smile widening with an infectious playfulness.

Rose shook her head, a smile breaking free in response. "No, something a bit more quaint." She could feel the atmosphere shifting around them, the air lightening as the tension in her shoulders dissipated. Though initially alien, this unfamiliar place gradually began to weave itself into the fabric of her heart, feeling more like home with each passing moment.

"But not this," Hugh said, a knowing chuckle escaping his lips. His eyes danced with a shared recognition of the past—one that both seemed to yearn for yet had been left behind. They stood in a port, a world apart from the frenetic pace of London they shared.

"Yes," Rose affirmed once more, her voice tinged with nostalgia as she pondered the winding paths ahead of them. Each step intertwined with the blossoming bond forming between her and Hugh. Her journey together with Rory—so full of possibilities—was beginning to unfold.

"It's different," Rory said, not wanting to be left out of the conversation. Rory tried to connect to their infectious enthusiasm.

"Yes," Rose and Hugh said in unison, laughter bubbling between them. The camaraderie felt genuine and comforting. Their shared British roots lent them a unique perspective that allowed them to compare their surroundings with London's lively, unpredictable energy.

They understood, perhaps better than anyone else ever could, the subtle yet profound changes one feels when moving from one city to another.

"Well, it's time to test our hotel," Hugh quipped, his usual playfulness shining through. Rose, matching Hugh's whimsical nature, replied with a knowing smile. "Midjal."

"Yes, but tonight is The Esplanade Hotel," he proudly announced. "The Esplanade?" Rory queried, the cost making him gasp.

"Yes, your Rose deserves a night of luxury before we whisk her into the wilds." Rose laughed. She liked Rory's jovial father.

Rory agreed with his father but knew the cost was something they could ill afford.

Hugh carried the whimsical belief that money, like leaves, grew on trees, yet had always managed to stay solvent through frugality—a lesson ingrained in him by his mother. She was a sturdy woman of the countryside, known for the relentless work that kept their farm running. Though Hugh's mining had provided the money through his gruelling work in the mines, his mother's tireless efforts sustained their livelihood.

To Rory, her unexpected death while he was stationed abroad during the war remained an open wound in his heart, gnawing at him with unresolved sorrow.

As Rory stood in the opulent hotel lobby, the grandeur surrounding him pressed down on his chest like a lead weight. Each marble floor tile and glistening chandelier was a stark contrast to the crushing reality of their financial plight. It was almost as though the place's elegance mocked him, reminding him of everything he lacked. The lavish fabrics and ornate decor only deepened the sense of longing within him, highlighting the vast gulf between this brief slice of luxury and the life he and his family were forced to endure.

His mother had been working tirelessly, fighting against the tide of bills and expenses, meticulously cutting corners and sacrificing her comforts in a formidable effort to keep alive the dream of a brighter future. Each month felt like a tightrope walk, the balance of their meagre bank account hovering precariously close to disaster. He could still remember the days when his father's mining fortune seemed to promise a never-ending abundance, but those days were nothing more than a faded memory now, lost to the relentless passage of time.

Yet as Rory watched Rose, her face aglow with delight and laughter echoing joyously throughout the gilded halls, he felt a flame ignite. A wild and fierce love surged forth, challenging the ingrained habits of thrift that were so deeply etched into his being. In that moment, he wrestled with his worries, pondering whether he could ignore the potential financial burdens just this once. Maybe the joy reflected on Rose's radiant face was worth the risk, a fleeting moment of happiness that needed to be cherished, even if it came at a price.

A nagging sensation crept into his mind. While his mother might have found the cost unsettling,

Rose could relish it without concern, thanks to Aunt Rosemary's affection.

Dinner was what Rose exuberantly termed 'fabulous.' The air was thick with the rich aroma of grilled steak, its tender, juicy texture practically melting in their mouths. Freshly harvested vegetables glistened with an irresistible sheen, bursting with colour and flavour that danced on the palate. They unfolded in a divine setting, where the flickering candlelight created an intimate ambience, wrapping them in warmth and delight as they savoured each exquisite bite.

After dinner, they settled into the lounge, the soft strains of a pianist conjuring melodies steeped in memories of war.

With a glass of wine cradled in her hand, Rose watched Rory closely, noting his steadfast refusal to indulge. A ripple of concern flitted through her mind—did he struggle with a drinking problem?

The thought lingered, heavy and unsettling, as she recalled that Hugh, for all his cheerful spirit, consumed alcohol more than any man might expect. She turned her gaze back to her father-in- law, a smile tugging at her lips.

Hugh's playful demeanour and magnetic personality felt like fresh air in a world long shrouded in conflict. Rose cherished these moments, intuitively understanding that the war had cast a long shadow over their lives, suffocating their joys and laughing spirits.

It was time for her family to chase away the darkness and reclaim their laughter amid the lingering gloom. Would they have the courage to move forward, casting aside the burdens they had carried for far too long?

Hugh had gone overboard with the luxury of a honeymoon suite. He was providing the newlyweds with the honeymoon they had missed.

Their tired looks did not go unnoticed. Always full of cheer, Hugh couldn't resist making a playful remark. "Good night, wasn't it?"

Rose responded with a mischievous smile. "The best," she said, causing her traditionally-minded husband to cringe slightly.

"It's something to remember and make up for the disappointment at the beach," Hugh quipped, grinning widely.

Rory locked eyes with his father, recalling the countless hours spent discussing their dreams and the relentless struggle to make ends meet.

He was acutely aware of the financial strain on their family but also knew that there were moments in life when the value far exceeded the cost.

His eternal optimist father had always embraced life with an unyielding passion, teaching Rory that love and joy often outshine practicality.

Rory recalled the countless nights his father had spent sitting by the fire, telling tales of resilience and whole-hearted living. He remembered his mother and him, rising to work the farm before dawn. There was the time they spent their entire savings to repair the family sheds after a fierce storm, refusing to let it fall into disrepair.

These memories fueled Rory's determination and commitment to uphold his mother's legacy. Every effort he made was a tribute to his mother's determination and his father's philosophy, a relentless pursuit to ensure their way of life survived and thrived.

With the rich aroma of freshly brewed coffee lingering in the air from their sumptuous breakfast, they embarked on their journey to Midjal. The gravel road, narrow and winding, crunched beneath the tyres with a rhythmic consistency as they ascended towards the Wheatbelt.

The crisp morning air carried the faint scent of gums, mingling with the sounds of nature awakening around them. Each turn of the road revealed sprawling fields, glistening under the early sunlight, painting the horizon warmly.

Rose watched the trees gradually thin, transitioning from dense clusters to lonely silhouettes etched against the horizon. The landscape starkly contrasted her lush, verdant Windermere— gone were the familiar emerald pastures of England.

Instead, a dry, barren terrain unfolded before her eyes. Fine dust swirled through the open windows, coating her skin and lips with a gritty film. The air tasted of parched earth, and each mile they travelled seemed to suck more moisture from the atmosphere, leaving behind a desolation where even the skeletons of trees grew scarce.

Hours later, Rose was woken by Hugh. "Your kingdom awaits," he quipped.

Rose surveyed a humble expanse of shops serving the vital needs of the local farming community. At the heart of this neighbourhood lay a general store, where families gathered, their shopping lists in hand. Shoppers could find everything from fruits and sturdy clothing to essential household items and even seeds and tools for their fields, all within these timeworn walls.

Nearby, the butcher stood proud, offering locally sourced meats displayed under the shop's soft glow. Of course, the bakery lured them with the aroma of warm, crusty bread, a staple for every household.

The post office serves not only as a place to send and receive mail but also as a hub for telegrams and financial transactions. The lively chatter of patrons would exchange the latest news.

For those seeking companionship, the local pub beckoned the men with its hearty atmosphere. At the same time, the café, adorned with delicate pastries and the rich aroma of coffee proved a favoured gathering spot for women. It was a perfect haven for catching up on friendships and discerning the latest whispers of town gossip.

"Everything a community needs," Rose responded with a smile.

She stood at the edge of the rail line, her gaze drifting over the modest homes that peppered the landscape. Each house, whether hewn from timber or brick, told a quiet story of resilience against the Wheatbelt's scorching summers, their corrugated iron roofs gleaming under the sun's relentless glare.

These homes were not just structures; they were havens filled with the whispers of life. Large verandas wrapped around the fronts and sides, inviting families to gather and share stories as the day faded into cooler evenings. Gardens with fruit trees and vegetable patches are a testament to the determination of families who nurtured both their plants and their bonds, cultivating not only food but a sense of community.

"See, we are not barbarians," Hugh chuckled, his voice breaking through her reverie. "No, far from it," Rose replied, her smile radiating warmth and familiarity, a spark of the connection that lightened her heart.

In her reflection, she peeled away the layers that masked Windermere's charm. Each town had its unique character, but beneath the surface, she discovered a tapestry woven with the duplicate threads of hard work and community spirit that defined her growing aspirations. As her apprehension began to fade, Rose found solace in the understanding that within the simplicity of life here lay a rich, shared humanity.

As she inhaled deeply, a rich, inviting aroma of freshly brewed coffee enveloped Rose, intertwining with the sun-warmed air like a soft, comforting embrace. No ordinary coffee; it was the kind that reached out, beckoning like a friendly welcome mat, exuding a warmth that seemed to breathe life into the vibrant street around her.

"Is that the scent of coffee I detect?" she asked, her senses heightened by the fragrant air.

"You certainly do," Hugh replied, a smile playing on his lips. He turned to his son Rory, who had been observing Rose's reaction with keen interest. "Well, come on, son, let's lead your wife into Lil's café," he urged, excitement twinkling in his eyes as the allure of the café promised a small haven of comfort and community.

CHAPTER 12 - MIDJAL

*Midjal's main street, set in rural Western Australia
along the Great Eastern Highway in 1946, reflects the
charm of a bustling post-war country town. Showcasing
Victorian and early 20th-century architecture, the street
includes local businesses like a café and a general store.
The scene captures the essence of a close-knit
community rebuilding and thriving in the wheatbelt.*

Hugh quiet contentment. "Home?"

Rose turned to him, her eyes sparkling with a burst of lively laughter. "It is like home," she breathed, her voice tinged with awe. The sunset cast a warm, golden glow across her face, highlighting her joy. "Just not Windermere," she added, a musical laugh escaping her lips.

Hugh held the door open for Rose and Rory to enter.

"Hugh, you're back already," Lil welcomed him. Grey-haired Lil's face showed years of hardship, which had etched lines into her, but her eyes sparkled with a kindness that had seen many through

"Hi Rory, you made it back!" she exclaimed, her

enthusiasm cutting through the afternoon air like a beam of sunlight. Curiosity shone in her eyes as she turned to Rose. "And who is this?" she asked with genuine interest.

"Lil, let me introduce my wife, Rose," Rory said, his voice brimming with pride and affection. He gently squeezed Rose's hand, a gesture that spoke of their deep bond. Rose, her eyes shining with warmth, felt an immediate connection to Lil, whose infectious spirit made her feel instantly at ease.

"Welcome, Rose," Lil greeted, her tone genuine and friendly. Rose recognised a kindred spirit, a woman whose forthright friendship offered a refreshing promise in the new town of Midjal.

For Lil, this encounter felt like the tender blossoming of a cherished friendship that would call upon all her strength and warmth to nurture in this distant, unfamiliar land. She could still recall the sound of the dry earth crunching beneath their boots when, years ago, she and Arthur had embarked on this same journey, their hearts brimming with the hope that something extraordinary awaited beyond the horizon.

"Thank you," Rose replied, her gratitude sincere despite her few words.

"I guess I am going to miss my best customer now that he has someone to cook for." Lil laughed, her eyes twinkling with a hint of mischief.

"Lil, don't give all my secrets away. I wanted

them to think of me as lonely," Hugh teased back, his ever-playful side emerging.

Rory couldn't help but feel the emotional spark that crackled between his father and Lil. As he watched their interaction unfold, a realisation began to blossom within him—his father's feelings for Lil ran deep, infused with warmth and unspoken recognition.

He pondered the transformation happening before him: Lil, with her kindness and vivacity, was gently weaving herself into the fabric of his father's heart.

Rory sensed a shared solace in their mutual singlehood, a silent understanding that flourished in their blossoming friendship. What did it mean for him, he wondered, to see his father find joy again, to watch this new chapter unfold?

"Take a seat. I'll get you some coffee," Lil responded, her suggestion met with enthusiastic nods. "I want to hear all about it." Her presence left a comforting imprint on the room as she walked away.

"She is a gem," Hugh said with a fondness that hinted at deeper feelings, his gaze lingering on Lil's vanishing silhouette. There was a certain warmth in his admiration, yet it teetered on the edge of something more complex.

Rose, sensing the undercurrent of tension, took the reins of the conversation while Rory sat in pensive silence.

His thoughts spiralled around the enigmatic connection between Lil and his father. Was she simply another fleeting romance for a man who seemed perpetually in search of affection, or did she reflect the same dutiful obligations he had observed in his mother's life—a relationship defined more by necessity than desire?

The truth clawed at him, each realisation more painful than the last. His parents' marriage had been a union forged in practicality; his mother's farming acumen made her an appropriate match in a world driven by survival. Yet, in this practical arrangement, had he forfeited his happiness? In that sacrificial moment, was he not also betraying the memory of his mother, a woman robust with love yet tethered by circumstance?

He felt a pang of nostalgia at the thought of the warm, gallant humour he had always shared with her, a ritual of affection. His heart ached, too, for Aunt Rosemary, whose unwavering support had woven a tapestry of love and understanding that he cherished deeply. The echo of a lingering sentiment drifted through his mind: "A man can't be a man without a woman." In that statement lay the heart of his struggles, revealing the intricate dance of longing and loss that defined his existence.

"Rory, what do you think?" Rose asked, her eyes scanning his face for any hint of his thoughts as Lil entered, balancing a tray of rich, aromatic coffee.

He turned to Lil with a genuine smile, a fleeting warmth that brought a glimmer of light to his otherwise reserved demeanour before he lifted the steaming cup to his lips with deliberate care. What myriad thoughts danced in the depths of those quiet eyes? Rose pondered, her mind racing as she struggled to unravel it.

He was momentarily spared from having to speak when the door swung open, and his neighbours entered.

"Rory," came the immediate, almost triumphant exclamation, the joy evident in Peter Harding's voice. "You are back."

"Peter," Rory responded quickly, grasping Peter's hand firmly. The way Peter clapped a reassuring hand on Rory's shoulder conveyed a bond forged through shared experiences, one that spoke volumes beyond mere words.

"I'm glad you're back," Peter repeated, his voice rich with heartfelt relief that wrapped around the moment like a warm embrace. It felt so right, like he was home, Peter's greeting, like he had never been away. But so much had happened.

"So am I," Rory said, a serene smile breaking over his face. The weight of absence lifted as a sense of belonging settled in his heart.

"Mr. Anderson." Peter turned, extending his hand toward Hugh. The atmosphere was thick with unspoken stories waiting to unfold.

Rose stood still, her heart wrestling with a tempest of emotions—confusion mingled with unexpected curiosity. She cast her gaze over the scene before her, her mind drifting back to Rory.

Only moments ago, he had appeared weighed down by the shadows of his thoughts. A man marooned in the depths of his worries. Yet now, he exuded an infectious joy that seemed almost alien to her. What event or revelation could have initiated such a striking transformation in him?

As Rose wrestled with the swirling questions in her mind, the atmosphere around her shifted. A soft, soothing voice gently penetrated her reverie, grounding her in the here and now.

"Don't look so perplexed. They've been inseparable since they were toddlers. This world, after all, has a way of drawing men together."

Curiosity sparked within her, compelling her to turn toward the voice. She found herself face to face with a woman whose smile felt like a warm embrace as if it had the power to melt away her uncertainty.

"Martha Harding," the woman said, her tone bright with the optimism that illuminated Rose's dim thoughts. We will be neighbours."

Her eyes twinkled with an inviting warmth, hinting at untold stories and shared laughter. Something in her gaze—a depth, perhaps— suggested that she had navigated her share of life's storms. As she extended her hand, it was not merely a gesture of friendship; it was an unspoken promise, a delicate invitation to embark on a journey of connection where their lives could share experiences and understanding.

The men quickly gathered themselves, their earlier fluster melting away. "Forgive me, this is my wife, Rose," he said, his voice steady yet warm, "and these are Peter and Martha Harding," he added, introducing them with deliberate care after a brief hesitation.

"Too late, Rory. I've already introduced myself," Martha chimed in with a playful laugh that danced between them. "And this," she said, gesturing affectionately toward her partner, "is my other half, Peter."

Rose's smile bloomed. At that moment, a quiet sense of camaraderie offered itself, one she felt invigorated to embrace.

The boys exchanged glances, a silent understanding passing between them as their eyes swept the room. "Let's put two tables together," Peter suggested, his enthusiasm infectious. "That way, we can really catch up."

"Come on, Rose. next to me," Martha suggested. "all these two will do is talk farm." Her tone carried a hint of resignation, blending with the low murmur of conversations and the gentle clink of cutlery. Reflecting a mixture of humour and quiet acceptance.

"Certainly." Rose welcomed the opportunity to solidify her bond with Martha. Perhaps this would be her chance to glean more about her enigmatic husband.

The men, already engrossed in their dialogue, their voices blending into the subtle hum permeating the room, paid no heed to them.

As they settled at the table, the delicate aroma of freshly brewed coffee enveloped them, offering a comforting embrace. Martha's curious yet kind eyes met Rose's. "Where are you from?" she inquired.

"Windermere in England," Rose replied, her voice tinged with a wistful nostalgia that painted memories of home in her mind.

"That is a coincidence Hugh's hometown," Martha said, her laughter—a friendly, melodic giggle—resonating through the cafe. Bringing a sense of hope and warmth to Rose, the first stirrings of friendship bloomed in this vast, unfamiliar land. It was the beginning of genuine camaraderie.

"Yes," Rose responded.

Martha was a source of much information. Rose soon discovered many things Rory had not mentioned, especially about the intricacies of farming in this rural expanse.

Martha shared tales of their trials with pride and an unmistakable love for the land. As she spoke, her eyes sparkled with memories of hard work and golden harvests. She revealed that she and her husband, Peter, had been married for three years, and she was a local girl rooted deeply in the community. Her husband, a figure often cloaked in the dust of distant fields, owned a farm further away.

Having exhausted her tale, Martha turned to Rose, her eyes inviting a new story. "Now, what about you? Where did you meet Rory?"

Rose took a deep breath, her thoughts drifting back to London's bustling, smoke-filled streets. Those streets, always alive with vendors and hurried footsteps, had a faint scent of coal and promise.

"I cared for Rory in London when he came in badly burnt," she began, her voice tinged with nostalgia and sorrow. Rory's haunting cries for Windamere—a serene countryside retreat that both of them cherished—lingered in her memory like a persistent ghost.

"You are a nurse," Martha interjected, her excitement palpable and eyes widening with admiration.

"Yes, at Queen Alexandra's," Rose confirmed, her tone shifting to pride as she continued, "My father was a Doctor." She wore her father's legacy, a compassionate man who dedicated his life to healing others with honour.

Martha, her weathered hands clasping Rose's across the wooden table, looked at her with earnest gratitude. "You are a gem. Out here, we need nurses," she said, her voice filled with hope and desperation. Rose's skills were a beacon of light in the vast and lonely countryside, where facilities were scarce. "In the case of emergencies, local care is very critical. Perth is the only place to get to specialist care, and you know how long that takes."

Lil arrived, cup in hand, to join the group. "A nurse, did you say?" she asked, her curiosity piqued. "Yes, from London," Martha elaborated, offering a warm smile. That's where she met Rory when they evacuated him. Her father was a doctor, too."

"Jody from the hospital is leaving at the end of the month," Lil mentioned casually. "She's marrying Harvey from Cooinda, so they'll look for a replacement."

Rose felt a familiar excitement surge through her. She knew this well; it felt as comforting as slipping into an old pair of slippers.

"Are you interested?" Martha inquired, her eyes twinkling with anticipation.

"Yes, but I'll have to discuss it with Rory," Rose added thoughtfully, recalling his initial reaction to her accepting the nursing position on the boat.

"There's the voice of a newlywed," Lil commented with a knowing nod, and Martha chuckled. "It will pass. Men aren't exactly known for making the best decisions."

Hugh slid into the chair, a curious glint in his eyes as he asked, "What are you laughing about?"

The warm glow of the café wrapped around them like a familiar blanket, creating an inviting atmosphere.

"Nothing much," Martha replied, her cheeky grin illuminating her face. "Just that Rose might get a job at the hospital." The excitement in her voice danced in the air, infusing it with a sense of hopeful anticipation.

"Now, ladies," Hugh interjected playfully, "I distinctly heard something about men and their decisions." His tone was teasing, yet there was a hint of introspection there—a fleeting thought about the complexities of choices and consequences that lingered behind his laughter.

They erupted into laughter, their shared joy echoing around the snug café, its walls filled with memories of countless conversations.

The camaraderie was thick, a warm tapestry woven from years of friendship, and Rose savoured the moment.

"Okay, we really must go," Martha said at last, her eyes drifting reluctantly to her watch. A mixture of obligation and genuine regret washed over her; they had promised Peter's parents they would bring one of her beloved apple pies to dinner. She turned to Val, a smile tinged with warmth. "But let's make a promise to catch up soon. There is a lot I have to share."

"Of course," Rose replied, her voice softening with understanding.

Martha shifted her gaze to Peter, her husband. "Time to go, love; Val is just fetching the apple pie, and your parents will start to worry if we delay any longer." The affection in her tone was palpable.

Peter looked up, an image of compliance mixed with affection. "Okay," he agreed quietly, the weight of the moment settling around them like a comforting cloak.

Rory chuckled, breaking the tension. "Look at you; she's got you well-trained."

Martha shot him an amused glance. "That's a lesson for you. It's always wiser to agree, especially when it comes to pie."

Just then, Val returned, cradling the pie like a treasure.

"That is our cue to leave and let Val quiet down for the day," Hugh suggested, his voice carrying both anticipation and a hint of trepidation. He felt a stirring in his chest as he thought of Windamere. He envisioned the countless hours of hard work that had finally taken shape, dreams he had nurtured through hardship now blossoming into reality.

He longed to share this moment with Rose, his daughter-in-law, to let her see what he had built from the ashes of the past.

The scars of war still tinged his memories, his family nearly wiped out, yet here he was, standing at the threshold of a new beginning. Would she recognise it? Would she see it as he did? The evolving fabric of his hope and determination for his family to have a better life?

The burden of his questions weighed heavily on his heart, a mix of excitement and longing swirling within him like a tempest. He longed for everything to unfold as he prepared to reveal their home to Rose—Rory's war bride.

A faint smile brushed his lips, a flicker of warmth amidst his turbulent thoughts. Rosemary's niece. Was it mere coincidence that their paths had crossed, or was it some invisible thread of fate

that bound them together?

It felt as if destiny itself had intervened, weaving their lives into a tapestry of hope and promise. It was the culmination of all his efforts and the pinnacle of his life's work. It mattered that she had the chance to step into the embrace of a family home. For without the warmth and love of family, he realised with a pang in his chest that all his hard-earned achievements would be rendered meaningless as whispers lost in the wind.

For here on the dust plains, it could be a lonely place.

As Rose looked out the car window, a smile blossomed on her lips, a rare moment of peace washing over her. For the first time in ages, she felt a sense of clarity, the conviction that she had made the right choice in following her heart.

Turning her gaze to Rory, she noticed the bright

smile illuminating his face, and the rhythmic hum of the engine provided a soothing soundtrack to their journey. In the backseat, Hugh animatedly shared a childhood anecdote that filled the air with laughter, his gestures so vivid they nearly pulled Rose into a fit of giggles. This shared moment of joy and connection wrapped around them, deepening the bond they all.

"Is this what friendship feels like?" Rose wondered, a twinge of disbelief flickering through her thoughts. It was an alien feeling, this seamless camaraderie. In London, friendships had been elusive, often shadowed by her guarded nature and the city's impersonal rush. Yet, she was embraced by Martha and Lil's openness, marvelling at how swiftly these bonds had formed.

She pondered the loneliness she'd carried to this new town; nursing was all she had considered since her parents' death. The nights were spent with only books and fleeting social interactions to keep her company. Now, it seemed, the universe had conspired to offer her a fresh start.

As the car navigated the winding roads, Rose couldn't help but think of the circumstances that had brought her here. "Perhaps," she mused, "this is where I was always meant to be." The thought filled her with quiet reassurance, a burgeoning hope that maybe, just maybe, she had finally found her place in the world.

Little did she know, her thoughts echoed those of Hugh's.

"Windermere," Hugh announced as they navigated the winding drive, the car tyres crunching over loose gravel.

It loomed on the desolate plains, a solitary sentinel against the vastness, its grandeur stealing Rose's breath away. Large and elegant, the home was characterised by a classic colonial or Victorian style. It was two stories tall, with wide, wrap-around verandas on both levels supported by intricately detailed, decorative posts. The roof has a distinct, corrugated iron featuring ornate finials at the peaks. Its colours, soft creams, and light browns blended harmoniously with the natural surroundings.

It was like her aunt's house. Rose's eyes danced over every architectural detail she could discern from this distance. Hot air bit her cheeks, and the scent of gums filled the air.

"You were right, Rory. It is like Aunt Rosemary's home," she whispered, her voice a fragile thread in the afternoon warm air. "But much more prominent and far more grand.

"Rosemary, a cherished part of her that I managed to bring with me," Hugh chuckled. "She couldn't come herself, but now we have two pieces of Rosemary: the house and her niece. Life has its quirks." Nostalgia shimmered in Hugh's eyes as memories of Rosemary washed over him; if only the past had unfolded differently.

"You have more than just two," Rory giggled. "Aunt Rosemary's gift is in our luggage—eight roses from Windermere."

Hugh laughed warmly, his thoughts momentarily transported to the days spent in Rosemary's company. "That woman," he said, feeling the intertwined threads of their long-shared history tug at his heart.

"An extraordinary woman," Rose responded.

"I agree," Hugh responded, shutting out the lingering memories. "We had better get inside. Those roses must be planted if they are to survive."

To Hugh, these roses were not merely plants; they had become his life's mission. He would tend to them with a devotion that suggested they held the key to his redemption.

Rory couldn't help but find it ironic, knowing his father had never been one to have a green thumb. Yet, in those roses, Hugh saw something worth nurturing that connected deeply to his past and purpose.

To Rose, they were a connection to Aunt Rosemary.

CHAPTER 13 - WINDAMERE

Hughs Wimdamere - a striking two-story house, set in rural Western Australia, exudes the charm of late 19th to early 20th-century Federation architecture. The home's elevated foundation and symmetrical design reflect the era's practicality and style, making it a centerpiece of the countryside. Its serene setting amidst open fields and native flora underscores its historical significance as a hallmark of rural Australian heritage, blending beauty with functionality in a timeless landscape.

Rose stood at the base of the steps, which curved upward, beckoning her to explore. The wide verandah unfolded before her, encased by beautifully ornate railings that whispered of both elegance and shelter. Shade poured down from above, inviting her into the embrace of this tranquil space.

Ahead, the solid wooden door loomed majestic and commanding, a sentinel to the interior. It was framed by tall windows that spilled warm, natural light into the shadows behind. As she ascended the steps, her gaze was drawn to the intricate carvings of the door, each detail telling a story of craftsmanship and time.

Once atop the verandah, she turned her eyes to the landscape before her. The gum trees offered some shade, and the vast, open horizon stretched out beyond the property, evoking a deep sense of peace and isolation typical of rural Australia. An expansive lake shimmered in the distance while paddocks stretched endlessly to the horizon.

It was a panorama unlike any she had ever. England's hills and valleys felt small in comparison, mere glimpses against the boundless expanse of this magnificent land. In that moment, she understood the sheer immensity that surrounded her, igniting a sense of awe within her heart.

Hugh swung the door wide, and the tender light of dusk cascaded into the room like a gentle embrace, softening the corners of the spa.

"Welcome to Windamere," he declared, his voice resonating with the echoes of untold stories and unfulfilled dreams. With a weight of solemnity that lingered in the air, he urged, "Son, do the right thing by your bride." Rory's face lit up with joy as he effortlessly lifted Rose into his arms, her laughter bubbling up like a sweet spring after a long winter. He carried her across the threshold, each step imbued with a promise of new beginnings.

As she stood on her own once again, a wave of slight disorientation washed over Rose, but it fluttered away as quickly as it came, replaced by the awe of her surroundings before she lay a grand hallway, its polished hardwood floors shimmering like sun-kissed rivers under the warm embrace of light streaming through the tall front windows. The ceiling soared majestically above her, where an antique chandelier hung like a constellation, casting a golden hue that danced along the walls.

Her gaze was drawn to the sweeping staircase, a graceful curve leading to the mysteries of the second floor. The intricate carvings of the mouldings whispered tales of artistry and time, compelling her to trace her fingers along their delicate patterns.

The house stood waiting, yearning for transformation—to be filled with laughter, warmth, and the chaos of life. It stood proudly against the backdrop of the rural landscape, harmonising with the gentle whispers of nature that surrounded it, waiting for those who would breathe life into its walls.

Rory, ever perceptive to her subtle cues, studied her reaction. "We're missing Rosemary's special touch," he murmured, sorrow colouring his voice.

As was his custom, Hugh quickly added his voice to the conversation.

"Joan had always been one for the outdoors," he reflected with a bittersweet smile. She was a remarkable farmer," he added, pausing to gather his emotions. She passed on so much wisdom to you boys. The war took all three of them from us." His words weighed heavily in the air as he struggled to continue, his eyes glistening with unshed tears. "Joan tried to manage everything independently, and in the end, it overwhelmed him too."

He carried a deep reservoir of sorrow, a weight that seemed to drag him down. Yet, nearly as if he had flicked a switch, his face broke into a warm, inviting smile. "It is up to us to make the most of our lives now they are 'gone,'" he declared out of respect, adding their names, "Joan, Albert, and Guy." He shrugged off his melancholy, adding that he turned his gaze to Rory with a newfound breath. "Thank God you survived. I feared I might be the last of the Andersons."

A knowing, affectionate wink followed, directed at "It's up to you now," she said, turning to Rose's laughter filled the room, a musical sound that momentarily lightened the heavy atmosphere. "Not just me," she said, her voice gentle but firm. But behind the coy reply, she noted this was the first time she had heard their names. There was a lot that her husband held locked away.

As the group shared the laughter, it was clear how significant this moment was for them. The family, once five strong, is now reduced to two; such is the relentless nature of war.

"Let's have a drink: tea or beer." Hugh's casual yet inviting voice broke the silence.

The choice of beer got the nod. With a playful

flourish, pulling open the fridge door and retrieved the bottles, thoughts flickering briefly to the many evenings spent in similar company.

"On the veranda," he proposed, his mind already wandering to the sunset that would soon paint the sky. As they settled onto the porch, the cool breeze swept past them, carrying with it the faint scent of blooming flowers and distant laughter.

"So, how was England?" Hugh inquired, beer now in hand, his curiosity piqued as he leaned slightly toward Rory, eager to catch every nuance in his response.

"Rose took me to Winde "mere," Rory replied, his eyes momentarily glazing over with the memories."

Hugh's grin revealed a hint of playfulness, yet his expression also held a more deep interest. "We explored the Andersons," Rose chimed in, her voice laced with a mix of nostalgia and gravity that made Hugh's.

"There are only us left now," Hugh murmured, his tone shifting subtly as the weight of the words settled around "hem. "There are no Windemere Andersons anymore, just graves." He felt a twinge in his chest, the loss tethering itself to a shared past that seemed to be an increasingly fragile future.

"Yes, the Vicar showed us where the plot was," Rory continued, with a touch of anxiety. He wrestled with the implications of sharing family secrets, unsure of how his father would respond. "I met Sir Reginald; he took me over his farm and even down a mine."

Hugh nodded, his gaze drifting over the landscape, the beer calm in his hand. "He is the exception to his father, a true gentleman," he remarked thoughtfully, studying the sunset. A slight tick in his cheek did not go unnoticed by Rory.

Rory turned to him. "You knew." He stated.

"Yes, nothing in Windermere passes without Rosemary letting me know." Suddenly, his face was brimming with amusement. "You don't have to have my permission to discover our family." He stated.

"I learnt a lot," Rory commented. "Mining is a hard life." "Rosemary's father enlightened me. His words were harsh but true."

"In that case," Rory commented, "it is time for me to show you to our bedroom." He said to Rose, finishing his beer.

"The main bedroom," Hugh instructed, with a nod to his son. It was his now, changing of the guard.

Rory opened the door, allowing Rose to enter first.

Stepping into the main bedroom, Rose was first struck by its spacious and serene feel. The high ceilings immediately give an arm glow over the space. In the centre, a grand wooden bed with an elegantly carved headboard draws her attention. Its crisp white linens and cozy quilt invite you to relax.

On her left was a small, decorative fireplace—its mantle adorned with a few personal items, giving the room a cozy, lived-in feel. The polished timber floors were softened by a large rug, making the room feel both elegant and welcoming. A large wardrobe with rich wooden detailing stood tall along the wall.

A comfortable armchair stood near the French doors that opened onto the balcony, from which there was a view of the vast countryside beyond.

Everything about the room exudes quiet luxury, blending the home's charm with a sense of peaceful rest. It's the kind of space where you immediately feel at ease, surrounded by beauty and tranquillity. "

"It is beautiful," Rose murmured. Never in her wildest dreams had she imagined this.

"You like it," Rory asked, his tone tinged with concern.

Rose responded with a tender kiss. "No, I love it. Your Windamere is very grand."

As she smiled at him, her eyes brimming with unyielding love, Rory felt a pang in his chest. He couldn't voice the pressing question that haunted him: Their empty coffers hung over him like a shadow, casting doubts. He was painfully aware of how little they had. Rose's unwavering faith made him want to believe they'd somehow find a way.

He took her arm gently, his eyes twinkling with anticipation. "Come, I will show you around before I check on the farm." Together, they strolled arm in arm.

Rose surveyed the kitchen first, starting with the massive stove that dominated the room. It exuded warmth, casting a cozy glow over the polished wooden countertops and the sturdy, well-worn benches.

"It burns all the time?" she asked, her curiosity piqued by the faint crackling sound of the flames.

"Yes, it heats the water as well. A slow burner Mum brought it," he replied, pride evident in his voice.

The refrigerator hummed softly, its interior stocked with provisions. Above, ample cupboards reached up to the ceiling, filled with essentials.

As Rory opened a door, revealing an austere bathroom. At the same time, Rose's eyes were drawn to the large clawfoot bathtub, its enamel gleaming in the soft light. A modest basin perched on a small table stood nearby, strategically linked to the stove's warmth.

"The toilet?" Rose asked, tilting her head.

Walking back inside, upon entering the dining room, you are immediately drawn to the sense of timeless elegance and warmth. The centrepiece is a long, polished wooden dining table, it's surface rich and smooth, surrounded by high-backed chairs with intricate carvings. The room feels expansive, with high ceilings and tall windows allowing natural light to flood in, casting a gentle glow on the space. Soft curtains frame the windows, adding a touch of refinement.

"Your father must have spent a fortune to build and furnish Windamere," she murmurs.

"Yes," Rory commented, not wanting to explain to what extent.

"Follow me," he said, a mischievous grin spreading across his face. He led Rose out the side door onto a winding path. In the distance, a small outhouse came into view. "We call it the dunny," Rory announced, his grin widening. "No sewerage out here."

Rose glanced toward the distant structure, a hint of disapproval in her eyes, but she remained silent. Instead, her gaze settled on a lush patch of green further out. "A vegetable garden?" she queried.

Still grinning, Rory says, "That is where drain water runs out. There is enough water to grow vegetables, but..."

"I know there is no sewerage out here," Rose responded with a smile as they continued on the tour. "or power."

"No Power?" Rose queried, thinking of the fridge and the lights. How would they live without it? He responded with a broad grin. "You're joking," she said, nudging him playfully.

"No, That's what the shed over there is for. We make our power," Rory explained, pointing to a small shed beside the house.

Rose could hear the low murmur of an engine. "You have your power plant," she said, relieved. "For a moment, I thought we were moving back a century."

"Are you calling us primitive?" Rory asked, raising an eyebrow.

Rose just nudged him again, choosing to drop the playful banter. In this mood, he reminded her of his father; at other times, he turned silent, realised that it was when a problem was worrying him.

Rory and Hugh went to inspect the farm. Leaving Rose to unpack, Rose decided to seek a breeze on the balcony.

Beads of sweat formed on her brow, mixing with the dust that clung to her skin. She squinted against the glaring sun, its relentless rays a stark reminder of the unforgiving days ahead. The dry earth lay sprawling before her, a desolate expanse that all the way to the distant horizon, the heat rising in layers like ghostly whispers, suffocating and relentless.

It was in that scorching moment that the heat wrapped around her like a suffocating blanket. The actual adversary in this sweltering expanse was not the biting chill as in England but the oppressive, unyielding heat. The warmth, once a source of comfort, had now transformed into an unrelenting foe that she had to learn to endure.

Her appreciation for the man she had married grew deeper as she gazed longer. The rugged landscape, harsh and unyielding, held his affection just as it had for his brothers, who were lost in the war. In the stillness, she began to comprehend his quiet nature. He was a man who endured, never seeking more, grounding himself in the here and now, making each moment significant.

Dust rose in lazy spirals from the paddock. They were back. Part of her wanted to ask and realise what she had asked. How was it? Rory had been itching to come home, back to his land.

Rose was a city girl, unsure what to ask on a farm like this. Rose pinned a smile to her lips as they got out of the ute and came towards her.

Hugh called up to her. "That hot; even the lizards have gone underground," he declared, his voice ringing with weary humour. "A beer, I think."

He disappeared inside, leaving Rose momentarily in heavy silence. Rose let out a bright, realising she had been holding it. I'm not sure if she should go down or if they would join her.

Rory stepped through the French doors, the soft creak of the hinges a familiar sound that welcomed him back. As he leaned in to kiss her cheek, the gentle brush of his lips conveyed a depth of emotion that words could scarcely capture. In that fleeting moment, his eyes sparkled with a mixture of relief and a glimmer of hope, pulling back just enough for their gazes to entwine.

"Are you glad to be back?" she asked, her voice

tinged with uncertainty that mirrored her heart—an anxious flutter that yearned for reassurance.

His lips curled into a faint smile, yet the shadow of something unspoken lingered in his expression, hinting at secrets buried deep within him. "Just as well I am back," he replied softly, each word heavy with emotions that hinted at stories untold, memories both sweet and bittersweet clinging to the corners of his mind.

Rory leaned against the balustrade, his gaze drifting over the expanse of the farm—a quilt of nostalgia and longing. Pride surged within him, intertwining with the relief of being home once more, yet his heart ached with the knowledge of all that had transpired in his absence.

The loss of his mother struck him with an unbearable weight. They attributed her passing to a heart attack, but he sensed it was more than that—a culmination of burdens borne silently.

She had always been the cornerstone of their lives, effortlessly managing the estate that had once thrived under the collective effort of the four of them: Guy, Albert, his mother, and himself. Now, he replayed moments in his mind—her gentle laughter during their long summer afternoons, the way her hands moved with grace as she tended to the garden. If only he had chosen to remain by her side instead of taking on the role of guardian to his younger brother, perhaps things would have unfolded differently.

"Why is that?" she probed once more, her curiosity a palpable force in the air between them, a silent plea for him to peel back the layers of his thoughts, to let her in on the tempest brewing inside him, much like the gentle rustling of leaves in the wind.

"The farm needed someone to run it," he replied, his voice calm and unwavering, yet the brief silence that followed belied a brewing storm of emotion beneath the surface. It was as if the very fields around them were not merely patches of land but mirrors reflecting the turbulence deep within his soul, the unease that lay coiled, waiting for just the right moment to break free. He was weighed down by responsibilities that were both visible and invisible, promises unfulfilled, and burdens too heavy to carry alone.

She felt a knot form in her throat, not knowing how to unravel it. "Is your father coming up?" she asked, her voice carrying an echo of concern.

"No, he's taking a shower, which is something I desperately need," he admitted, allowing a tired smile to flicker across his face, yet it didn't quite reach his eyes, which held a faraway sadness.

With a gentle determination, Rose rose from her chair, gliding behind him, her arms wrapping around him in a tender embrace. "I don't know; you smell appealing," she teased, her voice a soft melody meant to lighten the heavy air.

He chuckled, a fleeting sound that seemed to cut through the tension. "After, madam. I need to wash the earth off," he said, but beneath his jest lingered an undercurrent of weariness—a reminder of the toil etched into his skin and his soul.

CHAPTER 14 - THE TRUTH

Rory's Repairs - The towering windmill symbolizes the reliance on wind-powered water pumps to sustain crops and livestock in the arid landscape. The wide-open fields, dotted with trees and under a moody sky, reflect the resilience and determination of the farming communities. By 1946, the Wheatbelt had become a cornerstone of Western Australia's agricultural success and a testament to innovation and perseverance in rural Australia.

While Hugh had initially suggested planting Aunt Rosemary's roses right away, it was only the following day that they finally undertook the task, a subtle reminder of the unspoken dynamics in their relationship.

"Where do you think we should put them?" Hugh inquired, his voice tinged with uncertainty as he looked at the dirt that currently defined the garden. His attempts to engage in decision-making revealed both his eagerness to contribute and his awareness of his limitations in gardening.

"Let us start with along the front of the veranda,"

Rose said thoughtfully, recognizing that Hugh was out of his depth when it came to tending to plants. Her tone, gentle yet firm, reflected the lessons instilled in her by Aunt Rosemary, a figure that loomed large in their memories, symbolizing knowledge and care.

"Yes, that is a good idea," he praised her, grabbing his spade with a hint of admiration but also a trace of relief that she was taking the lead.

"First, we need to mark and prepare a bed for them," Rose suggested, understanding that Hugh's instinct was to bury them without further ado, an instinct that might stem from a desire to please rather than a genuine connection with the task.

"Ah!" he laughed lightly, attempting to cloak his ignorance with humour. "I detect an ounce or so of Aunt Rosemary in you." His statement was not just an observation; it was a bridge between them, a reminder of shared moments spent under the guidance of her beloved Aunt.

Rose stood from her crouched position, her gaze shifting from the soil to meet his eyes, a soft smile playing on her lips. "She is a good teacher," she replied, her heart swelling with nostalgia as she reflected on the wisdom passed down to her.

"That she is," Hugh said, his tone softening as if Aunt Rosemary's acknowledgment illuminated their collaboration. "Right, what are we going to need?" The weight of their shared history and unspoken feelings hung in the air, intertwining their actions and memories as they prepared to honour Aunt Rosemary's legacy through the act of planting.

It was lunchtime before they planted the roses across the front. First, they pegged the bed, then prepared the ground by adding manure (much to Hugh's disgust), and finally, they gave the roses a good watering.

Hugh surveyed their handiwork.

"Quite a job." He commented.

"But it will be worth it; next spring, they will prove me right," Rose responded with satisfaction. It had been what she needed, a chance to put her stamp on Windamere. "We will need a lawn, perhaps some lavender and trees lining the approach."

Hugh paled. This was Rosemary in full swing, and it meant a lot of work, and he felt he would not escape easily.

"Time for lunch," Hugh suggested with a spark of enthusiasm lighting his eyes. The kitchen felt alive with the scent of fresh herbs and the faint sound of the clock ticking in the background, a reminder that time was slipping away, yet this moment felt precious.

"I'm not sure what to make," Rose replied, her brow furrowed with uncertainty. Hugh noticed her hesitation, the way her fingers fidgeted with the hem of her shirt. It stirred something within him—a desire to support her, to show her that they could create something beautiful together.

Hugh smiled, feeling a rush of confidence. He was in his comfort zone, where he could reclaim a sense of control. "Right, my turn then. I may not be a gardener, but one thing I can do is cook." The proclamation felt good, and he relished the thought of taking charge, of introducing her to the joy of shared creation.

"We will make a good team," Rose laughed, her voice lightening the air around them. He loved that sound—the way her laughter wrapped around him like a warm embrace.

"Yes, we will." Hugh agreed, a swell of affection blooming in his chest. She was everything he had wanted—her spirit, her laughter, and more than he had ever anticipated for Rory's wife. In this simple act of cooking together, he felt the threads of connection deepen, weaving their lives more intricately.

"You're the chef; I am the assistant." Her playful tone was a stark contrast to the vulnerability he had sensed earlier. Her acceptance of their roles made him feel a rush of warmth. Together, amid the clatter of pots and the crackle of excitement, they were building something profound—an identity forged.

They prepared lunch just in time for Rory's arrival.

Ha! Rory sniffed the aroma of fresh bread and herbs wafted through the air, making his stomach rumble in anticipation. He had missed his father's cooking.

Rose met him at the steps, her eyes sparkling with excitement. "What do you think?" she asked, pointing to the new garden bed, a hint of pride in her voice.

As Rory glanced at the colourful blooms and neatly arranged plants, he couldn't help but admire the effort that had gone into it. "You have been busy," he replied, a smile creeping onto his face as he felt a warmth in his chest, pleased to see her creativity flourishing.

"And your father," Rose declared, her voice rising with enthusiasm. "We are going to plant a lawn!" The sheer joy in her eyes made Rory's heart swell; he could sense how much this meant to her.

Behind her, Hugh stood with an expression that hinted at both bemusement and resignation, hands cradling his head as he shook it slowly.

"Well, that will be something," he chuckled, the sound both affectionate and teasing. Rory couldn't help but feel a thrill at the thought of his father getting involved, the prospect that, with Rose's persistence, Hugh might even learn to embrace the land. The moment felt alive with possibility, a spark of hope that this simple endeavour could bring them all closer together.

"Perhaps later in the year," he suggested, striving to keep their spirits high despite the looming costs they could hardly bear.

"Yes, that sounds like a wise plan," Hugh replied, a hint of agreement sparking in the air. Waiting for the rains will allow the plants to settle in nicely before summer arrives.

"Perhaps," Rose mused, her mind wandering through the possibilities. A part of her craved immediate action, yet there was a logic to what he proposed. Still not ready to let go of her enthusiasm, she added, "But we could certainly fence the yard and prepare it in the meantime."

Hugh let out a resigned groan while Rory chuckled, the sound lifting the weight of the conversation.

Hugh soon found himself stepping into the role of her devoted apprentice in the garden, captivated by the wealth of ideas that flowed from her. Each vision of hers remained untouched, vibrant, and resolute, like a blossoming garden in spring. She dreamed of a quaint picket fence, its white slats promising a quaint charm, with a welcoming parking area nestled just beyond, offering an inviting sense of arrival.

As they marked the perfect locations for her dreams to materialize, Rose's keen eyes caught sight of the dilapidated hen house, a shadow of its former glory. The weathered wood, bleached by countless seasons, seemed to whisper secrets of days gone by.

Hugh swallowed hard, a knot forming in his

stomach. It had long been abandoned, yet the air crackled with hope as Rose's determination ignited the lifeless structure. With a spark in her eyes, she began to formulate plans, envisioning the hen house restored to life, bustling with the soft clucks of lively hens and fresh eggs.

Hugh reclined on the veranda, a beer cradled in his hand; he turned to Rory thoughtfully. "Your wife is truly resolute in her mission to breathe new life into Windamere."

Rory chuckled, a fond smile creeping across his face. Memories of the nurse he had encountered in the military hospital flooded back to him. "Indeed, she's got a knack for making things happen. I believe it was her tenacity that kept us all alive."

Concern etched on Hugh's face, he probed further, eager to grasp the trials his son had faced. "Was it really that severe?" He felt an urgent need to bridge the gap between the boy he had known and the man who had returned home.

"Yes," Rory replied, his gaze drifting towards the distant lake that glimmered under the sun. "There was another girl who had her eye on me—tall, dark, and handsome, she declared just her type. But Rose made it clear to her that my chances of surviving the night were slim." He paused, a glimmer of pride shading his voice. "It lit a fire in me, though; I fought like hell just to prove her wrong."

Their laughter echoed through the stillness, a

bittersweet reminder of the times when the family had been together.

As the week drew to a close, a rhythm emerged in the air of Windamere—an unspoken pact forged amid the challenges of daily life.

Rose, with her nurturing spirit, tackled the cleaning and gardening, drawing upon memories of her childhood spent in her mother's vibrant garden, where she learned to appreciate the simplicity of growing things from the earth.

Hugh, a man of the kitchen, found solace in the act of cooking, imparting to their meals the flavours he had learned from miners, where gatherings revolved around hearty feasts and laughter.

The only friction in their otherwise seamless collaboration was the laundry task. Rose, eager to shoulder the burden, proposed washing everything, but Hugh's independence flared at the suggestion. "I'm not asking for a servant," he declared with fierce pride; he wanted to retain his sense of self.

In the end, they reached a compromise, a testament to their adaptability and shared vision of partnership. Together, they stood firm under the expansive sky, embracing the magnitude of Windamere and all it demanded of them.

Meanwhile, Rory, the dedicated farmer, toiled alongside the spirited Fin O'Brien, a young Irish lad whose enigmatic past remained shrouded in secrecy. Though they never pried into the origins of his journey to Australia, a whisper of curiosity lingered—was he, perhaps, a product of the convict stories that haunted the land?

Despite the unsaid uncertainty, Rory appreciated Fin for his unwavering work ethic and the lighthearted camaraderie he brought to the fields. Residing in a cottage near the sheds, Fin quickly became a staple of their lunch routines, his laughter resonating across the tables cluttered with simple fare. Rose and Hugh often shared knowing glances, wondering if Fin indeed dined on anything beyond the midday meals, for his presence alone satisfied a hunger for community that filled the vast openness.

Hugh came to the rescue, providing him with snacks for later.

Rose's gaze lingered on Rory, noting the deepening lines of weariness and worry etched across his face. It was more than just fatigue—each furrow seemed to tell a story of burdens too heavy for one man to bear. She turned to Hugh, her voice barely above a whisper. "Have you noticed how much he's changing?"

Hugh nodded, a shadow of concern crossing his features. "He has a lot on his plate."

A sigh escaped Rose as she thought of the countless hours of toil and heartache weighing on him. "Yes, the work must be hard." Her mind drifted to the scars, the remnants of battles fought both externally and within. "I must check whether his skin grafts have held."

"Was Rory badly burnt?" Hugh's question brought her back to the present, but the memories lingered like an unwelcome guest. Through the haze of pain, she remembered Rory's brave smile.

"Yes," she replied, the heaviness in her chest tightening. "A bomb exploded from behind. Rory suffered 50% burns. If one could dare to find a silver lining amidst such horror, one could say he was fortunate. Had the explosion occurred in front of him..." Her voice trailed off, the thought too grim to articulate fully. The image of his face burnt by flames and the loss of vision haunted her.

"The war must have been tough for nurses, too," Hugh pressed, his curiosity raw and genuine. He wanted to understand and delve deeper into the unseen wounds that marked not only the soldiers but also those who took care of them.

"Yes," she conceded, her eyes glazing over as memories whisked her away. She found herself back in the sterile wards of the hospital, the acrid scent of charred flesh and blood a constant reminder of the horrors they faced. It was a stench forever etched in her mind, an indelible mark of her experiences.

Hugh sensed the bitterness of her recollections, the pain bubbling beneath the surface of her calm exterior. At that moment, he understood that the ghosts of the past loomed large, not just for the soldiers but also for those who had witnessed their suffering firsthand.

Hugh observed, "It must be tough for him to endure the harsh sun all day."

"I always ensure he's properly protected from the sun," came the reply, hinting at a more profound concern for the man's well-being and their bond.

Rory and Finn gazed up at the windmill, their faces etched with concern as the grinding sounds echoed ominously.

"Sounds like the bearings," Finn observed, the worry in his voice barely veiled.

Rory's brow furrowed. "When was the last time Dad greased it?" he asked threads of childhood memories weaving through his mind—a reminder of sunlit days spent under his father's watchful eye, learning the importance of maintenance and care.

"Not while I've been around," Finn answered, a hint of frustration in his tone.

Rory winced, his heart sinking at the thought of yet another breakdown. It was always something— the windmill had become a metaphor for their lives, always on the verge of collapse. Just then, Finn, quick and eager, darted up the struts, determined to inspect the gears at the top.

"Wait!" Finn shouted, adrenaline surging as he felt the rush of responsibility. "I need to apply the brake first!" He paused, suddenly aware of the stakes, as if the weight of their family legacy rested on his young shoulders. Sometimes, caution slipped

Finn's mind in his haste to oblige.

With careful hands, he turned the brake handle, feeling the satisfying resistance as the windmill gradually slowed. As the sails came to a gentle halt, he fully engaged the brake, an action both simple and profound in its significance.

"Okay, take a look," Rory declared. He wished to take that first glance himself. Memories flooded back of his mother's gentle reminders, teaching him the value of patience and the importance of teamwork. Finn meant well; the boy's heart was in the right place. Rory inhaled deeply, grounding himself as he resolved to be patient. It was not just mechanical labour; it was a lesson in loyalty and stewardship.

They needed to assess the damage—a process that held both peril and promise. Hopefully, they could give it a good grease and realign it. The last thing needed was a hefty bill.

Rory's mind wandered to the mounting bills. The sheep feed they desperately needed in the depths of December. Financial strains pressed down on him, yet amid the worries, he held onto hope that the repair wouldn't be too costly. After all, it was not just the windmill that required nurturing; it was the family's shared dream to make Windamere a commercial proposition, not just a beautiful home.

As he trudged through the door, exhaustion enveloped him like a heavy cloak. Rory spotted Rose and Hugh at the table, their laughter a stark contrast to the weight pressing on his shoulders. "You look tired," Rose said, her brow furrowing with concern, her eyes searching his face for the roots of his fatigue.

"Not a good day," he replied, the words barely escaping his lips as he braced himself for the inevitable follow-up. "Windmill in the south paddock broke down," he stated matter-of-factly. But the tremor in his voice betrayed his unease.

"How bad?" Hugh's heart sank, a hollow ache echoing in his chest.

"I hope we can grease it up and get it going. I will have to move the sheep," Rory said, eyeing the door as a means of escape.

"When?" Hugh pressed, urgency creeping into his tone, desperation blooming like a dark flower within him.

"Tomorrow. There's still a bit of water in the trough," Rory replied, his words wrapping around them like wisps of a fog that refused to dissipate. "I'm going for a shower," he muttered, retreating inside, seeking the solace of warm water to wash away the day's burdens.

"It's more than just the windmill, isn't it?" Rose's voice cut through the air, sharp and unyielding.

Hugh hesitated, the urge to keep their struggles hidden flaring within him. But as he glanced back at her—his family, his anchor—realization struck: honesty was non-negotiable. "My fortune only paid for the land and the house. Money ran out a long time ago," he confessed, the words tasting bitter as they left his lips.

Silence stretched between them, heavy and fraught with unspoken fear. Rose felt as if she were trapped in a gilded cage, beautiful yet devoid of actual substance. "Will it ever pay?" she asked, her voice barely above a whisper, though the question loomed large, bearing the weight of their shared dreams tied to Windamere.

"Perhaps if the market picks up and the seasons are good. Yes," Hugh replied softly, though doubt lingered in the corners of his mind.

At that moment, Rose realized she did not need to pry any further; the truth was etched in the shadows beneath Hugh's weary eyes, a world of uncertainty that she had come to understand all too well. Damn, Rory for not letting her know.

By the time they retreated to the sanctuary of their bedroom, uncertainty had churned within Rose, and her mind had flooded with burning questions. As the door softly clicked shut, she pivoted sharply to face Rory, her eyes aflame with a tempest of emotions. The anger emanating from her left him perplexed and uneasy. Where had things taken a wrong turn?

"Rory Anderson, tell me—am I your wife or not?" The demand erupted from her lips, her tone sharp and resolute.

"It's a tad late for such inquiries," he replied with

a nervous attempt at levity, trying to counter her storm with a wisp of humour.

"Then, am I?" she pressed, her intensity unyielding.

Involuntarily, Rory found himself admiring her fierce determination; this was his English Rose, her protective thorns now evident. "Yes, without a doubt. Aunt Rosemary made sure we're legally connected."

"In that case, stop shutting me out," she shot back, her voice now laced with a hint of vulnerability that cut through her anger.

Rory closed the distance between them, enveloping her in his arms, but she remained rigid, resisting the comfort he offered. "I would prefer we kiss and make up," he suggested, his voice softening with an earnest plea.

With defiance, she pushed him away, creating an aching space between them. She needed air, a moment to think without being swallowed by his overwhelming presence. "You won't get away that simply," she declared, making it clear that distance was essential.

"What have I done to deserve this?" he inquired, his hands raised in a gesture of surrender and confusion.

"You should have told me," Rose fired back, her frustration slicing through the air with each syllable.

A wave of dread crashed over Rory—he had dreaded this moment the instant she would face the unsettling truth about their grand home, a façade unsupported by reality.

"It's hot and dusty..." he stammered, his voice fading into the weight of unspoken truths.

"Yes, but I won't simply melt away! Have you forgotten who I am? I'm made of sterner stuff and deserve your honesty. So tell me what's bothering you," her words compelled him to search deep within.

His certainty about the heat, Windamere, and Midjal faded as he recognized that she sought the root of his unease; the thought of burdening her with his worries felt unbearable.

"No, Rory Anderson," she insisted, her gaze piercing and relentless, as if she could unearth his very soul. "Why did you fail to mention our financial troubles?"

"Windamere, the homestead," he began hesitantly, grappling for words among the chaos of his thoughts. "It's an illusion," he finally admitted.

"An illusion?" Rose echoed, finally grasping something tangible. "That's what your father said, yet it should have come from you."

"My dad's no farmer; he leads with his heart rather than his head. I can set things right," he murmured, his voice tremulous. "With patience and favourable seasons," he added, unaware that he echoed his father's sentiments, though his tone was woven with a note of optimism. "Most are in the same predicament."

"Yes, but they don't shoulder the burden of

Windamere. How much do you need?" she asked, her voice trembling with the gravity of the figure he would disclose. "I have some savings we can rely on," she offered, her demeanour steadfast.

"That's your money," he insisted firmly. "This is my burden to bear."

"It is our burden," Rose countered, her voice resolute, as unwavering as steel. "Windamere is not just mine or yours; it is our home, the future for our children."

Across the room, he held her gaze, feeling the weight of her resilience juxtaposed against his paralyzing fear of losing her.

A smile spread across his face as he spoke, "Ma'am," his tone laced with humility. Then, his voice smooth as silk, he added, "Shall we try to create something beautiful despite all of this?"

"Perhaps," she replied, but the fire in her eyes held firm. "But if you think I will forget, you are mistaken." With that, she whirled, tossing her blouse to the floor in frustration.

In an instant, he was behind her, nuzzling the nape of her neck. "I thrive in the heat; I'll navigate the thorns," he murmured, his breath warm against her skin.

"You had better, Mr. Anderson. Because I intend to hold you to that promise."

CHAPTER 15 - DAVID CROWLEY

Mijal Hospital - Circa 1946, showcases a modest yet functional design tailored to its remote setting. The hospital reflects the simplicity and resourcefulness of post-war rural healthcare facilities. It likely served as a central hub for medical care in the community, offering basic treatments, maternity services, and emergency care. Its serene surroundings and straightforward design symbolize the resilience of rural health services during a period of rebuilding and growth in Western Australia.

November 15, 1945

Hi, Aunt Rosemary

I hope you are well. Can you believe how quickly the time has flown? I know you are more interested in how I am going and Windamere.

I am fine. Hugh is everything you told me. He is light-hearted and fun. He helps me a lot, especially now that I am at Windamere.

Yes, it is built in the image of your cottage, but on a grander scale. It has a wide veranda to shield it from the

Rose stood on the balcony gazing out. This had become her favourite place to watch the sun dipping in the west, casting a warm, golden glow across the paddocks. How had she questioned going to

Australia?

The people of Midjal embraced her with open arms, wrapping her in a warmth and kindness she had seldom experienced.

She had left the relentless pace of London life, which turned every lost minute into a burden of wasted time. The air there was dense with the debris of war. Socially weighed down by centuries-old class distinctions, every social interaction is steeped in the rigid lines of an unyielding hierarchy.

But in Midjal, such barriers melted away; a shared pursuit of dreams and survival bound everyone.

Time here didn't rush; it meandered like a lazy river on a summer's day. Life intertwined seamlessly with nature—the trees, paddocks, and gums stood in harmonious symmetry. The expansive sky stretched endlessly to the horizon, a constant reminder of the boundless world they lived in. People were a small note in nature's grand symphony in this place. You had to live here beyond an artificial world to understand living with nature fully—the freedom to be yourself.

The only thing missing was Aunt Rosemary. How she wished she could see this.

As Rose prepared for bed, the soft glow of the bedside lamp enveloping the room in a warm embrace, Rory entered, his presence a gentle, loving intrusion. He kissed her with lips still dewy from the shower, carrying the crisp, refreshing scent of lemon that banished the day's dust and fatigue. "Mel has great plans for the garden," she remarked, her voice laced with admiration and hope.

"She is a remarkable gardener," Rory replied, sinking into the bed and sighing. He rested against the plush pillows, his body melting into the mattress, exhibiting a tranquillity more profound than Rose had ever witnessed in him.

"You look exhausted," she observed gently.

"Yes," he replied, a note of weariness in his voice, "but that's what I missed during the war—working out my frustrations alone in the world where no one gets hurt."

"I understand. Living here has granted me a freedom I could never find in London," she said with a small smile.

"I am glad you see it that way. But remember, this freedom comes with a cost—nature holds the reins of our destinies."

As she finished dressing, his words lingered in her mind. She seated herself delicately on the edge of the bed, her eyes searching his face for any trace of emotion. "On the subject of money," she murmured, "There is a vacancy at the hospital for a nurse."

"Do you want to apply to be a nurse or for the money?" He asked warily.

"Both," Rose responded. "I love nursing, and the money can put some pressure on my finances."

"Then you apply for that nursing position."

Rose laughed, leaning into him. "Yes, sir." Their lips met.

Though she had worked in far larger hospitals, an unfamiliar dread gnawed at her; memories of Queen Alexandra Hospital surfaced, where the echoing halls carried whispers of her past fears, the dilemma of wards where she'd once felt insignificant, each corner concealing anxieties she fought hard to subdue.

Did she want to give up the freedom that Windamere offered? This feeling of freedom was no longer confined by work hours.

She parked and got out of her car, looking across the hospital. Midjal Hospital was simple, constructed from weatherboard and with a corrugated iron roof. It was a world apart in terms of size from Queen Alexandra.

She took a breath, "Well, here I do."

Once inside, the receptionist suggested she take a seat. Looking around, she took the one next to a woman. Rose noted how tired she looked, as if she had already worked an entire shift.

"Are you here for the nursing position?" Rose asked, her voice edged with a blend of curiosity and apprehension.

"Yes." Her curt reply hung in the air, devoid of warmth, leaving an uncomfortable silence in its wake.

Unfazed, Rose pressed on. "Have you nursed before?"

"Yes, a while back, before I arrived in Midjal." Her words felt like pieces of a puzzle, but the picture was still incomplete.

"Rose Armstrong," she introduced herself, offering a hand in hopes of bridging the gap. "Jenny Tyler," the other woman replied, her tone slightly more inviting. "Are you also vying for the job?"

"Yes, I recently moved to Midjal." Rose's heart raced at the thought of new beginnings. "You are Rory Anderson's wife?" Jenny inquired, her eyes glinting with recognition. "That's right," Rose confirmed, feeling a swell of pride for her husband.

"You're lucky; Windamere is a beautiful home," Jenny remarked, her voice tinted with a hint of envy.

Rose's thoughts turned pragmatic. "You farm here?" she asked, her curiosity piqued.

"No, my husband's a shearer," came Jenny's response, tinged with a quiet determination. "He earns well when work is available."

Rose couldn't help but wonder about the challenges that came with such a life. "Do you have children?"

"Yes, five—two boys." Jenny's smile softened, revealing a glimpse of the joys and chaos that motherhood brought.

"That must be quite a handful," Rose commented, imagining the vibrant, bustling household. "Indeed, and a lot of mouths to feed," Jenny chuckled, the burden lightened by shared understanding.

Just then, the receptionist called Rose in for her interview, leaving behind the fleeting camaraderie they had forged.

Inside, there were a handful of wards with essential medical equipment to treat patients, primarily for routine illnesses, injuries, and maternity services. The hospital likely had a minor maternity ward, as rural hospitals in the 1940s played a critical role in childbirth for local families.

"Mrs. Anderson," the secretary called gently, breaking the silence of the waiting room.

Rose Anderson took a deep breath and entered the office, where two individuals awaited her. The matron, whose stern yet kind demeanour exuded authority, sat on one side of the desk.

Next to her was a strikingly dynamic man. His blue eyes, set in a sun-tanned face, exuded the vitality of someone who thrived in the great outdoors. His rugged appearance and the way his eyes sparkled signalled a life lived beyond the hospital's corridors.

"Let me introduce Matron Raymond and Mr. Crowley, head of our hospital board," the secretary announced.

David Crowley stood and towered over the room, every inch of him a commanding presence. Deep and filled with robust energy, his voice was contrasted by a playful hint of humour, visible in the slight twitch of his chiselled lips and the glint in his eyes.

Extending his hand towards Rose, his demeanour was disarming. "David Crowley. Call me David."

Rose felt a rush of nerves, chastising herself inwardly for reacting like a schoolgirl. She reminded herself to maintain her composure.

"Rose," she managed to respond, trying to meet his warm gaze.

"Welcome to Midjal. Rory's wife, I presume?" he remarked, seating himself comfortably. "How are you finding Midjal? It's quite a departure from your homeland." Rose smiled warmly, and David Crowley felt a pang of tension in his gut. This Englishwoman was genuinely captivating.

"It's different, but I love it. Not the heat, but the landscape and the people." Instantly, she appeared more at ease, her nervousness dissipating. That was the essence of Midjal; its inhabitants were known for their friendliness.

"Your credentials are quite impressive," the matron chimed in again. "Queen Alexandra is a well-known, large hospital. What will your transition to our much smaller establishment be like?"

"It's not the size of the hospital that matters, but the patients," Rose replied confidently. "I've nursed on the battlefields, as well. The scale of the hospital doesn't concern me."

"On the battlefields?" David Crowley inquired, astonishment lacing his voice. How could such a delicate-seeming woman have endured the ravages of war? "That must have been incredibly challenging." He internally chastised himself for his inadequate phrasing. Losing his composure was a rare and unsettling experience for him.

Rose's expression dimmed, her eyes momentarily distant. "Yes, we were inundated with patients, and it was heartbreaking to lose so many." She shook off the haunting images that filled her mind. "At least at the Queen, it was better equipped, but even there, we lost too many lives."

David scrutinised her anew. The fortitude required to withstand such trials bespoke hidden strength. "I don't know about you, Matron, but I believe Mrs. Anderson is the right fit for the position."

Matron Rymond's warm smile enveloped the room like a gentle embrace. "I concur, Mr. Crowley," she said, her voice laced with sincerity, hoping to bridge the divide between their differing opinions.

Rose glanced between the two, her heart heavy with concern. "You have another applicant outside who needs the job... a family is depending on them," she added, her tone carrying the weight of her empathy. She felt a knot tighten in her stomach, wishing to convey the urgency without seeming pushy.

David Crowley leaned back, his brow furrowing as he considered her words. "You are right," he murmured, a flicker of conflict crossing his face. "But someone with your credentials would be invaluable." He admired Rose's qualifications, yet he also felt the pressure of responsibility tugging at him, aware of the stakes involved.

"Perhaps you need to compromise. We could share the position," Rose proposed, a hint of hope threading through her voice. She did not want to come off as insistent, yet the thought of leaving a deserving applicant without a chance weighed heavily on her conscience. "It may be an alternative for everyone." Her heart raced as she awaited his response, craving a sense of unity in their decision.

"Thank you, Mrs. Anderson," David replied, his expression softening as he recognised the value of her suggestion. "We can give it some thought." But even as he spoke, a swirl of conflicting emotions churned within him, leaving him to wonder how they would reconcile the needs.

Had she blown her chances, Rose was not sure. But Rory's words rang in her head. "We are all doing it tough." But, it was not only the farmers but the workers whose jobs depended on them.

As Rose pulled into the driveway, a swell of determination surged within her, a palpable mix of excitement and anxiety coursing through her veins. She couldn't wait to share the news with Rory, was her touchstone, the one who grounded her in times of uncertainty. Her heart raced as she navigated the familiar dirt path leading to the far paddock, where she spotted his ute parked in the distance, a beacon of loyalty amidst the sprawling landscape.

When Rory approached her car, his brow furrowed with concern. She felt the weight of his question—the anticipation hanging heavy in the air. "Well, how did it go?" he inquired, his voice laced with an eagerness that made her pulse quicken.

Rose hesitated, her mind swirling with the right words to convey the turmoil inside her. "I'm... not entirely sure," she began, her voice wavering as she searched for clarity. "I could have taken the position, but then I ran into Jenny Tyler in reception. She's also in the running for the job, and I can't shake the feeling that she really needs it." She paused, gauging his reaction, the silence resonating with unspoken understanding.

"The Tylers are going through a rough patch," Rory mused, a flicker of amusement dancing in his eyes, yet his tone remained respectful. Rose felt an ache of solidarity for the family, the complexities of life intertwining in this moment.

"I suggested that we share the position," she finally admitted, her heart racing as she awaited his response. "What do you think?"

In response, he enveloped her in a warm hug, the world around them fading into the background. "I think Midjal will love you," he replied, his embrace infusing her with a rush of reassurance.

Rose pulled back slightly, searching his gaze for a hint of hesitation. "You don't mind?" she asked, the gravity of their debts pressing heavily on her mind.

Rory regarded her with a knowing sweetness tempered by the struggles they both recognised. "Yes, but the Tylers have five children to feed," he reminded her gently, leaning in to place a soft kiss on her lips. "We only have Dad's folly."

"Don't call it that." Rose admonished him. "Windamere is beautiful. It means so much to your father. He was providing his family with a home he never had."

"Try, and we will hold onto it one way or another until things come good. I would love to spend the afternoon with you, but I have to get back to work." He offered her a fleeting kiss, warmth blossoming for just a moment before he turned to assist Finn.

As she stood there, rooted in place, she followed his retreating figure, her heart heavy with unspoken words. Each step he took felt like a chisel against her chest, carving out the ache of absence.

He meant everything to her—her anchor, her reason to smile amidst the chaos. The world around her blurred, and all that remained was the echo of his laughter and the sensation of fleeting intimacy. She longed to call him back, to seize those precious moments, but instead, she was left watching him fade into the distance, wrapped in silence and the weight of her unsaid emotions.

She turned. She had to tell Hugh.

Hugh was waiting on the veranda. "well, how did it go."

"Different." She paused on the step, looking up. Her decision affected him, too. "I met Jenny Tyler. She was going for the job, too. I suggested we share it."

"Really, what did David say."

"He would think about it." She paused. "I know the money would have been helpful."

"Don't you worry, Rose? The world will be chasing our wool and wheat." Hugh predicted. "there will be a lot of changes, but we can make a go of it." He predicted.

Rose perched on the balcony, lost in thought when a cloud of dust signalled the arrival of a car. It rolled to a stop, and while the vehicle was unfamiliar, the driver was not - David Crowley stepped out. Surprised by his quick arrival, she made her way down to greet him. On the veranda, Hugh was handing David a cold beer, and as they noticed her presence, they turned to offer a warm welcome.

"Well, I'm sure you two have much to discuss," Hugh said, stepping back inside, leaving them to their conversation.

"Windamere is certainly a showstopper," David remarked, his gaze roaming over the expansive veranda.

"Indeed, it took my breath away the first time I saw it," Rose replied, recalling her awe.

David wasted no time. "I came with a proposition for you," he stated directly. "We're currently negotiating with St John's Ambulance to transfer it to the community. What we need is someone to spearhead this project." He took a slow sip of his beer, savouring the cool drink before continuing. "Initially, you'd handle the negotiations with St John's to ensure a seamless transition. Later, the focus would be organising, training, and recruiting volunteers. When I heard about your experience in the field, I thought of you. Are you interested?"

Rose felt her breath catch in her throat. "Yes," she answered, her words few as she contemplated the weight of what lay ahead. "You have taken me by surprise."

"The nursing position remains open if you're inclined. However, I sensed a yearning within you for something different," David remarked, his tone layered with unspoken concern.

"I cherish nursing; it has been my calling. Yet, Windamere has unveiled a sense of liberation I have long yearned for," Rose replied, her voice tinged with both excitement and trepidation. "This newfound freedom is a path I want to savour. The role you propose could offer a perfect bridge between my past and this new journey."

"That's good. Then we can catch up next week and go through the details," David concluded, standing to leave, a hint of anticipation lingering in his voice.

"Thank you," Rose replied, extending her hand, her heart racing at the prospect of their next meeting.

As he grasped her hand, a grin spread across his face, dazzling and magnetic—enough to steal her breath away in that fleeting moment.

"You may not realise how much it takes to get these things organised until you're in the thick of it," he chuckled from the steps, his laughter echoing with an undercurrent of sincerity.

Rose watched him depart, captivated by his effortless energy. He was a true man of action whose words were few but impactful. He was a force, a punch of vitality that lingered in the air long after he had vanished from view.

Hugh stepped into the doorway, his expression a mix of hope and apprehension. "So, did you get the job?" he asked, his voice thick with anticipation as if the answer could change everything for them both.

Roses, her laughter like a melody, echoed in the open air. "Oh, you know exactly what he said," she teased, a playful glimmer in her eyes. "You eavesdropper."

While Hugh might typically feel a flush of embarrassment at being caught, the lightness of their shared moment wrapped around him, and they both dissolved into laughter, a warm reminder of the bond that drew them together in the quiet of that evening.

"That's quite the compliment," he remarked, the admiration in his voice evident. "David has truly transformed Midjal with his relentless spirit. He crams more into a single day than most accomplish in a month, even though he barely has a moment to spare. Just think about it—he manages the largest property in the entire region." A hint of pride shone in his eyes as he continued, "Not too shabby for a young man who began with just 500 acres."

Rose's mind swirled with Hugh's observations, each word echoing in the chambers of her thoughts. David Crowley—a name that now loomed large in her consciousness. She began to delve into what it meant to be a man of many talents, the weight of leadership resting upon his shoulders.

Was it the charm of his every word that captivated those around him or the quiet strength that commanded respect? At that moment, Rose felt a mixture of admiration and uncertainty, questioning whether such qualities would be her downfall.

CHAPTER 16 - ST JOHN'S POSITION

Midjal's St. John Ambulance service 1946 - provided vital medical support to remote communities. The depot, a simple yet functional structure, served as the hub for emergency response and healthcare assistance. The ambulance, a robust vehicle equipped for medical transport, reflects the era's practicality and resilience. St. John Ambulance played a crucial role in connecting isolated areas to essential medical care, embodying dedication and service during a time of recovery and rebuilding.

Dear Aunt Rosemary

I hope you are well.

I have a chance at a nursing position, but first, I must ask Rory. He was non too [pleased when I accepted before getting his approval for the position on the boat, so this time, I am trying to do the right thing.

This marriage thing takes a bit of getting used to.

We have started the garden. Mel is great, and she is teaching me a lot. It is easy in England to grow things out here, but they must be strong to survive—like the people.

As Rose lingered in the embrace of the late morning, the stifling heat swept through the walls, cocooning her in an unsettling shroud. The atmosphere felt foreboding, a warning of the challenges waiting ahead. Hadn't she anticipated the comfort of Rory's presence this morning?

Exhaustion had claimed them both the night prior. But now, she couldn't shake the looming question of how Rory felt about St John's position. An unsettling weight settled in her stomach, a stone that gnawed at her insides. She hurried through her morning routine, her thoughts swirling with an anxious hope that their conversation would turn the tide in her favour.

Entering the kitchen, she found Hugh at the table, the familiar sound of the radio filling the air like a placeholder for the absence she felt. "Good morning," he greeted her, the warmth in his voice stark against the coldness pooling in her heart, dimming any semblance of joy.

"Morning," she murmured, her tone barely escaping as her eyes flickered around the room, desperately searching for a glimpse of Rory but knowing he would not be there.

Hugh read her mood and exhaled a sigh that punctuated the thick silence enveloping them. "No use looking for him. Just like his mother, farmers rise with the sun and return at dusk." His words struck her like a jolt, a stark reminder of the disappointment she tried to suppress and the simmering frustration that lurked beneath her carefully crafted exterior.

Taking a seat, she felt the weight of her emotions pressing upon her. The opportunity ahead shimmered with promise, a radiant beacon unlike anything nursing had ever offered. She yearned to immerse herself in the lives of these people, to connect and contribute, yet the shadow of Rory's approval loomed large.

Cursing her impulsiveness in accepting the position without consulting him, whispers of doubt echoed in her mind—she had been charting her course alone for too long, just like Aunt Rosemary.

Hugh noticed her frustration. "The kettle's on the stove if you want some tea and porridge," he offered gently. He observed her closely, uncertain if his words had registered, as she seemed lost in her thoughts.

Though miles apart, her thoughts drifted to Aunt

Rosemary, who remained cherished in her heart and mind. She wondered what wisdom her dear Aunt would impart if she were here. A warm, affectionate smile spread across her face, brightening the room like a ray of sunshine piercing the clouds.

Watching her as she gathered her breakfast and returned to the table, he asked what was causing her distress. "What's up? You should be buoyed by your new job, new challenge, and new husband, " he quipped.

"I was just thinking I should have asked Rory. I think I am too independent like Aunt Rosemary." She paused, caught in a web of memories. "How she would love Windamere."

He could vividly imagine Rosemary at Windamere. While some aspects of the girl were strikingly reminiscent of Rosemary, other aspects set them worlds apart. They shared that unwavering self-assurance and planning, but Rose had a sense of adventure and a need to explore, which Rosemary had lacked all those years ago. Rose was like the daughter they never had. He grinned, luckily; otherwise, who would have married Rory? It turned out better than he had ever dreamed; she was Windamere's Rose.

"Never one to let silence linger, he inquired, 'What weighs on your mind?' She nearly sputtered on her porridge, the intimate moment catching her off guard. Hugh chuckled though a shadow of concern hovered in his gaze. 'It must be something weighty if it has you choking like that.'

She composed herself, swallowing hard before taking a sip of her tea, deliberating how to articulate her thoughts.

'Come on, I'm here for you,' he implored softly, leaning in, his sincerity palpable.

'Perhaps I should have discussed it with Rory first,' she admitted, her voice thick with exasperation.

Hugh's laughter broke through the tension, an incredulous mixture of humour and disbelief. 'Is that truly what has you in such a tizzy?'

'It's just… I doubt Rory will approve,' Rose murmured, almost in a whisper. At Hugh's confused look, she divulged, 'He was upset when I accepted that position on the boat without consulting him.'

Understanding flickered in Hugh's expression, his demeanour shifting to one of empathy. 'My son is utterly captivated by you. I can't imagine he would stand in your way. Now, finish your breakfast; we've roses to tend to.'

'Indeed, Aunt Rosemary would surely disapprove if they withered away.'

'No doubt about it,' he chuckled. 'Afterward, why don't you take some tea and biscuits down to the paddock? It would give you both a chance to discuss things in private. A woman of your wisdom will figure it out.'

At that moment, she realized that Hugh was evolving into her confidant and steadfast support, taking on Aunt Rosemary's role—not that anyone could replace Aunt Rosemary.

She found Rory and Finn painstakingly repairing the windmill.

Looking up, Rory felt a mixture of frustration and longing. This interruption was the last thing he needed. The sight of the Holden almost made him scowl, a stark reminder of Hugh's reckless extravagance that they could scarcely afford, draining their already dwindling funds.

He harboured a complex blend of resentment and begrudging admiration for Hugh. At the same time, his emotions for Rose were deeply rooted in love, coupled with an intuitive `need to shield her from Hugh's reckless behaviour and financial troubles.

Rose walked towards him. She looked like an English lady in a crisp shirt and jeans. Her freshness contrasted with the dirt and heat here, although she did not seem to notice it.

"I have brought tea and biscuits." She said, smiling and waving the flask.

"You take a break under that tree over there, and I will look at this," Hugh suggested, stepping from the passenger seat.

"Yes, that sounds fine." He was relieved to learn that Hugh was taking a look, with his maze of complexities, was a skilled mechanic, particularly adept with windmills—expertise undoubtedly tied to his mining days.

Rory ambled towards the tree, wavering between hugging Rose or just offering a kiss on the cheek. "Sorry, I'm dirty and sweaty," he confessed, glancing nervously at her.

Rose looked up, a warm smile illuminating her face. "I've dealt with worse in hospitals," she teased gently.

"Yeah, I suppose you have," Rory admitted, his expression softening. "Different, but worse, at least emotionally."

They perched themselves on the branch of a gum tree, its rough surface hardly comfortable, but options were limited.

Rose spread out the biscuits and poured him a cup of tea. "I thought you might have preferred coffee," she remarked, eyeing him curiously.

"Tea is fine," Rory replied, though his mind briefly wandered to a cold beer he'd rather have had.

"You left early," Rose ventured, hoping to elicit a response, noticing the distant look in Rory's eyes.

"Yeah, wanted to get to this fixed," he said curtly, his gaze fixed more on the horizon than on her.

"Speaking of work," she began cautiously, "What do you think of David's offer."

He turned to her, a smile tugging at his lips. "I can see you getting them organised" he grinned.

"Yes, if it's alright with you," she said, lifting her

chin and looking him straight in the eye. She was prepared for any challenge.

"Sounds good," he responded calmly.

"But you didn't think so on the boat," she countered, her confusion evident.

He leaned in and pressed a quick kiss to her lips. "I've learned my lesson. You can no more do nothing than I can leave. Watch out, Midjal. Here comes Rose, just like Aunt Rosemary."

"I am not Aunt Rosemary." she replied, a mix of relief and apprehension coursing through her.

Rory chuckled heartily. Tilting his head to look closer at her. "Oh yes, you are."

All smiles, Rose returned to the home with Hugh. The sun blazed down, casting a heat haze over the surrounding paddocks. A gentle breeze rustled through the leaves, carrying the unmistakable scent of fresh earth and gum trees.

Hugh couldn't contain his excitement and amusement. "I told you so."

They both laughed, which echoed through the quiet countryside and made the air shimmer with happiness. "I would say Rory is pleased you have the position. He lives to farm, and it consumes his every working hour," Hugh continued, nodding to the vast stretches where the last of the wheat crop lay.

Flushed with excitement and a hint of scepticism, Rose shook her head slightly. "I still have to finalise the position," she pointed out, her eyes flickering with hope and doubt.

Hugh's eyes sparkled with unwavering confidence. "Oh yes, you do. In Midjal, what David declares is law," he reassured her—the conviction in his voice.

Warmth blossomed within Rose, seeping into her very soul. The promise of the homestead's cool embrace filled her with a burgeoning sense of belonging and anticipation for the intimate tapestry woven by this close-knit community.

As Hugh eased the Holden to a halt before the homestead, Rose's heart swelled with a cascade of memories. The familiar facade, resplendent in its timeless beauty, beckoned with echoes of joy and comfort. Yet, an inadequacy gnawed at her; it cried for a charming garden to crown its elegance.

"We need that lawn," Rose suggested, her eyes shimmering with vision.

"Not easy out here," Hugh remarked, his gaze drifting over the parched earth. But then, with a sigh, he conceded, "Yes, it does."

"It's such a beautiful home that it deserves it," Rose said, her voice brimming with an enthusiasm that quashed any thoughts of difficulty. "Imagine a lawn to set off Aunt Rosemary's roses."

Windamere was her haven, her sanctuary, and she was determined to render it as beautiful in reality as it was in her dreams.

Hugh kept his doubts to himself, choosing

silence as his companion. The land before him lay expansive and desolate, a stark departure from the lush, rolling hills of England's green countryside. Here, the unyielding sun bore down with relentless intensity, the dust swirling in the air like whispers of a bygone era.

Yet, amid this arid landscape, he couldn't help but notice the flicker of excitement in her eyes—a vibrant flame that ignited warmth within him. "Yes, we can do it," he proclaimed, his voice steady with determination. She would need every ounce of encouragement he could provide. If transforming this barren land into a reflection of her beloved Windermere would help her feel at home, he was resolved to see it through.

However, he soon found that his dedication was more taxing than he had anticipated. Once Rose set her mind to something, she became an unstoppable force. With a gleam in her eye, she leaped into action.

"First things first, where do we find lawn?" she inquired, her enthusiasm palpable.

"The finest gardener around is Mel Clement," he replied, a hint of optimism in his tone.

Rose's brows furrowed with curiosity. "And how do we reach her?"

"Simple," he answered with a playful smirk. "You fetch me a beer, along with whatever you desire, and I will ring her."

The next day, Mel arrived in a weathered ute, the

tray crowded with spades and gardening supplies. They clattered with each bump. She stepped out with a determined glint in her eye and surveyed the grounds with purpose.

"Hi, you must be Rose," Bounding from the ute, she greeted Rose, her broad smile exuding warmth and energy. She extended her hand to Rose, her grip firm and reassuring, before turning her attention to Hugh. "And how are you going, you old reprobate?"

"Hey, cut the old bit," Hugh replied with a hearty laugh, his eyes crinkling in amusement.

She turned to the house, sizing it up. "I have looked at Windamere since you built it, Hugh, itching to give it a garden," Mel said, her gaze sweeping over the landscape with a mixture of eagerness and contemplation.

"How about a drink? We can discuss it inside," Rose suggested, her voice carrying a note of hospitality.

"That sounds good, but let's have it on the veranda; then we can look at what we intend to do," Mel countered, her voice decisive yet friendly. "A beer for me, thanks."

"Me too," Hugh added, a hint of camaraderie.

When Rose returned, clutching the cold beers, she noticed the only available seat was a creaky, splintered chair. With a graceful, weary smile, she distributed the beers, then carefully lowered herself onto the precarious perch, the wooden slats groaning in protest. Sipping her now tepid tea, she gazed out over the veranda, mentally adding sturdy, comfortable chairs to the ever-growing list of tasks cluttering her mind.

Mel took a mouthful of beer before speaking. "I noticed you planted the roses."

"Yes," Rose replied, a hint of pride in her voice. "My Aunt gave them to me as a wedding present."

Mel stood, walking to the edge and examining their handy work. "Looks like you did a good job planting them, and placing them in front of the veranda is smart. They'll get a bit of protection from the sun."

Rose pondered momentarily, then said, "I was thinking of adding a lawn?"

Mel considered the idea, her mind drifting to images of lush greenery. "Yes, a lawn would look good. Are you thinking of an English garden?"

Before Rose could answer, Hugh chimed in. "Windamere is a replica of Rose's home in Windermere, England."

Mel nodded, a flicker of realization softening her features.

"Ah, that explains it." Her voice trailed off as she slipped into a quiet reverie, her thoughts weaving intricate patterns.

"Yes, it definitely needs a lawn," she murmured with a newfound certainty. "Hugh, you are going to have to get some water here." She commented.

Hugh gave her a weary look. Two bossy women, a man had to agree."

Mel's mind painted vivid images of the future—the lush garden bed brimming with roses and the vast expanse of vibrant green lawn. She pictured a few stately trees standing sentinel at the front, their branches forming an archway of welcome.

"I always like a grand entrance," she confessed, her voice conveying wistfulness as though she could already see herself walking through that majestic pathway to the veranda.

Rose stood in awe, her heart pounding at the audacity of Mel's meticulously crafted plan. A part of her embraced the ambition behind it, yet another voice whispered concerns about the hidden cost. Rory's warning about finances echoed in her mind—though she had the means, could she truly navigate this on her own? The house was her responsibility, but perhaps an arrangement with Rory was in order. She would manage the home while he tended to the farm.

"How much do you think this will cost?" Rose's voice was hesitant, laden with unspoken worry.

"Not much at all," Mel replied, her confidence palpable. "We can source some trees from the council—they owe me some. Locals will provide the lawn runners. A few hoses, pipes, and a tap will do the trick. If you can stretch the budget, sprinklers would be a boon for a garden this size."

Hugh chimed in, determination lighting his eyes. "I can rig up some pipes and sprinklers, maybe a gravity-fed system from the dam. Rose will be hard-pressed for time once she starts the job with David."

"What job are you referring to?" Mel's curiosity piqued, eager for fresh gossip. "Is it the nursing position?"

"No, David has something far bigger in mind for our Rose," Hugh declared, brimming with pride.

"Wait a minute! We need to sort out the details first," Rose interjected, her mind racing as new possibilities caused a flicker of excitement—and dread.

"Hugh disregarded her objection and continued. "David has our Rose earmarked to take over at St John's."

Mel scrutinized Rose, noting the underlying tension in her posture. David's judgment was astute; his choice of Rose was purposeful. "What he says is law," she echoed Hugh's earlier sentiment, firm in her conviction.

"How much do we owe you for your help?" Rose's anxieties were stark, vulnerability etched on her face.

"Nothing at all. Gardening is my passion, and Hugh here helps me out anytime—no charge," Mel remarked, a hint of offense coloring her tone. "This is Midjal; we look after one another."

"Apologies, I didn't mean to offend," Rose

replied, feeling marooned by her city-bred sensibilities.

"No offense taken. We're all in the same boat out here. Money's tight, but we make it work thanks to friends," Mel reassured her, her voice softening as she connected with Rose's unease.

"Thank you," Rose responded, acutely aware that her gratitude felt insufficient in the face of their kindness.

"Hold on—don't thank me just yet. This will require plenty of grit and hard work," Mel cautioned with an encouraging smile. With a wave, she bound down the steps and drove off in her weathered ute, leaving Rose and Hugh to watch the swirling dust settle behind her.

Hugh observed Rose's astonishment, a knowing smile on his face. "This land may be a realm for the young, but I assure you, it's the strong women who shape it."

CHAPTER 17 - A NEW CHALLENGE

The Wheatbelt of Western Australia - in 1946 was characterized by vast fields of wheat swaying in the breeze, dotted with small farms and sheds. Merino sheep grazed on the pastures, symbolizing the area's dual focus on grain and wool production. Rolling hills and scattered native trees formed a picturesque yet functional landscape. This region was pivotal to the state's economy, providing food and export commodities essential for post-war recovery and growth.

14 Dec 1945

Dear Aunt Rosemary

I know you will get a barrage of letters all at once, but writing to you makes it feel like we are still together.

We are working on the garden. There was no garden at all, but Mel will help me take photos shortly. I should have them for my following letter. It looks very fledgling, but Hugh and Mel assure me it will be perfect. She also insisted on a white picket fence. The fence is just for appearances. Out here, if rabbits or Kangaroos want to, they can get in, according to Mel.

I have not seen a kangaroo yet and am looking forward to it. Rory has offered to take me out in the evening to see them. He said they were busy eating his crops then, and he is unhappy with them. At the same time, I am looking forward to seeing them.

I have been offered a job setting up St John's Ambulance services, which is different from Nursing. The hospital board chairman, David Crowley, offered it to me. He has to be the most dynamic man I have ever met. You have to meet him.

Well, I had better get going things to do. Keep well. I love you.

Love Rose.

As Rose drew near the mirror, her heart danced with excitement, electrified by the anticipation of her reflection. The navy blue dress enveloped her figure like a gentle embrace, sculpting her silhouette with an air of authority and grace. The soft, luxurious fabric caressed her skin, its coolness a comforting balm against the flutter of nerves that stirred within her.

She tucked a wayward strand of hair behind her ear, the sensation of the dress soothing yet invigorating, and allowed a tentative smile to grace her lips, even as a whisper of uncertainty.

The anticipation of meeting David at the St. John's Ambulance depot sent a thrilling yet nervous energy coursing through her veins, like electricity crackling in the air. Though it might have seemed like an ordinary place to most, she understood its more profound significance – this was Midjal, alive with its unique vibrancy, a stark contrast to the sterile, grey expanse of London. A warm flicker ignited within her, stirring memories of past adventures and all the possibilities that beckoned on this sunny day. As she envisioned the unfolding moments ahead, a smile danced across her lips, hinting at the excitement swirling inside.

The gravel crunched pleasantly underfoot, a satisfying sound that echoed the feelings of anticipation swirling inside her as she moved toward the office. The sun bathed her shoulders in warmth, a gentle reminder of the summer's embrace, while a cool breeze tugged playfully at the hem of her dress.

Crossing the car park, she made her way toward the humble St. John's Ambulance depot. This unpretentious building sat snugly beside the fire station, its presence both reassuring and inviting.

Upon pushing open the door, she was enveloped by a distinctive medley of scents: the sharp, metallic tang of antiseptic mingled with the deeper, oilier aroma of grease. Her eyes were drawn to the two ambulances, their surfaces glinting and showcasing a meticulously arranged array of vital medical supplies, ready for any urgent call to action.

In the corner, an older man was hunched over an

engine, his hands stained and busy with repairs. He looked up, a grin breaking across his face. "You must be Rose; David mentioned you would be stopping by." He introduced himself. "John Watkins." He presented a hand covered in grease, which he quickly withdrew. "Sorry."

"Perhaps another time," Rose replied, laughter dancing in her voice. She noted the warmth and openness in his demeanour—a face that radiated kindness amidst the mechanical chaos.

"Yes. Follow me; I will take you to the office."

Just then, David stepped through the door. His presence imprinted itself on the surroundings. Rose drew her breath. This man was something.

"Rose, I see you have met our extraordinary volunteer, John," he said, a hint of humour lacing his voice.

"Yes, but I am a bit upset," John chuckled. "She would not shake my hand." He proudly displayed his greasy hands, an odd badge of honour that only drew a wry smile from Rose.

"I am certain Rose will adjust in time, that is, once you have washed it," David replied, his tone light and teasing, adding warmth to the moment as the camaraderie wrapped around them like a comforting blanket.

He stepped aside, letting her enter the small office. The space was almost camouflaged within the bustling environment, filled with towering stacks of files and scattered paperwork, each document holding the weight of life-saving missions waiting to be coordinated.

The air thrummed with an undercurrent of purpose, and Rose felt an exhilarating sense of belonging as if she were woven into the fabric of something profoundly significant. Just then, David stepped through the door, a presence that seemed to energize the room further.

David leaned back in his chair, studying Rose with a mix of curiosity and admiration. She had this fire in her eyes—a determination that sparked his ambitions. It reminded him of his younger self, a time when he, too, embraced the thrill of challenge without a second thought.

"So, are you ready to take it on?" he asked, gesturing towards the chair across from him. He was keen to see how Rose would navigate the complexities ahead.

"Yes, I like a challenge," Rose replied, her voice steady but carrying an undercurrent of excitement mixed with apprehension. In that moment, David could sense the weight of her past experiences pushing her forward. She had faced obstacles before, each one shaping her into the resolute woman sitting before him now. He admired her resilience, knowing her journey was more than just a quest for success— it was about proving to herself that she could rise above her fears.

"That you will certainly get," David assured her, feeling a rush of expectation. He recognized the potential in her passion, a beacon of hope that could illuminate even the darkest paths they might encounter together. As he exchanged glances with her, he wondered if she realized the depth of what lay ahead, not just from a professional standpoint but the personal growth that came with facing challenges head-on.

As they delved into the details of the job ahead, a palpable tension filled the air. Each word carried the weight of responsibility that rested heavily on their shoulders. David's voice resonated with the earnestness of a leader who understood the stakes: the lifeblood of the community depended on their careful coordination and unwavering commitment.

"Managing the volunteers isn't just about scheduling shifts; it's about building a family," he said, his gaze sweeping across the room, searching for connection. "We need to create a bond so that when emergencies strike, they're not just responding out of duty, but out of a profound sense of purpose."

The logistics were daunting. It wasn't merely about ensuring the vehicles were roadworthy or stocking first aid kits; it was about instilling a sense of pride in their work. "Every mechanical check isn't just a protocol," David emphasized. It's a promise to our neighbours that we'll be there when they need us most. In these harsh rural conditions, our vehicles are not just machines—they are our lifeline."

And when the calls of distress rang in, whether from frightened residents or overwhelmed medical professionals, the challenge became deeply personal. "Coordinating responses is a dance of urgency," he shared, tension threading through his voice. "It's crucial to ensure that every volunteer feels the weight of that call." His passion ignited in him an almost fervent need to reassure them: speed was not just an objective—it was a shared commitment to save lives.

"I envision training those in our community," he continued, his voice softening with hope. We must equip them with the skills to manage emergencies until help arrives. Each course taught isn't merely instruction; it's empowerment, a forging of connections that thrive in times of crisis."

David's vision extended to the fundraising drives, where he saw the heart of the community pulsing through every event. "Through these efforts, we weave a tapestry of belonging," he explained. "Every donation, every cheer at an event will create a profound sense of ownership and pride."

As he outlined the importance of meticulous records, it was evident that this was not just about numbers; it was about transparency and trust. "When we record our actions, it's a narrative of our commitment. Each entry speaks of our journey, the lives we touch, and the future we strive to build together."

David's thoughts turned to patient transport, the thread that connected individuals to hope. "Communication with hospitals is vital," he acknowledged. "In this remote area, we become their bridge to care. Each successful transport is a testament to our dedication."

Finally, he paused, the weight of responsibility etched on his features, and offered the question that lingered in the air, "So, what do you think, Rose Anderson?" His smile was enchanting, a beacon that drew her in, mingling hope with the seriousness of their mission. Would her heart resonate with the same commitment burning within him?

"Yes." Rose took a moment, her thoughts swirling like leaves caught in a gentle autumn breeze. "My father was a doctor, and in our home, the lessons of medicine were woven into the very fabric of my upbringing. I've come to appreciate the profound impact that early intervention can have on the patient's condition. While managing this situation will pose its own set of hurdles, I embrace the familiarity of such challenges. In Normandy, our survival hinged not on the shoulders of one but on the collective strength of us all. We learned the importance of collaboration, of relying on one another in moments of crisis." A warmth spread across her face as she met his gaze. "I relish the opportunity that lies ahead."

"Rose Anderson, I knew you would come

through for me." David extended his hand, a gesture filled with unspoken camaraderie and the weight of expectation. As he stood before her, the tension of the impending takeover hung in the air, a reminder of their shared ambition and the intricacies of their partnership. "Before we hand over everything, we'll need to focus on liaising and sorting out the details," he added, his brow furrowed in concentration. "To be honest, I'm not certain how much time this will demand, so we may need to keep our schedules flexible."

"Good," Rose replied, a sense of relief washing over her. The prospect of organizing Windamere brought a spark to her eyes. It was not merely a job; it was her legacy, a place that held the echoes of family laughter and the weight of history. "Having that flexibility will really help me get everything in order."

David chuckled, a warm sound that broke the seriousness of the moment. "Just keep an eye out for Rory and Hugh. They have a knack for complicating things."

With a playful smirk, Rose replied, "It'll be a piece of cake. Hugh's already on board, which is a blessing. He's familiar with my Aunt Rosemary, the very person he credits with my strategic planning skills." The mention of her aunt brought a swell of pride and nostalgia, memories of late-night conversations filled with laughter and wisdom.

Their shared laughter resonated, a comforting affirmation of their teamwork.

"I must meet your Aunt Rosemary someday," David remarked, his curiosity piqued. He sensed the affection in her words.

Rose's expression grew contemplative, a mixture of hope and longing welling up within her. "I truly hope you do. It would mean so much for her to visit Windamere." As she spoke, visions of her aunt walking through the grand home filled her mind, and the thought ignited a warmth in her heart, intertwining her present ambitions with cherished memories.

Arriving back at Windamere, Rose found Mel and Hugh engrossed in the labour of laying the reticulation. A mischievous smile crept across her face; their animated exchange was punctuated by lighthearted bickering. They paused to acknowledge her as she walked across. "How did it go?" they queried in perfect harmony, their eyes locking with a shared understanding as if they were safeguarding secrets meant only for her.

"It was good." Rose suppressed a chuckle, relishing the familiarity of their dynamic. With these two, formalities were unnecessary; they dove right into the heart of the matter. "We take over on the 9th of February," she announced, satisfying Mel's thirst for the latest gossip.

"That's excellent news. We should wrap this up

by then." A pointed look from Mel met Hugh's gaze, tension crackling in the air.

"Are there issues?" Rose probed, her curiosity piqued.

Hugh seized the moment, his voice a playful taunt. "Only one." His grin was infectious, but Mel's narrowed eyes spoke volumes of the unspoken troubles.

Mel's relentless pursuit of perfection was as unwavering as her dedication to her work; it was a trait that filled the void left by the death of her husband, Frank. In tending to her garden, she found solace and a sense of purpose, transforming grief into growth.

Hugh, observing her tireless efforts, couldn't help but feel a deep connection—a shared understanding of loss that resonated between them. They both carried the weight of absence, each in their own way, yet found an unexpected bond in their mutual heartache.

"Let's grab a drink on the veranda; I'll fill you in on all the details." Hugh's invitation was almost a dare.

"Great idea." Mel swiftly asserted her claim, eager to steer.

As Mel and Hugh lounged on the veranda, seeking refuge from the relentless sun, they each cradled a chilled beer in hand. Their conversation initially seemed trivial, characterized by playful bickering over the most minor details of their project. Yet, amid the lighthearted quarrels, a shared determination emerged: their system would be operational within the next two days.

"Right on schedule for that busy bee we talked about," Mel said, a glimmer of enthusiasm in her eyes. It was clear their previous camaraderie had been rekindled, if only for a moment.

"Working Bee?" Rose interjected, a look of surprise washing over her. The dynamic between Mel and Hugh intrigued her; their connection was unlike any she had witnessed before.

"Absolutely," Mel replied, her tone animated. "I believe it's the most effective way to tackle this. Plus, with everyone eager to meet Rory and his new bride, it's the perfect timing for such a gathering."

With the last sip of tea lingering in their cups, Rose and Rory nestled onto their beloved balcony, an oasis of intimacy amid a vast world. The evening unfolded before them, adorned by the silvery glow of the full moon casting a gentle luminescence over the twinkling stars, which sparkled like scattered diamonds across the velvet sky.

The soft rustle of night-time leaves accompanied the occasional haunting call of a curlew, a reminder of the wildlife awakening to the night's embrace. "It's beautiful and so peaceful," Rose murmured, her voice barely above a whisper, as if afraid to shatter the serenity surrounding them.

Rory reclined in his wicker chair. It's creaking a familiar comfort. "I agree. I missed this the most during the war," he said, his tone heavy with memories. "There was no relief, just a relentless barrage of chaos and fear."

Rose felt a shiver run down her spine at his admission. Rory rarely opened up about those dark times. "It still haunts you?" she asked, her heart aching with empathy.

"Always will," Rory replied, the weight of his words hanging in the air like the thick humidity before a summer storm. They both stared into the luminous abyss, the beauty of the night now steeped in a shadow of pain.

They sat enveloped in a heavy silence, each lost in the depths of their turbulent thoughts.

Rose's mind drifted to the harrowing scene of the field hospital in Normandy, where the air had been thick with the acrid scent of blood and desperation, and the cries of the wounded echoed like haunting melodies. The memories weighed heavily on her heart, and yet, she knew it had been even more unbearable for Rory.

Rory's reflections wandered to his brothers, the ghosts of their laughter now silenced forever. He clenched his fists, the dirt and grass of their shared childhood playing through his mind like a fading photograph. How had it come to this? He thought of their final resting places, far from Windamere's comforting embrace, a land that deserved to cradle them as they once roamed free.

Shaking off the weight of her melancholy, Rose turned towards Rory, the shadows of the room wrapping around them like a comforting cloak.

"Mel and Hugh are planning a working bee—or, rather, they're caught in a comical argument about it," she said, her voice laced with a hint of amusement.

Rory's grin surfaced in the dim light, a flicker of warmth against the cool air. "Yes, they're in constant competition for control, but deep down, neither truly wants to come out on top. The banter is far too enjoyable," he replied, his laughter echoing softly.

"They intend to organize it for this weekend. They've assured me that everything will be in place, and all precautions will be taken for this grand event." She paused, recalling the details. "They mentioned something about instead of our tin kettle?"

A rich chuckle escaped Rory's lips, reverberating in the cozy space around them. "Ah, a bit late for that charade, wouldn't you say?"

"What do you mean?" Rose asked, a puzzled expression crossing her face. Her curiosity was piqued.

"Picture this," he began, his eyes sparkling with mischief. "Imagine a wedding night blissfully unfolding, only to be shattered by a band of raucous hooligans outside, noisily clanging kerosene tins, pots, and cans—a cacophony of chaos," he elaborated, painting the scene vividly in her mind.

"I'm relieved we missed out on that wild interruption," Rose replied, laughter spilling from her as she envisioned the uproar. Her spirits rose amid the shared moment of mirth.

"How did your meeting with David go?" Rory asked, curiosity flickering in his eyes.

"Pretty well, actually. The handover isn't until February, so I'll have some time to pull everything together. It should be quite interesting, you know? I'll be in charge of coordinating the volunteers, handling promotions, overseeing training, and managing the funding. Honestly, I'm excited about the challenge," Rose replied, her voice brimming with anticipation.

"Sounds like something Aunt Rosemary would really support," Rory observed, a hint of admiration in his tone.

Rose laughed, her voice light and melodic. "Oh, I'm sure she would! Speaking of which, how did you get on with fixing the windmill?"

"I believe we've managed to get it operational without breaking the bank," Rory responded, a proud grin spreading across his face. "Tomorrow we will know for sure."

"Good." It sounds like a good day all around."

CHAPTER 18 - THE BUSY BEE

A country barbecue in 1946 captures the heart of rural Australian life, where families and friends gathered under the shade of trees to share a meal. Men in wide-brimmed hats tended to makeshift grills, cooking skewers of meat, while children sat on wooden benches, eagerly and women engaged in conversation. The community spirit was evident in the relaxed atmosphere. It reflected the self-sufficient, close-knit nature of post-war rural Australia, where food and fellowship were central to daily life.

17 Dec 1945

Dear Aunt Rosemary

I hope you are well.

I'm busy tomorrow, so I'm giving Windamere a garden. I'm not too sure what to expect, but I am confident it will be interesting.

Mel and Hugh have been marvellous, but they argue all the time. I think they enjoy it.

Hugh has been cooking up a storm. You never told me he was such a great cook.

Rose descended the stairs to breakfast, her mind gently churning with thoughts. She was aware that Rory had left for the day, and a part of her had hoped that Hugh would be seated at the table, just as he always was. Breakfast felt incomplete without his familiar presence. But as she entered the dining room, her heart sank; the table was empty. A flicker of worry passed through her. Hugh was a creature of habit—like clockwork, he was always there, a steady rock in the ever-shifting tides of her life.

Just as Rose's worry began to take hold, she contemplated knocking on Hugh's door. But then she heard the gentle creak of hinges, and there he was, his chef's pack slung casually over his shoulder.

"You're up," she said, feigning nonchalance, relief blooming beneath her words.

Hugh's warm grin brightened the morning. "Yes, I'm not going anywhere if you were wondering." His playful eyes eased her worries, though a nagging concern flickered in her mind. Something felt off.

"I thought it was a bit unusual." The honesty felt

good despite the discomfort it stirred within her. "So, are you off too?"

"Down to the shed. We need some meat for tomorrow's barbecue."

Her brows knitted together, confusion washing over her. "We kill our meat?" The thought sent a shiver through her, yet her curiosity piqued.

"Of course, where did you think it came from?" His question was straightforward, yet she sensed the teasing challenge behind it.

"The butcher shop," she replied defiantly.

"Ah, English Rose." The mischief in his tone coaxed a reluctant smile. "The bacon doesn't come from a shop if we're grilling beef or chicken, you know." The playful grin invited her into this unfamiliar world. "Want to come?"

"Not without breakfast first. I haven't seen the sheds, but I'll join you afterwards." She hesitated, seeking a moment to gather her thoughts about this unexpected adventure.

"Alright, I'll leave the car for you." He swaggered toward the door.

"I'll walk," she asserted, craving solitude to process the day ahead.

Hugh's gaze held hers, a mixture of concern and a quiet insistence to be present with her. "Then I'll take the car."

As he stepped out, Rose felt the weight of his concern settle on her, a comforting presence. She didn't know what the day held, but with Hugh nearby—or even insisting she could manage alone—she sensed something was about to change.

With each sip of her steaming tea, she savoured the warmth that spread through her, embracing the tranquil solitude enveloping the house. The faint aroma of the brewed leaves mingled with the cool, crisp air seeping through the partially open window, wrapping her in a cocoon of peace. Before venturing out to the sheds, she took a moment to relish the stillness, listening to the soft rustle of leaves outside and the gentle creak of the old wooden beams above her, each sound a reminder of her quiet sanctuary.

Rose peaked around the corner of the shed.

"Wow, you made it!" Hugh exclaimed, startling Rose as he suddenly appeared right behind her.

He flashed a grin that cut through the sweltering heat. "Care for a little tour?" His eyes sparkled mischievously as she nodded. "That's the thresher," he said, leading her to the adjoining shed. "We don't use it much anymore," he added, nostalgia creeping in. He gestured to the shearing shed, elevated on legs to keep it breezy. Rose laughed at his straightforwardness.

"These tools are ready for action when the season hits," he said, pointing at the neatly arranged shearing tools. He proudly tapped the wooden wool presses and sorting tables worn from hard work. "This is where we transform raw wool into marketable treasure."

As they strolled through, Rose noticed the farm tools along one wall. "What about these?" she asked, glancing at the organized spanners and hammers.

"Ah, essentials!" Hugh chuckled. "Each piece holds a story. And we can't forget the 'bush fix' supplies—things tend to break around here!" His practicality shone through, mixed with easy humour that relaxed Rose.

As her eyes drifted toward the two bags swaying gently from the rafters, a pang of unease settled in her stomach. "Is that for the barbecue?" she asked, heart racing at the implication.

"Absolutely!" he replied with unfettered enthusiasm, his grin broad. "I let them hang out to bleed before chopping them up. Just wait; it'll be worth it!" His cheerful demeanour almost made her smile, yet a shiver ran down her spine.

At that moment, she caught a glimpse of the sheep in the distance. The weight of reality crashed over her; once frolicking in the sun, she was now a silent participant in a gruesome ritual. The image lingered—its fate twisted in her imagination, blurring the lines between the charm of rustic life and an unsettling brutality she hadn't anticipated.

The joy of the barbecue danced mockingly in her mind as she grappled with the growing conflict inside her: a deep-seated fascination with the pastoral existence versus the unyielding truths of what that life entailed.

Stepping outside, Hugh pointed to the silo-like structures. "Those are our wheat silos," he declared proudly.

"They look simple," Rose remarked.

"Exactly!" Hugh replied, enthusiasm bubbling. "They're built to keep our grains safe—no spoilage allowed. Less time sewing bags in harvest season!" With a flourish, he finished, "Welcome to the headquarters of our farming operations!" His words echoed with pride.

"Are we heading back to the house?" Rose asked, uncertain.

"Absolutely, and I could really go for a beer," Hugh chimed, his bright enthusiasm jarring. A wave of unease washed over Rose; the group's ritualistic beer-guzzling felt like an overshadowing thirst, transforming camaraderie into something troubling.

Sitting in their cherished nook on the balcony, Rose felt a flutter of nervous excitement as she offered Rory an iced tea, her mind racing with the hope that this might entice him to reconsider his usual drink.

"I thought an alternative to beer might be a good choice," she said, her voice tinged with optimism, though she couldn't shake the slight tremor of doubt in her chest.

"Yes, nurse Rose," Rory replied, his tone carrying a hint of bemusement. He lifted the glass to his lips, savouring the coolness. "Not bad, but I think you will find most will stick with beer." His words felt like a wall, pushing back against her intentions.

"It can become addictive," she countered, her heart quickening as she carefully selected her following words. "Are there many cases in which people overindulge?" There was an underlying vulnerability in her question, a silent plea for a deeper connection.

"Yes, the occasional one." Rory's gaze drifted to the horizon, watching as the sun slowly surrendered to the night, its fading light mirroring the weight of his thoughts. "But you won't convert them. Most only drink in moderation." He sighed, his words steeped in resignation as he turned back to her, feeling the warmth of their camaraderie wrap around them like a familiar blanket.

They settled into an easy silence, one that brimmed with unspoken understanding—this time together had grown into something precious—a quiet sanctuary where they could share the minutiae of their days or be lost in the gradual, enveloping dusk.

"Hugh showed me the sheds," Rose ventured, her voice a soft invitation. She glanced at him, her curiosity genuine and eager. "There is so much I want to learn about your life."

"I should have shown you." A flush crept to Rory's cheeks, the embarrassment of his oversight weighing down on him. How could he have missed the chance to share a part of himself with her?

"You are busy with the farm; Hugh has the time to indulge me," she replied, reaching across the table to clasp his hand gently. A warmth surged between them, an unspoken connection that neither could fully articulate. "How was your day?"

"We moved the sheep back. The windmill is working fine." He answered before drawing back into silence.

"Tomorrow marks the Busy Bee," Rose remarked, her voice filled with anticipation.

"Yes," Rory responded, a flicker of hope lighting his eyes. "It will be good to catch up with everyone, to bridge the gap that the war has forced between us."

Rose could feel the weight of his unspoken thoughts—this gathering was more than to help them; it represented a chance to reconnect and finally put the ghosts of the war behind him.

As dawn broke, Rose awoke to the sun's gentle warmth filtering through her curtains. The fragrant woodsmoke wafted from the kitchen, mingling with the fresh scent of dew on the grass. Hugh's cheerful humming floated through their home, signalling the start of something special.

Today was the day of the barbecue, an event that filled the air with an excited buzz. The backyard, under the expansive branches of their cherished gum tree, had transformed into a cozy gathering spot. The warmth of the fire promised laughter and connection among friends and family. Hugh had meticulously set up the metal grate above the flames, and each time Rose glanced toward it, she could almost taste the smoky flavour it would lend to the sizzling meats.

The menu featured succulent lamb, beef, and sausages, all poised to grill outside. Hugh's eyes sparkled with enthusiasm as he spoke of his simple yet effective approach—lightly seasoning the meats with salt and unique spices, served alongside damper bread and a fresh, crisp salad.

"Do I look like I belong here?" Rose asked Rory as she adjusted her new King Gee jeans, a hint of nervousness in her voice.

He kissed her on the cheek. "Like a true Aussie," he remarked, holding the door for her to go downstairs.

As the Harding family arrived, Peter jumped into action alongside Rory, efficiently gathering tools. "What do we need for the garden beds?" he asked, glancing over the assortment of supplies.

"Shovels, hoes—anything we can get our hands on," Mel shouted, rallying the growing crowd. She glanced at the newcomers, excitement bubbling in his voice. "Everyone, we've got work to do! Let's make this garden come to life!"

Rose watched as locals she barely knew filtered in, their faces filled with determination and camaraderie. "Thanks for coming, everyone!" she called out, her heart swelling as they pooled their resources—seeds, plants, and wisdom—to nurture Windamere's garden.

"Together, we'll have this done in no time," Mel encouraged, pairing volunteers for the task of breaking ground. "Young and old, let's show this earth what we're made of!"

The sound of shovels hitting the soil harmonized with laughter and chatter, creating a symphony of community spirit. Rose thought it was therapeutic to witness the joy and relief in Rory's eyes as he reconnected with familiar faces, washing away the shadows of war.

Within three hours, they had transformed the landscape—what would have taken Rose and Hugh weeks to accomplish was now a vibrant garden in the making. "Time for the barbeque!" Mel announced, and cheers erupted, matching the warmth of the afternoon sun.

Rose took a moment to centre herself before stepping into the lively gathering, her heart fluttering with anticipation. She was not just Rory's wife; she longed to weave herself into the fabric of this community, finding her place as a vital member of St John's Ambulance.

Across the flickering glow of the fire, Hugh leaned forward, expertly stoking the coals that glowed with warmth and life, while Rory moved with casual grace, distributing drinks to eager hands.

Rose stamped her foot on thoughts of the poor

sheep. She was a farmer's wife. That was how they made their living: raising sheep for slaughter. She had to admit she preferred the wheat growing. But this was reality, and she had to accept it.

The adults received chilled beer, sweat glistening on the bottles as they emerged from the ice-filled metal tubs—those glistening vessels that seemed to embody the country's spirit, as if beer itself were a form of currency among them. The children, buzzing with excitement, clutched their cups of lemonade, their faces illuminated by the flames, laughter spilling forth like the sweetness in their drinks.

The circle of friends and neighbours grew comfortable around the fire. Some perched on rustic chairs while others stood leaning against the wooden posts, their conversations rich with laughter and shared history. Each story exchanged floated into the night air, a testament to the resilience and close-knit bonds that defined this post-war rural Australian life, informally knit together by the shared experiences and the warmth of community.

Rose's gaze danced across the group until it settled on David, who was encircled by a cluster of animated men. As she drew nearer, the vibrant conversations around them seemed to fade into the background.

David's eyes lit up with recognition, prompting him to part the throng with a warm smile and inviting gesture, granting her passage into their midst. "This is Rose," he announced, his voice rising above the lively chatter, "not just Rory's English wife, but the one who will be leading our efforts with the St. John Ambulance."

As she stepped into the circle, the air was thick with excitement. She was greeted with a flurry of handshakes and heartfelt congratulations, each voice blending into a symphony of welcome that echoed throughout the lively gathering. The warmth of the camaraderie enveloped her, making the moment feel even more significant.

After expressing my gratitude, she drifted towards a lively group that prominently featured Val.

"Thank you for coming," Rose's warm voice enveloped the air as she greeted her friend, the sunlight catching the glint of her smile.

"I would not have missed it," Val replied, her words imbued with genuine affection as she enveloped Rose in a brief and cheerful hug. "Let me introduce you," she continued, her eyes sparkling with excitement.

As she introduced each person, Rose's gaze was drawn towards David's wife, Mary, who stood with an almost otherworldly grace. She appeared ethereal, her golden hair fluttering like delicate tendrils in the gentle breeze, while her soft brown eyes held a depth that seemed to reflect the surrounding beauty of blooming wildflowers. At that moment, it was impossible not to acknowledge how ideally suited she was as a partner to David, their connection echoing through the vibrant atmosphere of the gathering.

The sun had long surrendered to the embrace of night, which wrapped the landscape in a soft and velvety cloak of darkness. Only the luminous moon and the scattered diamonds of stars punctuated the inky expanse above, casting a serene glow over the world. Yet, this tranquillity was abruptly shattered.

A fight erupted as Finn became locked in a fierce struggle, the air crackling with tension.

Rose's heart thundered in her chest as she watched the two grapple on the ground. Their movements were a whirlwind of energy, driven by beer-induced adrenaline and fury.

Around them, the partygoers remained oblivious, their laughter and chatter a distant murmur cloaked in ignorance. "Too much beer," Rose muttered, the irritation coursing through her veins like a sharp jolt of electricity.

"Take it back!" Finn growled, the rawness of his voice cutting through the night.

His opponent answered with a taunt—"Irish pig! Back to your spuds." The words were sharp and biting, slicing through the ambient noises like knives.

Rory and David pushed into the fray, their sturdy forms interposing between the combatants. With resolute gestures, they urged Finn and his adversary to pull back and retreat, their voices rising in an attempt to quell the tempest that threatened to engulf them.

With a fierce resolve that belied her inner turmoil, Rose waded into the turmoil surrounding her.

"Finn, you walk," she said, locking eyes with him, a spark of intensity illuminating her gaze. "No driving. And who's going to take you home?" Her attention flickered to the other fighter, suspicion clouding her features as if past encounters had imbued these moments with an unshakeable intensity.

"Bob, come on, it's time to go," a young girl chimed in, her voice unwavering in the midst of the chaos, a hint of exasperation colouring her tone. Her demeanour suggested that this was simply a chapter in their ongoing story, one that was all too familiar to her.

"Thank you. Please, take him to the car," Rose ordered, her voice firm yet tinged with an undercurrent of concern. As she placed a gentle hand on the girl's arm, it was meant to convey more than just authority; it was a silent acknowledgment of the burdens they shared and the unspoken struggles that shaped them both.

The evening bore a lingering shadow, a sense of discomfort that clung to the cool evening air. Soft murmurs of gratitude and farewells echoed among the guests, each voice a note in the symphony of our gathering, as one by one, familiar faces began to fade into the twilight, leaving behind the ghosts of our conversations.

Hugh, Rose, and Rory stood together in the yard, their eyes scanning the scattered remnants of the day.

"Looks pretty good. We can clean it up in the morning," Hugh said, a yawn punctuating his words—a small signal of his fatigue.

As they exchanged good nights, Rose felt her heart flutter strangely at the intimacy of the moment. The warmth of Rory's arm around her shoulders guided her up the stairs to their shared bedroom.

Yet, once nestled beneath the covers, sleep eluded Rose like a fleeting whisper. Her thoughts spun chaotically, and images of familiar faces and connections swirled in her mind. But it was the encounter with Finn that loomed largest, casting a shadow over her heart. What had his cryptic words meant? Did he harbour feelings, or was it all a mirage conjured by her?

Restless, Rose slipped out from under the cover and padded softly to the balcony. There, under the vast expanse of the night sky, she sat, surrounded by the stillness that contrasted starkly with the turmoil inside her. She breathed in the cool air, letting it fill her lungs, searching for clarity amid the confusion that clouded her thoughts.

Her thoughts spiralled back to the young girl's expression, a haunting blend of sorrow and resignation etched across her face. How frequently did such moments unfold in the shadows of their lives? More often than Rose dared to consider. Was it merely the effects of the beer clouding his judgment, or was there a more profound, more unsettling truth lurking beneath the surface? As she replayed his words in her mind, a bitter sting settled in her chest—a subtle yet cutting insult aimed at the very essence of Finn's heritage.

Indeed, not here, not in Australia.

CHAPTER 19 - FIRST CHRISTMAS

A Christmas feast in rural Western Australia, 1946, was a heartfelt gathering of family and friends, celebrating post-war hope and renewal. The long dining table, adorned with festive decorations and simple yet elegant place settings, reflected the warmth of the occasion. Traditional roasts, fresh farm produce, and homemade desserts filled the air with rich aromas. A decorated Christmas tree stood proudly in the corner. Despite the summer heat, the joy of togetherness, laughter, and gratitude made this a cherished holiday celebration in the heart of the Australian countryside.

As anticipation welled inside her, Rose felt a surge of excitement that tingled at her fingertips. The moment she had been waiting for since she first set foot in Fremantle had finally come—it was time for the call to Aunt Rosemary. Her heart beat faster with each breath, and the thrill was almost overwhelming. Despite the potential for static to distort their conversation, the mere idea of hearing her dear Aunt's familiar voice brought an irrepressible smile to her face. She could almost feel the warmth of Aunt

Rosemary's words wrapping around her like a comforting embrace, amplifying her eager joy.

The operator's voice crackled to life, prompting Rose to hold as the connection to Aunt Rosemary was established. A low hum filled the air, mingling with distant sounds, as excitement and anxiety coiled within her. Her fingers twitched around the receiver, tension rising with each heartbeat.

"Rose?" Aunt Rosemary's familiar voice sliced through the static, warm yet strained.

"Aunt Rosemary," Rose replied, her voice trembling. Emotions flooded her as tears spilled over—each drop a reminder of their prolonged separation. "I miss you so much," she confessed, nostalgia and grief weighing heavily.

"I know. I miss you too," came Aunt Rosemary's quavering response, each word a battle. "Read the letter… but no photos."

"I promise to send them soon. Mine haven't arrived yet." A silence stretched as worry seeped in. "How have you been? You sound different."

"Good. How are you?" The shift in her aunt's tone felt like a protective barrier against the heaviness of their past. "It's different here, but good. The people are friendly. You would love it."

Suddenly, a crackle interrupted, and panic gripped Rose—she couldn't lose this connection now.

Then came the operator's voice, cutting through

the silence, "I'm sorry, but there's been a disconnection."

"Can't you reconnect?" Rose's voice sharpened with desperation. "I'm sorry, but I cannot. There are no more calls booked."

Silence enveloped her, the line cut. "No!" she growled, the weight of her disappointment crashing down like a relentless wave. "Not like this."

Rory, whose arm had been gently draped around her waist, turned her toward him. She buried her face in his shoulder and cried and cried, releasing the pent-up sorrow swirling within her.

Her tears flowed for what once had been as she remembered the days when the world still held the person who meant the most to her.

In her darkest hour, she was lost and stunned by the sudden loss of her parents. A bleak future loomed, with no clear path ahead. But then Aunt Rosemary had stepped in, enveloping her in a comforting embrace. At that moment, cradled in her aunt's arms, she began to feel the first glimmer of solace, sensing that perhaps everything could be alright. She wanted to reach across the distance and hug her.

Aunt Rosemary

Carol gently removed the phone from Rosemary's hand, her mind awash with worry. Memories of past conversations and shared secrets filtered through her thoughts, making her heart pound a little more complicated.

Tears streamed down Rosemary's usually smiling face—a face known for its comforting warmth and unyielding optimism.

Carol's voice trembled as she addressed her friend, "Rosemary," she said with great concern. "It was a bit much for you." She reached out, attempting to dab at the tears cascading down Rosemary's cheeks.

Rosemary pushed her hand away with an unexpected force. Even as her younger years had given way to an age intertwined with wisdom, a firmness in her voice surprised Carol.

"I am going to Australia to Rose," she murmured, her voice fragile and trembling as if speaking might shatter her. The words carried the unbearable weight of her unfulfilled dreams. A determination filled her. With Rose was where she belonged. "Will you come with me?" Rosemary inquired, her voice surprisingly steady despite the tremor beneath it.

Carol felt her heart leap at the thought of Australia—a realm she had only imagined through the tales spun by relatives and friends who had ventured there; she never envisioned standing at the precipice of such a journey herself.

"Well?" Rosemary attempted a laugh, but it faltered into breathless huffs, her familiar warmth lost in the moment.

"Yes, in light of everything we've been through,

this is unexpected," Carol replied, her mind racing through the recent trials that had tested the fibres of their bond. Week after week, they faced emotional tempests and misinterpretations yet emerged with a more resilient friendship than ever.

"You mean the stroke?" Rosemary asked. I was lucky it was not too severe."

Carol disagreed. The recovery of the last months had been agonising. "you have recovered well, but do you think you are ready for this?"

For Rosemary, an unwavering beacon of independence, this moment was disorienting. Her voice, usually steady and infused with self-assurance, now trembled as she glanced at Carol. The foundation of their friendship, built on mutual respect and admiration, had shifted; never before had they leaned on one another so profoundly. "I want to go, Carol." Rosemary's voice wavered, and her spirited nature dimmed, revealing a vulnerability that contrasted sharply with her usual strength. "Yes or no?"

A thoughtful smile spread across Carol's face. "No, it's more like a 'probably yes.' Just allow me a little time to ponder it."

"Good," Rosemary's expression brightened, a flicker of her confident self breaking through the clouds of uncertainty, softened yet illuminated by the genuine challenges they had faced together.

Rory Anderson

"How is she?" Hugh asked, his gaze filled with an overwhelming concern as Rory stepped into the dimly lit kitchen. His voice quivered, each syllable heavy with unspoken fear. "She's in bed, probably crying," Rory replied, a whisper escaping his lips, laced with an anxiety that seemed to grip his heart. "I'll make her some tea; perhaps it will soothe her."

"There must be something troubling Rosemary," Hugh urged, his tone trembling with vulnerability. "I know her well—she's always been kind and caring. It's so unlike her to withdraw, to leave us in silence without a word. I've masked my worries from Rose; I just told her that sometimes the letters take longer to arrive."

Rory hesitated, his father's words penetrating the haze of his thoughts, a deep furrow etching itself on his brow. "Yes, it's truly unlike her. And her voice on the phone," he added, dread creeping into his expression, "it felt so different, so fragile."

They shared a lingering glance, a silent acknowledgment of their fear. "I will find out what is going on with Rose, "Hugh stated, heavy with uncertainty. The distance from them to Rosemary needed to be bridged, and he was sure he could do it.

"I will," Hugh asserted, his voice steady and unwavering. Though his confidence was founded on love, it cradled a more profound understanding—one forged from years of knowing Rosemary's resilience. Rosemary had always been a beacon of hope for them. Since childhood, her remarkable ability to navigate challenges that left even the elders confounded had illuminated their lives.

From solving intricate puzzles to tackling life's complexities, her insightful nature and serene composure were unfailingly the light that guided them through dark times. As they confronted another crisis, Hugh's faith in her was grounded in the countless instances where her strength had anchored them amid turbulent waters.

"Tomorrow is Christmas," Rory noted, concern tinging his voice. He recognised that it would take a miracle to transform this holiday into a celebration for Rose, especially after the past year's trials. Memories flooded his mind—the twinkle that once danced in her eyes, the effortless joy that simple things used to bring her.

"Yes, it is," Hugh replied, his voice imbued with assurance and a flicker of joy. Rory admired his father's unwavering optimism. I should get organised and make this first Christmas in Australia a special one for Rose," Hugh added, flashing a warm, encouraging smile that felt like a lifeline. "You look after Rose; she needs you," he instructed his son.

Rory watched him move toward the kitchen, a bittersweet wave washing over him. He wished he could channel some of his father's abundant spirit.

Instead, Rory sensed an immense weight of responsibility; he must find a way to span the growing emotional divide and craft a joyous Christmas for Rose.

Beneath his father's cheerful façade lay a reservoir of understanding and experience that Rory yearned to grasp as he navigated the choppy waters of their family's heart.

Rory found Rose on the balcony. Rose's smile was stiff as if pinned in place, although it looked as forced as the plastic holly on the mantel.

"He moved to the settee and sat, enclosing her in his arms. It was Christmas, and celebrations were mandatory, even if their heart wasn't quite in it.

"Come down. Dad is cooking up a treat." Rory encouraged her.

Full of boisterous energy, Hugh pranced around the kitchen, his high spirits making Rose wonder how much he'd imbibed.

Rory was already heading to the door when he turned back, almost as an afterthought. "Would you like to come?"

Rose looked up, startled. Why now? Why today, of all days? He never included her in his outings, yet her heart leapt at the unexpected invitation. "Yes."

Rory's brow raised, mirroring her bewilderment. "Then grab your hat, and I will meet you in the ute," he said—something almost tender in his voice made Rose's breath catch and hope flicker in her.

The vast expanse of the far paddock stretched before her, adorned in the golden hues of sunlit stubble where the kangaroos grazed. The sight was almost surreal; there they were kangaroos, moving with a grace that captivated her completely.

As the dusty ute rumbled into view, the kangaroos snapped to attention, their ears twitching with deliberation as they decided whether to flee or continue feeding. The tension between tranquillity and alertness hung like a palpable force.

"They are beautiful," she murmured with a sense of awe, her eyes wide as she took their sleek forms and powerful legs poised for a swift getaway.

"Pests," Rory grumbled under his breath, his voice tinged with a frustration born of mundane familiarity. He kept it to himself, not wanting to ruin this upturn in Rose.

Her admiration and his irritation clashed silently, a stark contrast that echoed their different perspectives. The kangaroos, startled by the intrusion, bounded with fluid agility toward the shelter of the trees.

"I just have to check the troughs, and we can head back," Rory smiled at her.

"Then lead the way." Rose was never one to let things keep her down.

Upon returning home, they discovered the dining table splendidly arranged for the Christmas feast. Continuously embodying elegance and grace, Hugh had painstakingly prepared the Christmas table for six.

"Six people?" Rose queried, her spirits still lifted by her recent encounter with the kangaroos, which had profoundly connected her to the land and its marvels.

Hugh's smile broadened, illuminated by a warmth and pride brightening the room. "Yes, Peter for Aaron, Martha for you, and Lil for me." His joy transcended the flawless table arrangement; it lay in the thoughtfulness behind each pairing, reflecting their deep bonds. Each name whispered unspoken tales, narratives of friendship and affection intricately interwoven.

"You have truly outdone yourself. It's astonishing," Rose praised him, her eyes reflecting both admiration and memories of England and Aunt Rosemary, brought vividly back through the simple sprig of mistletoe he had magically produced. The nostalgia tugged at her heart, but she resisted its pull.

"Thank you, Madam," he responded, bowing slightly, his gratitude shining through in his demeanour.

"Yes, Dad, it's truly remarkable," Rory added, his voice a blend of admiration and the burden of recollections. He was transported back to Christmases long gone, where the essence of the family was alive—Albert, Guy, his mother, and Hugh—all together. A swell of nostalgia enveloped him, and he blinked back tears that danced at the corners of his eyes.

Noticing his son's distress, Hugh placed a gentle hand on Rory's shoulder, his voice barely above a whisper, "Those were splendid days, son. Hold those memories close; let them offer warmth instead of casting shadows over your spirit."

"Yes, I should probably shower and get ready." Rory managed a smile, but it felt more like a mask than genuine cheer.

He stood under the shower, letting the water run over him. His thoughts wandered to the vow he had made to his mother before embarking on his quest to find Guy: "Mum. I promise to bring him home." Guy had been so young, with a bright future with promise. Now, they were gone.

The burden of his unfulfilled promise weighed heavily upon him, like an anchor pulling him into despair. The haunting image of his mother's hopeful eyes lingered in his thoughts, a poignant reminder of the trust he had broken. Guilt coiled within him, intertwined with an unyielding resolve.

He had to bring them home. He turned off the shower and stepped out. Now, he had to make it through Christmas without them—for Hugh, Rose, and himself.

Surrounded by the vibrant hum of conversation, the table became a nexus of warmth and delight. The gentle illumination created a play of shadows that wove seamlessly with the joyous laughter echoing throughout the space. The delightful fragrance of mulled wine intertwined with festive spices blended beautifully with the fresh scent of pine from the Christmas tree, elevating the spirit of the celebration.

Hugh's culinary wizardry surpassed all expectations. The turkey, roasted to a golden perfection, was tender and succulent, its juices pooling invitingly on the serving platter. Crisp potatoes, with skins crackling under the teeth, provided a delightful contrast. The crowning glory was a plum pudding, dense and rich, served with a dollop of cream that melted luxuriously, a symphony of texture and flavour that delighted.

As Rose watched Rory in silence, his relentless consumption of beer revealed layers of anguish hidden beneath the surface. Despite his attempts to engage Peter with lighthearted banter, Rose could feel the deep chasm of despair that was swallowing him whole. When the men retreated to the veranda, leaving Rose and Martha to handle the dishes, the gravity of Rory's sorrow lingered in the air, unspoken yet palpable.

Martha, observing the tension, gently raised the matter while scrubbing a plate. "Rory is struggling to adjust without them," she noted, her voice laced with empathy. "It must be incredibly difficult for him; they were such a vibrant family. Before you returned, Windamere felt like a tomb." She paused, allowing her words to settle before adding softly, "I really hope you can breathe life into it again."

Rose pondered Martha's words as the dishes clinked around them. "And what about Hugh?" she inquired, curiosity piqued.

Martha sighed, shaking her head. "He was almost never here..."

"But now he seems so upbeat," Rose interjected, her brow furrowing in confusion.

"He's putting on a brave face, trying to compensate for their absence. If anything were to happen to you or Rory, it would shatter him," Martha replied, her eyes reflecting a shared concern.

The thoughts lingered as Rose sat on the veranda, letting the conversation swirl around her. Sitting here, she could watch the interplay. Hugh was jovial, but was it as Martha had said and acted?

As their guests departed, Rory swayed slightly, his eyes shimmering with the haze of intoxication, yet his face remained a cool mask, a stoic facade.

"I'm going to have another," he murmured, his voice a low rumble, almost swallowed by the whispers of the night. He clutched the bottle tightly, its glass cool and slick against his palm, as he stepped back onto the veranda, where the soft breeze carried the mingled scents of eucalyptus and distant smoke.

Rose felt a surge of instinct to reach out, to pull him back from the ledge of his reverie, but Hugh's gentle grip on her arm froze her in place. The warmth of his touch contrasted sharply with the growing chill of the evening, grounding her amidst the turmoil.

"Let him be, Rose," he whispered, his voice a soothing balm. "Sometimes, it's the only way to quiet the ghosts that haunt us."

As Rose perched herself on the balcony, the cool evening breeze brushed against her skin, carrying with it the faint aroma of the eucalyptus. She gazed into the distance, her thoughts centring on Rory, who had yet to make an appearance. Although he typically sipped his drinks with restraint, tonight felt different, and an unsettling question flickered through her mind: had her discussion led him down this path?

She shivered slightly as the shadows of doubt crept in, pondering the allure of the frothy beer that seemed to flow like a river tonight.

Or perhaps Martha's words hung over her like a damp fog—was the weight of war truly pressing down on Rory, leaving him to navigate the loss of his mother and brothers? The air thickened with an unspoken tension, deepening the emotional landscape of the moment.

CHAPTER 20 - A NEW YEAR

New Year 1946*, were a joyful mix of optimism and community spirit as locals welcomed a new era after the war. Families and neighbors gathered in town halls, homesteads, and outdoor gatherings, with tables set for tea, cake, and home-cooked meals. Streamers and balloons decorated makeshift dance floors, where couples waltzed to the sounds of a local band or gramophone. At midnight, party horns and cheers filled the air as people toasted to a hopeful future, embracing the resilience and camaraderie of rural life.*

30 Dec 1945

Dear Aunt Rosemary

It was great to talk if only it had been longer. Are you well? The line was so crackly I could hardly hear you.

Can you believe it is almost another year? I look back, and I can not believe how much happened. The end of the war and the start of a new era. Then, Nursing at the Alexander meeting Rory, his connection to you and Windermere, getting married, coming to Australia, meeting Hugh, and so much more.

As the final breath of the year lingered in the air, Rose inhaled deeply, preparing herself for the closing chapter of 1945—a year that had reshaped lives and severed dreams. The horizon shimmered with the promise of a new beginning, filled with uncharted possibilities and potential transformations just waiting to be seized. She couldn't help but wonder: what would this fresh start carry in its embrace?

Rose glanced over the arid landscape from her balcony, the day's heat wrapping around her like a heavy cloak. This last day of 1945 marked not just the end of a calendar year but the conclusion of an agonizing. But as she turned to Rory, she wondered if their paths could ever untangle from the past or if they were destined to be haunted by it forever.

"What a year," she whispered to herself, the words heavy journey that had tested the very fibres of her soul. The scars of war clung to her and everyone she knew, memories etched in the air like the bitter scent of gunfire and loss. It was a time she longed to bury, one she hoped would never rear its dark head again. with the weight of reflection. "No, I must correct myself—at long last, the war is over, and we can start anew." They had endured the brutality of conflict together, and now the fragile thread of hope they clung to began to weave a tapestry of possibility, precious and tentative as it was.

Rory's firm voice broke through her thoughts, imbued with a shadow of sorrow. "Yes, for us." His words hung in the air like a ghost—that haunting reminder of his brothers, who now rested in a lonely field doomed to eternal silence. The pain of their absence gnawed at him, a wound that no amount of time could heal.

Together, Rose and him were survivors, yet amid the promise of the new year, a part of them remained forever tethered to the past.

His words pulled Rose back to that haunting day when a Nazi bomb shattered their home, claiming the lives of his parents.

A palpable sadness enveloped her, creeping into her heart like a slow, relentless tide. They were so young, robbed of the chance to witness the end of the war and the hope of a brighter future—they would never know the sweetness of freedom that lay ahead. This sorrow would always linger, a shadowed hue in her memories, yet she firmly clung to her determination; she refused to let their absence stifle the potential of her days.

She and Aunt Rosemary often reminisced,

sharing stories that warmed them like a cherished blanket.

Each recall was a spark, illuminating the good times they had shared, moments of laughter that danced in stark contrast to their grief. Their bond was a fragile thread, woven in the crucible of conflict—a connection profoundly deepened by the shared scars of loss.

In that moment, Rose felt the weight of their intertwined lives; laughter resonated alongside tears, and dreams lay splintered, stark against the harsh realities they had faced together. Yet through it all, hope flickered like a distant star, illuminating the path forward.

Rory could not escape the shadows of his past, the memories clinging to him like a persistent fog. This lingering experience loomed large in his mind, an unhealed wound that yearned for closure. Without addressing it, he feared it would only deepen, turning from a mere scar into a festering source of pain that would not heal.

As he gazed into the distance, Rose couldn't shake the feeling that darkness loomed closer than she dared to admit.

"I guess we'd better get dressed," Rory grumbled, the heaviness of his spirit seeping through his voice, a bitter reminder of the battles they'd waged lately.

She hoped Christmas Day would not be a repeat. He was so sick the next day, but would that should deter him?

"Yes," Rose replied, a sigh escaping her lips, relief mingled with worry threading through her tone.

Her mind raced with the weight of their recent struggles—the silent arguments and unspoken words left in the wake of their discord. Would this evening serve as a bridge towards the peace she yearned for? In the quiet corners of her mind, she nurtured the fragile hope that this small step might kindle a change in him, alleviating the shadows that had crept into their relationship.

Martha's persuasive charm had drawn them into the golf club's New Year Dinner, a decision that felt both exciting and daunting. "Maybe Peter could work his magic on Rory," Rose mused, her thoughts swirling with memories of Rory's once-passionate love for the sport, a light now dimmed to an echo.

With his usual diplomatic grace, could Peter coax Rory into stepping back into the swing of life? Rose's heart ached, hoping that Peter might manage it, igniting a spark that could stitch their frayed connections back together. Yet, in the back of Rose's mind lingered a question: would tonight's festivities bring them closer or drive an even wider wedge between them?

As Rose descended the graceful staircase, the soft light filtering through the ornate window cast a warm glow around her. Hugh stood at the foot of the stairs, his presence exuding charm and mischief. "You look simply enchanting, my dear Rose," he proclaimed with a theatrical flourish, extending his arm in an elegant gesture to escort her toward the waiting car, gleaming softly under the evening sky.

She shot him a teasing glance, a playful smile dancing on her lips. "You say that to every woman," she replied, her voice light yet tinged with curiosity.

Hugh paused, pondering her words as amusement sparkled in his eyes. "That may indeed be the case," he said with a whimsical grin. But at my age, we seize every chance to spread a little cheer, don't we?"

Their laughter rang out, echoing like music through the spacious hall, imbuing the atmosphere with a sense of joy and camaraderie that lingered in the air.

But Rory lingered at the edges of their banter like a wisp of smoke, unnoticed yet deeply present, silently craving connection in their shared warmth. If he could be jovial, it kept pulling him back to Normandy.

With pomp, Hugh led Rose through the door, gently placing her in the car. He tossed the keys to Rory. "Cheer up, son. I am letting you drive. That should brighten you up."

Rory caught the keys. "Yes, Sir. "He got into the mood. There was no time for ghosts tonight; it was New Year's Eve.

"Just don't forget we are picking up Val and Mel," he ordered from the back seat.

Rory smiled; his father had a soft spot for those alone, and that was the case, both widows and now single. He made sure they were not left alone on a night of celebration.

As they stepped into the hall, Rose rested her hand on Rory's arm, her pulse quickening in anticipation of the evening's festivities. Hugh, Mel, and Val flanked them, the air buzzing excitedly. Mel mirrored their enthusiasm, and a bright smile lit her face.

Rory's gaze swept the room, and a wave of nervous energy washed over him when he spotted Martha and Peter near the crowd's edge, their table waiting like a sanctuary amidst the swirling chaos.

He felt a knot tighten in his stomach at the thought of getting a good spot. After all, at these dances, being first meant everything, especially on a night as electric as New Year's Eve, where every moment promised a thrill amidst the crowd of jubilant revellers.

The air buzzed with energy as the early birds filtered in, the vibrant sound of the band, the Cowan Boys, filling the atmosphere with an infectious rhythm. Mel's eyes sparkled with eagerness as she turned to Rose, her voice bubbling with excitement. "It's the Cowan Boys," she exclaimed, the warmth of local pride in her tone.

Hugh nodded appreciatively, the steady heartbeat of the music thrumming through him. "They play a good rhythm," he remarked, the lively beat reverberating in his chest. His gaze swept over the scene, catching the flicker of lights and the glint of smiles. "So what are we standing here for? Let's get to the table and dance the night away."

As they greeted Martha and Peter Harding, a warmth filled the air, wrapping around them like a familiar embrace. Their laughter mingled, a gentle symphony of connection that drew attention to David Crowley seated at the nearby table. With a shared glance and a spark of recognition, they leaned in, enthusiasm bubbling between them as they exchanged friendly words, inviting David to join their gathering.

The atmosphere shifted as David brought along his wife, Mary, whose bright smile filled the space with light, and Dan Curley, his foreman, whose steady presence grounded the group. As David's other guests began to arrive, the blend of personalities and stories promised to weave a rich tapestry of camaraderie, drawing them closer, as if each shared moment built upon the last, deepening their bond in this bustling, shared chapter of their lives.

As the haunting melody of the Circular Waltz filled the air, the atmosphere shifted, pulling them onto the dance floor like moths drawn to an enchanting flame. With every graceful twirl, they glided from partner to partner, the scent of polished wood mingling with the warm embrace of bodies swaying in unison.

Rose soon found herself trapped in David Crowley's magnetic aura. His proximity was a heady blend of tension and allure, leaving her heart racing in a disconcerting dance of unease.

Just as the moment reached its climax, she was gently drawn into Dan's embrace, his serene presence washing over her like a balm against the storm of her swirling emotions. His steady grip became her anchor, a beacon of quiet reliability that offered solace amidst the chaotic electricity of David's charisma. In her heart, Rose recognized that both men exuded compelling confidence. Yet, Dan's steadfastness served as the foundation for David's magnetic success, creating an intricate tapestry of connection and conflict that left her yearning for clarity.

She twirled gracefully amidst the swirl of laughter and music, the vibrant colours of dresses and suits merging like a living tapestry around her. Peter, with his warm smile, and Hugh, his cheerful spirit infectious, joined the crowd of revellers—faces unfamiliar yet somehow intoxicating. The air crackled with excitement, the scent of champagne mingling with festive snacks as twinkling lights danced above like stars descending to join the celebration. What a breathtaking way to embrace the dawn of the New Year, each heartbeat resonating with joy and anticipation.

Wrapped in a rush of exhilaration, she felt the warmth of Rory's embrace enveloping her, creating a sanctuary from the chaotic world outside. His scent—a heady mix of earthiness and something uniquely his—enveloped her senses like a welcome homecoming. As she gazed up into his eyes, those deep pools reflecting shared laughter and silent promises, the realization washed over her like a comforting tide: at this moment, she had indeed found her soul mate. The shadows of war still hovered at the edges of their reunion, a distant echo of struggles past, yet amidst the lingering unease, there was a profound certainty: there was no other place she would rather be than nestled.

The atmosphere at the table mirrored the ebb and flow of dance, each guest shifting like partners in a well-rehearsed waltz. To Rose's delight, she sat beside the matron, a comforting presence amidst the swirling conversations.

"Matron, it's so wonderful to see you! How is Jenny faring?" she inquired, her heart lifting at the familiar sight.

"Quite well," the matron replied with a knowing smile. "The moment he spotted you, I sensed a plan stirring. David is quite the one to make swift moves."

A ripple of laughter escaped Rose, light and

buoyant. "I can hardly wait for the St. John's challenge," she said, anticipation dancing in her chest.

"Always ready to dive into a challenge, that's our Rose," Hugh chimed in, his voice infused with merriment. A touch of drink bolstered the good-natured warmth of the evening. But tonight, Rose felt an unusual sense of ease regarding his level of intoxication. Hugh had a knack for moderation; she often wondered if he kept a mental tally of his sips, knowing precisely when to curb his enthusiasm.

A gentle tap on her shoulder jolted Rose from her thoughts. She turned to find Dan. "May I steal you for this dance?" he asked, and a rush of delight surged through Rose as she accepted his invitation, ready to twirl into the rhythm.

As the lively barn dance began, Rose and her partner stepped onto the floor, their movements intertwined with the vibrant rhythm. In that swirling midst of laughter and twirling skirts, Rose found herself drawn to understanding this man, the one she instinctively knew was David's right-hand confidant. "Have you and David been together long?" she ventured, uncertain if her words would land as intended.

"Yes, we went to Ag College together," he replied, his voice steady, yet a hint of nostalgia lingered between them.

She liked him; it was an instinctive reaction. He

exuded a calm confidence that felt almost at odds with the role he played throughout his life. As they glided through the dance steps, Rose couldn't help but appreciate the way he moved, each step solid, each motion purposeful, unlike so many others lost in the chaos of the celebration.

"So you are David's choice to head the St John's organization," he observed, his tone implying a deeper understanding.

His gaze held her, probing and perceptive, as if he were measuring the depths of her aspirations. Did he see the nerves beneath her composed exterior?

"Yes, I am looking forward to it," Rose affirmed, though uncertainty flickered beneath her calm facade.

"David mentioned you did fieldwork in Normandy," he continued, quizzing her, seeking to peel back the layers.

"Yes, although this position will be entirely different." A pause hung in the air, rich with what lay ahead. "A new challenge."

"Rory is a lucky man; you are following him out here. It must be a big change." His words were like a gentle nudge, encouraging her to share more.

"I think I am the lucky one." The words flowed from her, imbued with the weight of experience. "Rory and I have come through the same hardships. War teaches you what truly matters in life."

As Dan nodded, she sensed a shift in him; he

seemed to relax. What had he been searching for in this exchange? In that fleeting moment, she felt she had answered his unasked questions, Even though she was uncertain what he sorted.

Later that night, as the stars twinkled above them, Rose and Rory settled onto the balcony's edge, the soft night air cradling them in an intimate hush. She couldn't shake the lingering thoughts from earlier, the weight of the conversation still pressing on her mind.

"He was testing you," Rory said, his tone light yet somehow more profound, as if hinting at a seriousness beneath the surface.

Rose's brow furrowed in confusion. "Testing me? About what?" she asked, her voice barely above a whisper, curiosity knitting her brows together. She felt a knot of unease form in her stomach.

Rory chuckled, a warm, melodic sound always comforting her. "Dan looks after the family, especially Mary," he explained, the moonlight catching the glint in his eyes.

"But she is his David's wife?" Rose replied, the confusion shifting to concern. The implications of that situation stirred a storm within her.

"Yes, and a very loyal one," Rory added, his amusement evident. She could see him struggling to maintain his composure, that mischievous glint never far from his gaze.

"So?" Rose prodded, playfully jabbing her elbow

into his ribs to coax out the whole story. "Explain yourself, Rory Anderson."

Rory leaned back slightly, considering her challenge. "Let's say David isn't quite so faithful," he finally revealed, the gravity of his words hanging between them.

Silence wrapped around Rose as she processed this. Her heart raced, recalling her instinctual responses to David earlier. "He was checking if I would be David's next conquest," she murmured, realization dawning like the first light of dawn.

"Yes," Rory nodded, a knowing grin spreading across his face as he turned his gaze skyward, lost in the vastness of the universe. "I'd say so. Nice guy, Dan."

Rose released a breath she hadn't realized she was holding. "Then you can rest easy," she said, feeling a surge of confidence. "I sensed I passed his test." The words played in her mind, echoing with certainty: *I think I am the lucky one. Rory and I have emerged from the same trials. War teaches you what truly matters in life.*

Rory's laughter danced through the air, rich with affection and pride. "So, you passed, did you, Mrs. Anderson?"

"Yes, consider yourself fortunate," she replied with a mischievous smile lighting her face. "David is undeniably a dynamic man, but at the end of the day, I am married to you." In that moment, she felt the weight of their bond reaffirmed, as solid and enduring as the stars above.

As they sat together, the air thick with unspoken tensions and tangled thoughts, Rose was submerged in a storm of confusion. Everyone revered David, a man of many accolades, yet whispers of his infidelities gnawed at her conscience. "Why is it," she ventured, her voice barely above a whisper, "that David garners such admiration despite his flaws?"

Keenly aware of the layered affections surrounding their discussion, Rory offered a measured response. "His accomplishments cast a long shadow over his indiscretions," he remarked, choosing each word carefully. "Women are drawn to him, and he reciprocates their affections willingly. It's a daring dance that few would dare embrace, yet he thrives, not just for himself but for Midjal. He's woven his success into the very fabric of our community." A beat passed, and before continuing, he emphasized, "He has built more than just a farming empire; he has nurtured this town, earning our respect in ways we can hardly measure."

Rose processed Rory's observations, a bittersweet cocktail of admiration and pity swirling within her. "But does Mary know?" The question trembled on her lips, a frail attempt to grasp the total weight of the situation.

"In such a small town, how could she not?" Rory replied, his tone laced with an unsettling inevitability.

A deep ache settled in Rose's heart for Mary, who radiated beauty and grace yet stood on the precipice of profound betrayal. She couldn't fathom enduring such humiliation. "I couldn't bear to face that," she admitted, a shiver of empathy coursing through her.

Rory's laughter rang out, bright yet tinged with an edge of condescension. "Don't fool yourself into thinking that you ever will."

CHAPTER 21 - TAKING UP THE CHALLENGE

*In 1946, letters from family in **England to Australia** carried heartfelt messages of love, longing, and post-war resilience. They shared news of rationing, rebuilding efforts, and cherished memories. Many letters expressed excitement about migration, updates on loved ones, and hopes for better days ahead. For Australian families, these letters were a vital link to home, treasured and read repeatedly, bridging the vast distance between two worlds through words of warmth and connection.*

January was suffocatingly hot, the oppressive air wrapping around Rose like a heavy blanket. There was a stillness that seemed to carry the weight of the heat, and even the occasional gust that broke the silence felt as though it had travelled straight from Kalgoorlie, the dreaded "Blower" they warned about. Rose rolled her eyes at the exaggerated tales, dismissing them as mere exaggeration—until Rory pointed out that Kalgoorlie was so far inland it was a furnace.

As the days passed, she found it hard to fathom

that it was already the 12th. Just the anticipation—
and dread—of starting at St. John's loomed before
her, intertwined with thoughts of David. He had
taken her breath away from when they met in the
matron's office, then again at the New Year's Eve
Ball.

At the mere utterance of his name, a maelstrom
of conflicting emotions surged through her; working
alongside him was like walking a precarious
tightrope delicately balanced between intrigue and
wariness. Did she dare confront the tangled feelings
that she felt?

It would serve her well to explore the depths of
her internal turmoil as she grapples with this
emotional tug-of-war. David, perchance to wander,
loomed over her, casting long shadows on the
palpable chemistry that sparked between them. It is
utter folly to entertain these feelings. But his
magnetic appeal was potent.

With sharp clarity, she recognised that crossing
the threshold from mere attraction to authentic desire
would complicate her life in ways too risky to
contemplate. Her steadfast loyalty to Rory, the one
she believed to be her destined partner, tightened its
grip on her even as she struggled through this
turbulent ocean of emotions. Ultimately, she would
need to unearth a way to harmonise these conflicting
desires.

She felt a rushing tide of thoughts swirl in her

mind, a storm that urged her to act rather than linger in the chaos. The rhythm of work had always provided her with a sense of clarity and solace. With purpose in her stride, she gathered the dusters and polish, her hands trembling s as she cleaned the lounge room. Pouring herself into the task as if striving to scrub away her turmoil, she felt a sense of clarity and solace.

Later, Hugh's familiar voice broke through her reverie as he popped his head around the corner. "How about a tea?" he offered a hint of playfulness in his tone. "Careful with that polish; you'll wear it away."

A small smile flickered on her lips as she wiped the sweat from her brow, the warmth of his presence a comforting distraction. "Yes, sounds good," she replied, though she longed for something more than mere tea—it was the warmth she craved in this chilly solitude.

As she entered the kitchen, the sight of a bundle of letters on the table jolted her from her thoughts. Aunt Rosemary? A gasp escaped her lips, and she tore into the first envelope with trembling fingers, anticipation mingling with a flutter of anxiety in her chest.

"I truly despise being unsociable," Rose confessed, her voice a mixture of determination and vulnerability. "But I need to take these upstairs. I want the freedom to read and cry without holding back." She rose from her seat, a look of resolve in her eyes.

Hugh chuckled softly, sensing the weight of her words. "Here, take this with you," he said, handing her a cold beer. "Sometimes, a chilled drink is what you need to accompany those tears."

She paused, a flicker of gratitude crossing her face as she accepted the gesture, silently acknowledging the warmth of his understanding. "Thank you, Hugh," she replied, her voice softening. "Good advice." She turned at the door. "On this occasion, in moderation," she clarified.

As Rory stepped outside, he found Rose still perched on the balcony, her gaze lingering on the horizon, lost in thought. He approached and offered her a beer, a simple gesture loaded with unspoken understanding. Her smile broke through the mist in her eyes—two beers in one day, a tiny indulgence.

"Dad said Aunt Rosemary's letters arrived," he remarked, motioning toward the jumble of opened envelopes draped across her lap. Like a doorway to the past, each letter whispered secrets of family and nostalgia.

Rose turned to him, a soft light illuminating her features, mingled with the remnants of sadness deep within. "Yes," she replied, her voice barely above a whisper. Yet, she knew that words were insufficient to convey the weight of her emotions; the warmth creeping into her cheeks spoke volumes, and the gentle curve of her smile revealed the bittersweet tale she carried inside her heart. Memories of laughter shared and tears shed, of ties that bound them all, echoed quietly in her mind, creating a richness to the moment that words alone could never capture.

"I miss her," she whispered, her voice a fragile thread in the stillness that enveloped them. They lingered in the quiet, the clinking of beer bottles punctuating the heavy air. "You know how long you long for your mother and brothers. Your grief weighs more than mine," she added, the unspoken truth of their absence hanging between them like a ghost.

He turned to the distant horizon, where the sky kissed the earth. "I've been reflecting on that," he said, a quiet resolve settling in his chest. "I want to bring them home." His choice of words was deliberate—he avoided "bodies," instead envisioning a place of rest in Midjal, where their spirits could dwell together. He imagined them all reunited, enveloped in the warmth of shared memories, as if he could finally bridge the chasm of loss by bringing them back to where they belonged, to her. He had promised his mother.

Rose had sensed it all along; the silence wrapped around Rory like a shroud when the memories overwhelmed him.

"It haunts you? Is it the war that still grips you?" Her eyes pierced through his, filled with a desperate longing for connection.

"Yeah," he breathed out, his voice rushing out as if it had been held captive. He took a steadying breath as if trying to capture the swirling shadows of his thoughts. "But it's mostly what it did to our family."

"What part of the war haunts you most? The battles?" Her inquiry hung in the air, thick and heavy, as if every word weighed down by shared heartache.

As her question lingered, it stirred the murky waters of torment lurking within him—the agonizing memories of the day Guy was snatched away by fate amid the relentless clamour of gunfire and chaos. How could he even begin to express the depth of despair that had since become his constant companion?

He had fought against the cruel hand of destiny, desperate to save Guy, yet every effort had crumbled beneath the weight of reality. The losses clawed at his heart, each one rendering the entire experience all the more senseless—both in the throes of battle.

"Why did you go to war?" she whispered, wanting to understand.

He hesitated, the weight of the question settling heavily on his chest like an unyielding boulder. "I didn't want to. Guy, my younger brother—just sixteen, but he sprinted off and enlisted." The quiver in his voice gave way to a torrent of memories, each one crashing over him like waves. He could picture his mother's anxious face, eyes wide and glistening with unshed tears, her hands gripping the fabric of his shirt as if trying to anchor him to her, pleading for him to stay.

"You went after him to save him," she murmured, the pieces of his puzzle slotting into place, concern etched in her gaze.

"Yes, I promised Mother I'd bring him back." His voice faltered, choked by the weight of that vow, heavy with guilt and sorrow.

"And you could not," she said softly, understanding the unspoken pain.

"Yes," he confessed, the words falling like ashes. "I promised her, and she died knowing I failed." Emotionless yet burdened, he buried the tumult deep within, shielding himself from the storm.

"He was ready to set sail." That day flashed before him, and he saw the moment when he had to choose between his mother's plea and his brother's folly. He had made the wrong choice; nothing he did on the battlefield could save his brother.

"Your mother wouldn't blame you," Rose reassured him, reaching for the part of him that ached most.

"Perhaps," he whispered, regret thick in the air. "But I failed them both— I could not keep Guy from death. My mother's heart gave out, whether that was due to hard work or the toll of Albert and Guy's deaths. We will never know. Probably both." Guilt was a dark cloud, shadowing every thought.

"Your father and I are happy you lived. We can

be a family again. Tell your children about your mother and brothers," she said gently, her hand warming his across the table. The touch sparked connections to buried memories, long forgotten but never truly gone. Her eyes mirrored years of pain and resilience—a silent testament to the enduring power of love amidst the trials.

She hoped to remind him that his existence still held value, even amidst the shadows of his past, every scar a silent testament to the strength that had brought him back to this moment. Her words were the echoes of countless nights waiting for his recovery and the unspoken promise that his story was far from over.

"I need to bring them home for closure." Rory's voice whispered through the silent night. "Then the family will be together again. Mum will have them with her."

Rose gently clasped his hand with tender resolve, her lips brushing against his palm in a soft, lingering kiss that spoke of unspoken promises. "I know you do."

"Yes, tomorrow I will go and see Mum's grave." He paused and then admitted, "I have put it off too long."

Rose gazed across the cemetery, where the stark, cold gravestones stood solemnly amidst the gnarled branches of spindly trees, their twisted limbs clawing at the grey sky. The air was heavy with the scent of dust, a stark contrast to the vibrant greens of Windermere Cemetery back in England, where both Rory's and her ancestors rested peacefully. Here, the horizon loomed in the distance, a reminder of the vast world beyond, yet the atmosphere felt suffocatingly intimate, as if the very ground beneath her was steeped in whispered memories and lingering sorrows.

It had been three long years since Joan's death, yet for Rory, the ache of her absence lingered, sharp and relentless. The echoes of her laughter that filled their days now wrapped around him like a ghostly whisper, leaving an emptiness that choked him. On afternoons like this, when the sky hung heavy with slate-grey clouds, mirroring his sorrow, he could almost feel the world weeping alongside him, each droplet of rain a reminder of the warmth he had lost.

The sombre atmosphere weighed heavily on their hearts as they approached the graveyard.

"I need to do this, Rose." It was as if his determination needed a boost.

Rose took a deep breath and squeezed his hand gently. "I know it's hard, Rory, but this is the first step. You have to say goodbye properly."

Rory clenched his fists, his knuckles turning white. "Mother was everything to me," he whispered, eyes filling with unshed tears. "How am I supposed to do this without her?"

"You don't have to do it alone," Rose reassured

him, her eyes wet with emotion. "We're in this together, remember? Your mother would want us to be strong for each other."

As they reached Joan's grave, Rory hesitated. "Do you think she'd be proud of me?" he asked, his voice barely audible.

Rose turned to him, her expression soft. "I have no doubt," she said earnestly. "Your mother wanted the best for you, Rory. She always would."

The wind rustled through the trees, echoing Joan's laughter. Rose stood beside the grave, placing a bouquet of Joan's favourite flowers. "We'll get through this, Rory," she vowed. "One step at a time."

Rory nodded, his resolve hardening. "For Mother," he murmured, taking a deep breath as he stood beside Rose. Together, they faced the bittersweet task of saying goodbye, strengthened by the bond Joan had left behind.

Rory felt like he was drowning in his Memories—his mother—her warm embraces, the way she always knew the right things to say, the way she always strove to keep them going. It's not easy with a husband like Hugh.

He loved his father but was not blind to his faults. In another world, they may not have been necessary. But here, it was a struggle to survive, and that was something his mother had taught him. Their future was tied to the land and if the rains came.

They found the spot halfway down the hill.

Unlike other graves, his father had made a family plot, just like the one at Windamere Cementry, which is all those miles away.

The primary headstone is inscribed "The Anderson Family Plot," and beside it, a single headstone is inscribed:

Standing there, the earth beneath his feet, he found himself in front of her grave. The modest headstone bore an inscription that he stared at until his tears rendered it illegible.

"Dad got it right," he whispered, his voice trembling. It's just how she was—a simple, loving mother devoted to the land." The breeze rustled the leaves, echoing his sentiment. Rose stood beside him, her arm a comforting weight around his waist.

"I wish I had known her. Do you have any photos?" she asked softly, her voice blending with the whisper of the wind through the trees.

"Yes, I think so," he murmured, his eyes still locked on the headstone. Despite the flood of emotion, a serene calm washed over him as if the earth offered solace.

That night, they pored over the handful of photos Rory could find. There were few, each a fleeting glimpse into Joan's spartan life. Joan had been an outdoor person, practical and no-nonsense, with little room for frivolities.

Among the scarce collection were a few images of Guy and Albert, frozen moments amidst a backdrop of wilderness and toil.

Rose recalled the overflowing pages of her family album, bursting with life and memories, contrasting starkly with the scanty photos boxed away, bereft of the warmth of an album. Each photograph seemed to whisper tales of ceaseless labour and stark solitude.

This stark portrayal of Joan's life felt incongruous with Hugh, a man of social vigour, always surrounded by camaraderie. Rose's thoughts wandered again to the enigmatic union of Joan and Hugh, their marriage a joining of two such divergent souls.

They came from such different backgrounds,

Rory and her. She was the daughter of an English doctor, and he was born into a farming family.

Their lives would have never intersected without the war, a storm that had ravaged their separate existence but bound them together in shared survival.

Windamere stood as a testament to their entwined fates, rooted in a history that predated their union but had now found new life through their combined saga.

In the quiet moments, she reflected on their differences and the unseen threads of hardship and hope that stitched their lives into one tapestry.

Rory sat transfixed, a handful of photos of his brothers spread across the table. They were laughing, playing, and fighting. Each picture was a portal to a time now lost, a poignant reminder of the lives cut tragically short.

His eyes welled up with unshed tears as he lifted his gaze to meet Rose's. Rose, his wife and unwavering confidante, is a silent anchor in this storm of sorrow. She had not known his brothers. Now, as Rory confronted the ghosts of his memories, he found solace in Rose's steady understanding.

"I have to bring them home," he murmured, his voice breaking with determination and sorrow. The weight of his words hung in the air, leaving Rose stunned by the gravity of his revelation. "They deserve to come home," he continued, "to rest in peace and have a proper burial." The resolve in Rory's voice was unwavering, though the pain in his heart was as raw as ever.

"That is a monumental undertaking," Rose murmured, her mind reeling as she tried to grasp the enormity of the task ahead. The weight of what lay before them seemed almost crushing, like an invisible force pressing down on her chest.

"Do you know where they perished?" she asked, an unexpected boldness tinging her voice, betraying her astonishment at her daring.

"Yes," came the solemn reply, each word carrying the gravity of the knowledge held. "I know the place where they met their end. It will not be a simple endeavour, fraught with challenges, but I am determined to find them." The determination in his voice was as palpable as the tension that filled the room, each syllable echoing a silent vow to see the task through.

An unyielding fire had ignited within him. His childhood had been marked by warmth and laughter, his mother's strength, and his father's infectious love.

Yet, the cruel hands of war had scattered them across the unkind corners of the world. The memory of brothers Albert and Guy growing up together fighting, playing, and laughing, and the collective heartbeat of their unity haunted his every waking moment.

Rory's determination was not merely a resolute decision; it was the very essence of his being. He was driven by the longing to heal the fractured remnants of his past, to gather those he loved once more back into the ghostly echo of a family that once was.

Every step he took, every plan he made, was laced with the unshakeable belief that no force on earth could deter him from mending it.

Hugh returned home, the air thick with memories as he found them poring over old photographs. He settled at the table, his heart lightened by nostalgia. "Do you remember this?" he chuckled, lifting a photo of Albert, caked in mud, immortalised in an instant by the joy of childhood. "One of the rare moments you bested your older brother."

"Ah, yes," Rory replied, his gaze drifting over the image, a bittersweet smile forming. "He was never an easy opponent."

In the corner, Rose remained still, acutely aware that this was a sacred moment for the men in her life, a bridge to their past they needed to cross together.

"No, but you were the rock, the one who always found a way to rise above," Hugh said softly, his thoughts wandering to the children he cherished. "Guy may have been too young to understand, but his laughter filled our hearts."

Rory's smile wavered as he recalled the sound of his younger brother's joy. "He was always laughing, wasn't he?"

"And your mother, June, she was truly the best," Hugh said, his voice thickening with emotion as he fingered a photo of her. "She worked tirelessly, too hard perhaps," he murmured, regret lacing his words.

"I visited her grave today," Rory shared, his voice

almost whispering.

"I'm glad," Hugh replied, warmth flooding his heart. "She would have so wanted to see you. You've always reminded me of her: steadfast and loyal." He paused, swallowing back the sense of loss. "It was her spirit that drew you back to us."

"I promised her I would bring them home," Rory confessed, his eyes shadowed by regret. "Son, the war—none of us could have fathomed how brutal it would be," Hugh said, a profound empathy binding them in shared sorrow.

They sat in silence, fingering through the photos before Rory spoke.

"I am going to bring Albert and Guy back," Rory declared, his voice steady yet betraying an undercurrent of profound sorrow. Each word was a weight he carried, a mixture of hope and despair mingling within him as he spoke. He felt the ache of loss and the desperate need to rectify his past decisions, knowing that the lives entwined with his own deserved more than mere regret.

Hugh's reaction was immediate, his voice slicing through the tension like a blade. "I'm going with you." His resolve was palpable, a fortress built on layers of unyielding loyalty and hidden grief. There was no room for doubt in his declaration; it was as if he was resurrecting an unspoken promise among them, a vow that family, however fragmented, would not be abandoned.

"It's the right thing to do," he continued, his tone

softening yet imbued with an ironclad strength. Each word reverberated with the weight of timeless ties, echoing the shared laughter and whispered fears that had once filled their home. "This is their home; they belong with June." His assertion hung heavy in the air, suffused with the silent acknowledgment of their collective history and unvoiced emotions. "We are a family."

Rory and Rose exchanged glances, both startled and drawn into a deeper understanding of Hugh. The jovial facade he often wore slipped away, revealing a raw vulnerability that resonated with their hidden sorrow. In that moment, Rory realized how much grief still lingered, quietly woven into the fabric of their lives. It was a deeper connection forged through shared pain, awakening a sense of urgency within him—a need not just to find Albert and Guy but to mend the frayed threads of their bond.

"Indeed," he replied, his eyes glistening as he envisioned their future. "It's reminiscent of Windermere, a continuation of our legacy." As the image of the barren plot filled his mind, memories of the fallen miners surfaced, intertwining with his hopes. "This chapter will bring us joy and prosperity, far beyond what they ever knew."

CHAPTER 22 - ST JOHN'S

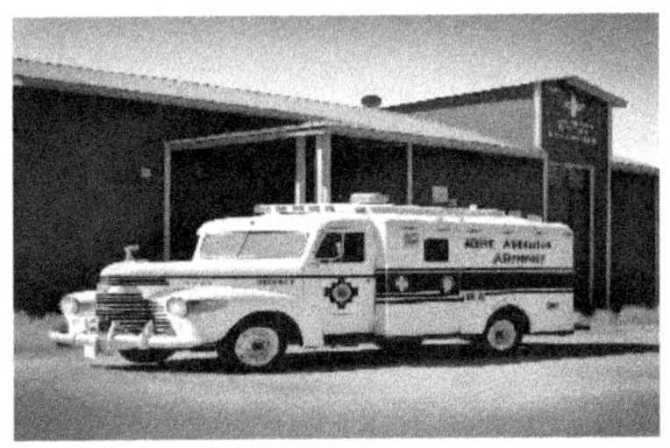

In 1946, the St. John Ambulance service in rural Western Australia provided vital medical support to remote communities. The depot, a served as the hub for emergency response and healthcare assistance. The ambulance, equipped for medical transport, reflects the era's practicality and resilience. St. John Ambulance played a crucial role in connecting isolated areas to essential medical care, embodying dedication and service during a time of recovery and rebuilding.

Hugh sat at the table, his gaze intent as he broke the silence. "Nervous?" he inquired, perceptively noting the tension in the air.

"Yes, I am," Rose confessed, her voice barely above a whisper. It wasn't the job that brought about her anxiety; it was David Crowley. The temptation he represented loomed large, an alluring yet dangerous distraction from the life she had envisioned with Rory—a future she was not willing to jeopardize for a fleeting flirtation.

"The job?" he probed, watching as she returned to the table, porridge and tea in hand.

"Partly," she deflected, skirting the depth of her feelings.

A playful smile spread across Hugh's face. "The other part wouldn't happen to concern Mr. Crowley, would it?" he teased a hint of mischief in his eyes.

"You've been talking to Rory," she shot back, betraying a mix of annoyance and amusement. "No, he's magnetic; he knows how to wield that charm," Hugh mused, his brow furrowed in contemplative thought. The weight of memory hung in the air between them. "But that's all in the past. The locals? They have long memories."

"How long?" Rose's voice trembled slightly, eager yet cautious, as if she feared the answer might shift the ground beneath her.

"Way back," he replied, his eyes glazing over with the film of nostalgia. "David's early years were nothing short of brutal. He and Dan rode into town like wild stallions, two young lads on rumbling motorbikes, with nothing but a legacy of five hundred acres of salt lake country left by his uncle."

"The lake in the distance?" Rose prodded, her imagination capturing an image of shimmering water, its allure both haunting and inviting.

"Yes, but further around," Hugh continued, a hint of sadness threading his words. "You might think this land is harsh, but believe me, salt country is far worse. They had very little to start with, but somehow, Dan and he managed to make a life here."

"What about Mary?" Rose's curiosity sparked, a thread of urgency compelling her to piece together the storied tapestry of this man's life.

"She was the daughter of one of the pioneer families. They met at a dance in the countryside, and he fell for her almost immediately. Just twenty, far too young for such a commitment. But Mary… she defied her father, and they married in the city."

"She ran away?" Rose's mind struggled to reconcile the image of a calm beauty with the notion of rebellion.

"Yes," Hugh replied, nodding with a mixture of admiration and melancholy. "Her father eventually forgave her, even offering David a hand in those tumultuous early years—a bit of advice and the financial support to bail him out when he faltered." He finished his tea, the cup clinking softly against the saucer as he rose. "But now, all of that is history. David has transformed Midjal into a community, owning over twenty thousand acres. He is a leader."

"And the affair?" Rose asked, needing to know the details, the shadows lingering in David's past that might illuminate the present.

"A minor fling," Hugh shrugged, a weight hanging in the silence that followed. "With a toddler and another on the way, Dan and Mary's father intervened, and since then, David has stayed well within the lines. As I said, the locals remember these things."

He gathered his plates and took them to the sink, the mundane act punctuating the gravity of their conversation.

"Thank you," she murmured, the clarity of it all settling over her like a soft blanket. It struck her that Rory had missed these crucial details. Why?

"You need to set the tone from the outset," Hugh advised, his gaze steady and severe. "With David, honesty is crucial; he'll respect you for it."

Those words lingered, wrapping around her thoughts like an unbidden melody, echoing through her mind, urging her to embrace the truth.

Upon her arrival at the depot, her mind was a tumultuous sea of doubt and yearning. Did Hugh, in all his earnestness, truly comprehends the depth of her struggle. She ached for this job— not merely for the responsibilities it would entail but for the wisdom and growth that lay within each challenge. David Crowley, her superior, had bestowed this chance upon her, and yet…

It seemed Hugh viewed the world through a lens tinted by the confines of his own experiences—man to man as if gender were a mere backdrop in their unfolding story.

For her, it was more than just a gap; it was an abyss that threatened to swallow her whole if the tumult of her desires surged beyond her grasp. This sensation was unlike anything she had encountered before, a powerful force that both exhilarated and terrified her.

David was not merely another name; he was an intoxicating temptation that stirred a yearning deep within her soul. Rory, in stark contrast, felt like a safe harbour, a man who had gifted her a lifetime together. At the same time, David represented nothing more than the allure of a fleeting affair—a seductive whisper distracting her from the life she really craved.

Hugh had hit upon a truth: David Crowley wielded a magnetic charm that was uniquely his. There was no need for him to exert control; women gravitated toward him effortlessly, and he revelled in the attention. But beneath that veneer of allure lay the unsettling realization that with every flirtation, every enticing smile, there was a risk of losing herself entirely, caught in a web of desire that could unravel everything.

A wave of clarity washed over Rose, stirring turmoil within her. It wasn't David who sparked her distrust; it was the reflection of her insecurities that loomed large. Doubt gnawed at her, whispering that she was the one to be wary of, and deep down, she feared the shadows of her own heart more than the potential flaws of those around her.

With a fierce resolve, she crossed the threshold into the depot to be confronted by the men hard at work surrounding her. The air, heavy with the gritty aroma of engine oil entwined with the sharp sterility of antiseptic, enveloped her like a familiar shroud. It could have been Normandy, but here, the ghosts of smoke danced among the shadows while echoes of past journeys murmured age- old tales, each unspoken story weaving a rich tapestry of experience and emotion yet to unfold.

John Watkins stepped back from the engine he was diligently tending to, grease on his hands and a focused look on his face.

"Good morning, Boss," he greeted cheerfully, the sound of his voice cutting through the hum of machinery. "Good morning, John. I see you've immersed yourself in the motors again," Rose replied, a hint of warmth in her tone as she studied his committed demeanour.

"Absolutely. We have to ensure they're always in peak condition," he said. His pride in his work was evident as he wiped his brow with the back of his hand.

He gestured toward the office door. "Inside," John indicated, a slight nod revealing his understanding of the dynamics at play.

"Thank you. I'll catch up with you later," Rose replied, her voice laced with a confidence that surprised even her. As she made her way toward the office, a warm sense of tranquillity enveloped her; this was not merely a job; it felt like stepping into a long-lost home.

Hugh had an uncanny ability to soothe her

anxieties, dissipating the tempest of uncertainty that once clouded her thoughts. However, upon entering the office, she was greeted not by David, as she'd anticipated, but by an unfamiliar face—an elderly woman with kind eyes. "Good morning! You must be Rose Anderson, our new Head of Operations. Welcome to the depot!" The woman beamed, extending her hand in a warm handshake. "I'm Janice Stone, and I've been holding the fort until the transition is completed."

"It's a pleasure to meet you. Thank you! I'm genuinely thrilled to be here and eager to absorb everything I can today. How is the transition progressing?"

Janice checked her watch, her expression shifting to one of mild urgency. "That's precisely what we're doing today. There's a meeting scheduled with the Shire President and the lotteries. We have about thirty minutes; perhaps we can grab a quick coffee before heading over."

"I'm afraid I haven't had the chance to meet the Shire President yet," Rose admitted, her curiosity piqued.

Janice raised an eyebrow, a hint of amusement dancing in her eyes. "Of course, you have met him. It's David."

"David? Are there any positions he doesn't occupy in Midjal?" The words slipped from Rose's lips before she could rein them in.

"No," Janice responded. "Or at least none he has not held at some time."

They settled into the seats at the board table. The atmosphere pulsed with anticipation. David looked around, a familiar warmth in his eyes before he initiated the meeting. "Thank you all for coming today. Before we officially hand over the ambulance, I wanted to share a few thoughts. This moment signifies more than just a vehicle; it embodies the spirit of our community. Dr Holland, having you here to represent St John Ambulance is truly an honour."

Dr. Holland smiled, sensing the weight of the occasion. "Thank you. It's genuinely a privilege to stand with you today. Throughout my years working with various communities, I've witnessed the unbreakable thread of resilience that binds rural towns. Midjal's determination to secure this ambulance reflects an incredible collective spirit."

David nodded, his gaze sweeping across the faces gathered around him. "Indeed, it has been a true community endeavour. From our farmers offering support to families digging deep to contribute whatever they could, every hand played a crucial role. Thanks to the collaboration between St John and the Lotteries Commission, we are finally on the brink of enhancing emergency services here."

Major Hunt, with a sense of pride in his voice, added, "The Lotteries Commission is honoured to back this initiative. The commitment of Midjal's residents highlights just how much you value safety and well-being. It's a pleasure for us to be part of such an inspiring effort."

Dr. Holland interjected, "And let's not forget that this new ambulance equips your depot to respond faster to emergencies—especially in those hard-to-reach areas. Your volunteers will now be prepared to provide first aid swiftly, saving critical time before a hospital transfer can occur."

Janice's eyes gleamed with unbridled hope, reflecting the promise of a brighter future. "This is exactly what we need. We've persevered through the toughest of times with scant resources, but this ambulance signals the beginning of something monumental. Our team of passionate volunteers is itching for training, ready to leap into action. And I can't think of anyone better than Rose to lead us." She turned to include Rose in her fervent declaration, a silent solidarity bonding them.

"Rest easy, Rose," Dr. Holland said, his voice imbued with warmth and encouragement. "You won't be facing this challenge alone. St. John is committed to providing continuous support and training for your volunteers. The rugged terrain and expansive distances may seem daunting, yet your unwavering determination is nothing short of inspiring."

With a steadfast resolve in his voice, David interjected, "Thank you, Dr. Holland, and you as well, Major Hunt. We are wholeheartedly dedicated to making this endeavour successful for Midjal. Today isn't merely about receiving an ambulance; it's a profound affirmation of our commitment to each other's health and well-being." His words echoed with an intensity that filled the room, igniting a shared sense of purpose.

"Well expressed, David," Dr. Holland replied, his tone rich with appreciation. "Now, let's make this moment official."

"Excuse me for interrupting," David said, his enthusiasm palpable. "If it's alright, I'd prefer to do that at the depot; we've organized a reception for the volunteers."

"An excellent suggestion," Dr. Holland responded.

As they arrived at the depot, the sight that greeted them was warm and inviting: a table brimming with hearty country fare while the urn beside it gurgled delightedly, releasing the scent of fresh brew into the air.

"Thank you all for coming to witness the handover of our new ambulance," David addressed the crowd. His voice was steady though tinged with excitement. "Without further ado, I will now turn it over to Dr. Holland so we can wrap up these formalities before personally welcoming both Dr. Holland and Major Hunt."

He took a moment, smoothing the front of his

jacket, his eyes scanning the eager faces before him. "Thank you all for gathering. Let's get this part over with so I can truly enjoy the hospitality of your fine country," he said, a flicker of a smile breaking his formal demeanour. "On behalf of St John Ambulance, I am proud to present Midjal with this ambulance. May it shine as a beacon of hope and service in the years to come."

David stepped forward to accept the keys, a mixture of pride and anticipation coursing through him. "Thank you, Dr. Holland. I'm certain there isn't a person in this room who hasn't been eagerly waiting for this day." His heart swelled as the weight of the moment settled around them, binding them all in shared purpose and hope.

Formalities concluded, David ushered Rose into the company of Dr. Holland and Major Hunt, the weight of past shadows lingering in her heart.

"We were fortunate to have Rose join us. She served as a nurse during the Normandy campaign," David stated, pride lacing his tone.

"That must have been a truly harrowing experience," Dr. Holland remarked, his voice tinged with empathy.

At his words, Rose felt an involuntary shudder ripple through her as memories clawed their way to the surface—chaotic days spent amidst the screams and the relentless tide of blood, the faces of the lost still haunting her. "At times," she replied, her voice steadier than her thoughts. It was a struggle to keep the floodgates closed, memories she desperately wished to banish. "But I'd prefer if we focused on the future, specifically our new St. John's service in Midjal."

"I completely understand," Dr. Holland said softly, recognizing the walls she had erected. Far from being offended, they soon found themselves deep in discussion of the service and its benefits in rural areas, a favourite topic of Dr. Holland's.

Back home, Rose sat at the table, her gaze settled on the plate that Hugh had placed before her, a smile breaking across her face. "Hugh, you are a genius. I can't wait to devour every bite."

"Then do just that," Hugh chuckled, his warmth filling the air as Rose savoured her first mouthful, a satisfied murmur escaping her lips.

Rory, sitting nearby, leaned in slightly, his voice steady but laced with an undercurrent of concern. "How did the handover go?"

"It went well," Rose replied, her tone carrying a blend of cautious optimism and quiet pride. "After the formal meeting, we gathered at the depot for a more informal exchange. I had an extensive discussion with Dr. Holland. He possesses a visionary outlook for our service's future in rural areas. He's advocating for a network of rural depots, aiming to bridge the gap and ensure that critical ambulance services reach the remote towns—those places that have been all but forgotten by urgent medical assistance."

"Sounds like you have a daunting task ahead of you," Rory suggested, his protective instincts kicking in as he observed the tension that knitted Rose's brow. He could sense the tremor of uncertainty beneath her confident exterior, the weight of the responsibility already pressing heavily on her shoulders.

"Indeed, but I'll have substantial support from St. Johns," she replied, her voice steadier than she felt. The thought of tackling the needs of isolated communities stirred a mixture of excitement and apprehension within her. "Their backup and training are a bonus. He wants the most isolated communities to have people who can provide basic medical care until professional help arrives." Rose shifted her gaze, briefly lost in the vision of those communities, their faces reflecting both hope and desperation.

"He said a number of towns have them already, and they are working well," Hugh interjected as if to lift some of the turmoil swirling in her heart.

Rory studied her closely, acutely aware of the burden she carried. "What about the volunteers?" he asked, the concern lacing his tone intertwining with admiration for her courage.

"Yes, I'll be immersed in recruiting, training, and fundraising." Rose chuckled softly, a sound that felt almost foreign as it masked the creeping anxiety underlying her laughter. "Aunt Rosemary's expertise will prove invaluable." She remembered the faces of the devoted volunteers she had met that day, each one a testament to humanity's resilience, even as her heart ached with the gravity of what lay ahead.

"It takes a special kind of person to commit to that," Hugh remarked, his mind swirling with the harrowing realities those volunteers might face as visions of grizzly scenes danced uninvited across his thoughts.

Rory nodded in agreement, a solemnity settling between them. "Not something we all could do." His acknowledgment hung in the air, a silent understanding of the magnitude of her endeavour.

"No, but my job will entail a lot more on the organizational side," Rose replied, steeling herself against the wave of trepidation that threatened to drown her resolve. Determined to pivot the conversation, she asked, "How did you go about finding out about bringing Arthur and Guy home?" Her curiosity masked a flicker of anxiety, signalling her desire to delve into the familiar.

"There's not much progress to share," Rory said, a hint of frustration lacing his voice. "The government has decreed that soldiers won't be repatriated; instead, they are to be laid to rest in the very grounds where they fell."

Hugh's brow furrowed as he grasped the implication. "So, Albert and Guy will never even share the same cemetery," he interjected softly, his heart heavy at the thought of their separation, miles apart in different countries.

Rose's expression turned pained as she sought understanding. "Albert wasn't in your unit?" Rory shook his head, memories flickering in his eyes. "No, he deployed six months before Guy, and he fell in Italy."

"That's so unjust," Hugh responded, a simmering anger rising within him. "They should be together." The thought of the brothers being denied each other's company in death stung like a fresh wound. "We have to go to Perth and confront the military about this."

"Yes," Rory replied, his resolve hardening. "At least we'll know what we're facing."

Rose felt a warmth spread through her chest, a flicker of hope igniting within the group. They were united in purpose, ready to stand against the tide of bureaucracy in their fight for what was right.

CHAPTER 23 - RED TAPE

*In **1946, Australia**, continuing the tradition of memorializing loved ones with **ornate family plots and Celtic-inspired gravestones** carried deep significance, particularly among British and Irish immigrants. These traditions, rooted in the homeland, symbolized a **connection to ancestry**, respect for the deceased, and the preservation of cultural identity in a new land. Marking the sacrifices made in settling rural Australia.*

Aunt Rosemary

How time flies. Can you believe I have started at St John's already?

Christmas and New Year are gon15 Feb 1946

Dear e.

Rory and Hugh want to bring Albert and Guy home for burial, but the government has a ruling against it.

I went to Rory's mother's grave. Hugh has set up a plot for the Andersons, just like at Windermere Cemetery. He says this is where the next generations will be.

As they confronted the dilemma before them, the
emotional stakes rose palpably. The urgency of their
trip to Perth to liaise with the military weighed
heavily on Hugh, not only as a matter of duty but as
a means to secure their future. Yet, the reality of
leaving Rose without a means of transportation
loomed large, raising the stakes for her employment
and sense of independence.

"It is not just while we are away, but Rose needs
a vehicle to get to work." Rory pointed out.

Hugh, driven by a desire to find a solution,
suggested the reliability of a Holden, believing it
would serve them well in the long run. However,
Rose's practical mindset sparked a spirited debate;
she leaned toward the more economical choice of a
green Austin 8—its affordability at under three
hundred pounds was a compelling argument in a time
of financial uncertainty. Finally, they agreed to place
an order for the Austin with the local Midjal Motors.

"Listen, Hugh," Murray began, leaning against
the polished counter at Midjal Motors, his tone firm
yet understanding. "With the surge in demand after
the war, our inventory of new Austins is nearly
depleted. Delivery times are stretching out, with wait

periods now ranging from twelve to eighteen months, depending on what we can get shipped in."

Rory's brow furrowed in frustration. "Twelve to eighteen months? That's absurd! Is there anything else we can look at?" His impatience bubbled to the surface, reflecting the urgency of their need.

Murray paused, tapping a finger on the counter thoughtfully. "Actually, I just had a cancellation come through for a Ford Ute. Wouldn't be my first choice either, but it's available now."

Hugh crossed his arms, his expression hardening. "A Ford? Really, Murray? You know I'm a Holden man through and through. They're better vehicles, reliable for long hauls on the back roads." Rory, trying to keep the conversation flowing in a productive direction, weighed his options.

"What's the price of this Ford Ute? It might be worth considering," he asked, probing for details. Murray sighed, the weight of the dirt-covered roads and heavy machinery of the farm echoing in his voice. "It'll set you back five to six hundred dollars."

Hugh scoffed, shaking his head vehemently. "That's nearly double what we'd pay for an Austin! How can we afford to invest that much?"

Yet Rory interjected, his voice calm but resolute. "Dad, think about it. A Ute could really serve its purpose around the farm. We need something we can rely on for hauling supplies and maneuvering around those fields. It might even save us money in the long run."

Hugh stared out the dealership window, contemplating the prospect. "We'll think about it," he muttered, annoyed, as he turned to leave, a sense of defeat hanging in the air. That's a lot of money to consider." He left the office, leaving Rory standing facing the agent.

"Hold it. I will check the finances and confirm tomorrow." They shook hands on the arrangement. Rory was well aware he had to convince his father and find finance.

That night, as a gentle breeze rustled the leaves, Rory leaned against the balcony railing, his eyes fixed on the distant horizon. He turned to Rose, the weight of his following words evident in his tone. "I've put a hold on the ute," he revealed, the practical advantages of the vehicle hanging heavily in the air between them. "It'll serve us well on the farm and also on the road. Dad's Holden will be just for trips into town."

Rose, eager to absorb everything about the life that awaited her on the farm, furrowed her brow. "What about the jeep? Can't we use that?"

Rory shook his head, his voice steady and firm. "No, we can't drive it on public roads; it isn't licensed."

"Then the ute seems essential," Rose affirmed, understanding the dual purpose it would fulfil.

Rory contemplated their financial situation for a

moment, then added, "I think we can manage the financing—if we squeeze it a bit."

"How much are we talking about?" Rose pressed, her curiosity piqued by the intricacies of their budding partnership.

"Five hundred and fifty," he replied, watching her process the amount.

After a brief hesitation, she realised she could pay for it. Then Rose realised a handout was not what Rory needed. Arranging the finances was far more critical; it was a challenge Rory needed. "What are our chances?"

Rory contemplated her question. "Yes and no. We Andersons might seem well-off with our grand mansion, but we're always a bit cash-strapped."

"I know you can do it." She laughed.

"Let them know about my wage." Rory's eyebrows lifted, a playful smirk forming on his lips. "You can bet on it, Mrs. Anderson."

"But somehow, I think it will be yours." she shot back, playful defiance shining in her eyes.

The conversation uncovered the complexities of their backgrounds—Rory felt a strong sense of responsibility due to his family's financial struggles, while Rose understood the significance of their current situation. Their motivations intertwined, setting the stage for the journey they were about to undertake together.

"It's in Perth, so Dad and I can pick it up when

we are there to see the military about Abert and Guy."

It took some convincing, Hugh, but finally, they agreed to add picking up when they were in Perth after the meeting with the military.

"I am sorry, Rory, but we have strict rules regarding the repatriation of bodies," the Sergeant began, his voice heavy with the weight of countless similar conversations. "No, Australian families can bring their soldiers' bodies back. The Australian government has determined that the remains of military personnel who died overseas will be interred in Commonwealth War Graves located in the countries where they fell." Rory's eyes widened in disbelief and sorrow, searching the Sergeant's face for any trace of leniency or understanding. But the Sergeant's expression remained resolute, though a glimmer of empathy broke his otherwise stern facade.

"The practical challenges of repatriation," he continued, his voice softening as he acknowledged Rory's visible anguish, "such as transportation costs and the logistics of moving so many bodies across the world, influenced this decision. Instead, soldiers are to be buried in cemeteries managed by the Commonwealth War Graves Commission."

"They deserve to be home," Rory uttered, almost to himself, his voice cracking under the strain of unshed grief. The Sergeant nodded, knowing that no words could genuinely ease the deep pain felt by families who had sacrificed so much.

"I comprehend your emotions, but this is the decision made by the Government," he explained softly, sensing the weight of Rory's distress.

"Then the Government is mistaken. My sons, our dutiful sons, were taken from us, and now we are denied the right to bring them home," Hugh's voice trembled with grief and anger, his eyes pleading for understanding.

"I realise this feels deeply unjust," he responded, his tone carrying a finality that seemed to close the door on further debate yet revealing a hint of regret.

"Feel deeply!" Rory yelled, his anger boiling over. "You took us, killed us in this horrific war. I want my brother home."

Hugh placed a calming hand on Rory's arm. "We will fight this, Rory. I promise you." Then he turned to address the officer. "The government has turned its back on its soldiers. You will hear from us."

He guided Rory out of the room.

The officer tailed them. "There have been instances where Australian soldiers have been repatriated," he said, his concern evident."

Hugh faced him. "What action do we need to take?"

The officer took a deep breath. "Some families launched long-term campaigns, lobbying government officials, seeking media attention, and garnering community support. Occasionally, these efforts resulted in the return of their loved ones' remains."

"And?" Hugh prodded. "Families often found greater solace if their soldier was interred in a local civilian cemetery rather than an official war grave," the officer clarified. "Though it was infrequent, it occurred when townspeople took it upon themselves to lay a soldier to rest instead of having the body moved to a formal burial site."

Hugh pressed his lips into a tight, grateful smile as he respectfully nodded to the officer. "Thank you," he said, his voice strained with the weight of the evening's events.

Glancing over at his son, who stood a few paces away with wide, weary eyes, Hugh felt a surge of urgency. The boy's small hand was clutching a threadbare stuffed toy, his innocent face marred by shadows of fatigue and confusion. "I need to get my son home."

"Well, come on, let's pick that ute up. It's yours so that you can drive it home."

As Rory glided into the driveway, the sight of Rose elegantly perched on the balcony ignited a rush of warmth in his chest. The drive home had enveloped him in an uplifting buoyancy, a delightful energy that clung to him like a second skin.

With a smile dancing on his lips, he swung the car door open for her as if unveiling a treasure. "It's spacious," he announced with a note of vitality, his voice shimmering with joy. Although Rose didn't share the same enthusiasm for cars, the effervescence radiating from Rory wrapped around her, allowing her to feel the sheer delight that this vehicle brought him.

Sliding into the plush leather seat beside her, he sank back, savouring the luxurious embrace of the interior. "I can stretch my legs out—what a bonus!" His fingers instinctively curled around the polished steering wheel, igniting a glowing warmth within him. "And look how easy it is to read the dash," he said, eyes sparkling as he gestured toward the gleaming controls, his excitement bubbling to the surface. "The steering wheel feels solid, a steadfast companion ready to tackle whatever the road throws our way." Turning to Rose, he nodded toward the spacious tray in the back, his enthusiasm infectious. "And this tray? It'll carry everything we need, saving us precious time, just like our adventures together."

A smile danced across Rose's face as she saw his infectious joy; he was captivated by his new acquisition. "Is this your first car?" she asked, a teasing glint in her eye.

He cast her a sideways glance, a smirk playing on his lips.

"Thought as much," she chuckled, but beneath their laughter lingered an unspoken truth—a bittersweet acknowledgment of the joys the war had robbed them of.

"Home, let me make us some tea. Your dad should be along any moment now," Rose gently urged, her voice warm with encouragement.

"Before that, I need to see how Finn is doing. I'll be back in a bit," he replied, a grin on his face.

Rose watched the dust rising as he drove towards the paddock. He most likely wanted to show it to Finn.

Rose stood on the veranda, her heart racing as she watched Hugh pull into the drive. Getting out, he made his way across the yard, each step laden with unspoken tension. The roar of the ute's engine echoed in her mind, a stark reminder of Rory's Departure, the dust trailing behind him like a fleeting memory.

As Hugh approached, his footsteps were soft yet deliberate, a stark contrast to his normal jaunty ones. Her gaze remained fixed on the receding vehicle, an overwhelming sense of loss washing over her. "It didn't do well," she murmured, her voice trembling with emotion. A tight knot of regret and worry coiled within her, threatening to spill over.

"No," Hugh replied, his voice steady yet coloured with an undercurrent of determination. "Let Rory work it off." Despite his attempt to sound calm, the flicker of anxiety in his eyes betrayed his true feelings.

"Don't fret about Rory. He has a new toy," Rose

quipped, her laughter mingling with the settling dust from the departing ute.

A smile broke across Hugh's face. "I forgot he's never had a car of his own," he chuckled.

"That's more like it; I prefer the jovial Hugh," Rose retorted. "You remind us that life is meant to be enjoyed and that nothing is insurmountable."

Hugh enveloped her in a fatherly embrace. "Thank you, Rose. With you by our side, I believe we can mend this family."

The discussion was left until all three sat together around the dinner table; a heavy pallor hung in the air, reflecting the weight of their conversation. The outcome of the meeting loomed over them like a storm cloud, casting shadows on their already fragile hearts.

Hugh's stark and unyielding voice broke the silence. "They don't have legislation stopping the repatriation of bodies; it is only an agreement between the commonwealth countries." The bluntness of his statement struck Rose like a cold gust of wind, sending a shiver down her spine.

"How can we fight this?" she asked, her voice barely above a whisper, as the depths of her concern seeped into the room.

"Some families have launched long-term campaigns," Hugh explained, tracing the contours of his grief with every word. "They lobby government officials, seek media attention, and muster community support. Occasionally, these efforts bore fruit, resulting in the return of their loved ones."

At that moment, Rose's eyes flickered with a glimmer of hope—a slight reprieve amidst the despair. "It has been done then," she murmured. "That is good."

Yet Rory's response was a blaze of determination that caught her off guard. "Yes, it will be a battle." His fierce resolve, shaped by personal loss and the promise he made to those he loved, resonated deeply within her. Her heart raced as she realised what he was willing to risk. "But we will get them back," he asserted, his voice imbued with an intensity that mirrored the urgency of his commitment.

Rose's heart ached with the enormity of Rory's mission. It wasn't merely a battle; it was a harrowing quest to reclaim fragments of their spirits, parts of themselves that the cruel hands of fate had wrenched away. She shivered at the thought that failure would not only mean losing cherished family and friends but would also cast Rory into a chasm of despair, one so deep and consuming that he might never find his way back to her. The very thought of him enveloped in that darkness ripped at her insides, igniting a fierce determination within her to ensure he emerged victorious.

"Where do we start?" Hugh asked, his furrowed brow hinting at the toll this impending battle was taking on him as well.

In that moment of shared resolve, they embraced the idea of an all-out attack; it was the only path they could conceive to secure not just their loved ones but also any semblance of peace amidst their raging turmoil. Together, they readied themselves for the fight ahead, stealing their hearts.

The first significant breakthrough occurred when Rory reached out to Noel, driven by his relentless ambition and unyielding dedication to his craft. Noel's remarkable talent in photography earned him a coveted position at the prestigious Melbourne Age, where every snapshot he took told a compelling story.

Despite the competitive nature of journalism, Noel's motivation was unwavering as he meticulously investigated potential avenues to publish an article.

Harnessing his network from college connections, Noel deftly maneuvered through the media landscape, ultimately securing valuable coverage in the West Australian Newspaper. Each step he took was motivated by a desire to create a significant impact.

Rose pondered what they must do to ensure the boys could come home. Winning approval would not be easy.

When David Crowley first saw Rose at the depot, an electric tension sizzled in the air, a brewing storm hidden deep in her gaze—an unsettling distraction that suggested layers beneath her weary exterior.

"Rose, you seem down," he remarked, his voice wrapped in a gentle timbre imbued with a palpable concern that made the space between them thrum with unspoken understanding.

"Yes, a bit," she replied, the corners of her lips attempting a smile, but the effort crumbled, betraying the storm of emotions roiling inside her. She knew the battle ahead was a hard one, but one that they had to win.

"Is there anything I can help with?" David asked, his gaze unwavering, keen as a hawk, sensing that her sorrow was merely a thin veil draped over a much more formidable struggle.

"Yes," Rose said, her voice trembling slightly as the words tumbled forth. "Rory wants to bring his brother's bodies back to Midjal. They spoke to the military, but in Australia, the policy is to leave soldiers where they fell. It is not a formal decree but a fragile consensus among Commonwealth nations." She paused, her eyes glistening with unshed tears, conjuring images of her lost loved ones. "This means Rory's brothers lie not only miles from home but alone, scattered across different countries."

David's brow creased as empathy washed over him, his chest tightening with the weight of her revelation. He recalled the deep scars etched into the Anderson family, their sorrow a heavy cloak they wore for far too long. The yearning for closure, for families to be reunited with their cherished ones, tugged insistently at his heart, a relentless pull that would not let go.

"That hardly seems fair," he mused after a moment, a sense of determination sharpening his voice, cutting through the heavy air. "Let me see what I can do." His words transcended mere promises; they became a solemn oath infused with a fierce sense of justice and compassion that enveloped the room like the warmth of a flickering flame in the dark.

A mix of gratitude and embarrassment washed over her as she remembered the conversation with Rory. It was only thanks to Hugh that she had come face-to-face with the real David Crowley—the man whom the town of Midjal had come to revere. Here stood a man who was not just a figurehead but genuinely invested in their struggle, exuding the same passion for their cause as he did in all his endeavours. David Crowley, the very individual she had started to admire deeply, was more than just an advocate; he was the living, breathing representation of the unity they yearned for in their fight for justice.

Hugh also worked with meticulous focus, digging through his acquaintances for people whose assistance he may be able to convert to their cause. His determination was palpable. Each detail he unearthed seemed to build an unshakeable foundation for their hopes, connecting them even more to their struggle. After some thought, he concluded that the most influential work would take place in Perth.

"I can discuss things in person," he mused, "Far better than through a letter that goes unread." This revelation took both Rose and Rory by surprise.

"Who exactly are you planning to talk to?" Rose asked, her curiosity piqued.

Hugh smiled, a glimmer of hope in his eyes. "An old friend of mine is in town—someone who has come through for us before. It's the perfect opportunity to reconnect and see what we can accomplish together."

Rose looked at him sceptically. He was up to something.

CHAPTER 24 - THE ACCIDENT

*In **rural Australia**, the **grain silo** has been a vital structure since the early 20th century, playing a crucial role in **storing and preserving wheat** for domestic use and export. By 1946, as Australia recovered from WWII, silos symbolized **agricultural resilience and economic stability**, ensuring efficient grain storage before transport to markets. These structures became community landmarks, central to **harvest logistics, rural employment, and the expansion of Australia's wheat industry** in the post-war era.*

With a sense of accomplishment washing over her, Rose gazed across the desk, feeling a growing confidence in her abilities. The transition from nursing to a coordinator role at St John's had been daunting, yet her struggles were gradually transforming into a source of pride. Embracing the challenges tested her resilience and ignited a passion within her, deepening her connection to her work and the lives she touched.

A sharp knock resonated through the room, pulling Rose's attention.

John slipped his head in, his expression taut with urgency. "I just got off the line with David's place," he said, breath hitching slightly. "There's been a silo accident—one of the contractor's kids. James isn't here yet." He gestured as if to highlight the growing concern in his eyes.

"I'm coming with you," she declared, the words spilling forth with an instinctual determination that surprised even herself. A sense of responsibility ignited within her, overshadowing any hesitation.

"Who's going to handle the depot while we're gone?" he countered, his voice laced with worry, the weight of their shared duties evident in his furrowed brow.

"I'll call Janice," she replied, her fingers already reaching for the phone, the resolve in her voice firm. The need to understand their work, to delve into the realities they faced beyond their office walls, surged within her like a tidal wave. She knew this was a chance to confront the truths of their world. A brief conversation flashed by, "She will cover the depot." Resolved, they were in the ambulance and on their way.

John pressed down on the accelerator, urgency spiking in his veins. Each passing second stretched into an agonizing eternity as he battled against the relentless tick of the clock, knowing the journey before him was a gruelling thirty minutes that felt like a lifetime.

Upon their arrival at the silo, an unsettling stillness descended, wrapping the area in an almost tangible cloak of silence. The men remained motionless, their rigid postures and downcast eyes betraying the weight of their unuttered fears.

"We're too late," Rose breathed, her voice a fragile shard piercing the thick, oppressive air surrounding them.

"Seems that way," John murmured, his words laced with a heavy sense of defeat, each syllable hanging in the cool breeze like a mournful echo.

"This is all too familiar for me," Rose said, her eyes glazed over. She stared into the abyss of her memories as if peering through a fogged window into a past she wished to forget.

It still struck Rose with an agonizing jolt, a brutal twist of fate that seemed almost surreal. A boy, no more than six, with wide eyes that had gleamed with innocence and joy, now lifeless. She could picture him perched atop the aged wooden beams of the silo, his small frame silhouetted against the vast sky, as he watched his father's toil with innocent amazement. That moment of blissful observation he had quickly turned into a harrowing nightmare—a swift descent into suffocating grain, where laughter vanished, replaced by silence.

Her heart ached for the father, who sat there in stunned disbelief, clutching his son's still body as if holding on to the last shreds of a fleeting dream. Rose approached him slowly, the weight of despair settling heavily on her chest. She wrapped her arm around his trembling shoulders, feeling the shivers of anguish ripple through him as he rocked back and forth, lost in a storm of sorrow.

Tears stung Rose's eyes, threatening to spill over, but she fought to contain them. The scent of fresh wheat mingled with the bitter tang of grief, overwhelming her senses. Memories surged forth, unbidden—the countless faces of children she had cradled during her time in London, their laughter silenced by the horrors of war. The pang of recollection cut deep, pulling her back to those frantic days spent racing against time, where hope was often a fleeting shadow, and the sound of doomed cries still echoed in her mind.

"Rose, we must return the ambulance," John urged, gently tapping her shoulder.

But Rose was lost in her resolve and shook her head slightly. "Just a moment," she murmured, the weight of the boy's life pressing heavily on her heart. Though powerless to save him, she recognized the profound need to offer solace to the father who stood at the precipice of despair.

At last, her voice broke the thick silence. "Would you like me to take him?" Rose offered to hold the little boy's body.

He offered no reply, his head shaking gently, a movement heavy with unspoken sorrow.

"Perhaps you'd prefer to board the ambulance," she continued softly, "that way, you can cradle him on the journey back to Madjal."

This time, he stood unmoving, tears tracing silently down his cheeks. Clutching the boy close, he began his slow, deliberate march toward the ambulance. It was a scene seared into Rose's memory, one she knew would never fade.

She assisted him into the back of the vehicle, gesturing toward a seat. "But if you wish, you may lie with him in your arms," she suggested, nodding towards the cot.

"Yes," he replied, a simple word steeped in longing.

"Do you want me to stay, or would you prefer to be alone with him?"

"Stay. I need your strength," came his answer, raw and earnest.

"Of course," she said. "I will do whatever I can— no matter how small." As she turned to John to close the door, her gaze caught a glimpse of David overhead. A deep, haunting sadness lingered there, a shadow that would also shade his heart.

As they returned the ambulance to the depot, Janice stepped forward, her warm demeanour cutting through the heavy air. A sense of finality hung around them, and the gravity of the situation settled like a dark cloud.

"He did not make it," John whispered, his voice

barely rising above the station's hum. The words felt like stones dropped into a still pond, sending ripples of despair through the room. "He was gone before we even arrived."

They sank into the familiar comfort of the staff lounge, the weight of their shared grief palpable. The ceiling loomed overhead as Rose reclined, her heart aching as she broke the silence. "If only we hadn't taken so long to get there…" Her voice trailed off, thick with emotion, each word a reminder of the urgency they had faced.

Janice interjected softly, her eyes reflecting the pain etched in their expressions. "That's one thing we can't overcome." The heaviness of her statement resonated with the others, drawing them into a contemplative silence. "I gathered that little Tom's chances were slim, even if you'd arrived sooner."

Rose nodded, a tumult of regret and frustration swirling inside her. It was a constant struggle within her mind—a battle between what was and what could have been. Yet amidst the sorrow, she clung to a flicker of resolve. They had to look at the bigger picture. "We need to learn from this," she said, her voice steadier now, a determination brewing beneath her grief. "Something good has to come from little Tom's death."

"Yes, but not today," Janice said thoughtfully, her voice tinged with concern. She paused, her mind racing as she considered the turmoil swirling around them. "The emotions are too high right now. It would help if you had time to process everything," she added, feeling the weight of their shared trauma pressing heavily on her chest. Memories of their ordeal flooded her thoughts, amplifying her empathy and her desire to shield her friend from further pain.

Rose was trapped in an endless loop of memories, each replay more haunting than the last. The weight of the tragedy pressed heavily on her heart; a child should not have had to endure such an end.

But in the wake of this calamity, someone had to bear the blame, and instinctively, she realized his father would be consumed by guilt, forever questioning his own choices. Should little Tom have ventured near the silo? Was it wise to let him ascend to such dangerous heights? Could they have saved him when they pulled him from the wheat? Each question echoed relentlessly in her mind, a haunting refrain of decisions made and missed opportunities.

But she also knew that wallowing in regret was a futile endeavour; it could never bring back the light that was lost. Yet perhaps this heartbreak could serve as a stark lesson for other families—a brutal reminder of the fragility of life and the importance of vigilance. Even in her sorrow, Rose clung to the hope that such a lesson could prevent further tragedies, illuminating the path for others to tread more carefully in the shadows of consequence.

Though it extended beyond her official duties at St John's, she recognized the absence of a grief counsellor in Midjal. Despite lacking formal training, she wanted to make a difference. One casualty was already too many. Perhaps her efforts, however unpolished, could provide solace to him in his time of need.

There was so much more she could do. While St. John Ambulance was an essential initial step, it was only the beginning. She recognized the pressing need for various services tailored to the unique challenges faced by residents in remote rural areas. These included grief counselling to support those coping with loss and specialized programs for mothers and babies. Additionally, she could implement training initiatives that utilized lessons, informative pamphlets, and radio broadcasts.

Perched on the balcony, Rose grappled with the weight of her day as she confided in Rory. "We couldn't do anything for little Tom; he was already lost to us," she murmured, deliberately sidestepping the harshness of the word "dead." A shroud of sorrow enveloped her, but she clung to the fragile hope that his passing could herald a greater purpose—that his short life could resonate in the lives he might yet save.

Rory pushed away from the balcony post, his brow furrowing with concern. "Yes, my thoughts drift toward Don Marshall."

Rose felt a shift within her; the man she had comforted now wore a name, a life beyond being little Tom's father. Her heart ached with the realization that Don was someone in desperate need of support, an echo of shared grief.

"Midjal is in dire need of more health services," Rose declared, a hint of urgency lacing her voice. "This accident should never have occurred; it serves as a stark reminder that we must raise awareness about the lurking dangers."

Rory's expression softened as memories flooded back, igniting a nostalgic spark in his eyes. "Most children spend their days out in the paddocks with their fathers. I did, too, but even more so alongside my mother." A grin broke across his face as he recalled the sun-drenched afternoons in the paddocks, chasing after her, feeding the animals, and riding together on the tractor. "It's how we connect," he added with a heartfelt emphasis. "It's why we cherish this land."

Rose pondered his words, her brow furrowed in thought. "Indeed, you have a point," she replied slowly, each word weighing with significance. "But we have to remain vigilant about the risks involved. It's not about hindering those moments of connection; rather, it's about staying aware." She paused for a moment, letting her thoughts crystallize. "Sometimes, the ordinary blinds us, and we overlook the perils surrounding us."

Rory nodded, recognizing the wisdom in her reflection. "Yes, you are right."

As Rose sat at her desk, she meticulously outlined her priorities—first on her list was reaching out to Don Marshall, who desperately needed support.

John had supplied her with Don's address and painted a picture of the man and his family. Don, a dedicated worker and a beloved figure in his community, was also a fierce fighter against life's adversities. His four children, the oldest merely eight years old, now faced the weight of despair following the recent loss of young Tom, a tragedy that would inevitably stretch the family's resilience to its limits.

When Rose arrived at Don's home, a wave of hesitation washed over her as she struggled to compose her thoughts on how best to engage with the grieving family. Would they be open to her presence, or would her visit be seen as unwelcome?

The house loomed before her, shrouded in shadows, its old lounge languishing on the front veranda, while a sturdy shed stood in the backyard, somehow more robust than the fading structure of their home. The contrast reflected the burdens the family carried, a visual testament to their struggles and the emotional turmoil that lay within.

She rapped softly on the door, the sound echoing her anxious heartbeat. From within, she could detect a scuttling noise, a rustle of movement before the door creaked open to reveal a small girl, her delicate features framed by wild, dark curls. Concern flickered across her innocent face.

"Is Daddy home?" Rose asked, her voice steady despite the unease settling in her stomach.

The girl shook her head slowly.

"What about Mummy?" Rose pressed, her heart aching at the thought of the sorrow that must be woven through this household.

"Who is it?" a voice called from inside, tinged with weariness.

"Rose Anderson," she replied, the words tumbling out before she could hold them back. "I was the ambulance driver who attended your son. I'm just checking to see if there's anything I can do." The statement felt inadequate, almost clumsy, but it had the desired effect; the door widened slightly.

On the threshold stood a woman, perhaps in her mid-twenties, yet her face bore the weight of countless burdens, age etched into every line of her harrowed expression. Life had clearly carved deep scars into her spirit.

"No," the woman murmured, her cheeks glistening with unshed tears, a silent testament to her struggle.

Stricken by the palpable pain radiating from her, Rose instinctively reached out her hand, a gentle gesture of solidarity. "Let me help. How about I make you a cup of tea?" she offered, the warmth of her voice a fragile thread woven through the heavy atmosphere.

The woman was about to reject her, when a voice from behind. "Let her in, Shirley."

Rose turned, her heart quickening at the sight of Don Marshall. Just yesterday, he had loomed large in her mind, a bastion of confidence amid a swirling storm of grief. But today, he appeared diminished, as if the tragedy had siphoned away not only his spirit but also the very essence of his being. The weight of loss was etched into his features, and the fragility of his mental state was laid bare before her.

"Good morning, Rose," he said, his voice faltering. Each syllable was a testament to the turmoil roiling within him. She caught a glimpse of the turmoil in his eyes, a haunting reflection of the sorrow that enveloped him.

"I just came to see how you were coping," she ventured, her concern genuine yet underscored by a sharp tug of her unease. She felt a swell of empathy, knowing that beneath his resilient façade lay a tapestry of heartache, the threads of which were unravelling painfully.

"Thank you," he replied, the words barely escaping his lips—a dry, monotone acknowledgement that conveyed a deep well of emotion left unaddressed. It reminded her of the arid landscape left in the wake of a storm; everything was scorched and desolate. Rose could almost feel her own heart aching in response to his, wishing desperately to bridge the chasm of grief that had opened between them.

"Rose." The sound of her name cut through the silence like a whisper of a fading storm. Both she and Don turned instinctively to find David approaching—his presence a beacon of familiarity amidst the uncertainty that hung in the air like a thick fog.

"Don." David extended his hand, an invitation wrapped in unspoken comfort. Don accepted the gesture, the movement so automatic that it bypassed conscious thought. "Is there anything we can do for Shirley and you?" His gaze drifted toward Shirley, seeking her in this moment of shared struggle.

Rose stepped back, her heart thrumming in her chest as she observed. This was territory David had travelled many times before; he was their stalwart friend, while she felt like an outsider, a mere shadow in the warm glow of their camaraderie.

"We are coping as best we can," Shirley replied, a flicker of light igniting in her eyes at the sight of David. His arrival was a balm, easing the raw edges of their grief, and Rose could sense how much he meant to them and how deeply rooted their connection was.

"Then we will leave you, but remember, both Rose and I are available to help in any way we can." David's voice was steady, a lifeline thrown into turbulent waters.

As they moved toward their cars, Rose couldn't shake the feeling of unease that settled in her stomach. Turning to David, he glanced back, the weight of their shared experience lingering between them. "I will meet you at the depot," he said with a nod before taking his leave.

Driving back, every mile stretched out in front of her like a question mark. Rose's mind spun—had her earlier actions inadvertently offended him? The thought gnawed at her, intertwining with the worry that perhaps she had stepped too far into a world where she didn't fully belong.

At the depot, they cradled steaming cups of coffee, the aroma mingling with the cool morning air.

"I wish to do more," Rose began, her voice steady yet laced with the undercurrent of her unspoken fears. "St. Johns is just the beginning. It's not only for the Marshalls; it's for everyone in Midjal." She met David's gaze, her own eyes reflecting a resolve she didn't entirely feel. "There's an array of services we desperately need. I know these can not be fully provided, but by raising awareness and empowering the community, we can learn to cover the gap ourselves."

David tilted his head, curiosity mingling with scepticism. "How do you plan to achieve that?" His expression was thoughtful, an unspoken challenge lurking beneath his words.

"I need a radio spot," she declared, her determination crystal clear. Then, I can reach more people both for training and provide answers for any questions they need answering." She paused before adding, " I don't know all the answers, but I will find them."

David's eyebrow arched, a mix of surprise and admiration crossing his features, a grin breaking through the tension.

As John leaned against the doorframe, he couldn't help but break the silence. "It seems we've stumbled upon Midjal's interpretation of Florence Nightingale."

David chuckled in response, his eyes sparkling with amusement. "You hit the nail on the head, John. That would be none other than Rose Anderson."

CHAPTER 25 - A VISITOR

In 1946, Aunt Rosemary joined Rose. Joining the farming community in rural Western Australia. With determination and a pioneering spirit, they embraced the harsh yet rewarding life, working the land, tending livestock, and becoming part of a close-knit community. Through seasons of drought and prosperity, they built a legacy rooted in hard work, perseverance, and a deep connection to the rugged beauty of the Australian countryside.

As Rose pulled into the driveway, a wave of emotion washed over her—Hugh had returned.

He stood on the veranda, framed by the soft golden light of the setting sun.

"How was Perth?" she asked, ascending the steps.

"All went to plan," he replied, a broad grin lighting up his face, his eyes crinkling with delight.

"I can tell you're up to something," Rose teased, catching the glint of mischief in his gaze.

He laughed, a sound like tinkling chimes. "Then you'd better come inside and find out."

Entering Windamere, the ornate woodwork and faint scent of aged books wrapped around her. She inhaled deeply—the house always welcomed her home.

Rose caught sight of the unexpected visitor sitting in the lounge.

"Aunt Rosemary!" Rose exclaimed, her face illuminating with pure joy. "I can hardly believe you are here to see me!"

"Of course, my dear," Aunt Rosemary replied, her eyes shining warmly. "Your letters were so deeply moving; I simply had to experience your journey in person."

Rose's laughter filled the air, rich with warmth and unbridled freedom. This reunion felt different from before. Then, their embraces were drenched in tears; now, it was a swift, joyful hug followed by a tender kiss on her cheek.

Rose's keen observation noted the change in her Aunt. "You had a stroke!"

"Indeed, I did." Aunt Rosemary responded. Her voice had changed now slower and with the slightest slur.

"And you came all this way alone?" Rose gasped.

"No, with Emily's assistance." Rose searched the room for her. "She's in the kitchen preparing tea for us," Aunt Rosemary added. "Emily is a relative of Carol's who views this as quite the adventure."

"Indeed, I do," Emily declared, expertly

balancing a tray in her slender hand. Rose's gaze drew upward to meet the vibrant eyes of a girl with curly ginger hair and an exuberant smile that could light up the room. At first glance, Emily appeared so youthful that it struck Rose; then, with a pang of realization, she noted that the girl was likely only a few years her junior.

"Welcome, Emily," Rose said, her voice tinged with a subtle unease as she measured her Aunt Rosemary's choice of companion for such a lengthy journey.

A tumult of emotions swirled within her, and she felt a pang of resentment—indeed, it should be her caring for her aging Aunt, not Emily. Yet, Rose grappled with her ambitions, yearning for the opportunity to forge her path amidst the swirling dynamics of duty and desire. She had already started on a new path.

"Alright, who would like some tea?" Emily chirped, raising the teapot high, embodying a warmth that momentarily dulled Rose's uncertainties.

"I would love a beer?" Hugh inquired, a playful smirk dancing across his lips, his eyes twinkling with mischief.

"Hugh!" Aunt Rosemary chided gently, her voice laced with mock disapproval. Yet, as if a switch had flipped, her stern demeanour softened into a warm smile as she shifted her gaze to Emily. "Why don't you fetch him one? I have no doubt he has a hidden stash tucked away in the fridge," she instructed, her tone now playful before turning back to Hugh with an eyebrow arched mischievously. "Some things, it seems, never change."

Hugh let out a low chuckle, resonating with familiarity and comfort. "Never," he replied, the warmth of shared history flooding the space between them.

Rose absorbed the conversation as if the years between them had evaporated. This moment felt like a glimpse into a reality that might have been had it not been for the weight of Rosemary's father's Decree. They would have shared countless years in that alternate life, free from the shadow of his ruling. Without the Decree, there would have been no Rory, and without Aunt Rosemary's nurturing presence, where would she have found her compass?

They looked out the window as the distinctive sound of crunching gravel heralded the arrival of a vehicle. A flutter of anticipation stirred within Rose as she recognized it. "It is David," she called out, rising to meet him, her heart quickening at the sight of him.

On the veranda, their eyes met, and she sensed the warmth of his presence. "I came to give you the name to contact at the radio station in Bellara. Most of us listen to it. Contact Ray Ingram at 6MD," he said, his voice steady, yet there was an underlying tension that Rose could not ignore.

"Thank you," she replied, smiling, but her mind raced with thoughts of how to bridge the distance that seemed to grow between them. "Would you like to come inside? My Aunt has just arrived from England." Her offer was born from a desire to extend their time together, to share in the joy of reunion, yet she felt an unspoken heaviness in the air.

David shook his head slowly, the refusal a small dagger to her hopes. "Another time. I promised Mary I would be home for tea." He squeezed her arm reassuringly, but that brief contact sent a ripple of emotion through her—an intense mix of longing and regret. "Good luck," he added, his tone softening.

But then, as if sensing a shift in the atmosphere, David's gaze froze, and she followed his line of sight to see Rory standing at the far end of the veranda. His hands were planted firmly on his hips, a storm brewing in his expression. At that moment, a pang of fear gripped her; she could feel the tension tightening around them.

David glanced at her, and she caught a fleeting glimpse of his anguish, which only deepened her own. "I will be off," he stated, his posture straightening as he turned away, a silent act of defiance as he walked back to his car. He was not fleeing the altercation, preferring to save Rose the embarrassment. But Rose was left standing, her heart heavy with unexpressed words and the stark reality of the churning emotions surrounding them.

Rose advanced along the veranda. Fury was evident in her posture. "How dare you," she stated, her voice sharp.

Rory stood firm, defiance clear on his face. "How long has this been going on?" he retorted, anger simmering in his tone.

"This is about David and me working together. Don't insinuate anything else!" Rose stepped closer, their bodies inches apart as they locked eyes. "You owe him an apology," she demanded, a protector's authority in her voice.

For a brief moment, Rory hesitated, taken aback by her intensity. Yet, pride reasserted itself. "He has a history, and everyone knows that," he replied, the words heavy in the air.

"That was years ago when he was still young. He's not that person anymore," Rose shot back, her disdain unmistakable. Rory's stance was a direct challenge to her respect for David — a respected member of their community. "You've insulted not just a friend but someone who means a lot to us," she asserted, barely containing her frustration.

Taking a breath, she added, "Go shower and cool down. Aunt Rosemary has arrived." With that, she turned on her heel, determined to maintain her composure. As she strode toward the front door, she cast a final look over her shoulder, leaving Rory to contend with the tension between them.

After a frosty tea, Rosemary and Hugh retired to

the wicker chairs on the veranda, their eyes sweeping over the sprawling estate. The sun beating on dry land, the gums drooping in the heat, was so vast it made you blink.

"Your Windamere is truly enchanting, Hugh. You possess everything my father once claimed you would never achieve," Rosemary remarked, her voice laced with admiration and a tinge of disbelief.

"That was the goal," Hugh replied, his tone tinged with a hint of regret. "Yet, it hasn't unfolded quite as we imagined."

"No, indeed. Those were remarkable times, moments woven into the very fabric of my being, keeping me afloat during my darkest days," Rosemary reflected, her thoughts meandering back to a distant past when they were so in love.

"The finest moments," Hugh agreed, a softness entering his voice. "Who could have predicted that your niece and my son would tie the knot?"

Rosemary chuckled, the laughter dancing in her eyes. "Not even in our wildest dreams could we have envisioned that!"

"I've taken to calling her Windemere's Rose because she has revitalized this place with her spirit," Hugh said, a proud smile gracing his lips.

"My little girl has transformed so beautifully. This place has been a blessing for her," Aunt Rosemary said gently, her gaze shimmering with pride and affection.

Hugh laughed heartily, agreement evident in his mirth. "Indeed, she has truly flourished here."

Aunt Rosemary's smile widened, radiating pure joy. "Yes, it's palpable in her every movement. She walks with a newfound confidence, a trait she often struggled to embody. My little Rose no longer requires my counsel," she murmured, nostalgia tinging her words as she savoured the bittersweet passage of time.

While upstairs on the balcony, Rose sat stiffly on the lounge, her anger simmering just beneath the surface. The sting of Rory's insult lingered in her mind, a cruel reminder of how easily words could cut. She could feel the sun's warmth on her skin, but it did little to thaw the icy resentment building inside her.

Rory approached cautiously, a mix of determination and uncertainty in his posture as he leaned against the post.

"We need to get past this," he suggested, his tone mild but lacking the conviction Rose sought. Her response was sharp, almost instinctual: "When you apologise to David." The words flew from her lips before she could temper them, reflecting the tumult of her emotions.

He paused, the weight of her demand settling heavily on his shoulders. Did he trust David? Earlier in the day, his answer would have been a firm 'no,' but now doubt flickered in his mind. Yet, there was

Rose—loyal, unwavering Rose. Her fidelity was a beacon in his muddled thoughts.

"How do you suggest I do that without offending him further?" Rory asked, his frustration bubbling beneath his calm facade. He felt at a loss; the path forward seemed shrouded in shadow.

Rose's gaze was unyielding, her resolve hardening. "You should have thought about that earlier. Then we wouldn't be having this conversation." Each word was a stone, adding to the fortress of misunderstanding between them. She could sense his struggle, but her heart insisted that he reconcile with David first—a principle too important to let slide. "You will get your chance tomorrow night when David promotes your cause - to bring your brothers home."

Rory cringed. He had insulted the man.

Rose delicately smoothed the hem of her maroon dress, a modest yet elegant piece that seemed to whisper promises of comfort and style—exactly what she needed for the upcoming golf club social. As she adjusted the fabric, she felt a twinge of unease, her heart heavy with unresolved tension.

On the other side of the room, Rory stood dressed and ready, yet his mind was a whirlpool of regret and uncertainty. The invitation to the social loomed over him like a storm cloud. Deep down, he would have preferred to remain where he was, nestled in the isolation of his thoughts.

However, the weight of his desire to regain Rose's love propelled him forward; he knew that he first needed to confront David to achieve that. The word "amends" rang hollow in his ears, a mere excuse to mask the bitterness that marred his spirit. The mere thought of mingling in a lively gathering felt jarringly out of sync with the sorrow that clung to him.

From the shadows of his troubled mind emerged the figure of Rose—a jagged silhouette of concern. He could envision her lying awake in their bed, tossing and turning, wrestling with thoughts that mirrored his own. She worried for him, her heart tethered to his turmoil.

With a heavy sigh, Rory approached her, wrapping his arms around her in an attempt to offer solace. Yet she stiffened, palpable rejection radiating from her. Undeterred, he held on tighter. "I apologise to you, and tonight, I will do the same with David," he whispered, his voice a mix of desperation and hope, clinging to the words as a lifeline.

She pushed him away, her gaze steady, icy determination etched on her face. "You had better," she warned, her voice cutting through the air with unwavering resolve, making it clear that she would not yield even an inch in this battle of hearts.

"It's quite the crowd," Hugh remarked, his voice almost swallowed by the laughter that floated through the summer evening. Rory's gaze drifted across the lively lawn, where small clusters of friends danced between tables burdened with a feast of smoky grilled meats, vibrant salads bursting with colour, and hearty crusty loaves, each scent weaving a nostalgic tapestry in the warm air.

"Indeed," Rory replied, the words escaping him wrapped in a thin veil of hesitation as if the jubilant atmosphere were a distant melody, soothing yet far removed from him. He looked for David Crowley; that was his priority.

Spying him entering with Mary on his arm, he made his way across, hoping to get him alone, but he knew it was a forlorn hope. People flocked to David, as they always did.

Val waylaid him, carrying a plate. The aroma of rich and savoury grilled lamb attacked his senses, pulling at the edges of his memory. It reminded him of family barbeques, filled with laughter, his siblings teasing one another over piled plates, their affectionate jibes softening any lingering tensions. The recollection tightened in his chest, sharp against the backdrop of his solitude as he observed the scene before him, where connection flourished, and he remained a sole spectre amidst the warmth.

Val's words fractured his thoughts.

"Get yourself a plate. " Val Smiled. "Where are Hugh and Rose?"

He pointed towards the entrance, where they were talking in a group. "Aunt Rosemary joined us,

" he added. "Come, I will escort you."

"Rose's Aunt." Val queried. A dash of uncertainty crossed her face.

"Yes." Making room for them to pass, he was almost in the crowd when he recognised whom they were talking to.

A flicker of warmth momentarily illuminated his features as Noel turned.

"Noel!" Rory's laughter bubbled forth, surprising even himself. The sound was a brief echo of the joy that the party buzzed around them.

Noel, beaming widely as he closed the distance, stretched his hand towards Rory. Their connection was warm and unique amidst the joyful chaos surrounding them.

"Noel, what brings you here?" Rory's chuckle danced with layers of surprise mixed with uncertainty.

"Well, when duty calls and all that," Noel replied, his eyes glimmering with camaraderie, hinting at deeper ties that bound them together.

"Duty?" Rory raised an eyebrow, the noise of the celebration swirling around him, a world away.

"Yes, I'm here to interview a local legend."

"David Crowley," Rory quipped with a grin, thoughts of the festive spirit he once was now drifting alongside the laughter surrounding him.

"No, not him, although he did put in a request," Noel began, but his words were swallowed by a glass clinking sharply, a request for quiet resonating throughout the gathering.

As Rory watched David Crowley take the stage, he couldn't shake the reminder that he still owed him an apology.

"Thank you all for joining us tonight," David's voice resonated, a blend of warmth and authority. "What I cherish most is our Midgal community and its relentless spirit of support."

A wave of gratitude washed over Rory; Crowley's relentless efforts to bring his brothers home had touched him deeply.

With a nod to the man beside him, David introduced their Member of Parliament, John Gilbert, inviting the crowd to engage with him this evening—an act woven with camaraderie. Rory noticed the laughter that followed Crowley's jest about local gossip, a sharp reminder of the biases he had held.

As the crowd settled, David brought the focus back. "The Andersons' plea to retrieve their sons, Albert and Guy, has been denied by the government. This is simply unjust," he proclaimed, igniting a spark of defiance within Rory.

This was Crowley's essence—relentlessly championing what was right. "I urge you to support their petition, which John will present in Parliament to ensure it gets the attention it deserves."

A ripple of agreement coursed through the

audience—a collective acknowledgment of the weight of his words. As David encouraged everyone to enjoy the evening and connect with John, Rory felt a surge of purpose. Crowley's presence illuminated the strength of their community and rekindled the belief.

He approached them with purpose, but Aunt Rosemary quickly intercepted him. "I am Rosemary Ashford, Rose's aunt," she introduced herself with a firm nod. "And you must be David Crowley, the man I've long anticipated meeting."

"From England, I presume?" David replied, flashing a captivating smile. "That's quite a journey just for an introduction."

"I didn't walk," she retorted sharply. "I took a boat."

David chuckled. "I'm sure you kept everyone on edge during the voyage."

Aunt Rosemary stepped back to better scrutinise him. "I must say, I like you," she admitted with a knowing smile. "Just save that charm for me and not my dear Rose."

"Do you know how many people adore your Rose?" he asked with a playful tone.

"She has a natural inclination for caring," Aunt Rosemary acknowledged.

"Indeed, she does. She's our gain an Australian triumph over England, much like our victories in cricket," David pointed out with a grin.

The light dimmed as the sun set, casting elongated shadows across the lawn, where the sweet aroma of grilled lamb and beer permeated the evening air.

She leaned closer, her eyes sparkling with mischief. "That may be short-lived. Bradman is getting old," she retorted, a playful smirk curling her lips.

He chuckled, the sound rich and warm resonating as he glanced down. "I think we are more than you English can handle," he said, his words dripping with amusement. He savoured the lively exchange as the hum of evening chatter surrounded them.

She gave him a knowing look, the faint trace of a smile dancing at the corner of her mouth. "Well, at least you are." She let her words hang in the thickening dusk, full of unspoken meaning.

Rory stood in stunned silence, his heart racing as he absorbed the gesture. They had indeed done this for him, and the weight of their sacrifice filled him with a fragile hope. In that moment, he dared to envision a future where he could lead them safely back home.

Yet, amidst the flicker of optimism, shadows of doubt lingered; the war had exacted a heavy toll, and each setback weighed on him like an anchor. Caution became his constant companion, a reminder of the harsh realities that still loomed ahead.

He turned to Noel, a curious look in his eyes.

"You came to help me?"

Noel nodded, a knowing glimmer in his gaze. "The paper sent us, thanks to a bit of encouragement from a friend of yours—a rather influential friend, I might add." His voice held a hint of disbelief as he wrestled with the complexities of David Crowley, a man whose influence reached far and wide, weaving through the threads of various lives and decisions.

"Indeed, I owe a debt of gratitude to David," Rory admitted, embarrassed at his blunder.

He then turned his gaze, and there was David, who was engrossed in a discussion with Aunt Rosemary.

"Right now, she's giving him some sound advice," Rory continued, a hint of admiration in his voice. 'Aunt Rosemary has a way of peeling back the layers of confusion; she truly leaves no stone unturned."

Noal nodded appreciatively, his eyes flickering between Rory and the pair, deep in conversation. "You certainly have some remarkable friends," he remarked.

Noticing that David was moving on, he excused himself and cut him off.

"David, I want a word." He tapped him on the arm.

"Yes, Rory?" David asked.

"I owe you an apology," Rory said.

David laughed, "Rose got to you, did she?" His

grin was broad. "Our Rose has sharp thorns, believe me."

"Yes," Rory admitted, feeling the flaying she had given him.

"I have to admit it sent me into a spin. A long time ago, I made an error of judgement." He paused, thinking back to that evening long ago. Dan straightened me out in more ways than one. Forget it, I have. David admitted, ready to move on.

"I am not sure Rose will, "Rory murmured.

CHAPTER 26 - ON AIR

*A **rural radio station in Western Australia, 1946**. The scene captures a broadcaster in a small wooden studio, speaking into a vintage microphone with an **"On Air"** sign illuminated. Through the window, the vast farmland and a windmill highlight the **importance of radio in connecting isolated communities** with news, music, and essential updates in post-war Australia.*

Rose sank into the familiar embrace of the well-worn chair at her desk, its fabric imbued with the scent of aged wood and countless memories.

An unsettling wave of apprehension washed over her, a shadowy echo of her past. Shouldn't she be by her Aunt's side now, offering comfort instead of remaining trapped within these four walls? Just the day before, she had crossed the threshold of Windamere, and the vivid clarity of their long-awaited reunion still danced in her mind, a bittersweet symphony of laughter and tears.

Hugh had assured her all would be well, that he would manage everything while she was at work.

Yet, as she gazed out of the window framed by

cotton curtains, a tight knot twisted in her stomach, echoing the uncertainty within her. Would the deep-rooted bonds they once treasured— those clandestine afternoon teas and whispered secrets beneath the stars—be strong enough to bridge the expansive chasm carved by the relentless march of time?

What if her absence transformed into a heavy shroud, leaving her Aunt to dim memories of their shared past, burdened by the weight of loneliness? Was that what had brought her all these miles so they could be together? The thought shivered through Rose, sending her back into the swirling labyrinth of memories they had built together, now tinged with the threat of distance.

Her phone buzzed. She was lifting the handset she spoke. "Rose speaking." "It's Emily, about your Aunt."

Roses had dreaded such a moment. Her heart raced. "What is the matter? " she asked, stressed.

"Your Aunt fell out of bed." Rose rose from her chair, ready to go.

Then she heard a voice in the background. "Emily, give me the phone." It was Aunt Rosemary, and she certainly did not sound like she was at death's door.

"Silly girl. I am fine, Rose." Aunt Rosemary exclaimed with annoyance. "Are you sure?" Rose sunk back into her chair.

"My ego is bruised, especially when Hugh came

to the rescue, hauling me up in my nightly.

Hardly appropriate." Her Aunt huffed.

Rose laughed as she released her plenty of anguish.

"It was not a laughing matter." Aunt Rosemary grumbled. "You get back to work, and I will get dressed." She put down the phone with a clunk.

As David walked into the room, Rose's eyes shifted toward him. Her thoughts lingered on their silence from the night before and how Rory's earlier actions might have affected David.

"Good morning! You're up early," he greeted her with a cheerful smile.

"Indeed, I have much to address," Rose responded calmly. "I apologise for Rory's behaviour." She knew she needed to address the issue directly.

David chuckled softly. "No need for that. Rory has already apologized." His smile faded for a moment. "It's time for you to forgive him. Life moves on."

"It was awkward for both of us," Rose admitted, still feeling the discomfort.

"True," David agreed, reflecting on his past. "I once made a mistake, too. Thankfully, Dan helped me see it differently. I learned to prioritize what matters—my family and friends. It wasn't easy, but it taught me a valuable lesson." He paused. "We have a strong connection, yet the consequences would be too great for our families."

"Agreed," Rose replied, returning his smile. "Now, let's turn our attention to what needs to be done."

David glanced at his watch. "Yes, I have a council meeting, and you have your tasks to handle."

As he departed, Rose observed the subtle shift in their dynamic. She sensed the gradual distance between them in the days ahead, but perhaps this change would benefit them both, creating space for growth and self-discovery.

As the gentle morning light spilled into the room, illuminating every corner, Rose looked up to see an unexpected visitor at her door confronted by an unforeseen visitor—Noel. He settled into the chair opposite her, his casual demeanour laced with unmistakable intent.

"I've come to discover the story behind the woman dubbed Midjal's Florence Nightingale," he announced, bypassing any pleasantries. A spark of amusement flickered in Rose's eyes as a smile broke through her composed facade. "I gather David has been filling you in," she quipped, arching an eyebrow, a knowing glimmer dancing in her expression.

"Indeed," Noel replied, a mischievous grin tugging at the corners of his mouth. "He's quite the fellow."

"Yes, he is," Rose acknowledged, her smile

momentarily betraying a deeper contemplation—a whisper of doubt that hinted, "Perhaps overly kind." Dismissing the thought, she steered the conversation anew. "So, you're still seeking a story? I assumed you would be immersing yourself in Rory's world."

"No worries; eventually, I shall," Noel said, his gaze momentarily drifting toward the door as if searching for inspiration beyond its frame. "But first, I sense a compelling narrative that chronicles Rose Anderson's ascent as a local heroine. How did this English woman elicit such profound emotions in such a brief span? I can already envision the headlines."

Rose laughed. "No, you can't."

"Oh yes, I can, "Windermere's Rose to the Rescue." Noel expanded writing in the air.

She felt sad when she remembered the sight of little Tommy lying in his father's arms. "That was far too personal for the newspapers," Rose said, dampening her character.

Noel looked at her in Surprise. "What was?" He sniffed a story here.

"No, Noel, she warned. "A little boy died, and we did not make it in time to save him."

"How?"

"He drowned in a wheat silo." Rose's eyes misted over. "There is so much to do; it was avoidable with more awareness and training. Suppose we had got there quicker. It may never have happened. We need to highlight the need for caution. As Rory pointed out, that is how they live out here. The danger is all around them."

Noel sensed her sorrow. So he suggested. "How about a tour of the place?" "It won't take long," she commented. "I'll show him around," John mentioned from the door.

Rose watched them go. How often did John listen at her door? How much would Noel glean from him?

They burst back into her office, the strong bond of friendship unmistakable between them.

As they re-entered the room, Rose felt a wave of protectiveness wash over her. "I don't want to see any more harm come to the Marshalls," she warned, her voice steady but laced with concern.

Noel placed a hand over his heart, sincerity etched in his features. "I swear I won't."

Yet, doubt lingered in Rose's eyes. A journalist stood before her, skilled and assured, yet those like him often lacked the gentleness necessary in such fragile situations. Questions swirled in her mind— could he truly navigate this with the care it deserved?

His confident smile dimmed as he sank into a chair, the weight of his own words pressing down. "I've endured war; I am not without compassion. What I seek is to ensure that the tragic loss of the boy leads to meaningful change." He paused, the gravity of his statement hanging between them. "If that means you taking up this cause, then Little Tom's life served a purpose and could spare others from a similar fate."

Would she be his ally in this endeavour?

John stepped forward, an advocate in Noel's corner. "That is what you need, and I am sure Don will agree. Perhaps the three of us could discuss it with him?" He looked at Rose, hopeful yet uncertain.

Rose's mind whirred, battling with her thoughts. "It could be too soon; they only buried Tom yesterday." The words felt heavy; grief was still fresh, and she could almost hear the echoes of sorrow in the distance.

"I want to help you," Noel said earnestly, a playful grin attempting to lighten the atmosphere, but Rose remained firm in her resolve.

"It's a message that needs to be spread," John interjected, determination. "You could save a hundred little boys that way."

"I can unlock many opportunities, granting you access to those who matter," Noel added, a hint of urgency creeping into his tone.

"I will consider it if I get my radio post at 6MD," Rose replied, setting the terms with a steely determination. The stalling had been a test, a struggle to find clarity in the chaos. "And certainly not without his family's consent."

As Noel looked at her, he realized he had gained the go-ahead he sought, but it was tempered with caution. This was not the naive young nurse he once knew from the war-torn streets of London; this was a formidable woman, steadfast and unwavering in her principles. He wondered what had changed within her, yet he could not ignore the strength she now possessed.

With each mile Rose drove towards Windamere, a growing sense of unease settled within her. The day had been a whirlwind of achievements, yet her campaign lay untouched, a looming spectre in her mind.

David's presence had once buoyed her spirits, infusing her with a renewed sense of purpose. But as she approached solitude, the comforting echo of his encouragement faded, leaving her with doubts. A stark realization washed over her—she had leaned far too heavily on him for strength and affirmation. Now, faced with the daunting task before her, the weight of this dependency pressed heavily on her chest. How could she stand firm when the very foundation of her confidence felt so precarious?

Windemere towered before her, its imposing structure a testament to Hugh's ambition. The house, far too glorious for a simple wheatbelt farm, stood as a symbol of his dreams realized. Even as he skated memories of Aunt Rosemary's father's scorn, he found solace in the familiarity of this grand abode.

Her eyes drifted up to the veranda, and an unexpected chill washed over her as she noted the absence of a warm reception. The hire car parked out front stirred a tumult of emotions within her—a stark reminder that Noel was inside.

What could compel him to come here? A fleeting thought crossed her mind—he was Rory's friend, their groomsman. Yet, that connection felt overshadowed by the weight of his profession—a journalist. That title alone ignited a storm of distrust, bringing back memories of her parents' tragic end, accompanied by the invasive photos and tell-all articles that had plagued their lives.

She wrestled with the urge to cling to the fond memory of Noel from her time at Queen Alexandra Hospital—a vibrant and friendly man who had breathed joy into the room. That version of him felt almost mythical now, steeped in a past that had grown unbearably distant.

But now, her focus shifted to safeguarding the Marshall family's privacy, ensuring they could mourn free from the judgmental eyes of the press. They deserved their peace.

As she stepped through the door, laughter wrapped around her like a warm embrace, grounding her in the familiar family chaos. Emily's eyes sparkled as she jumped up, breaking the moment with her exuberance. "Tea to a Beer, Rose," she called a playful challenge shimmering beneath her words.

"A tea would be nice. Thank you, Emily," Rose replied, though internally, she felt the gentle tug of nostalgia—a reminder of simpler times, painted with the colours of shared conversations and laughter.

Aunt Rosemary turned with enthusiasm, her voice cutting through the warm chatter. "Noel was just telling us about when you were all at the hospital," she said, directing her gaze at Rose, a knowing smile on her lips.

"Remember V-Day?" Noel chimed in, and at the mention, Rose was transported back to that pivotal moment, emotions swirling—the joy, the love, and the hope enveloping them as fiercely as the hospital walls had surrounded them.

"Yes, when Rory proposed," she responded, the memory resurfacing vividly, soft yet piercing in its clarity.

"You have no idea how much encouragement it took from all of us to get him over the line," Noel said, his tone teasing yet imbued with genuine sincerity.

Rory's laughter rang out, buoyant and carefree. "That is what you think. I just chose the right time," he countered, a playful grin dancing across his face, masking the nervous energy that had once churned within him that day."That's what he says. I know otherwise," Noel replied, his words cloaked in playful secrecy, his mouth hidden behind his hand as if sharing a deliberate whisper. Laughter spilled over the

table, a network of shared understanding and

subtle teasing that warmed the air.

"He always needed a bit of a push," Hugh interjected, nostalgia brightening his face. He leaned back slightly, a fond smile emerging as he continued, "I remember when he was a toddler— Albert was the one who got him moving. Pushed him right down the front steps."

As Hugh shared his tale, Rose could almost feel the echoes of that afternoon, the children's laughter ringing in her ears. "Joan had indulged Albert's whim, but it had worked. After that daring tumble, Rory had learned to walk, his little legs carrying him into new adventures." Hugh concluded, laughter resonated again, a chorus of shared memories creating a tapestry of happiness. It was a good moment for confessions and remembrances, and soon, they settled down for tea. The intoxicating scent of one of Hugh's special creations swirled around them, offering timeless comfort and connection.

As Aunt Rosemary finally entered retirement, she remarked playfully about it being past her bedtime. With a knowing nod, Emily offered her assistance, while High felt the pull of time's passage and knew he had his affairs to attend to.

Once alone, Noel, Rory, and Rose drifted toward the veranda, drawn by the shimmering contours of the landscape bathed in the soft glow of the moonlight. It was a sight that inspired reflection.

"Never imagined you had something like this," Noel mused, a hint of disbelief in his voice. "I always thought you were just a dirt farmer."

Rory chuckled, shaking his head. "Well, I am a dirt farmer. Windamere, however, is my father's dream—a testament to his aspirations." His words hinted at a larger narrative, one woven into the fabric of his upbringing.

There was a glimmer of curiosity in Noel's eyes. "There had to be something driving him to build this out here. Not to mention its sheer audacity—brass and all."

Rose, always keen on her family history, chimed in. "He found inspiration in Aunt Rosemary's father. That's where it all began." Her voice carried the weight of legacy, a connection to a lineage shaped by ambition and sacrifice.

Rory leaned in, his instincts sharp as he added, "And the brass? That came from the mining in Kalgoorlie." He had a knack for piecing together the fragments of the past, his curiosity a bridge to the stories hidden beneath the surface.

A playful grin spread across Noel's face as he sensed the puzzles unravelling before him. "I sense a story here." The air around him seemed charged with the promise of discovery, like a bloodhound on the scent of an intriguing tale.

"You and your stories," Rose laughed, finding joy in Noel's relentless pursuit of the narrative.

Despite Noel's identity as a reporter, in that moment, it was clear he was just one of them—an integral part of their shared exploration of history, identity, and connection.

"Well, I had better be making tracks," Noel said, his voice tinged with a hint of reluctance. The thought of leaving felt like a tug at his heart, but he knew the evening had to come to an end.

"You should have stayed here," Rory remarked, his tone playful yet laced with genuine concern. The camaraderie was comforting, and he couldn't shake the feeling of missing out on more shared laughter.

"Next time," Noel promised, trying to project optimism even as a sense of longing washed over him. His curiosity piqued, he turned to Rose. Rose, do you have a busy day tomorrow?" He hoped for an opportunity to spend more time with her.

"Every day is full," Rose replied, her smile bright. Yet Noel could sense the weight behind her words. It was as if she was referring to her tasks and responsibilities that pressed against her spirit. There is so much that needs doing."

Can she spare me just a sliver of her time? He wondered, hoping the answer would lean in his favour. "Can you spare half a day for me?" he ventured, holding his breath.

For a brief moment, Rose hesitated, the 'no' lingering on her lips like unspoken thoughts. But then, she relented, and something in Noel's chest lifted. "Yes, I will fit you in." Her willingness to accommodate him sparked a warmth within him, a genuine delight, and he wanted to see Rose fulfil her destiny.

"Good. I will pick you up at eleven o'clock," Noel said, the excitement in his voice rising like a tide. The thought of spending that time together filled him with anticipation. "Should be just enough time to reach 6MD; after all, we are taking Ray Ingram to lunch, an event that could open new doors for both of us."

"How did you organise that?" Rose asked a note of surprise in her question. He could see the spark of intrigue in her eyes, which delighted him, igniting a warmth of pride in his chest.

"We media people stick together," he replied with a casual smile, though inside, he revelled in the fleeting sense of connection they shared. He stood and walked to the veranda's edge, letting the night air brush against him as he took a moment to reflect. "Thank you for a great evening— one I won't forget for a long time." The words hung in the air, carrying a more profound significance, a promise of things yet to come.

Ray Ingram was not what I had pictured. His radio voice, with warmth and charisma, hinted at a vitality that felt almost youthful. Yet, standing before him, I was struck by the weight of his years—nearly sixty, he bore the telltale signs of a life steeped in the rugged realities of rural existence. While his voice might glide through the airwaves unnoticed, in the flesh, he radiated a formidable presence that demanded attention.

His sharp gaze pierced the air between us as he cut straight to the chase. "So you want a spot on my station," he stated in his direct and probing tone. It was a voice I had grown familiar with, yet now it was accompanied by a face etched with lines of experience and unspoken stories. "Why?"

I felt a twinge of hesitation before I spoke, my emotions swirling like a storm. "I want to connect with rural people," I explained, forcing my voice to remain steady despite the gravity of my words. "As Midjal's St Johns coordinator, I train, inform, and provide immediate professional aid." I wanted him to see my resolve and understand the passion behind my purpose.

His reaction was as blunt as a hammer striking an iron anvil. "So?" The dismissal stung, and for a fleeting moment, I considered backing down.

But the memory of the boy pierced deeper than any critique. "Right," I continued, pushing through the discomfort. "So, I recently attended an accident where we lost a young boy who was out with his father. It could have been prevented. He might have been saved had some intermediate medical aid been available from those on the scene." My heart raced, the weight of that loss crashing over me. "I want to instil that knowledge and preparedness." I searched his eyes, hoping to find a fraction of understanding, a glimpse of shared purpose in the depths of his weathered soul.

"That could work as a temporary spot on air," Ingram responded, his brow furrowed with concern. "But we need to consider much more for a permanent fixture."

"We're missing so many essential health services in remote areas," I continued, my voice tinged with urgency. "And we have to brace ourselves for the long haul. These services will be introduced, but waiting won't be an option for some, like Little Tom."

A smile broke across Ingram's face for the first time, a flicker of hope igniting his eyes. "Noel, you just might be onto something."

Noel, who had remained silent until then, couldn't resist the opportunity to inject a bit of bravado into the conversation. "Told you so," he quipped, a mixture of pride and challenge lacing his tone.

CHAPTER 27 - PERMISSION GRANTED

*In **rural Western Australia**, newspapers were a **lifeline for isolated communities** in 1946. With limited access to radio and no television, they provided essential **news on global events, government policies, and local happenings**, helping farmers, workers, and families stay informed. They connected rural Australians with the broader world, delivering updates on markets, weather forecasts, and advertisements for farm supplies. They fostered a sense of **community identity**, preserving local stories, achievements, and social events, making them an indispensable part of daily life in the bush.*

Rose's heart thrummed with exhilaration as she stepped onto the porch, a joyful pulse that felt like it might open her chest. She had news that shimmered like sunlight on water, and the urge to share it with her family quickened her steps. But there, waiting on the veranda, was Rory.

His broad smile was an open invitation to happiness that calmed the flurry of emotions inside her. "Good day?" he inquired, his tone playful yet warm, igniting a spark of hope.

"The best," she replied, laughter bubbling forth as she grasped the moment tightly. "I have a trail of three on 6MD." In that instant, joy surged through her, compelling her to wrap her arms around him, pressing her lips against his in a kiss that tasted of sweet anticipation. It was the start of a new journey for her, and the challenge drew her in.

Rory's breath caught in his throat, surprise lighting up his eyes momentarily. Then, he steadied himself, pulling her gently toward him, his arm resting comfortably around her shoulders. "That calls for a celebration," he proclaimed, his voice resonating with a newfound camaraderie. Rose felt the warmth of his enthusiasm as he continued, "I got the green light to bring Albert and Guy home."

Her heart swelled even further, delighting at the thought of their loved ones reuniting. "That is marvellous, Rory."

Rose's laughter danced through the open door, a melodic cascade that drew smiles from all. Its clarity lit up the atmosphere like sunlight filtering through leaves, enveloping those around in an embrace of warmth and shared joy. The day sparkled with the radiant glow of unspoken victories, each chuckle weaving a tapestry of delightful camaraderie.

As the festivities unfolded within the warm embrace of the room, a palpable sense of anticipation filled the air. Aunt Rosemary, her eyes twinkling with joy, sat poised at the table alongside Hugh, Emily, and Noel. Everyone clutched their glasses tightly, excitement and nerves flickering across their faces.

Noel broke the momentary silence, his voice steady but imbued with heartfelt emotion. "To both of you." He lifted his glass high, his smile radiating genuine pride. "Congratulations." The words hung briefly in the air, their simplicity underscoring the depth of their meaning.

At his side, Emily beamed, her heart swelling with happiness as she exchanged knowing glances with Hugh. Together, they raised their glasses, immersed in a shared celebration transcending mere formality. The traditional salute felt more profound; it was a bond forged through trials and triumphs, a testament to their collective journey.

Then Emily, her enthusiasm palpable, handed a glass to Rory, whose expression shifted from surprise to resolve. With a deep breath, he lifted his glass with intention, the moment's gravity echoing as he declared, "To our joint efforts." A flicker of determination danced in his eyes, and the room seemed to pulse with unspoken promises for the future, their emotions woven together in an intricate tapestry of hope and unity.

"Ah, so when do you plan to begin, Rose?" Aunt Rosemary asked, her curiosity stirring with eagerness and concern.

"There isn't a set schedule just yet; I'll be on next month's roster," Rose replied, her voice tinged with anticipation, the excitement palpable as it wrapped around her words. "I'm truly thankful for the chance to dive into this."

Aunt Rosemary turned her gaze towards Rory and Hugh, her expression a mix of concern and curiosity. "And what about you two?" she asked, her voice gentle but probing.

Rory's brow knitted in worry as though the world's weight hung heavily on his shoulders. "I need to concentrate on my crops first," he said, his tone taut with stress. "I have a lead on Guy; however, Albert... he was lost in the Battle of Crete. I have to discover where he rests now." His admission hung like a solemn tide, vulnerability washing over him.

Rose leaned forward, her eyes wide and earnest. "How can we find exactly where he fell during the Battle of Crete?" Determination blossomed within her, a garden of resolve amid the uncertainty.

Aunt Rosemary mulled this over, her fingers tapping lightly against her chin. "A great place to start would be the soldier's military service records. An Australian soldier's record often details deployments and sometimes even the circumstances surrounding their deaths."

"That's an excellent point!" Hugh interjected, a spark of enthusiasm lighting his face. "Those records can be a treasure trove of context. Plus, the Commonwealth War Graves Commission keeps records that specify where soldiers are buried or commemorated—especially if their final resting place remains unknown. A good number of those who perished in Crete are interred at the Suda Bay War Cemetery," he added, pride bubbling forth as he revealed, "I've been researching this."

"Yes, the CWGC could be a goldmine, particularly for tracing down cemeteries or memorial sites," Rory added, his excitement growing like a flame in his chest. "If we dive deeper, we might also want to review unit war diaries and operational records."

"Exactly," Noel chimed in eagerly, his mind racing. "By tracing the movements of Albert's unit during those pivotal moments, we could zero in on where he might have met his fate."

Aunt Rosemary nodded, her voice brimming with purpose. "Absolutely. We could even visit local memorials or cemeteries in Crete for a more targeted approach. For instance, the Suda Bay War Cemetery has a commemorated soldiers registry. There may be critical information on-site regarding the battles and where individual soldiers fell."

"But how will we do that from here?" Rose asked, a thread of worry weaving through her words.

Aunt Rosemary's determination did not falter. "True, but what if we can reach out to families with old letters, diaries, or soldiers who returned from his unit? Soldiers used to detail their locations in their letters home, and families might have received specific updates about their last known whereabouts."

"Combining these resources could greatly enhance our chances of uncovering where Albert is buried in Crete or pinpointing a close approximation," Rory mused, his desire for closure ringing clear and true.

"I can gather a lot of this through my job," Noel offered, his enthusiasm tangible. "With the right resources, we could map out his final movements and identify possible locations where he fell. But I'll need assistance to tie it all together," he proposed.

"That will be Hugh and me. As the older statesmen here, we've got the time on our hands," Aunt Rosemary responded with a chuckle, her spirits lifting. At that moment, she felt more than just a visitor; she felt a vital piece of the family puzzle, eager to contribute to their quest.

"Indeed, I am here to assist," Hugh replied, though his words barely disguised the weight on his mind. Each day served as a fresh reminder of time's relentless march, starkly contrasting with the vigour of his youth.

The labour of mining—once a source of rejuvenation—now resonated as the weary creaks of his joints and the fatigue draped heavily across his shoulders. With every ache, he pondered the fleeting nature of strength. His weathered hands, once symbols of power and agility, now told stories of resilience waning.

Deep within him lay a yearning to contribute, to feel helpful in a world all too often blind to the wisdom age offers. In reaching out to help, he sought not just to fulfil his obligations but to reclaim fleeting moments of purpose in a life waning too swiftly.

"That sounds like a plan," Rose finalized with a nod of agreement.

"Yes, and I know someone who can assist us on the ground in Crete," Aunt Rosemary said triumphantly. "Sir Reginald. He had indicated to you, Rory, that if there was anything he could do to help, he would." Perhaps his intentions weren't exactly aligned with her grand vision, but Aunt Rosemary decided that was a minor detail, hardly worth raising.

As fortune would have it, the heavens opened, showering the parched earth with relentless drops of rain, igniting a spark of joy in the hearts of Rory and Hugh while leaving Rose and Aunt Rosemary utterly astonished, having long since abandoned any hope of witnessing such a phenomenon again.

They stood spellbound on the weathered wooden veranda as the sky unleashed its bounty. Each large raindrop plummeted to the ground, bursting forth clouds of fine, earthy dust that danced in the air before settling quietly. This land was alien to them and starkly contrasted with England, where rain was an almost daily companion.

Enveloped in the rhythm of nature's applause, Hugh and Rory toasted their good fortune with a frosty beer.

"Well, that means seeding is about to commence," Rory declared, a glimmer of excitement lighting up his eyes as he envisioned the renewal ahead.

"Your enthusiasm will wane; it's been four years since your last," Hugh replied, his voice tinged with a weariness borne from experience, aware of the relentless toil the seasons demand.

"It feels like a fresh start," Rory reflected on the weight of his words, which was heavy with longing. He found himself lost momentarily in memories of days gone by, where laughter and life once filled the air, now replaced by an aching solitude. His mother and brothers had departed, leaving him surrounded by the familiar contours of the land. This landscape stood resolute, unchanged, even as time marched forward, echoing the ghosts of his past.

Hugh raised his glass. "To a new start. And may the past never be repeated."

They were leaving. As Aunt Rosemary and Rose stood on the steps, the fading silhouette of the car pulled away, enveloping them in a palpable silence. "It's hard to fathom that everything is finally falling into place," Rose whispered, her voice barely above a sigh, as uncertainty clung to her words like morning mist.

Aunt Rosemary was lost in the echo of Hugh's kiss as he departed, and she felt her heart stir with nostalgic warmth. It was as if time had folded back on itself, reconnecting her with her past's vibrant, youthful passion—a past filled with promise and heart-fluttering excitement. She shook her head gently, trying to dispel the wistful thoughts that began to bloom unbidden. How foolish, she chided herself to still be ensnared by such fanciful daydreams at her age.

"Yes, and if we hold onto that belief, perhaps we can preserve this fleeting joy," Aunt Rosemary replied, hesitating momentarily as the weight of her emotions settled in her chest. With a deep breath, she turned to retreat inside, her heart a canvas of mixed feelings—hope intertwined with the bittersweet memories of what once was.

Aunt Rosemary approached the breakfast table, her voice bright but edged with an urgency that made the air crackle. "Do you know what day it is?"

Emily and Rose glanced up from their plates, a flicker of concern flashing between them. Had she forgotten? The two of them chimed together, a forced cheerfulness in their tone, "Sunday." "Yes, indeed. And what do we do on Sundays?" Aunt Rosemary probed, her eyes glinting with expectation.

Emily hesitated, her voice uncertain as she

responded, "Church." The word felt alien on her tongue, laden with unspoken doubts.

Surprise etched itself onto Rose's face. After all, since their arrival in Australia, the comforting familiarity of the church had faded from her routine. Memories of hymns and prayers felt like distant echoes, overshadowed by the storm of her past.

"The service begins at ten o'clock, so you both better get ready," Aunt Rosemary commanded, her tone leaving no room for argument.

A mix of rebellion and turmoil churned within Rose. She longed to voice her dissent, to articulate how the very idea of the church felt like a betrayal to her memories, to all she had endured during the war. But the determined look in her aunt's eyes silenced her. Deep down, Rose grappled with her lost faith; after everything she had witnessed, she often wondered if there was a God to believe in—or if that was merely a comforting illusion. Yet here she was, trapped beneath the weight of expectation, suffocated by the norm.

A glance at Aunt Rosemary extinguished Rose's objections entirely as if tethered by an invisible thread. A tumult of frustration churned within her; this was a journey she had never wished to take.

Yet, beneath the current of dissent, a spark of elation flickered at the sight of Aunt Rosemary's spirit rekindled, a vibrant echo of the past. She felt herself being pulled between the weight of her reluctance and the warmth of her aunt's regained vitality, even as uncertainty gnawed at her thoughts.

As Rose stepped into the church, she felt a new complexity within herself; it was a space that stirred echoes of her past, even in the absence of her faith. The hymns filled her with a bittersweet nostalgia, their familiar melodies wrapping around her like a warm embrace.

Amid the congregation, she found a connection—not just with the joyous strains of song, but with people who welcomed her with open arms: David, Mary, Val, Mel, and so many new faces who sought her company.

Yet, beneath the surface, joy and subtle unrest tugged at her heart. How could she savour these moments of community while grappling with her spiritual emptiness? When Rose returned to Windamere, it was not merely with contentment; she carried a growing awareness that her journey was far from complete, and perhaps there was more to uncover within herself than mere fleeting happiness.

Rose was soon ensnared in a tangled web of memories, her mind drifting back to Aunt Rosemary of yesteryears. Once, her heart had eagerly answered every request, every plea from her beloved Aunt.

But now, a fierce yearning for independence tugged at her spirit, igniting an inner conflict.

The chasm between their shared history and her newfound aspirations loomed large, demanding that she grapple with the delicate threads.

"Right, we need to set some rules while the boys are away," Aunt Rosemary stated, her voice firm yet laced with an undercurrent of goodwill. "I'll handle the cooking."

Rose felt a reluctant knot twist in her stomach at this pronouncement. It wasn't merely the assignment of duties that troubled her; it was the unspoken truth that echoed in her mind—this was her home, Windamere, and it felt disheartening not to have a say.

Memories of a similar arrangement with Hugh surfaced, where the unbalanced sharing of chores had become second nature: "I'll take care of the cleaning."

"It's a big house, and you have your work. Let Emily and me handle the bottom section," Aunt Rosemary proposed, her keen eyes catching the flicker of discomfort on Rose's face. She could sense the turmoil within her niece, that unvoiced yearning for a voice, for control. "I have plenty of time to potter around."

After a moment's hesitation, Rose sighed, her shoulders relaxing ever so slightly. "Okay, I'll feed the chooks and collect the eggs." The agreement flowed almost as a concession, yet it felt like a shared truce—a silent acknowledgment of their intertwined lives.

At that moment, they reached an unspoken

resolution, two women navigating the complexities of their relationship as they divided the tasks. Each held their private thoughts as they moved forward, bound by a blend of love, duty, and the lingering shadows of their pasts.

As Emily stepped into the familiar yet altered environment, she felt a surge of anxiety mingled with excitement wash over her. The moment's weight pressed heavily upon her chest, and she sat at the table, her fingers nervously tracing the grain of the wood beneath them.

"I want to let you know there's a job coming up at the hospital for an assistant. I would like to apply," she blurted out, urgency lacing her words. Yet, beneath that urgency lay a gaping chasm of doubt. She hesitated, gathering the bits of her scattered thoughts, before gazing at Aunt Rosemary. "If you can cope without me..."

Aunt Rosemary's expression shifted as she mulled over the question. "Yes, I am okay to look after myself," she replied, her smile warm but tinged with an inscrutable uncertainty. She took Emily's hand, grounding her in that moment. "Dear, it is a great chance to get that new start you have been looking for."

Emily felt a flicker of hope sparking within her— a longing for independence battling against the fear of being left alone. Her face brightened with a genuine smile, yet it concealed the turmoil beneath.

"I will always be here for you, grateful for the start you gave me." Her heart swelled with gratitude, but the complexity of her emotions—the push and pull between ambition and loyalty—left her feeling vulnerable.

"Go on, write that application. I will check it and give you a letter of recommendation to accompany it." Aunt Rosemary's encouragement hitched a ride on Emily's apprehension, offering a glimmer of security.

"I will see if I can open a few doors, too," Rose said. She could sense the underlying worry in her Aunt's voice—an unsteady thread woven through their conversation that hinted at the struggle to maintain independence.

In that moment, Emily stood at the crossroads of her aspirations and love, each path enticing yet fraught with unspoken fears.

On Monday morning, Rose was engulfed by fatigue, her mind reeling from the tumult of recent events. It was time to regain her focus and return to her duties. Just then, Noel strolled in, his infectious smile lighting up the room.

"Good morning, Noel. What brings you here today?" Rose asked, curious. It felt like he had another life that tethered him to this place.

"I've heard the news—you got the gig," he replied, his tone filled with enthusiasm. "It's just a three-week trial," Rose corrected gently, trying to temper his excitement. "In that case, we'd better roll up our sleeves. We need to get the word out and ensure everyone tunes in to hear you on air," he asserted, his determination palpable.

At that moment, Rose sensed an underlying motive in Noel's eagerness. He was drawn to Midjal in a way that felt deeper than mere professional interest. "You're banking your future on me," she stated, meeting his gaze directly.

Noel replied with a playful, lopsided grin, "I'm hitching my wagon to a rising star." He paused thoughtfully, continuing, "I'm joining the Western Mail."

"Are you relocating to Perth?" Rose asked, her curiosity piqued.

"Yep, I'm going to be part of their editorial team," Noel said, a grin spreading across his face. "The Western Mail has really made a name for itself, thanks to all the amazing Western Australian writers and artists. I mean, just look at the annual editions! They always showcase the best in art, photography, and literature from local talent. I'm hoping to sneak a few of my own photos in there, too."

Noel chuckled, feeling a warm sense of camaraderie between them. "You know, the war taught us both a lot," he said, his voice taking on a serious tone. He spoke about the publication with a kind of respect that made it seem almost sacred. "It started out helping farmers stay informed," he explained, reflecting on its origins, "but now it's turned into so much more. It's like a lifeline for people living in remote areas."

He could almost picture the faces of those who depended on this connection, and it filled him with purpose. "And those sections for women and children? They didn't just get added on— they really became key to keeping the paper afloat."

Noel's eyes sparkled with excitement and a touch of nostalgia. "I'll be working with this amazing network of contributors, reaching out to readers from rural and urban backgrounds." Just thinking about diving into that vibrant community made him feel hopeful. "I can't wait to spend some quality time in and around Midjal," he added quietly, sensing that new beginnings were on the horizon.

Rose chuckled, her laughter breaking through the solemnity. "I thought we lived in the sticks; I remember you telling Rory he was a 'dirt farmer.'" The memory hung in the air, a playful jab that tugged at their shared past.

Noel joined in her laughter, the camaraderie warming him. "The war taught us both what is important." It was a bittersweet realization but grounded him in what truly mattered now.

Rose's expression turned contemplative. "Mr. Smith, have we changed that much?" she mused, her mind racing back to those earlier days. Just a few months had passed, yet she felt the weight of transformation—both in herself and the world around them. It was remarkable how quickly life could shift, leaving them grappling with what had been and what lay ahead.

Rose turned to Noel, her smile tinged with the weight of their shared memories. "We should start working soon; there's much to reclaim after the devastation the war has wrought on our lives and this place."

CHAPTER 28 - THE ANDERSON FAMILY REUNITED

***Two soldiers' coffins being unloaded from a train in rural Western Australia, 1946**. The solemn scene captures uniformed servicemen carefully carrying flag-draped coffins while a small group of mourners, including grieving family members and a chaplain, stand nearby. The **simple wooden train station** and vast open farmland in the background reflect the **quiet dignity of the moment**, honoring the sacrifices of war.*

Aunt Rosemary and Rose stood together on the platform, a quiet tension hanging in the air between them. The message had arrived just yesterday, heavy with unspoken implications. They were back. No details, no reassurances—just those words that echoed in Rose's mind.

"Three months, and they are back," Rose murmured, a blend of amazement and confusion swirling in her chest. Their return sparked hope, but anxiety lurked beneath.

"That is good. It must have gone well," Aunt Rosemary responded, her gaze fixed intently down the line, searching for the train that would bring them home. Her tone was steady, but Rose could sense how Aunt Rosemary's calm facade barely masked the racing pulse of her heart, revealing her raw vulnerability.

"Maybe," Rose replied, uncertainty lacing her voice. The sparse letters they had received in those months had been more like echoes than conversations, leaving her restless with questions. All they knew was that they had met with Sir Reginald and learned of Albert's whereabouts, yet even this fragment felt insufficient. Rose's mind was a tumult of hope and fear, drawn towards the faces she had longed for while bracing herself for whatever revelations their return might bring.

"Here it comes," Aunt Rosemary announced, her voice tinged with an uncertainty that made her fingers twitch nervously at her side. A flicker of anxiety crossed her face as she braced herself, the air thick with anticipation and unspoken fears.

Suddenly, they were enveloped in the present moment. Rose found herself cradled in Rory's embrace, a brief but poignant reality coalescing around them, while Aunt Rosemary stood lost in a bittersweet memory with Hugh.

As the warmth of the kiss lingered, Aunt Rosemary jolted back to awareness. The exhilaration of the platform beneath her feet reminded her of that long-ago moment when they kissed moments before he departed, leaving her with a heart full of love and longing.

Her dishevelled appearance contrasted sharply with Hugh's radiant smile, a grin that seemed to echo with memories of their shared past. "Quite the welcome, wouldn't you say?" he teased, his playful tone barely masking the depth of nostalgic emotion swirling between them.

His words gently tugged Rose away from Rory's warmth, like a soft breeze breaking the stillness of a summer day. Their kiss—a rare bloom of intimacy amid the crowd—ignited the air with unspoken longing.

Yet, instead of disapproval, the spectators around them beamed, their smiles radiating a sense of shared happiness. The air was thick with joy, a reminder that genuine affection can illuminate even the most ordinary moments.

"Let's go home," Rory murmured, his voice barely rising above the crowd's hum. He wrapped an arm around Rose, the warmth of the gesture offering comfort that belied his swirling thoughts. A sense of urgency tinged his words; he longed for the familiar solace of their shared space, where secrets could spill forth like the evening's fading light.

"Yes, we have so much to tell and catch up on," Hugh agreed, his tone imbued with excitement and apprehension. He felt the weight of Aunt Rosemary's past stories pressing against the edges of his mind, and as he gently guided her off the platform, he couldn't help but worry about the revelations that awaited them at home. Each step was heavy with the unspoken, and he silently prayed they would be ready to face whatever memories lingered just beyond the threshold.

"Windamere!" Hugh whispered, his breath catching in his throat as the familiar silhouette of his home emerged from behind the trees.

The sun wrapped Windamere in its golden arms, it stood proud and regal, a beacon of ambition amidst the surrounding landscape. The golden rays danced upon its elegant facade, highlighting every intricate detail he had painstakingly crafted. A swell of emotion flooded through him, his heart expanding with pride and longing.

This was more than just a house; it embodied his dreams, a testament to what he could achieve. Yet, the shadows of uncertainty loomed still as the final chapter of his aspirations hung delicately in the balance, tantalizingly close yet just out of reach. Or were they? He glanced at Rosemary, who sat stiffly, looking straight ahead.

Hugh and Rosemary sat waiting for Rose and Rory to stash their bags upstairs.

"Where to start?" Hugh pondered, the weight of unspoken worries settling heavily on his shoulders. "But where is Emily?" The emptiness of the room around him mirrored the absence of her cheerful presence.

"She has a job as a nursing aide at the hospital," Aunt Rosemarie replied, her voice steady but harbouring an undercurrent of concern.

Hugh's heart tightened as he asked, "How are you?" The question felt inadequate, knowing the challenges Rosemarie faced alone.

"Fine, I can look after myself," she asserted, yet the way her eyes briefly flickered with doubt told a different story. "It is good for Emily to spread her wings. She is far too young to be looking after an old lady like me." Aunt Rosemarie's laughter echoed but carried a hint of forced lightness, revealing her struggles beneath the surface.

"You aren't that old; remember, I am five years older," Hugh teased, attempting to lighten the mood, though he sensed a shared understanding of their mortality creeping in. "We have years to go."

"What about the news?" she questioned, her tone shifting as if she sensed a deeper conversation looming, one intertwined with their family ties.

"Let's wait for them to return. I will get some refreshments," Hugh decided, making his way to the kitchen, though his thoughts lingered on the impending departure.

As Rosemarie observed him walk away, a wave of loneliness washed over her. Soon, she would have to return to England, a thought laden with a bittersweet pang. Despite her wide circle of friends, the familiarity and warmth of family grounded her in a way that solitude never could.

"Well?" Aunt Rosemary prompted, her voice sharp and direct as if she had little patience for lingering thoughts or emotions. "They are coming home," Rory replied, a weight lifting from his chest as he spoke. There was a bittersweet reassurance in the fact that they would retrieve the bodies before shipping them back together. It was a grim task, yet one that promised closure.

"That is amazing," Rose said, a smile breaking across her face as she took Rory's hand. At that moment, he felt the warmth of her touch, a fleeting solace amidst the heavy reality surrounding them. "No, what is amazing are the strings Sir Reginald pulls to make this all happen," Hugh interjected, his mind drifting to the dimly lit mines where he had spent long days toiling under a weight far greater than stone. "He was a good boss, a beacon of light in that shadowy place. But his brother?

He was the opposite—a true tyrant."

"Yes, Richard was a nasty piece," Aunt Rosemary reflected, her eyes clouding with memories that implied deeper scars, not just from the mines but from the bitter clash of familial bonds.

"So when will they be back?" she asked, her gaze turning hopeful yet tinged with anxiety. "In a couple of months," Rory said, his voice barely above a whisper, yet it was suffused with an unexpected relief.

The first part had gone so well, but as the thought settled in, a flicker of apprehension crossed his mind—what would they face when the bodies returned? Would they be prepared for the weight of memories flooding back?

A small crowd of locals gathered at the platform, their faces etched with solemnity and reverence as they awaited the train's arrival.

This time, however, their anticipation was shadowed by grief; they stood not to welcome home loved ones but to bear witness to a poignant farewell. A profound silence enveloped the scene as the train rolled to a halt.

Twelve soldiers stepped down, their movements deliberate and purposeful, as they began to unload the draped coffins from the carriage. Each coffin was draped in the vibrant Australian flag, a poignant tapestry of sacrifice. Topped with a slouch hat that spoke of pride and sacrifice. The air was thick with unspoken sorrow; these men were honoured with a full military funeral, a final tribute to their bravery.

"How beautiful," Rose whispered, her heart clenching at the sight. The elegant folds of the flags seemed to flutter gently as if embracing the souls they housed. She felt a wave of emotion wash over her—pride mingled with profound loss.

"They shall be laid to rest with the dignity afforded to heroes," Rory whispered next to her, the gravity of his statement hanging in the air like a heavy shroud.

He paused, allowing himself to absorb the solemnity of the military presence—their crisp uniforms and upright postures a stark reminder of both respect and the sacrifices made. Yet, beneath his calm exterior, a profound sorrow gnawed at him; the honour was steeped in a heart-wrenching cost.

At that moment, they existed in a cocoon of shared silence, their unspoken grief intertwining with that of the fallen, weaving a tapestry of remembrance that bound their lives forever. The army had meticulously orchestrated every detail of the ceremony, from the timing of their arrival to the solemnity of the burial.

Noel had taken it upon himself to announce their coming in the Western Mail, and his story was a poignant reminder of the senseless deaths in a war for freedom that they would never know.

It ignited a collective spirit in the Midjal community. They gathered in solidarity to bid farewell to two of their own—young men who pulsed with the dreams of a tragically short future.

Aunt Rosemary and Hugh lingered on the veranda, their glasses clinking softly as they sipped their drinks. The air hung heavy with the remnants of an emotionally charged day that had drawn them closer yet left them aching inside.

Hugh gazed into the distance, his mind drifting to

his sons, who lay with June. They represented not just family but the lifeblood of his existence—vivid reminders of a warmth he had always coveted but seldom felt. In that ephemeral moment, it felt like they were a complete family, a delicate harmony flourishing in a fragile bubble of hope. Yet, that sense of unity teetered dangerously on the brink of an impending storm.

Beneath their seemingly serene facade lay a haunting truth: they were bound by the chains of their past, each carrying the weighty shadows of grief and regret. The future lurked in the periphery, threatening to unravel the fragile bonds they had fought so hard to weave. With every step forward, they felt the ghosts of their shared history tugging at their hearts, urging them to confront the pain they longed to escape.

Aunt Rosemary shattered the stillness with a voice that echoed with both longing and familiarity. "It's over; it's time for me to return home," she said, her words laden with a bittersweet nostalgia that clung to the air like a lingering perfume.

Windamere had transcended mere geography, intertwining itself with her spirit, becoming a refuge far more comforting than Windermere's faded, distant memories in England. Even surrounded by friends, England had no family. She felt the gnawing ache of solitude she had stowed away, just out of sight.

"No." Hugh's voice cut through his swirling emotions with the clarity of a freshly sharpened blade. The urgency in his tone bore the burden of decades filled with unspoken wishes and hidden hurt. "It took me over forty years to get you here. Now you are staying." His fierce resolve was a tapestry woven from threads of love and a relentless craving to craft a new story—one where heartache faded beneath the shimmering possibility of joy.

"That is an old story," she retorted, folding her arms defensively, memories flickering in her mind like shadows.

"All the more reason to end it," he replied, gently enclosing her hand. "Rosemary Ashford, will you marry me?"

"Don't be silly." Rosemary's laughter rang out, bright yet tinged with uncertainty. "We are way too old for this."

"I won't settle for anything less than a yes this time," Hugh insisted, his gaze firm, seeking to pierce through the veil of doubt between them.

Rosemary giggled, surprise mingling with long-buried dreams. Marrying Hugh had always been a cherished dream that sat nestled in her heart but never blossomed into reality. They were older now; the passionate fire seemed but a flicker in the cavern of her soul, yet love—the deep, abiding kind— remained steadfast.

"Yes, Hugh Anderson, I will marry you," she

finally murmured.

Hugh exhaled a deep sigh that unfurled like a long-held breath. "At last," he whispered, his heart swelling with hope and the possibility of a new beginning.

As the sun dipped below the horizon, casting a warm glow over Windamere, Hugh, and Rosemary stood hand in hand, feeling the gentle weight of the promise they had just made.

Around them, the whispers of the past mingled with the laughter of family members nearby, echoing the life they had built together.

The spectres of loss would always accompany them, but together, they would weave those threads of grief into a tapestry of new memories.

"Let us celebrate," Hugh said, a newfound lightness in his voice. "Today marks more than just a promise; it is the beginning of our journey."

"Yes," Rosemary replied, her eyes shimmering with unshed tears of hope. Let us honour their memories and create a future filled with love and laughter."

As the stars began to twinkle above, they moved towards their loved ones, ready to forge a new path together, their love a beacon for the memories that shaped them.

My new book coming soon

"Between Dust and Dreams"

9798897952199